J.

SPECIAL MESSAGE TO READERS

THE ULVERSCROFT FOUNDATION
(registered UK charity number 264873)
was established in 1972 to provide funds for
research, diagnosis and treatment of eye diseases.
Examples of major projects funded by
the Ulverscroft Foundation are:-

- The Children's Eye Unit at Moorfields Eye Hospital, London
- The Ulverscroft Children's Eye Unit at Great Ormond Street Hospital for Sick Children
- Funding research into eye diseases and treatment at the Department of Ophthalmology, University of Leicester
- The Ulverscroft Vision Research Group, Institute of Child Health
- Twin operating theatres at the Western Ophthalmic Hospital, London
- The Chair of Ophthalmology at the Royal Australian College of Ophthalmologists

You can help further the work of the Foundation
by making a donation or leaving a legacy.
Every contribution is gratefully received. If you
would like to help support the Foundation or
require further information, please contact:

THE ULVERSCROFT FOUNDATION
The Green, Bradgate Road, Anstey
Leicester LE7 7FU, England
Tel: (0116) 236 4325

website: www.foundation.ulverscroft.com

David Donachie was born in Edinburgh in 1944. He has always had an abiding interest in the naval history of the eighteenth and nineteenth centuries as well as the Roman Republic, and has published a number of historical adventure novels. David lives in Deal with his partner, the novelist Sarah Grazebrook.

ON A PARTICULAR SERVICE

1796: Lieutenant John Pearce is going home aboard a hospital ship crammed with human cargo. But added to the difficulties of insufficient ballast to match the heavy swells of the Mediterranean in midwinter, Pearce must also avoid capture by an Algerine warship. His problems soon mount when in attempting to steer his disparate band of friends, the Pelicans, clear of being pressed into service aboard a British frigate, the group risk being hanged for desertion once home. By cunning and bluff, Pearce seeks to protect his friends, but his troubled love life with Emily suffers. In a whirlwind of action, there are forged wills, devious trades, contrived murders and dangerous spy missions, with so much deceit that Pearce does not know who to trust. All he can hope to do is survive.

DAVID DONACHIE

ON A PARTICULAR SERVICE

Complete and Unabridged

CHARNWOOD
Leicester

First published in Great Britain in 2017 by
Allison & Busby
London

First Charnwood Edition
published 2018
by arrangement with
Allison & Busby Limited
London

A catalogue record for this book is available
from the British Library.

ISBN 978–1–4448–3925–8

Published by
F. A. Thorpe (Publishing)
Anstey, Leicestershire

Set by Words & Graphics Ltd.
Anstey, Leicestershire
Printed and bound in Great Britain by
T. J. International Ltd., Padstow, Cornwall

This book is printed on acid-free paper

To Phil Birch,
for many years of friendship
and no shortage of sound advice

1

John Pearce knew it was unreasonable to expect decent weather at this time of year. That being accepted, he held the opinion the Mediterranean, even in midwinter, was being particularly perverse in giving him constant headwinds. In addition, a continuous heavy swell, on a contrary east-running current, slowed his progress towards the Straits of Gibraltar, forcing the ship of which he had titular command to endlessly tack and wear which was tiring for the crew, while the heavy seas made the transport vessel *Tarvit*, lacking in ballast, pitch and roll like a cork.

Even if he bore no responsibility for the matter, it outlined to him the gaps he still had in his knowledge of ships and sailing. It was a requirement he should have examined and remedied. The vessel had come out from Britain heavily laden, packed with stores for the Mediterranean Fleet. She was going home as a hospital ship with human cargo, men suffering from various wounds and afflictions, so in terms of payload was seriously light.

The remedy, a common one for a merchant vessel, would have been to seek a cargo or take on quantities of gravel or lead with which to weight the hull. Michael Hawker, the master and the man actually sailing the ship, had not done so. Challenged as to why, he provided a ready excuse: the company who chartered *Tarvit* to the

Navy Board had declined to provide him with the authority to purchase such necessities.

That lay in the hands of the company agent, a fellow called Tobias Fuller. He had met the most pressing needs of the vessel in terms of canvas and cordage, but had not been forthcoming with the funds necessary to buy ballast, as well as that needed to see it brought out into the anchorage to be loaded.

'The ship is fully insured under its contract, Mr Pearce.'

'How gratifying that must be for the owners, Mr Fuller, to know that they will not lose a penny if we founder. Not much comfort for those of us who will go down with her.'

Both had to take a firm grip on the edge of the table as the stern dipped into a deep trough caused by the ship wearing onto another tack, only eye contact being maintained with Pearce trying to keep the papers that lay on his desk safe. Everything of a furnishing nature had to be fixed in such a situation, but that did not apply to humanity. If the Pearce glare was not benign, Fuller declined to be embarrassed by the implication of laxity.

'It may have escaped your notice, sir,' he insisted, while seeking to reset his wire-rimmed glasses, dislodged by the panicky need to take a grip, 'that I am aboard this vessel and as at much risk as anyone.'

'Hardly enough to provide ease to the minds of either the crew, the passengers or the casualties we are tasked to take home and, hopefully, seek to deliver to their cure.'

Pearce was being a little disingenuous in that statement; the 'tween decks were full of injured men, some wounded in battle, most victims of a shipboard life endemic in the nature of its danger. Many more sailors expired from maladies or accidents than fell to roundshot, a musket ball or a slash from a cutlass.

The provision of medical facilities on station was not wanting; it was as good as the navy could make it, with treatment ashore at Leghorn provided where necessary, with the aim of rapidly returning men to a service in a fleet short of hands. What they had aboard *Tarvit* were the serious cases, incurables, the accumulated results of two years of sea service.

The ship was carrying home those who, whatever the cause of their confinement, were too badly injured to ever again be of use to the navy. It was assumed some would not survive the sea journey which, even with clement weather, was held to be inimical to a patient's well-being, though the tossing about the ship was undergoing was thankfully relieved for the patients by hammocks. Once home those who still lived would, at best, be released as invalids. At worst they would lie in the naval hospital at Haslar and no doubt, in time, expire there.

'The weather, Mr Pearce, cannot stay this way for ever. We all pray daily for alleviation.'

'Since I do not pretend to believe in divine oversight, Mr Fuller, I will leave the begging for a better future to you. But I will say this: if the weather deteriorates further, we may have to come about and return to Leghorn.'

'Surely a decision for Mr Hawker?'

'I, sir, am not on board for adornment. If the service insists on a naval officer taking a place aboard a chartered vessel it is, I must inform you, one of ultimate responsibility.'

That got a pinched look from a small fellow with ginger hair and bad, blotched skin. Pearce, taller by far, even sitting, was not about to admit it was a discussion in which he and Hawker had already engaged. They found themselves in agreement as to what might be necessary if the present weather showed any sign of deteriorating, although neither was happy to adopt such a course. Certainly they had no need to consult a fellow who was held to be no more than a counter of beans.

That said, the ship's master was an employee of the company and might be sanctioned by them for his actions, especially if the Navy Board sought recompense for a contract questionably executed. John Pearce had his own concerns, which made the notion of a return to Leghorn unpalatable. Yet right now he was more anxious to cover himself, given he was returning to England and an uncertain future.

'I require from you, sir, a written explanation as to why you declined to see to the proper trim of the ship. It has already suffered damage to wood, canvas and cordage, which will cost money to repair. That, given the cause, is not something that should fall as an expense to the King's Navy.'

'And I sir, decline to provide it. I have done

4

my duty by my employers and that is where my obligation lies.'

'Then I must tell you it is a daily entry in my log and that will be true of today. Your refusal will be noted.'

That got a sly smile exposing uneven and yellowing teeth. 'While I, sir, will record your threat. It is a habit among naval officers, sir, and a bad one, to think their orders are Holy Writ. The man who held your post on the voyage out shared the fault. I daresay you and your kind would flog me if you had the freedom to employ the cat.'

Pearce was thinking a ducking in the sea would do this, irritating sprat the world of good, while being well aware he did not have the power to act in such a manner. In conversation with Hawker, it had been suggested that Fuller may well have pocketed the money that would have gone to pay for ballast.

In short, he could be risking the lives of everyone aboard for personal gain. If they got home safely his peculation might not be questioned, even in the unlikely event his employers discovered it; the matter would have to be kept from those paying for the charter.

'I have good reason to think you believe in an all-seeing God, Mr Fuller.'

'Who does not, sir?'

Pearce declined to reply 'Me for one', only to be interrupted in what he was about to say — that if anything untoward should happen, Fuller was bound for perdition. The outbreak of high-pitched wailing was a sound that struck at

5

the Pearce heart but was not allowed to show in his features; indeed, he tried to appear irritated. Few aboard knew the crying infant was his own son, which meant a fiction of seeming indifference had to be maintained.

To all who had seen him since birth he was the child of the late captain and still living Mrs Ralph Barclay, given space in the great cabin out of both sympathy and regard, as well as on the orders of Admiral Sir John Jervis, Commander-in-Chief of the Mediterranean Fleet. Fuller had pulled a face full of insincere concern at the sound of infant discomfort and, given their conversation had achieved nothing, Pearce was desirous of getting rid of him. The wailing ceased abruptly, for the baby would now be at his mother's breast.

His father liked nothing more than observing the way young Adam fed with lusty endeavour, but Fuller being present precluded it. The same sound brought Michael O'Hagan out of his pantry, to enter within seconds while having to take a good grip on a bulkhead in order to prevent a fall. He looked at Pearce in a way that seemed to imply he might want something and this provided a degree of amusement. If John Pearce was enamoured of his son, his friend Michael, who masqueraded as a servant, seemed to be equally stricken.

'Did you call, your honour? A cup of coffee, happen?'

'No, Michael, thank you.' The kindly look disappeared to be replaced by a glare, as Pearce's attention shifted from Michael back to the agent.

6

'I think Mr Fuller is about to return to his own quarters.'

Fuller's face was showing a hint of anticipation at the thought of coffee. That quickly resorted to a sour look when Pearce made it plain he wanted him gone. As he rose to depart, staggering unsteadily towards the door, he was gifted with an acerbic farewell.

'Do use the manropes on your way, Mr Fuller. It would be very unfortunate if you fell victim to your own parsimony.'

'My proper sense of responsibility is to my employers, sir.'

'So you say.'

'Sure he's built for a purser, John-boy,' Michael said softly, once the door was closed behind him. 'Should I be askin' if Mrs Barclay wants anything?'

The use of the Barclay name got O'Hagan a crabbed look, but nothing was said, there being no point. To Michael, Emily had always been Mrs Barclay. He maintained now it was necessary to still term her so, despite many requests by his friend not to talk of her in such a way. The grounds were that to make habitual any other form of address risked a slip of the tongue in public, which could make anyone listening curious if not downright suspicious.

'I think I best see to that, don't you, Michael?'

The huge Irishman smiled but there was disappointment in it too. 'As you wish, John-boy.'

It had been edifying to observe his friend cradling Adam, as he had many times these last few days. Massive in his frame, a bruiser in his

7

looks as well as his scars, and a man well capable of telling John Pearce he was wrong, it was a delight to watch a gentler side to him.

That great square face would soften, taking on a wholly different cast, eyes too, while to hear him intone soft lullabies was charming, even if it seemed totally out of character and was in his unfamiliar Erse tongue. Yet it had to be recalled that Michael came from a large family and had been the second eldest of his brood; he would probably have held and caressed his small siblings in the same manner.

'Never fear, Michael; Emily would not wish that you should miss a chance to sing to our son.'

'Which would have me say, as I have afore, she is, for sure, near a saint.'

Tempted to reply she had not been so virtuous and glad of the fact, Pearce held his tongue. Strong in his papist beliefs, it was doubtful whether Michael saw their affair as a sin — Pearce had never asked him — but there was a whole world out there prepared to do so and take great pleasure in the social condemnation that would thus be inflicted.

They had first become lovers in England and, to avoid both scandal and the nefarious machinations of her late husband, Emily had come out to the Mediterranean with him. The journey was blissful, but the term 'plain sailing' could not be applied to what had happened subsequently and that was before she became pregnant, especially when that became very obvious. The lax morality said to pertain in Italy

8

did not extend to the British community, whether serving officers or resident civilians, and Emily felt keenly the risk of disgrace from such a quarter.

Pearce suspected many people might have guessed at their association but held their tongue. The likes of Lady Hamilton and her husband Sir William had openly condoned their liaison and aided both where they could. But there were others who had to be kept in the dark and the recollection of such people, most recently the ladies of the English community in Leghorn, as well as the steps he had taken to avoid their censure, went some way to dent the good feeling he had just experienced.

As of now he and Emily were in limbo, as much for being aboard ship as any other reason. But waiting for them, as soon as they landed anywhere, was a seemingly insoluble difference of opinion. Within the cabin, as long as there were no visitors, they could act as what they were, although intimacy was barred by the time needed to recover from delivery. Both avoided the subject of what would come later, taking advantage of this interlude.

'Mr Pearce, your arm if you please.'

On hearing the call, Pearce executed some well-measured steps over to the sleeping cabin and threw open the door. Emily was sat up in her swaying cot, with Adam laying on her now clothed breast. He helped her up and guided both into the main cabin, where she assured herself no one else was present. Then she smiled at Michael, accepting that he too should escort mother and child to the safety of a casement seat.

O'Hagan was quick to fetch the cushions which, laid on one side, would protect them from a fall when the ship dipped its stern. Pearce took up his place on the other side to look down into a pair of large blue eyes intently examining his face, made more obvious when Adam was passed into his arms where a presented finger was tightly taken.

'He's a strong fellow, Emily. What a grip for his size.'

Pride was not allowed to overcome necessity. 'He needs to be winded, John.'

Having just raised Adam to his shoulder, and about to pat his back, Pearce was annoyed to hear a knock at the door, which meant he had to immediately pass the child back to his mother. It should never be intimated that he was anything other than an acquaintance; to be seen winding the infant would not fit with such a pretence. He was back at his desk before he shouted that whoever had knocked should enter.

'Mr Hawker?' he said as the master's large frame filled the doorway, his face far from happy.

'A sail has been spotted to the south of us, Mr Pearce. A fair way off, mind, but I reckon it would serve if you were to examine it.'

Hawker threw a very swift glance at Emily before bringing his gaze back to his naval counterpart. As a way of saying what had been spotted portended possible danger, he could not have been more explicit. Ladies, as was the custom, must not be alarmed. In Emily he had

10

misread the person; she was as fearless as any man John Pearce had ever met.

'I will join you presently. Michael, stay with madam and the child and see to their needs.'

'Happy to, your honour,' came the reply, as the Irishman gathered up the required outdoor clothing.

At moments like this Pearce sought to check whether the subterfuge was holding up. Were the crew, from Hawker down, curious or suspicious of the relationship? The woman they knew as Mrs Barclay was still in the full bloom of youth and strikingly beautiful; the lieutenant sent to sail with them was a tall, strong-looking cove, handsome with it, as well as confident.

If they had doubts as to the association it bothered him not one whit, but it would mortify Emily if they were seen as anything other than strangers. For a brief moment their previous dispute upon a shared future bubbled up in his mind, but the way Hawker was looking at him left little time for such contemplation. He took his boat cloak and hat from Michael, nodded to the master and, with irregular steps, followed him out of the door.

The motion of the ship made getting to a secure place on the deck impossible without the use of the rigged manropes. Once on the quarterdeck it was even harder to employ a telescope with the kind of application needed to keep it steady. In addition, the ship Pearce sought, given the heavy swell, had to rise on a wave at the same time as the deck on which he was standing.

The first sight was of a streaming pennant, and that, being red with a crescent on it, brought from John Pearce an angry curse. 'Barbary.'

Hawker had his mouth pressed to the Pearce ear to confirm that had been his first conclusion; he had to in order to be heard over the whistling sound of the wind in the rigging. His listener continued to blaspheme, for he had been afflicted by the sight of such an ensign too many times in the last couple of years.

As both ships rose on the swell at the same time, he could see and examine more than the flag. Now there was the sight of the hull and it was substantial which, being brief, told him little of real substance, which had him divesting himself of his hat, cloak and finally his uniform jacket, the chill on his skin through his cambric shirt immediate.

'I must go aloft for a proper sight.'

The look on Hawker's face said *rather you than me*. To climb the rigging on a calm sea was not without risk, proof of which was occupying some of the hammocks below: men who had fallen from yards and the like to be seriously maimed. Given the way the ship was acting now it was not really sensible. Yet Pearce knew he had no choice; if there was a threat, he needed to know in detail what it was.

2

He took care to approach the rigging in the way he had learnt when first set to do so as a pressed seaman, aiming to climb with the wind on his back. He had been taught then by a fellow named Robert Sykes, the bosun aboard the frigate HMS *Brilliant*, into which he had been illegally taken up. Sykes had cajoled rather than shouted his instructions, encouraged instead of ordered, for which he had been chastised by his captain, Ralph Barclay.

The bosun was a man to be recalled fondly, for he never altered his manner to please authority. Added to that he had saved John Pearce from a possible heavy flogging when he sought to desert the frigate off Deal, for Barclay — a man free with the cat in any event — would have taken the chance to make an example of him to the rest of the crew.

Before he got to the point where the ratlines joined the bulwarks, he was approached by two more old friends, Charlie Taverner and Rufus Dommet, both looking anxious. They, along with him and Michael O'Hagan, had gone through the same baptism under the beady eye of Bosun Sykes as well as the basilisk one of the late Ralph Barclay. Both had been pressed with him and, with only a short break, they had served together ever since, though not as common seamen, following on from Pearce's rise to his present rank.

'They's saying it's the same devils as we came foul of afore, John,' Charlie shouted, sure no one else was close enough to hear. 'It be Satan's work.'

'Who's saying that, Charlie?' Pearce yelled in reply.

'The *Tarvit* hands.'

'And how would they know?' It was the look on Rufus's freckled face that gave the game away. 'It could only be because you were tall-tale-telling.'

'Can't fault us for that,' Dommet protested.

Pearce shook his head, as much to ponder as respond. Asking sailors not to tell exaggerated stories of real or imagined exploits was like crying for the moon and they would have had good fun scaring the crew of *Tarvit*. How much had this pair, and maybe Michael as well, gilded their previous adventures and the dangers they had faced against that crescent motif? The truth was bad enough when it came to Barbary pirates, but embellishment would render it terrifying.

'And the crew now?' he demanded.

'Shaking to a man and ready to slit their own gullets,' Charlie shouted.

Looking back towards the quarterdeck, Pearce saw Hawker observing this exchange with a degree of curiosity. He knew all three to be navy, yet he must reckon it strange to see an officer and two seamen conversing in such a public and easy-going manner. Such familiarity was not even common on a merchantman.

14

'The tale you have to tell them now is that we all survived, not that they would be in ignorance given you are not ghosts.' Jamming the telescope in his waistband, he gave them a look full of exasperation. 'Now, stand back so I can go aloft and get a better look at what we face.'

Clambering onto the hammock nettings, Pearce grabbed the tarred rigging and swung round to climb, the wind pressing him forward, feeling his foot sink as he put pressure on the lowest rung of the rope ladder, his hands reaching up to those running to the masthead, narrowing the further up he went. It had been some time since he had done this and it was rare for anyone in a blue coat, midshipmen besides, to risk their dignity in such a way.

But he was young and fit, though he cursed such attributes when halfway to the cap, as the *Tarvit* dipped heavily to leeward, leaving him, thanks to sheer gravity, hanging on for dear life. The lubber's hole served to get him onto the mainmast cap and, once there, he could steady himself with an arm around the base of the upper mast, that also aiding him in steadying and focusing the telescope.

What he saw could not be fixed — both vessels were too much in motion — but then it was scarce necessary. He observed enough of the other ship to tell him it was a large galleass, part-sailing ship, part-galley, with what looked to be ten gun ports on the visible beam which would be replicated on the far side, with other cannon in the prow and pointing astern.

Lateen-rigged on three masts, and barred from

oars by the sea state, it was sailing under as much canvas as the weather would allow, tacking and wearing into a wind especially unfavourable to its type. That it was foul for a fore-and-aft-rigged vessel meant little; the wind was just as bad for a square-rigged, broad-beamed merchant vessel like *Tarvit*.

But one fact was obvious; whoever commanded her was holding to precisely the same course and, as a destination for a North African ship, Port Mahon in Minorca, home to the fighting vessels of Spain and Pearce's first port of call, was unlikely.

He swept round the horizon, hoping he would spy one of the British warships tasked with protecting the route from Italy to Minorca, where mercantile security until Gibraltar became a Spanish responsibility. All he observed was an empty, grey and heaving seascape, which left only calculation.

In this wind the galleass would struggle to overhaul them, but the earlier words of Tobias Fuller came to him and it provided no comfort that the man was right: the weather must at some time moderate. There was no way for a merchant tub to outrun a galleass in normal conditions.

It looked too substantial to be a pirate ship of the kind he had faced previously, though the only safe assumption said it might be. Given its armament and the probable size of the crew, it was also too formidable an opponent for a trading vessel to contest with; indeed, it would give a good account of itself against anything smaller than a frigate.

Yet knowing that did not provide any answer as to how it was going to be dealt with. At that point Pearce recalled the searching blue eyes of his son so recently looking up into his own, as well as the scent of Emily, sat beside him. Whatever it was and whatever its intentions, an answer had to be found.

For all his claims to superiority of rank, Pearce knew any action would have to be agreed between those who held responsibility. For reasons of discretion, the necessary discussion had to be held in Hawker's cabin. There it was made more obvious, by the confined space, that the ship's master gave little away in size and build to Michael O'Hagan; he too was a bear of a man and again, like the Irishman, not one to employ his bulk to distress people.

In the short time they had sailed together Pearce had grown to esteem him, for he lacked bombast and had a friendly nature, while being prepared to listen to any advice proffered by his naval counterpart without any hint of resentment. They had engaged in a quiet conversation prior to this gathering, to make a joint assessment of the time they would have to decide on a course of action.

Whatever threat was faced, it would require better weather before they risked any chance of being intercepted. The present heavy swell dictated what was possible and no captain in his right mind would seek to come close to another vessel in such a sea. There was no chance, given the respective armaments, of a fight with cannon, so the risk was a shot across the bows, followed by a demand to surrender. Such an ultimatum could be refused until the weather moderated. Time was a friend, not an enemy.

The presence of Fuller, when they did finally assemble, was technically superfluous and was certain to prove annoying. Yet Pearce felt he had no choice but to include him, given his role acting on behalf of the owners. Also called to Hawker's cabin was Stephen Byford, the naval surgeon who had charge of *Tarvit*'s patients. He too would contribute little in the nautical line, but he might add something of use when he chose to speak on behalf of those under his care.

Pearce opened proceedings by describing the vessel he had seen from the masthead, while also outlining the advantages as well as the drawbacks of a galleass.

'They can use either oars or sail to move and manoeuvre and in certain conditions that can be an advantage, but in open water with anything like a running sea it cannot contest with a square-rigged warship.'

'Which we are not,' Fuller stated. He was determined to participate in the conversation to the point of stating the obvious, which Pearce made a point of ignoring.

'Our friend is substantial, close to the size of a small frigate, and not of the kind I would associate with brigandage. Old-fashioned it might be, but it is a fighting ship, and may well be a state vessel of Algiers.'

The agent butted in again, his pale-skinned face showing the blotches that marred his cheeks: evidence of high dudgeon. 'I feel I must point out to you, Lieutenant Pearce, that is hardly reassuring. I would also add the responsibility you were earlier so keen to emphasise, that of your right to command, lies at your door. You have an obligation to keep us safe.'

'It is the responsibility of us all, Mr Fuller,' Hawker insisted, before turning his attention to Pearce. 'Even if they are not inclined to outright piracy that does not mean we will be allowed to just sail on.'

'Sadly true, Mr Hawker. The reputation of those who fly under such a flag is not one to reassure.'

'Perhaps you would care to explain,' Fuller demanded, clearly confused. Given there was a pause while Hawker gathered his thoughts, it brought forth a point driven by both fear and frustration. 'I doubt we are gifted with time for reflection.'

Pearce cut in, his tone severe. 'You might reflect that while you are an ignoramus in this matter, Mr Hawker is not. You would serve us all by remaining silent.'

'As will I,' added Surgeon Byford, which even with a bit of a West Country drawl was enough to cut off Fuller's protests, 'and for that very reason.'

That double put-down got a quiet smile from Hawker as he went on to explain.

'Even if it is a national vessel of Algiers that does not render us secure. It is their habit to seize ships of both sides in the present conflict and seek ransom for the crew, as well as any passengers they may be carrying. The Bey of Algiers claims to decry the practice and to punish those who transgress, but no one doubts he profits from it.'

'And the vessel itself?' Fuller demanded.

'British ships are insured, so they know the loss will be made good. I am told the practice is to take them to a small, unimportant harbour, out of sight of prying eyes. There any cargo will be unloaded to be carried to a major centre and sold. The hull will be renamed and hawked to traders whose sole occupation comes from facilitating such dubious transactions. A few alterations to the upper works, a new figurehead and you have a different vessel.'

'Like a doctored racehorse?' Byford asked.

'The same,' Pearce replied. 'As for us, it will be said we were saved from a vessel sinking beneath our feet, which allows the Algerines to demand recompense for our return. A lie, but who will challenge it?'

'I have confidence those I represent will move with alacrity to get us freed.'

Pearce was savage in his response to such a smug attitude. 'A company that declines to lay out for some very necessary ballast, Mr Fuller, might take a sweet time indeed to expend coin for the likes of you.'

Fuller was about to say something to counter that — it was in the expression on his face — but it was swallowed. Had he been about to blurt out a truth about that ballast, or just protest at being so addressed? There was no way to know as, fiddling with his wire spectacles, he switched back to a look of irascibility.

'We are not expected at Gibraltar,' Hawker continued, 'or even at home, so it could be months before anyone is aware we are missing.'

Byford interrupted, 'Surely our departure, as well as our cargo of invalids, will be mentioned in the despatches sent from the Mediterranean Fleet?'

'Which will take many weeks to reach home,' Hawker insisted. 'And that tells those in England nothing except we could still be at sea. Any packet ship would easily overhaul us without catching sight of our sails, never mind our name.'

'There are British consuls in the main North African ports, Mr Hawker, to which we would probably be taken,' Pearce countered. 'Admiral Jervis will know of what occurred within a very short time and, given we are carrying naval personnel, he will be bound to act to get us free.'

'My crew and I are not navy, Mr Pearce.'

'He would scarce move to free one without the other.'

'You talk as if this is commonplace,' Fuller protested.

'Suffice to say,' Pearce replied, with a look designed to cause discomfort, 'it is not singular.'

'Then surely the situation demands that they be chastised. This is nothing short of official piracy. What is our fleet for, if not to protect British trade?'

'Quite apart,' was the mordant reply, 'of the small matter of a large and powerful French fleet in Toulon, added to an enemy army camped at

Nice, intent on attacking Italy.'

Tempted to explain further, Pearce decided against it for it would be wasted on this poltroon. King George's Navy had a multitude of tasks to perform in a sea full of potential adversaries and questionable allies. Algiers might profess neutrality but they were ever happy to take advantage of opportunity, safe in the knowledge that an understrength British fleet, supported by the less than energetic Spaniards, lacked the means to both contain the French and risk making of them an enemy.

Such a problem was not confined to the North African littoral. A prime example, of which John Pearce had very recent personal experience, lay in the mercantile Republic of Genoa, sat between the forces of the Revolution and the coalition led by Austria on its borders, supported by the Royal Navy at sea.

They too had declared neutrality, while in reality depending on protection from the very same forces of the coalition, despite the fact that French republicanism was very different to their oligarchical kind. More troubling, they also turned a blind eye to anyone who sought to trade for profit with Britain's enemies.

'That said,' Pearce added, 'even if Jervis finds out we have been taken, it will be some time before the situation can be resolved. It will have to be negotiated.'

'Hardly beneficial to my patients,' the surgeon said.

'It's worse than that, Mr Byford. As it has been imparted to me by those who have witnessed them, the conditions in which we would all be held would not be of the kind to be beneficial to men already suffering from injuries or other afflictions. It would scarce be fit to keep healthy ourselves or the men of the crew.'

'We must also consider Mrs Barclay and her baby, Mr Pearce,' Hawker said. 'The child is at a very delicate age and I need hardly point out to anyone present, as well, that Mrs Barclay is a rare beauty.'

Pearce was grateful to the ship's master for raising it, having thought of little else since he came down from the masthead. The point about two-week-old Adam was well made but the other was just as worrying. The pamphlet stories of European women being cast into harems or sexual servitude by Barbary pirates were rife.

They were titillating to the type who would pay a penny for a salacious tract. They also created a frisson of exhilarating fear in the breast of females who were never going to leave the safety of their own hearths. There was, however, a factual basis for these tales and it had existed over centuries, which meant the risk could not be taken.

The kidnapping of comely females, as well as the enslavement of European ship's crews to man commercial galleys, was not singular — it was so commonplace that charitable entities had been set up in most trading countries to raise funds for ransom.

The consuls of various nations in Ottoman ports had a standing duty to use the funds raised to get free any captives but they were not always successful and that applied more to women than men, which made Hawker's point regarding Emily very pertinent.

These thoughts were followed by a tinge of guilt: he was putting his private concerns above the needs of the whole. Such a feeling was not helped when Hawker went on to articulate the hazard.

'A handsome young European woman is considered a rare trophy for a rich man and, once hidden away, which she could most certainly be, it would be damned hard to get her released, even for payment.'

'Mr Pearce,' Byford interjected, for once speaking both rapidly and with real emphasis. 'For Mrs Barclay's sake, if for no other — and we must not forget the infant — I fear you must provide us with a solution.'

'We are all equally at risk here,' Fuller insisted. 'Mrs Barclay is but one.'

'Such chivalry,' the surgeon responded. 'But I think you must admit they are a pair.'

'You should have a mind for your charges, Mr Byford. They, surely, are your prime concern.'

Byford, usually a study in calm demeanour, broke that now. His response was hard in tone and uncompromising in opinion.

'Many of what you call 'my charges' may not see Spithead, and those who do are in for a sorry existence, in which death might serve them better. You may find that callous, sir, but I am a man of my profession and have been so for enough years to prohibit any avoidance of the realities. I therefore say we must turn our minds

24

to what is best for the people here present, the mother and child in the great cabin, ourselves of course, but also the crew, who as of this moment, I am told, are near to despair and are sure they are facing a horrible death.'

Damn the Pelicans and their tales, Pearce thought, just before he spoke. 'If it falls to me to solve what seems intractable, I require some peace to think it through.'

3

Michael O'Hagan was the first to be consulted on a way to respond and, as was his habit, he was all for fighting whatever the odds, a notion swiftly scotched by his friend.

'We have a total of eight old, small-calibre cannon and few men trained to handle them. Between us Pelicans we can ply one, but with only half a gun crew, little in the way of speed. The rest? One shot would be all I would expect before confusion set in and the whole notion of firing at all would be lost.'

O'Hagan nodded in reluctant agreement, but proffered no solution. Pearce had come to the tiny pantry to talk, in the hope that to do so would provide enlightenment, it being probably the only place on the ship in which he could speak freely, although they needed to be quiet. His cabin was barred by the presence of Emily but the pantry was close, too much so to allow loud talk. It also had the advantage, in being so cramped, of making it possible to remain upright without worrying about the pitch and roll of the ship.

'*Tarvit* is not built for manoeuvre — not that many vessels would be compared to a galleass.' Pearce looked at the bulkhead, lost in thought. 'Though it is of an aged design and she might be difficult to handle.'

'It's at sea, John-boy, and as you tell me

26

making as much way as this barky in foul weather. Best not to go straw clutching and assume it to be in good enough order to be plied as it needs.'

Pearce acknowledged the truth of that, to then remain silent for some time. They had already covered the previous discussion in Hawker's cabin, including where the closest source of salvation lay, which got a sceptical response from the Irishman.

'I would beg to be unsure of that. Jervis, hearing your name, will not be afire to set you free. Sure, Mrs Barclay might sway him, but not you.'

Pearce responded with a grim smile to what was the plain truth. He had never been a friend to admirals. Even with his lowly rank, he had disputed with Vice Admiral Lord Hood, then fallen foul of the malice of his successor, Sir William Hotham. But Sir John Jervis was of a different order to both. Hood had been a man of fair, if snappish disposition, albeit with a sneaking admiration for those prepared to stand up to him. Hotham was a weak fellow fond of his belly. If he was devious, he was disinclined to face open confrontation.

Jervis was neither; he was forthright and something of a martinet, added to which he had wanted John Pearce out of his area of command from the moment he realised he was present, openly referring to the dubious way he had reached his rank without the customary examination and at the personal insistence of King George. If he did not allude to a possible recurrence of the madness of his sovereign, it was plain he thought His Majesty to be both deluded and acting above his responsibilities.

'Dislike cannot come into it, Michael. Even if he sees me as not much of one, I am a King's officer. Jervis wouldn't dare leave me in the hands of the Mussulmen, for to do so would not sit well with those he commands. We both know it would be common gossip throughout the fleet in a day that we were captives. And that applies just as much to you, Charlie and Rufus.'

'And Mrs Barclay?'

'You have the right of it. Quite apart from his partiality to young ladies, he should be doubly keen to rescue the widow of a post captain who recently died in battle. The only question is how long it will take and what might be faced in the meantime.'

'I doubt it runs to comfort and well-being.'

'And can that be countenanced?'

Another silence followed; Michael O'Hagan knew when to keep quiet. Intent on Pearce's face, he was aware, as the eyes took on a certain look, that his friend had formed some kind of notion of a way to proceed.

'It seems to me, if those fellows shadowing *Tarvit* are intent on taking us, profit must sit as their motive. What is it they would see as being of most value, us or the vessel?'

'Jesus, how would I know?'

'We are a merchantman to their eyes, so they will assume a saleable cargo. But what happens when they find we carry nothing but broken and maimed bodies? They'll want the hull for certain,

28

but will they want a shipload of invalids, all of them navy and many of whom are bound to expire in their hands?'

The canvas screen that acted as a flap to the pantry was drawn back to reveal Emily, a slightly pinched look on her face. 'I will not enquire as to why you're skulking in Michael's pantry, John, but there is a messenger come from Mr Hawker and the fellow sent to deliver it is waiting in your cabin.'

'Then I best attend to it.'

'While you're at it, you might attend to me and at least give me some indication of what is going on.' Faced with a blushing lover, she did not wait for an explanation. 'You may think you're protecting me, but such a hope is a false one. The whole ship is aware of something you seem to wish to keep me in ignorance of, namely that there is a possible hostile vessel on the same course as us.'

'There is no certainty we are at risk.'

'But no certainty we are not?'

'No.'

'Then I wait to be enlightened.'

The screen dropped and she was gone. Pearce turned to O'Hagan with a grim expression to whisper, 'Whatever happened to the sweet creature I once knew?'

Michael's face broke into a broad grin. 'She bore a child, John-boy, which means, in the pecking order, you're not first to the grain seeds any more.'

The message from Hawker was not welcome. The sky was clearing to the north-west and the first hint of a change of wind was being felt on deck, a shift that would make sailing easier. Night would come soon and with it a change of course, but it was fully expected the state of the weather in the morning would be much altered.

'Please tell Mr Hawker I will be on deck presently.'

Emily having retired to her sleeping cabin, he was then obliged to totter over to the door and gently knock before opening it. She was perched on the cot above which Adam lay asleep in a smaller version knocked up by the ship's carpenter. Fixed by ropes to the overhead beams, both cots were still while the deck moved, so the subsequent conversation was carried out with both mother and child in some comfort while he had to hang on to the door jamb.

Knowing her as he did, Pearce was well aware that there could be no gilding it. Emily would want the truth, which he gave to her unvarnished, once more, as he had with Michael, reprising the discussion in which he had been engaged in Hawker's cabin. If he also reiterated the view that all was speculation, yet there was no diminution of what the ship faced or what she might also need to contend with.

'I will, of course, if they seek to board us, provide you with a loaded pistol.'

'The purpose of which is?'

'To allow you the freedom to choose your own fate.'

'Are you saying you intend to fight, John?'

'I hope not to, but we may not be given the choice. If I must, it's unlikely I will survive.

Which leaves you and Adam unprotected.'

'Unlike you John, I have my prayers to protect me.'

'All I am guilty of is seeking not to cause you anxiety.'

'When will we know?'

'At dawn. Mr Hawker will change course overnight. There is a faint hope that the Barbary vessel is on some mission or other, that holding the same course as us is coincidence. But if they are in sight at first light . . . '

There was no need to finish and very quickly her expression softened, her hand being proffered to draw him close, one eagerly if awkwardly taken. There was just room on the cot for him too, though he had to crouch a bit to avoid the one that held his son. He and Emily sat for some time in a silent embrace, until she began to talk of the strange circumstances of how they had met, her initial reluctance to admit being attracted to him and what he, along with their child, meant to her now.

'Perhaps, John, it would be best just to surrender to our fate, which is in God's hands.' Emily must have felt him stiffen at the mention of the deity, about which he had serious reservations, for she was quick to add, 'Life is everything, even for those under Mr Byford's care.'

'Then — ' He had cried out too loudly for Emily, who abjured him to remember the sleeping infant, which meant the rest of what he had to say was a whisper. 'Let us secure it for them.'

His confident response confused her, obvious from her expression, as he stood, using one of the cot ropes to steady himself, before bending to kiss her on the brow.

'I am no more given to surrender than I am to pray, Emily, but if I find it hard to share your faith, this I will admit to believing. Where there's a will, there's a way.'

★   ★   ★

They were all on deck before first light: Hawker, Fuller and Byford, plus the Pelicans and, barring the cook and those who feared to know, almost the entire crew, though they did not, like the navy, run out their guns. Nor, when dawn did come, would they swab the decks and flog them dry, it not being seen as a daily need; truly, a vessel occupied in trade operated in a very different way to a warship.

Not that a merchant crewman was always happier for the lack of such burdens. Too often the pay was poor, the accommodation cramped, while the number of hands commonly could be rated as inadequate, especially in foul weather, while the provision of sustenance was nothing like as regular and filling as that on a King's Ship.

Most shipping companies put profit before the welfare of those they employed and nothing demonstrated this more — East Indiamen excluded — than the paucity of the means to defend themselves. *Tarvit's* eight cannon were old pieces lacking in flints to fire them and dependent on slow match, the sold-off property of an Admiralty that saw such ordnance as too worn out for royal service, with their accuracy questionable.

The practice of pressing hands returning to British ports might be decried, but such protests often came from the owners; some of the supposed victims were happy to swap decks as long as they could do so with outstanding pay. Likewise ashore and in the ports: as soon as a new war was declared the merchant fleet would be decimated as those who preferred the King's service sought out captains with whom they had served before, or those with a reputation for profitable activity. Added to that was an immediate cash bounty.

To many a blue water sailor, the navy was — the risk of being flogged and blown to bits apart — a better place to be for camaraderie, pay, albeit intermittent in provision, a full belly and regular grog. Added to that was the chance that they might, in some successful battle, make enough prize money to set themselves up when peace came. It was a pipe dream in too many cases, given the propensity of tars to quickly spend any money they acquired.

The crew of *Tarvit* enjoyed the best of both worlds: all the benefits of being aboard a hired naval vessel with none of the disadvantages that came with royal service, from which they carried exemptions. The way the work, ordered by Pearce, had been carried out overnight drove home the main difference lay in discipline.

On a man-o'-war an order was just that and

had to be obeyed, though a crew were not beyond making their displeasure felt if such an instruction bordered on stupidity, or it appeared someone was coming on a bit high. But a sullen naval tar was one thing, the men aboard *Tarvit* quite another, made worse given the man telling them what to do had no time for lengthy explanation regarding the eventual purpose of his varied dispositions.

In this, the bulk and appearance of Michael O'Hagan, backed by a bellicose Rufus Dommet — he too had become a bit of a bruiser — added to the seductive blandishments of Charlie Taverner, using a combination of threats and wheedling, had got completed what needed to be done. Now the moment was fast approaching to see if all that effort had been worthwhile.

Hawker, having reversed course in darkness, made the most of what remained of the westerly wind to create what was hoped would be enough to distance from their assumed difficulties and nail the intent. As expected, the weather had changed and with it the sea state, though there was still a telling pitch and roll on *Tarvit* from the following sea.

Pearce, as he worked both on and below decks, had come to realise that, riding so high out of the water, it would be plain the ship was lacking in full holds. Would that in itself be enough to discourage a potential seeker after booty?

The eastern sky was a slowly increasing grey on what promised to be a clear day, which had John Pearce back aloft with his telescope to search to the south and west, there being no sign of the pursuit. This cheered him, but not for long. Just as he was about to shout down to the deck, to say they could resume a course for Port Mahon, the tip of a sail on the horizon checked him.

With a growing feeling of dejection, caused by increasing daylight and increasing proximity, he watched as the vessel slowly revealed itself. The point came when he could just make out the crimson of the flag, this confirming the chase was deliberate. He remained in place, harbouring a deep reluctance to let on to those below what he had seen, even more so to initiate the course agreed on should this happen: to come about and close with a vessel they could not outrun.

He sat for a time on the mainmast cap to review what he had planned, not least the fact that it was based on a number of variables and so much guesswork as to be close to dangerous speculation. If it turned out not to be a state vessel he would be utterly thrown, yet given the rate at which the two vessels would close, he had no time to alter his dispositions.

'Mr Hawker,' he yelled. 'What we feared has come to pass.'

A blast of a cannon echoed within seconds, sending forth a cloud of acrid smoke, though not of aggressive intent. Sound travelled well at sea, so setting off regular shots with powder might attract any naval vessels picking up the echo, it being one no fighting captain would ignore.

As for his aim to close with Barbary, the

chosen course for *Tarvit* would surely cause confusion, it being an act totally singular from a ship that should be doing all it could to delay seizure. Given his presence on deck was not immediately required, Pearce stayed in place, watching as the rudder worked to begin the turn, this as the falls were loosed on the yards to let them swing free.

In this position he was better placed to calculate the time it would take to close, a point at which he would need to be on deck to ensure what he had decided upon was executed to the letter, by a crew both fearful and bound to be muddled.

The hands that came aloft to reset the sails did not race up the ratlines, navy-fashion. They ascended in a deliberate, steady progress, ready when the order came to loose the reefs on the courses, while others headed on for the topsails to let them drop. These had been clewed against the previous headwinds and would now be set to gain a little extra speed, again exactly the opposite of what would be expected.

As the falls were secured, the sails billowed and the speed of *Tarvit* increased markedly. The galleass almost immediately let fly its own sheets; the lateen sails were then lowered, before turning to oars for propulsion. The act of coming about and adding canvas had clearly created suspicion. Positions reversed, he would have suspected another vessel, quite possibly a man-o'-war, somewhere well astern of *Tarvit* and as yet invisible to the Barbary vessel.

The man in command was being cautious,

wondering why this potential prize was speeding to its own capture, putting himself in a position to come about and flee if need be. There was advantage in that: with many of the crew on those sticks, it would reduce the numbers available to board — not that they were likely to be short. Warships were always well-manned, whichever polity they represented, and no corsair sailed short-handed or with slaves on their oars.

Sure the galleass would now be visible from the deck, Pearce made his way back to the quarterdeck by sliding down a backstay, hardly surprised that not one of the crew, having completed their tasks, had gone below. They stood in groups as another blast of black, acrid, spent powder swept over them, suspiciously eyeing this blue-coated naval officer who had hatched a hare-brained scheme that would very likely see them all perish. The huge yawn he produced, as he approached Michael Hawker, might have been taken to be for effect. It was not: John Pearce was seriously weary.

'We have created doubt,' he said, to a raised and questioning eyebrow.

'Then it is time to haul in the boats.'

Pearce nodded at yet another part of his plan. With the bulk of *Tarvit* hiding what was being towed behind, they could be brought onto the stern and lashed below the cabin casements. Overnight, two of the boats had been loaded with casks of water, still reasonably fresh from Leghorn, biscuit, peas and cured meats likewise, each one stepped with a mast as well as the canvas required to raise a sail, including the means with which to fish for fresh food.

Was it a wise precaution or a forlorn hope they might get at least a number of their ambulant beings free in that fashion? Whatever, it would not include him, Michael Hawker, most of the crew or any of the patients. Fuller had insisted he must go, in sharp contrast to Byford, who was adamant his post lay with those under his care.

The response, not taken well, had been that the agent must take his chances along with everyone else, which had opened John Pearce to the accusation of putting his own interests to the fore, given he had planned that Emily and the baby would seek to escape in the cutter.

The largest of the ship's boats had been loaded overnight with her possessions as well as provender. A dozen of the crew, chosen by lots and the most muscular, would also go to man the oars. Their instructions were to row hard until well clear and only turn to propulsion by sail if it seemed advantageous.

At Pearce's insistence, given Michael O'Hagan flatly refused to leave him, the numbers would include Rufus and Charlie, to ensure the mother and child were well-cared-for: not a thing to entrust to strangers. They had been, like him, pressed seamen once and useless with it, but time at sea had changed that. Both were now well able to sail a boat and read a compass, which would allow them to follow a simple course set for them by Michael Hawker.

The rest aboard had one of the other two boats, which left a chance for some to do likewise. Pearce hoped it provided some reassurance that the possibility of flight instead of capture and incarceration existed.

4

'The flag?' Pearce said this as half a question, half a statement, just after he heard Hawker order the cannon to cease firing; if the navy had not heard by now, it was unlikely to change. 'Time to raise it, I think.'

'Let us hope they comprehend it, Mr Pearce,' barked Fuller. 'I would take a plain flag to denote an unwillingness to engage in tricks, which I would recommend as the proper course of action.'

The man worried John Pearce and he had enough of those anyway. His aim would succeed only if everyone stuck to what had been agreed. The slightest hint of dissent could ruin everything and he was far from sure Fuller was as convinced as he needed to be.

'If they have aboard anyone with a smattering of English or French, they will be told its meaning beforehand.'

'And if they do not?'

'Mr Fuller,' he replied, with a smile he knew to be forced, 'some things, though it pains me to say it, are in the lap of the gods.'

An arm was taken by Michael O'Hagan to drag him out of earshot, which got a look of surprise from Fuller; in the agent's world, servants did not manhandle their masters. Nor did they dare to whisper in their ear like a familiar.

'There's a pair of pistols, John-boy, primed and loaded, by the way into the carpenter's walk and another pair in my pantry. Will you be wanting your own to hand?'

'No. I can't even allow myself a sword, Michael.'

'Sure there's little to stop me and I can stay close?'

'Ever willing to fight,' Pearce said with a wry grin, which got a more fulsome one in response. 'Michael, I require you to smile upon these sons of the Prophet as you would on little Adam and ensure the task I have outlined to you is carried out.'

A cry came from the cap, sent by the man replacing John Pearce. 'Barbary has raised sail again.'

'I am curious to know how you see things, Mr Pearce,' said Byford, as he rejoined the senior group. 'Are matters proceeding as you hoped?'

Turning to the surgeon, Pearce made no attempt at false promise, nor was he in any way dismissive. The man had been exemplary in the way he had deferred to the expertise of the sailors, which would have been fine if either he or Hawker had been sure of a good outcome.

'The time to answer that question, Mr Byford, is when I can look into the eye of the man I must deal with. What have you told your patients?'

'I had no need to tell them anything: the sailors saw to that well before I had a chance.'

'And?'

'The mind-afflicted apart, who show no sign of reaction, I am astounded by the stoic manner

41

in which they have accepted that, as they express in an Italian phrase, 'What must be, must be.' I wish I could be so sanguine.'

'The British tar will put up with a great deal, Mr Byford. Just to take the King's shilling is to assent to the risk of death, as sure as the making of your mark.'

Whatever response Byford had in mind was cut off by the distant rumble of cannon fire, followed in several seconds by a rising plume of seawater at least half a cable off the bow. It had been made as a signal that *Tarvit* should heave to, which would be the sensible thing to do.

That was the moment when the flag, in truth a plain piece of bedding stitched into one, was hauled up to break out at the masthead, which had Hawker make a slight alteration to his course to keep the approach of the galleass to the larboard side. Over the stern the ship's boats were being moved to the starboard side to keep them hidden from view.

Pearce took hold of the speaking trumpet and made for the larboard bulwarks, there to clamber up by the mainmast ratlines, the instrument by which his voice would be amplified held out as an indication he wanted to parley. As yet, the man he would need to address was still too far off to identify, but the two vessels were closing at a fair rate. Pearce must be visible, but would his intention be evident?

Another ball hit the intervening sea to send up more white water, though well away from *Tarvit*. To Pearce, his opposite number was wasting his time yet it was telling: there was no way the other captain was going to fire into the hull, which implied he wished to preserve it intact. Those long oars appeared again as the lateen sails, having been earlier reset, were clewed up, Pearce noting there were several men aloft scanning the horizon for a potential rescuer.

'Ahoy, do you have anyone aboard who speaks English, *ou une personne qui parle français?*'

That was a call that had to be repeated several times — the galleass was too far off for Pearce's question to carry clearly, but he kept shouting through the trumpet so it would elicit an answer as soon as possible. Eventually he heard a response, which though unclear sounded as if it might be in English.

'Then know this. We carry no cargo, but are a hospital ship carrying wounded and sick men home from His Britannic Majesty's Mediterranean Fleet. We have no value other than the poor souls we are transporting. If you wish to send over a party to inspect below decks, we will make no attempt to impede your coming aboard.'

There was a long wait, but the hoped-for answer was unforthcoming, not that the lack of it came as a shock, it being only an opening gambit in the hope of deflecting their purpose. If Pearce added more it was in hope rather than for effect.

'Should you act the brigand, you will have on your hands men in need of care and attention, as well as those held in high esteem by the commanding admiral of the British Fleet, this for the service they have given. He will not take kindly to the notion any of them should suffer and possibly expire due to being held for

43

monetary exchange.'

The reply came eventually, not in words but in action, as the galleass began to swing in a wide arc to come on to a matching course, a prelude to boarding. Once round she began, with care, to close the gap, the decks and rigging of *Tarvit* being carefully examined by several people on her quarterdeck, giving him the sense there was a degree of apprehension. The actions he had initiated so far had put them on their guard.

A body of boarders, some two dozen in number, emerged onto the deck: dark-skinned coves in turbans who, as much to animate themselves as send a message to him, brandished and waved their weapons, this accompanied by much shouting. But it was the voice, which up till now had only uttered the indistinct but affirmative word regarding being a speaker of English, which surprised Pearce, for what he heard made him doubt his ears.

'Clear the starboard side,' came the command, in what was, very clearly, a West Country accent.

If it made him curious, he was not about to meekly accept the instruction, working hard to get into his voice a warning growl. 'What value can sick men have to Barbary? Is that, and this hull, worth the price you might pay for a nefarious intention? Britannia is aware of your habits, which angers the nation and our sovereign. One day retribution must follow.'

A musket was fired, the route of the ball established by the plume of black smoke which rose into the air. Pearce was not going to risk another being aimed at him, so he clambered down and went to join the others on the far side of the quarterdeck.

'Round one to the Prophet,' was his mordant comment.

The faces were clear across the water now, the rank of the fellow surely in command established by a glittering bauble stuck on the front and centre of his turban, red on the cap and wrapped at the base with tightly bound white. Once close enough, and the oars withdrawn, grappling irons were thrown to hook onto *Tarvit*'s bulwarks, muscle power employed to bring the galleass hull to hull with its intended prize. A grinding sound of wood on wood signalled that had been achieved.

'I desire to parley with my opposite number, please. So English speaker, if it is not you, pass that on to him in his own tongue.'

Again the reply was not a verbal one; a party of men clambered onto their own bulwarks to run out planks by which they could safely cross the gap created by the tumblehome of both vessels, one they would have been obliged to try and jump while simultaneously fighting if they had been opposed.

Pearce and his quarterdeck party had moved to the opposite side, leaving the way clear, and all made it plain, by holding out their arms from their sides, that they carried no weapons. He had to suppress a feeling of absurdity, not least because of what was utterly inappropriate in the circumstances. The boarders were nervous too: it was almost a minute before the first one put a foot on the deck, others following until all were standing, silent, with weapons ready.

A path was cleared, this to allow the fellow with the bauble to cross. He wore a huge curved sword on his waist, which proved awkward as he was helped down on to *Tarvit*'s deck. Once there, he spread his feet to keep his balance. Concentrating on his face, which was youthful but set to look forbidding, it was a moment before Pearce glanced at the man behind and following: a fellow plainly clad, with a countenance less dark than his companions — tanned yes, but a golden colour instead of nut brown.

As their eyes met, Pearce received a gesture of the head, imperceptible to others but very plain to him. It said 'you do not know me!' But he did and an urgent whisper came from Michael O'Hagan to tell him he was not alone in recognition.

'Holy Mary, Mother of Christ, John-boy, it's Ben Walker.'

Pearce had a very strong feeling Ben did not want to be acknowledged, yet the sight of a man who had been pressed, with him and the others, out of the Pelican Tavern hard by the River Thames, was hard to absorb without reaction and he was not sure he managed it, having to force his features into a bland expression.

That a friend he had last seen as a physical and emaciated wreck, slaving on the dockside in Tunis in a way that would in a short time see him expire from endless toil, should turn up on the deck of *Tarvit* was, in itself, remarkable. His being in full health, cheeks full and body restored, dressed in baggy pantaloons and wearing a turban was even more so, making it hard to concentrate on the matter to which Pearce immediately had to attend.

He dragged his eyes away from Ben and on to the face of the man with whom he must deal, first identifying himself. 'I am Lieutenant John Pearce, of His Britannic Majesty's Royal Navy, presently in command of the transport vessel *Tarvit*.'

There was a pause as the fellow before him, of medium height, slender build and much the same age as he, with a full moustache drooping to either side of pink sensual lips, carried out a studied and silent examination — to Pearce's way of thinking as a means of establishing his superiority.

He too was scrutinising: taking in smooth skin on an attractive brown face, the steady black eyes, the way the clothing differed from that of his men, finer in both quality and fit, while the hilt of the long sword at his side was heavily bejewelled. In his twisted waistband he had a silver-handled knife and a pistol with filigree silver work on the butt, while the air of easy command was palatable and effortlessly worn.

When his head moved it inclined towards Ben Walker, an indication that he should interpret, instructions given in a deep and rasping voice, oddly attractive given it displayed no malevolence. Ben did so, to then ask Pearce a question in that distinctly West Country burr.

'The Amir al Bihar, His Excellency Raïs Hamidou, wishes to know why you do not offer him your sword.'

47

The title established the truth of what Pearce had suspected; this was no corsair but an Algerine state vessel. The man possessed an Ottoman naval title, something above a captain which, in a fellow who looked to be, like Pearce, in his early twenties, hinted at a man held in high esteem by his Bey.

'The gentleman will observe I am not wearing one.'

Pearce was stalling, still trying to get over the sight of Ben while seeking to make sense of it. His old shipmates on HMS *Brilliant* had reported him as fallen overboard in an engagement with an Algerine galleass, perhaps the very one now lashed alongside *Tarvit*.

This had been early in the present war, at a time when the neutrality of the Barbary Principality had yet to be agreed with the French-leaning sultan in Constantinople. It was assumed he had drowned, but he had survived to be picked up and this was the second time his one-time shipmate had been astounded to come across him.

'I am not prepared to just surrender the ship,' he added, knowing he could not string matters out too long. 'The Bey of Algiers, on the orders of the Sultan Selim, has signed a solemn and binding treaty with my government to respect the flag of our nation. So I am at a loss to know why we are being pursued, with what looks like an intention to take us as a prize.'

The response took some time to translate and, during the explanation, the Amir al Bihar glanced up at the unmarked flag, still fluttering in the breeze above their heads. His remark on that had to be held in check until Ben Walker finished speaking.

'That is a request to parley, not a flag of submission,' Pearce responded.

'What is there to parley?' Ben asked, once instructed to do so.

With frequent pauses, so it could be translated, Pearce launched into a fuller explanation of what they carried, how furious a man like Sir John Jervis and the fleet itself would be to see their casualties intercepted and their well-being endangered.

'If the Amir al Bihar is seeking ransoms, the greatest number aboard are men who have suffered in the service of King George, so they will have to be returned to his gracious person, by the terms of the treaty, both alive and for free. As for the merchant crew, I doubt, given we are sailing under Admiralty orders, they will be treated any differently to the poor creatures laying in their hammocks below decks.'

Pearce paused to see if his words were having any effect. Those black eyes had hardened, to become positively gimlet-like at the notion Pearce would refuse to meekly surrender. The time had come to drive home the possible consequences.

'If you are engaged in an act of piracy, it would not surprise me to see the Bey being obliged to pay a high price for your actions and the breach of his obligations, even to the point of having his city of Algiers suffer bombardment.'

The threat of retribution against Algiers

turned his mood into one of fury, which had Pearce adding quickly, to soften his point, 'My first request is that the Amir al Bihar inspects what we carry, so he knows I speak the truth.'

The deep voice spoke with a rapidity and tone hitherto avoided, evidence he had been made livid and his tirade was lengthy. It was also enough to bring a touch of rouge to Ben Walker's cheeks, evidence he took no pleasure in passing on to John Pearce, when his Amir finished speaking, that His Excellency was contemplating hanging him from his own main yard.

'A crime which could have only one outcome,' Pearce growled, staring straight at the Amir, refusing to be cowed, on the very good grounds it would serve them ill. 'And that is likely to be retribution. Hang me and the King's Navy will do likewise to you.'

'Have a care, Mr Pearce, you're not alone in this predicament.'

Fuller's protest had Pearce's hackles rise, it being exactly the wrong thing for the man to do. Yet he declined to turn and check him, for to do so might imply he had a stature on the ship he did not possess. It was pleasing to hear it was not required, as an even-toned and soft Irish voice spoke up.

'Sure now, one more toot from your whistle and it will be seawater putting a stopper to it.'

'I will — '

'Be silent, Mr Fuller,' Hawker said, 'as our Irish friend suggests, or it will be two sets of hands chucking you over the side.'

'Three,' countered Byford.

The Amir wanted to know what was being said. Pearce had a distinct impression, from the sideways cast of Ben Walker's eye, he was not getting the entire truth, so he spoke to cover for the interpretation.

'I will also, if the Amir accompanies me, show him what steps I have taken to respond, if he is intent on breaking the obligations of that treaty.'

'Raïs Hamidou thinks you are either a brave man or a fool,' Ben said, following on from a rapid burst of Arabic.

'You may tell him I am very likely both.'

Even if the Amir tried to hide it, the response amused him slightly, evidenced by a twitch of those full lips. When he spoke it was loudly, aimed over his shoulder at his boarders. With a swift movement he hauled out his sword, the long blade engraved with symbols in Arabic, to speak once more, with Ben deepening his own voice, seeking to endow his message with the same gravity as his master.

'Have a care, for you will die if you indulge in deceit.' That was driven home by Ben producing from his thick-coloured waistband a long knife. 'I will be close behind you and I have been told what I must do.'

'Mr Hawker,' Pearce hissed, spinning round to speak quietly, he hoped without being overheard, 'I ask that you keep everyone silent and still, for I reckon us to be at a delicate point. Michael: with some discretion, to your place.'

He could see by the look he got that no further explanation was necessary; Hawker knew Pearce had scored a small gain by having the

51

Amir agree to inspect what they carried. The why mattered less than the fact of it being conceded. O'Hagan knew what to do.

'Mr Byford, I think it fitting that you accompany us.' That had him turn back to Ben Walker to say he would be doing so. 'Please inform the Amir al Bihar that he is the ship's surgeon.'

The point conceded, Pearce headed towards the companionway leading down to the main deck, Hamidou stopping to look along towards the prow for a few seconds. Was he wondering what Pearce meant when he said he had taken steps to avoid capture? The man who had issued those words had been surprised to get no reaction; it was as if he had not been believed. The only thing visible was a crew, nervously gathered in the forepeak. Apart from that there was no sign of anything untoward.

The indication to move on was a sharp jerk of the head. Another companionway led the party to the lower deck and the rows of hammocks that contained Byford's charges, their pale faces lit by tallow lanterns. As they passed each one, crisscrossing from side to side and hammock to hammock, the surgeon gave Ben Walker a description of the particular ailment by which they were afflicted, this passed on, though for those lacking limbs explanation was scarcely necessary.

Hamidou was careful in his scrutiny, not willing to be rushed, even getting Ben to ask the more sentient some questions as to how they had come about their hurts. With one or two it was pointless; all they did was stare with blank eyes at the overhead beams. The inspection finished at a rear bulkhead with Byford opening the door to stand aside, allowing Pearce to enter.

5

'Damn you, Pearce, what am I doing here? Give me back my deck at once and confine yourself to your cabin.'

Lieutenant Henry Digby was dressed in a long, flapping and far from clean shirt, with no breeches or footwear. His hair was unkempt and wild, as were his eyes, as he positively spat out these words. For so long the man who had commanded the brig HMS *Flirt*, he had tried and failed to also command John Pearce. Normally ranting at the bulkheads and calling down God on those he saw as his enemies, Digby was enjoying one of his slightly more lucid moments, evidenced when Pearce stood aside to reveal Raïs Hamidou.

'Who is this damned fellow and how did he get aboard without my permission? You have been exceeding your position again, sir. Wait till I get you before a court, I'll see you drummed out of the service.'

The Amir moved further into the separated sickbay to look at this fellow with bulging eyes and spittle-flecked lips, with a sideways glance at the other officer mentally afflicted, lying silently in his cot, seemingly unaware of the disturbance. That also brought forward Ben Walker, which had Digby peering at him for several seconds.

'You, I know you!'

Pearce cursed himself. He had forgotten that

Digby had also served aboard HMS *Brilliant*. He had been the divisional officer of the newly pressed Pelicans, so had been close to Ben Walker as much as he had been to the others, this as they went about their unfamiliar shipboard duties under his direction. These had generally been carried out in a cack-handed fashion, in need of close and sometimes physical instruction, which also occasioned a high degree of familiarity.

Compared to Ralph Barclay, Digby had been a benign presence, more inclined to quiet aid than barking orders, a fact that had not endeared him to his bellicose and hard-hearted superior. When Pearce left HMS *Brilliant* off Brittany, in the company of the other three now aboard *Tarvit*, Ben had chosen to stay aboard the frigate under Digby's eye.

He could not have failed to mark him for his decision and they had remained in proximity until Digby himself shifted to Admiral Hotham's flagship at Lisbon. By the look he was not fooled by the garb or the skin colour, but he registered the shock of surprise.

'Your name, man,' Digby barked, 'which I struggle to recall. And drop your insolent glare when in the presence of an officer.'

Pearce moved a fraction to cut Ben off from Digby's line of sight, turning to address Hamidou. 'Tell the Amir this officer used to command me, but he lost all sense of his responsibilities or of reality. He is being taken home in the hope that a cure can be found for his malaise of the mind.'

Raïs Hamidou looked at Digby, then Ben Walker and finally Pearce, who was surprised to feel a hand moving him aside as the Amir came close to his one-time captain. An arm came out to let the fingers very gently touch his forehead. Even if he could not see those of the Mussulman, Pearce knew he was holding Digby's gaze because that was fixed. He watched as they went from fury and an attempt to recoil, over several seconds, to a look of confusion, this as the Amir mumbled a low and steady incantation.

'What is he saying?' asked Byford.

'He's a'calling down the blessing of Allah on the troubled mind. Such men, in Islam, are often seen as Holy Fools, closer to God than creatures who appear sound.'

'And you,' the surgeon continued softly, 'what of you?'

Ben's tone of voice was different, sharper and no gentle burr. 'It'll not be something to concern yourself about.'

'Does Lieutenant Digby know you?'

Pearce cut in before Ben could respond. 'The man is mad, Mr Byford, and seeing apparitions that do not exist. No doubt Mr Digby is mistaken.'

'He seemed very sure,' was a vexed reply. 'I am obliged to seek alleviation to his condition on the way home, Mr Pearce, and not just hand him over to Bedlam as he is. If I have with me someone who knew him before his senses went, it may help to begin to bring him back to some form of lucidity.'

'I knew him,' Pearce growled, 'and that will suffice.'

'You most certainly did, and I have never before alluded to the fact that it may have been you and your actions that tilted his mind into disorder. When he rants it is your name he most often employs, your actions and insubordination reprised repeatedly. Your presence signifies anxiety. This fellow, who is clearly one of our countrymen, may do the opposite.'

If he was desperate, Pearce was stymied for a response to this animated observation, so at odds with the surgeon's normally composed demeanour. He had always accepted he might have had a hand in tipping Digby over the edge, but to be held responsible by a medical cove was at another level entirely.

There was no time to argue; he had to stop Stephen Byford unintentionally exposing Ben Walker, because if Digby did name him, he might also let on that Pearce knew him too, which was hardly likely to provide an advantage. Luckily the Amir finished his incantation and turned to Ben, with a request to be taken to the great cabin.

That being the last place Pearce wanted to go, he spoke quickly, only realising his protest against the necessity was a mistake when the Amir's eyes narrowed, to soon be followed by a rasp he knew to be a demand that brooked no argument. There was no choice but to oblige and, advising Byford to stay with his charges, he led the way up to the main deck and the cabin door.

He had to pass close to the pantry and those pistols Michael had planted. Was this the time to get his hands on them and perhaps take this Amir as hostage? Ben Walker's knife was closer and Pearce had no idea if it would be employed. He entered the main cabin to find it empty, to then position himself in front of the door that led to the quarter gallery, which Emily used as her nursery, his expression as non-committal as he could make it, even if his heart was pounding.

'If you wish to examine my orders and despatches,' he said, pointing to the bundle on his desk, 'I took the precaution of putting them out. There the Amir will see those that are not sealed are signed by Sir Hyde Parker, Captain of the Fleet to Sir John Jervis.'

That was translated to an opponent looking about him with an expression impossible to read; in fact Pearce realised it had been mostly like that from the moment he came on deck. Even if Hamidou had been made angry, it had manifested itself in a controlled way, to be quickly shielded. He went to the desk, picked up one of the separate bundles tied with red tape, seeming to weigh them before dropping them back.

There followed a series of questions, none asked with much in the way of emphasis by either the Amir or his interpreter. When *Tarvit* sailed and from where, with no need to ask a destination, which had to be Gibraltar followed by England. Then Hamidou turned to look out of the rear casements in apparent contemplation.

Pearce was tempted to speak, to say that

taking possession of the vessel would scarce do the reputation of Islam and Algiers much good in a world that already held them in low esteem. It was an impulse he resisted and continued to resist even when Hamidou picked up one of the casement cushions and lifted it to his face, holding it to his nose for a while.

There were two quarter galleries off the main cabin and with no great haste, and to Pearce's surprise, Hamidou opened the one he should have had as a private dining cabin, but had been using to sleep. When the Amir turned it was obvious he wished to look in on the other quarter gallery, the door of which Pearce was blocking and one on which he had just planted a discreet knock shielded by his body. A gesture to move aside produced a minimal look of impatience, repeated at Pearce's attempt to look uncomprehending.

'He says you are to stand aside.'

When Pearce still did not move it was turned into an abrupt and unmistakable demand that required no interpreter to make it plain, Even then his response was slow, which made Hamidou suspicious enough to order Ben to enter first. The door, when opened, revealed Emily, wrapped in a boat cloak, sitting on the main cot with a sleeping Adam on her lap, wrapped in swaddling clothes under a tarpaulin shawl.

Ben was so shocked at the sight he let out not only a Christian expletive, but another name from HMS *Brilliant*. 'Holy Christ, Mrs Barclay.'

The need to observe a reaction made Pearce

spin to see the Amir smiling. Then Walker turned, to be faced with a question that required a long, detailed answer, which left Pearce at a stand. It was, being in Arabic, incomprehensible, not that there was much doubt as to the content, proven when Ben addressed him, having clearly been given permission to do so.

'I had to tell him, John, but you will not like to be told he suspected something a'forehand.'

'Did I give it away?'

'Not 'it', something. It were the look on your face when we came aboard. And then there was Lieutenant Digby and you disputing with that surgeon fellow. You'll find there's a trace of scent — womanly — on the cushion he was sniffing, so he guessed something was being hidden. He's a sharp cove, my Amir.'

'Not too much so, with you spitting out the Barclay name.'

The sharp one had entered the cabin to look at a woman who responded to his stare with one of her own. With him blocking the doorway, Pearce did not see him place a finger on the cloths surrounding Adam's head, to gaze into the sleeping baby's face before he spoke over his shoulder.

'He wants you to know that Islam respects women and children,' Ben said.

Pearce did not respond to say that was far from the truth as known; it would not serve to antagonise Hamidou, who had come out to go back to the desk and look at him and Ben in turn. Pearce held his gaze but he addressed his old shipmate.

'What did you tell him?'

'Everything. He knew already I were pressed and where, for he's curious of England and our customs. About you in the main.' Pearce raised an eyebrow. 'I said you was a good and honest man.'

'And . . . ?' came the next question, a gesture being made to the quarter gallery.

'What could I say? The lady is the wife of the captain who pressed us, and only Allah knows how she is where she is now and with a child.'

'Barclay's dead.'

'Allah be praised,' Ben cried, before adding in a softer tone, 'for he was a man with a black heart.'

'She and the child are being taken home.'

'Odd that it should be by you, John.'

Why would Ben say that? Yet he must recall what he had seen, the way Emily Barclay had shown clear displeasure at her husband's treatment of him, as well as the way his pressed shipmate had, against all the tenets of the service and society, sought to engage her in a conversation that brought him to the grating. Pearce had been attracted to her; that was impossible to hide.

'Coincidence, Ben, nothing more,' was the response.

Emily had laid Adam in her cot to come to stand in the doorway of the quarter gallery and, having heard the exchange, she addressed Ben. 'Forgive me if I did not recognise you. Mr Pearce has spoken to me of you, as well as of your struggles.'

61

'Best, Mrs Barclay, if I had not done the same to you.'

Pearce thought Emily was being too polite and too open. Her words hinted at intimate conversations, so he spoke himself to stop her carrying on. 'Ben, I need to know what the Amir is thinking.'

'Which I can't tell ye, John. He ain't one to let on.'

'Ask him, on my behalf.'

The response when it came, was a question, one which showed Hamidou to be a fellow in full control of his mind. He recalled the first conversation with Pearce on the quarterdeck, as well as the threat issued, and wanted to know what steps Pearce and all the others aboard had taken to avoid the ship being secured as a prize.

'Which I will tell him, upon his bounden word we will be allowed to sail on in peace.'

'He says you are in no position to bargain.'

'Tell him that you know me well enough to be sure I am not inclined to bluff and exaggerate, if you have to. But know this: I have taken steps that will most certainly make this hull near to worthless and might indeed oblige the Amir to take on board those lucky enough not to drown.'

'He would be curious to see this.'

Pearce forced a smile and shook his head, to hear what sounded like another question posed to Ben — one which, when it failed to be translated, had Pearce asking Ben what it portended.

'He's asking me what I would do, John.'

'Then I hope you would give him an answer that satisfies me.'

'Us,' Emily added softly.

'Might be a trap.'

Ben spoke quickly to explain how he had been saved from slavery and certain death by Raïs Hamidou's uncle. Well-cared-for, brought back to health, he had been instructed in religion, which led him to become a convert to Islam. Of necessity it was not extensive and it was delivered with Ben looking at the nephew of the man who had rescued him. All John Pearce cared about was one thing: would he now favour his old religion over the new?

'Happen if I said the wrong thing, I'd end up in the same dungeon as might be waiting for you. Or swinging.'

'So he's asking if you would renounce Islam and side with us?'

'Reckon that's the drift.'

'And would you?'

Ben shook his head slowly. 'Why would I, when I found peace there? You will recall I was ever an unhappy fellow — '

'Down at the mouth, Ben,' Pearce interrupted, 'but who would not have been aboard *Brilliant?*'

'Weren't just the ship. The others must have told you I was that way even before we met. I carried a troubled conscience, for the things I had done a 'fore I came to London and the Savoy Liberties.'

Ben dropped his head; his voice, which had been sombre till now, became positively mournful.

63

'You can hide from the law but never from your remembrances. I did murder out of passion, John, a poor girl I was sweet on and the man who took her into his arms, to be granted favours never given to me, but those I hankered for. They both paid for my sin of jealousy and I lived with it. That is till I made my peace with Allah.'

'A Christian God is just as forgiving,' Emily said, to get in response a wan smile. Then Ben spoke to the Amir before relating it to Pearce and Emily. 'I have told him I will abide by whatever he wants to do.'

'You would abandon us?' Pearce asked, seeking to hide his astonishment. 'Michael, Charlie and Rufus?'

The reply was forceful, from a man who had never been that way in the past. 'It's that or abandon myself.'

Hamidou spoke again, Pearce recognising the name of the Prophet in what he said. Ben's face, which had been closed up like a child's, immediately cleared.

'He will not do you or anyone aboard harm. Islam does not make war on the afflicted, or a woman and her child.'

Pearce had to ask, but he did pause before doing so. 'Can I trust him, Ben?'

The look that got was angry enough to nearly make Pearce recoil. 'Ours is an honest faith, not like the Christian with its lying priests who glutton while poor folks starve.'

'There are honest and sincere divines, Mr Walker,' Emily insisted, 'just as there has to be

64

men less so in Islam.'

The Amir asked about that exchange which, when provided, made Hamidou emit a quiet chuckle. Ben was then obliged to pass on a new communication only to be in receipt of another enquiry.

'But he still wishes to know what you would have done to try and stop him.'

'It may be wise to keep that to myself.'

Ben Walker was careful in his response. 'I would say, sir, even if'n I don't know you that close of old, it will be by way of a condition. It would not do to let the Amir think you do not believe him.'

'As a naval officer it fell to me to decide on ways to prevent being taken, so I reckon it falls to me to either comply or decline his request.'

A sharp stream of words had Ben saying, 'He is waiting.'

Pearce did not reply for several seconds and, when he did, if he spoke words requiring translation, they were delivered direct to the Amir. There was a description of his official position, followed by a precis of the discussion as to how they were to first try to throw off the pursuit and, if that proved impossible, to confound the notion of capture.

The wailing of Adam John Pearce interrupted the explanation and it was instructive. Both the Amir and Pearce looked put out, which indicated he too was a parent. It served to allow the infant's father to decide on one thing. This was a man whose word he could trust. He had, at some point, intended to show this corsair that he could

65

not act with impunity and that point was quickly made.

'If the Amir will follow me, I will show him my dispositions.'

Hamidou was taken back onto the main deck to be shown and have explained the barrels of powder stored in the carpenter's walk, hard against the scantlings on the starboard side, clear of the waterline in such a high-riding vessel, with a line of slow match set to be ignited by a lantern there for the purpose. They were packed tightly against the side by canvas, as well as full barrels of water, beef and pork, set to ensure the force of the blast went outwards.

'It would blow a hole in our planking for certain and it would not have been kind to your own, Ben. Not enough to sink you, but enough to do serious damage.'

That was why Michael O'Hagan had put two pistols for defence by the entrance: so the man setting the fuse alight, very likely Pearce himself, could not be stopped from acting. Whether he would survive was not mentioned and so he declined to reference the weapons.

Next, the Amir was then taken on deck to be shown the fire engine hose, lashed to the starboard bulwarks and covered with a tarpaulin. It was not rigged to draw seawater but turpentine from a concealed barrel. This would have been sprayed on the deck of the galleass before being ignited. Once a fire had been started, the primary task of the Algerine crew would be to extinguish it.

The conversation that followed was, of

necessity, stilted by translation. The Amir spoke about the level of retribution such acts would have brought down on the crew of *Tarvit*, even the lady and her child. He was then taken to look down on the boats ready to depart in the ensuing confusion of both fire and explosion. They would carry news of the illegal interception of the ship to those who would act on the information, while Raïs Hamidou with a blaze to contend with would be in no state to effect a pursuit.

'Tell him this, Ben. I think his desire for bloody vengeance would have been tempered by the knowledge of the price to be paid, once news of it reached Sir John Jervis.'

Hamidou stood looking at the deck, obviously in deep contemplation. When he raised his head and spoke, it was to tell Ben Walker to pass on his belief that Pearce had engaged in nothing but an elaborate bluff that he would never have carried out.

'The problem for him, Ben, is that he will now never know.'

That got the first full smile since the man came aboard and, having ranged his gaze of the knot of people on the quarterdeck, all with worried expressions, he indicated to his boarders to get back aboard the galleass before aiming more words at Pearce.

'He wonders if you might meet again, John. Indeed, he hopes for it and in well-matched vessels.'

'You are welcome to sail on with us, Ben.'

'If I did John, it would be to confess my crime, and that could only lead to the gallows.'

'You're sure?'

His answer was a fervent, '*Allahu Akbar.*'

The next shout came from the Amir al Bihar and it sent his sailors to rig the sails. Once Hamidou and Ben followed the boarders, the grappling irons were cast off by the crew of *Tarvit* and the two vessels began to drift apart, with the merchantman's boats let go to drift into its wake. Soon both were sheeting home canvas and moving, the galleass swinging onto a southerly course, *Tarvit* heading west.

On both decks the men in command stood gazing, no doubt wondering at what might have been. All that was needed was the smallest misunderstanding, a point made by Byford, in ignorance of what had taken place in the cabin, but well aware of the preparations made to confound the Algerine.

'I am tempted to ask if it was all a bluff, Mr Pearce.'

'While I ask myself why he gave us his word. It may be, having seen what we carried, he reckoned the game not worth the candle. What would he gain from a crock of invalids — and navy at that? If he cannot be sure I was bluffing, I cannot be sure his motives were as pure as he wishes us to think.'

6

It seemed as if all their difficulties disappeared at once; the sea state had become as benign as the wind, making progress steady if still far from truly comfortable. Pearce noticed that the merchant seamen on board, who had hitherto more or less avoided him, now looked at him with a greater degree of respect, which led him to suspect that his actions reacting to the Algerine had grown in the telling.

The Pelicans would have been claiming inside knowledge of his thinking and his actions and they would not be shy to make him sound masterful. They would never know that, in reflecting on what he had done, the man they now seemed to admire was having severe doubts as to whether he had been right to take the risks he had.

The only problem to emerge in the following days lay in the great cabin, where Adam was showing signs of an affliction of the skin, with a naval surgeon useless when it came to providing remedies for an infant. As soon as they raised Port Mahon Emily took him ashore to consult, in a very stilted fashion, with the local equivalent of a midwife, to then return aboard with a nanny goat.

'I believe, although I cannot be certain, my mother's milk is sometimes too potent, too rich. She had no English, no French and I have not a word of Spanish. We can only hope her remedy is the correct one and he does not suffer to be blemished for life.'

'I do hope so too, Emily,' Pearce responded, 'but I also hope you are not asking me for an opinion.'

The brow furrowed. 'I feel I should know these things without recourse to a wet nurse. I handled enough babies when my mother and I did our charitable duty to the poor.'

The reference to her prior life, to which she was determined to return, put paid to that conversation.

★   ★   ★

Pearce had been ashore too, dragging with him a protesting Fuller to insist he purchase ballast on the very good grounds that, as a troubled sea, the Atlantic was a great deal more temperamental than the Mediterranean at any time of year, winter especially.

Once the purchase had been completed and arrangements made to get it out to *Tarvit* and loaded, he went to call upon the Spanish admiral, which he was bound to do out of respect for an ally. He knew he would be quizzed on what was happening with Jervis's fleet and he had his replies ready. They were of a positive nature, with caveats regarding the lack of warships for the number of tasks the fleet had to perform.

There was, of course, another purpose: to report on his recent adventures and advise the

Spaniards that there was a possible corsair sailing the waters between Italy and his command. On the way he could not help but notice the number of frigates, brigs and sloops in the anchorage: vessels which, if they could not aid Jervis, would have been better employed on the sea lanes to make safer the journeys of those engaged in commerce.

Again conversation required an interpreter as Admiral Lángara, a portly fellow who gave out no great sense of seeking activity, quizzed him regarding recent events in Piedmont and the Genoese Republic. Pearce, somewhat distracted by the difference between a portrait of a much younger and thinner Lángara, set against the more substantial fellow before him, could only say that matters were at a stand.

After one failed incursion against the Austrian lines, General Kellermann had retired to his base at Nice and, as far as Pearce knew, the army of the Revolution was once more static. Tempted to enquire as to why such a powerful fleet, which would have greatly increased the ability of the coalition to fight the Army of Italy or any French fleet that emerged from Toulon, was anchored so far from the scene of conflict, Pearce held his tongue.

Not that he lacked an opinion, and it was quite a common one. It was generally held amongst British naval officers that Spain had no great desire to see triumphant a nation that had so often been its mortal enemy. A France utterly humbled would mean the balance of naval forces in the Mediterranean would be severely altered and not to Spain's advantage, the same applying to French supremacy. Let Britannia and the Revolution do battle with each other, which must weaken them both.

'His Excellency has heard of this Raïs Hamidou, Lieutenant,' Lángara's English-speaking aide explained. 'He comes from a prominent family, so high rank is his by right. It is reported the Bey of Algiers greatly admires him and has promoted him to command at a very young age.'

'Could I recommend, sir, that the sight of some of your warships on the horizon would severely curtail his ability to act?'

He watched Lángara's overfed face as this was imparted to him, wondering if the admiral would see it as impertinent. He felt it needed to be said: the British Fleet was overstretched in the number of tasks it had to perform, and besides, if he did object, Pearce didn't care. He had bearded his own elevated superiors, why not a Don?

The irritated reaction was in the eyes only and it was a brief flash at that. The voice, when he spoke, was even, his words being translated as they were uttered. If they were platitudes, Pearce was later to discover that Lángara would have been off to Toulon in a flash if he had not had instructions from Madrid to stay in Port Mahon. Thus he was later to reason the admiral's annoyance was with his political masters, not this upstart British lieutenant.

With the ship's water and wood restored to Leghorn levels and stores of fresh food brought aboard, *Tarvit* raised anchor for Gibraltar, to enter a current that ran favourably for the Straits. Ships had no trouble exiting the Mediterranean; it was getting in that took time, effort and a helpful wind. The stop there would be of longer duration as the crew went ashore to sample the ninety-odd watering holes-cum-brothels the colony boasted. Time to recover from their debaucheries had to be allowed for as well.

Michael, Charlie and Rufus also desired to take the opportunity for pleasure, with their friend and source of funds cautioning the latter pair to mind out for O'Hagan, who was a demon when he was in drink and prone to fighting anyone who came into his arc. He had been in that state when Pearce first clapped eyes on him in the Pelican Tavern, an occasion when the Irishman had thrown a punch at a fellow who was then a stranger, one that would have probably broken his jaw at the very least if it had connected. Luckily, his vision blurred by an excess of ale, O'Hagan missed.

The presence of Adam, now fortunately restored to unblemished skin through goat's milk, prevented Emily going ashore, not that she had much desire to do so and face possible questioning about sharing a cabin with a handsome young lieutenant with a raffish reputation.

Pearce was obliged, once more, to present himself first to the admiral of the squadron based at Gibraltar, then to the governor. The former, when his name was sent in, declined to see him, but he got a better reception at the

Convent, home to the military governor of the Rock.

This turned out to be the newly arrived Lieutenant General Sir David Rose, an old acquaintance last seen when he was on his way back from India. The ship carrying him home had picked up the previously shipwrecked Pearce and his Pelicans and the two had bonded. So the welcome he got was fulsome from a man who was, by nature, both hearty and friendly.

'Damn me, Pearce, you young rogue, you're the colour of a nabob.'

'Too much Mediterranean sun, Sir David.'

'You ain't come across anything to compare with the heat in India. Drains a fellow so much he needs to drink just to stay on his feet.'

'I had always understood that the result of consumption was the opposite, sir.'

That got twinkling agreement and a booming laugh as a servant came in to place wine and goblets between them. 'I daresay I allowed myself the odd stagger. The bottle stands before you, sir, and is in need of sampling. Spanish it is, and as good a substitute for claret as the Dons can manage. They do a fine brandy to boot.'

The goblet before Pearce was filled with wine when Rose nodded to the servant. 'Time for you to rate this first.'

The general being a definite four-bottle man, it was an occasion when Pearce would be obliged to consume more than his normal quantity. At least it was in the company of a cheerful companion, a man with no side and little time for the follies of hierarchy, making it a convivial

74

occasion as much as a serious one. Having drunk with Rose previously, Pearce was quick to get the business end out of the way, only managed after his goblet was filled for the third time.

He got a quick report on the situation over the border, with Spain having concluded a peace in the far north in order to restore its Pyrenean border with France. From the information Sir David had, the talking was still going on, with his visitor then alluding to the inactivity of the Spanish fleet.

'Lángara has his hands tied. The government in Madrid is run by a scoundrel called Godoy, who is said to be bedding the queen. He is no friend to Albion, so Spain could turn from an ally to an enemy in a blink.'

'Hopefully not before we are out of their waters.'

'Come, Pearce, you simply must sample their brandy.'

Tarvit plucked her anchor after two days with a sore-headed crew, which included their naval officer. He had been forbidden to breathe brandy fumes on his son, while being subject to jaundiced remarks from his paramour as to it being sinful to imbibe so much. At least Michael O'Hagan was prevented from ribbing him; he too was in a delicate way.

It was necessary to sail close to the Spanish shore and the formidable fortress of Tarifa, with no sign of danger from its forbidding cannon. Byford was on deck using a borrowed telescope to study the sky, more factually the birds wheeling around the cliffs, an activity he continued to engage in until they left proximity to land.

Emily was on deck too, taking the air, carrying Adam in a crooked arm with Michael O'Hagan at her side, hand ready to steady her should she stumble. Proximity to John Pearce, stood on the quarterdeck with Michael Hawker, had to be avoided but he was watching her out of the corner of his eye and not just her.

There was Tobias Fuller, he seeking to disguise the fact that he was watching Emily carefully and making a poor fist of it. It was something that had become commonplace now the motion of the ship had eased. Not that Pearce was concerned; if anything it was an irritant and one he could ignore, but it did add to the low opinion of a man who had not stood tall for some time.

Given reasonable conditions and a favourable wind it was decided to eschew another stop at Lisbon so they headed straight out into the Atlantic. In the open sea, on a course that would take them well to the west of Biscay, they had the sensation of being the only vessel on the water, rarely seeing another sail. In three weeks, having weathered the Scilly Isles, they raised the Lizard before putting up the helm for the run up the Channel to Portsmouth.

'Sail two points off the larboard quarter.'

The cry coming through the skylight had Pearce handing his son back to his mother, to go on deck: this was a stretch of water regularly used by French privateers but it was also well-patrolled by ships of King George's Navy to

76

ensure they did not enjoy success. What anxiety Pearce harboured evaporated when he was told from the masthead the approaching ship was a frigate, with the pennant of an admiral of the Red Squadron at the main.

'Not Channel Fleet, then.'

'Unless Lord Howe has been replaced,' Hawker replied.

'The tale going the rounds in Leghorn was that he was commanding the fleet from Bath, basking in the glory of the First of June as well as taking the waters.'

'And counting his prize money from the battle.'

The remark had John Pearce thinking about that sea fight, for Emily's husband had been a participant. The success against the French had brought great rewards to the captains who sailed under Howe and it had been added to Ralph Barclay's other achievements, so he was, by the time of his death, quite a rich man. It was one of their bones of contention: Emily wanted him to live off Barclay's money; Pearce was adamant he would not.

'Our friend is coming on,' Hawker said, breaking the train of thought. 'Perhaps he thinks our flag false.'

The remark occasioned a quick glance at the red duster streaming out above his head, yet what had been a jest turned to reality as the frigate increased sail on a course to close. They watched it for some time, wondering if some other sighting had brought this on, but eventually there was no mistaking the intent and nor was anyone in doubt as to the reason. The frigate swung south to then come round on a course to bring them alongside.

'I reckon I am going to finally justify my presence aboard, Mr Hawker.'

'So it seems.'

'Best put on my dress coat,' Pearce said to Michael O'Hagan, as he re-entered the cabin. 'Must look our best for this visit.'

'Do you recall John-boy, it was in these very waters we were pressed for the second time? A bad omen.'

'How can I forget, Michael?' He turned to address Emily, sat once more on the casements, knitting a baby comforter that would keep Adam warm in chilly England. 'That, Emily, was all down to Toby Burns, your nephew, our supposed hero.'

'I doubt I required to be reminded, John. And it is a truism. You can choose your friends but not your relatives.'

'I wonder how you will describe him when you are asked of his progress, which is bound to happen?'

'I will be the soul of discretion.'

Pearce changed the subject, it being perilously close to their ongoing argument about the future. 'Michael, I daresay it would be in order to uncork a bottle of that Spanish wine gifted to me by Sir David.'

'Sure it's a good job he's not aboard. There'd scarce be a drop left.'

'And we would be dining on net-caught sprats. I recall he has a fondness for the creatures.'

78

'More'n a fondness.'

'He was good company, Michael.'

'So I recall, but given what you drank in his company, I'm surprised you can.'

'Physician heal thyself. I don't recall you coming aboard at Gibraltar in a fit state to do your duty.'

Michael adopted a faraway look. 'Gibraltar, sure now, there's a name to ring a bell. Was I there?'

The faint sound of another shout, faint and incomprehensible coming through the skylight, was followed within seconds by a messenger. 'Mr Hawker's compliments, we's being told to heave to.'

Pearce eased on his scraper before making for the deck, there to take hold of a speaking trumpet and give his name, rank and purpose of both the ship and himself, this to a warship now half a cable off the larboard beam. He automatically registered she carried twenty-eight cannon, making her of the smaller variety, which would imply a commander of no great seniority. As soon as she hove to, a boat was lowered into the water and the frigate's gangway was opened.

'I require to examine your papers, Lieutenant.'

'To whom am I speaking?'

'Captain Warren of HMS *Bellona*.'

'I can assure you, sir, upon my honour as a fellow naval officer, the papers of this vessel require no perusal. We are a hospital ship.'

The reply came after a long pause. 'You say your name is Pearce?'

'It is.'

'I seem to know it.' There was another pause before Warren spoke again and now he was plainly visible it could be observed he was conversing with his officers. 'Are you the scoundrel that was given a lieutenancy by the King?'

'Damn,' was the under-the-breath reaction of Pearce, but he was obliged to reply. 'I am, sir. And I would remind you it was done for what His Majesty saw as an act of conspicuous bravery.'

It was a boast Pearce rarely allowed himself, it being blatantly immodest; indeed, forced to tell the tale many times, he had always downplayed his own actions. It was said now to deflect the tone of antagonism apparent in Warren's voice, obvious even imparted through a speaking trumpet. Also induced was a sinking feeling: it had been a forlorn hope he had harboured that the navy at home, unlike the Mediterranean when he was present, would have forgotten his name and how he had come about his rank.

Turning to glance at Hawker, he wondered if the man knew of it. If he did, and it was very possible for he had been ashore at Leghorn, he had made no allusion to it over their weeks at sea. Now the man would not meet his eye, making it obvious he had been regaled with the tale; no doubt it had been termed as scandalous.

'Prepare to receive a party aboard. In fact, I shall come aboard personally.'

No name used, no courtesy in the manner. 'Then I have no choice but to welcome you, sir, and hope once you're satisfied that you will take a glass of wine with me in the great cabin. It is fresh from Spain.'

'Damn you, get about your duties.'

This stricture was not aimed at Pearce but at the hands on *Bellona*, some of whom had come to look over the hammock nettings at this man of whom their captain obviously had a low opinion. Captains did not undertake tasks such as inspection; that was for lieutenants. On close examination Pearce got the distinct impression that, due to the shoulder belts, which could only be for cutlasses, they were armed.

'Sir, I would remind you that a vessel sailing under Admiralty charter is free from the activities of the press. All men aboard bear exemptions.'

'Which I will most assiduously scrutinise.'

'Bar my own personal servants and followers,' Pearce added swiftly; there were a trio on board who did not: his Pelicans.

Warren failed to acknowledge that last part. He was already clambering down the battens to board the boat, now with a dozen armed men at the oars. O'Hagan having come up to observe, he was immediately and quietly addressed by his friend.

'Load my pistols and fetch my sword on deck too.'

'It's the King's Navy, John-boy,' was the whispered response.

'As of this moment, they are as dangerous to us as that Algerine.'

'And you reckon I like a fight?'

'They are going to try and press hands out of

this ship. I intend it should not happen. I need hardly tell you who are without exemptions and are thus at most risk.'

'Happen I should arm myself?'

'No, Michael. You, the navy can hang. Me? All I risk is dismissal from the service. And oblige me by telling Emily what is happening and what, it is possible, might follow.'

'And what, John-boy, would that be?'

'Threatening to take up a weapon against a superior officer. Now I suggest we do not have much time.' As Michael departed, Pearce addressed Hawker. 'We need to open the gangway, Mr Hawker.'

'If he takes any of my men,' was the hissed and angry response, 'it will be not only illegal, it will be an outrage.'

'I agree, and I intend it should not happen.'

'I will report the fellow.'

'Mr Hawker, it is my guess that HMS *Bellona* is not, as I first surmised, cruising these waters to protect against French privateers. Given his admiral's pennant he must be heading to another station and the choice of those could extend to either the East or West Indies, or the Cape of Good Hope.'

'So he could be away from England for a year or more.'

'Just so. Many more if it is the East Indies. Vessels remain on that station for up to a decade. Complain you may, an apology might even come your way. But if men taken from *Tarvit* are transported to such a far-off station, you will wish in vain to see them again.'

Just then Michael appeared, sword in hand, two pistols in his belt, which clearly alarmed Hawker, who spoke as Pearce clipped on the sword.

'I doubt, sir, violence is an answer. Not only are we not in soundings, where impressment may be condoned, if not welcomed, my men have the protections issued by the Navy Board and that should suffice.'

'You have a charming trust in the navy, Mr Hawker, whose officers are adept at ignoring such things as protections, especially when they know they will not face censure until the whole sorry business is forgotten. But I will say this to you. The weapons are not to keep safe your crew, they are required to keep by my side men whom I call friends.'

With that Pearce went towards the gangway.

7

Pearce kept an eye on the men rowing their captain. There was, in the thwarts, beside his superior, the obligatory midshipman whom he could discount. But on such a duty Warren would have loaded his boat with the hard bargains: men who liked a scrap and who delighted in pressing their fellow seamen. If they were not always faced with violence, it was more common in these waters than elsewhere, for the crew of *Tarvit* had accumulated pay that would be as good as forfeit if they were taken aboard *Bellona*.

The sound of bustle momentarily distracted him, making him quick to realise that those crewmen were taking up weapons, cudgels and marlinspikes. What Warren proposed would not happen without violence, for which he was obviously prepared. Thus, Pearce reckoned, he had to be prevented from bringing his men aboard. As the boat swung round to hook on by the *Tarvit*'s battens, he moved right to the gangway.

'Captain Warren, you may bring your mid aboard with you, but I must ask that your rowers remain where they are.'

The face, close up, was red and heavily pockmarked, the hair at the side of the man's scraper a very obvious blonde though it lacked any quality of refinement, being coarse. Indeed, in the round, that was the word to describe an officer with thick lips, hard blue eyes and a bellicose look.

'You may request all you wish, sir, but I, as your superior officer, order you to stand aside.'

'While I must politely refuse.'

'Damn you, have a care.'

'I reckon it to be you who must have that, sir, for I am sure of my ground and the rights granted to me by being given this command.'

The response was an angry bark, one that added more blood to that already cherry countenance. 'A fitting one for a poltroon in the guise of a lieutenant.'

'You may outrank me on the Navy List, sir, but with what Admiral Jervis has gifted me I stand, at present, as your equal. You command your ship, I command mine. You are free to come aboard; your men are not, for they can only do so for one purpose and that is to press men out of a vessel, which it is forbidden to do.'

'I will not dispute with you, Pearce, for you don't rate the privilege, but I am off to fight the nation's foes and that takes precedence over your pretensions. Stand aside, or face the consequences.'

Pearce's sword came out swiftly. 'I fear it is your men who might face the consequences. The only way you can come on to this deck is by assault, one which I assure you will be fiercely opposed, and not just by me. I am prepared for bloodshed, but I wonder if you should be so sanguine, since this vessel will be in harbour in two days where your depredations will become common knowledge.'

'Mr Pearce.'

He had to turn to face Hawker, who looked concerned and well he might be. It was not impossible, if there was bloodshed, that he could be blamed for it along with this titular commander. He would know enough of the vagaries of British courts, not least the Admiralty one, to post much faith in an honest outcome.

'I have seen this Captain Warren close up, Mr Hawker, and I now have no doubt he will take from us as many men as he needs while ignoring their certificates. I have observed a martinet, sir, who cares not for the law.'

'Are you going to do as ordered, Pearce, and stand aside?'

The question was ignored. He kept his sword out with the blade showing to those below, to continue to address Hawker.

'It has been my misfortune to meet Warren's type before; indeed, if you knew the full extent of my tale you would be aware it was such as he who first pressed me into the navy. It might aid your thinking to know that his act was doubly illegal in the nature of those he took up and the location in which it happened. He faced a court for it, made up of fellow transgressors, and was acquitted. The law will not aid you in this, so if you care for your men, you must back me.'

The pause was not of long duration, given the truth of what Pearce was saying registered. Hawker stepped up to the gangway and spoke in a firm voice, repeating what had already been said about the nature of the ship and its cargo, as well as its immunity from what was obviously being planned.

'I must tell you, sir,' was his valediction, 'if you persist in seeking to bring a boarding party onto this deck, I must tell my crew to oppose you.'

'Happen you'll be the second head we break,' Warren snarled.

'So,' Pearce responded, with a smile that infuriated even more a man already in spleen. 'Your true colours, at last. You have a choice, sir. Either come aboard with just your midshipman or return to your own deck.'

'I've a mind to put a ball or two into your hull, to be followed by some grape to clear your deck.'

'I invite you do so, Captain, for that would most certainly condemn you to the Marshalsea. I have had experience of prison and I can say with confidence you would not relish it.'

'Cutlasses, lads,' Warren spat. 'We are going to have to teach these wretches a lesson.'

Pearce swept his gaze along the crew. 'I wonder which one of you will strike at me, an offence for which you, as common seamen, can hang?'

'They will do so under my instructions.'

How short of a full complement was this man? What he was proposing smacked not just of pique but a degree of desperation. It had been the same for Ralph Barclay, tasked to take an undercrewed frigate to sea at the very opening of a new conflict. Not that Pearce was inclined to forgive him; Barclay had brought his men into the Liberties of the Savoy knowing it was outside the law to press there. War had brought him opportunity after five years without a ship and he was short on money. His need was greater than his fear.

Was Warren in a like situation? The navy never had enough men to man its ships in time of war and this one had now been going on for over three years. The pool of volunteers, never in truth large enough, must be exhausted, made more acute by the numbers required to both sail and fight a man-o'-war: over eight hundred for a first rate of a hundred guns, including officers and warrants.

Warren waved to HMS *Bellona* in what must have been a prearranged act. A cannon was fired immediately, aimed at the prow, high and wide enough to be harmless, the plume of disturbed water conveying the message. Warren held the eye of John Pearce with a look that was designed to imply the next shot would be properly aimed.

'How I wish I had asked Mr Hawker to load one of our cannon so we could return the courtesy.'

'Feel free to do so now, Pearce.'

'To provide for you an excuse? I think not. And if you address me at all, please do so in my official capacity. The proper form of address is 'Captain'.'

'You may dream of it sir, but you will never hear me address you with such a title. You are a common seaman who got his step through royal folly. The proper place for you is at the grating, so you may learn some manners.'

As ordered, his boat crew now had their weapons to hand. Worse, a second manned boat was departing *Bellona*. The gangway Pearce knew he could defend, but if Warren was prepared to undertake a full-out assault it would not just be here, but either over the bows or the stern and so spread out it would be impossible to contain, even if every member of the crew opposed it.

It always troubled Pearce that in every naval vessel there were men who relished such a task, though it was often the case of doing so for a cash reward. Yet it seemed as if they, serving themselves, could not abide the notion of others escaping it. Those boarding, chosen by their commanding officer, would do so with gusto and if they were not of a mind to kill, they would not hesitate to break a skull or two.

Occupied dealing with this fresh threat would leave Warren free to bring his own party aboard through the gangway and do as he liked. Pearce reckoned they would be lucky to find themselves with enough crew to get the ship to port.

'I repeat my invitation, Captain Warren. Come aboard and inspect the 'tween decks and my orders.'

Unknown to Pearce, Byford had come up behind him, only to step forward and face Warren, giving his name and occupation, to also add that he found what was being planned to be reprehensible.

'Go back to your probes, sir, and perhaps use one to clear your arse as well as your throat of constipation.'

'I would rather use it, sir,' the surgeon responded in his West Country drawl, which

89

made it more telling than it would have been in fury, 'to produce from your innards a dose of the manners you so clearly lack.'

'That, Mr Byford, will scarce help,' interjected Tobias Fuller.

'This area of the deck is becoming somewhat crowded,' Pearce remarked on hearing the voice. If the agent was aware of the glare he received when Pearce turned to face him, he ignored it, going to a place where he could address Warren.

'It would be folly if all this fell to bloodshed and broken bones. Perhaps if you were to provide us, on a promise of no more, with a number, we could accommodate your requirements.'

'And into whose pocket would go the wages not drawn on when we land?'

'Mr Hawker, that is a base suggestion,' Fuller protested. 'I act only to find a compromise in which no harm will come to anyone.'

'Mr Fuller,' Pearce snarled, swishing his sword through the air. 'If you do not get off this deck you will be the first victim and at my hand.'

'Tell him, Mr Pearce,' came a cry from one of the crew. 'Greedy sod's only seeking to fill his purse with our money.'

'I require twenty men,' Warren called up. 'I will give an undertaking to take no more.'

'Half a year's pay, Fuller,' Hawker said, his distaste obvious. 'I daresay, with your bean-counting mind, you will have already calculated that to the penny.'

Warren had actually and incongruously pulled out a watch. 'You have no more than two minutes to decide, Pearce, but be assured I would be inclined to include those you term your servants.'

'Followers, as I told you. So you would even break the conventions of the service to get your way.'

Warren was smiling now through wet lips. 'By the accords I adhere to, captains have followers; lieutenants do not.'

The sound of a pistol shot startled everyone, making even Warren recoil as he feared himself the target. Every head turned to see Michael O'Hagan holding a pistol with the barrel pointing into the air. He was grinning at John Pearce, who quickly got the message and passed it on.

'I should send back to your ship for muskets, Captain Warren; you will need them to get on this deck. Swords and cudgels will not suffice.'

'You would not dare fire on a King's Officer, not even a scrub like you.'

'I find you free with your insults, sir, but I must warn you there is a price for such laxity should we ever meet ashore.'

'You think I would deign to duel with you?'

'I had no intention to seek such an encounter, sir, but should we ever be in the same place, either this day or another, I will, assuredly, box your ears.'

As expected, that brought another rush of blood to that heavily pockmarked face, but that was not all: unseen by Warren, some of his oarsmen were smiling.

'Is anyone going to be good enough to tell me

what is going on and what has rudely awoken my son from his slumbers?'

Pearce had to stop himself addressing her as Emily, while he refused to term her Mrs Barclay. He also had to adopt a tone he reckoned suitable to the occasion and one loud enough to carry to the boat at the bottom of the gangway. Not even the likes of Warren would seek to board with a lady on the deck.

'Madam, I suggest it would be best if you return to your cabin. The disturbance of your child does not rate with that which Mr Hawker and I have to deal with.'

'Which is?'

It was necessary to produce false exasperation. 'I would say it is not your concern.'

Having ignored his instruction and moved forward, Emily could obviously make some appreciation of what was going on. She was not a sailor but she had voyaged with Ralph Barclay in HMS *Brilliant*, and, given his ways and attitudes, she arrived at an accurate conclusion very rapidly.

'They are seeking to press some hands?'

'Illegally press, Mrs Barclay,' Hawker replied. 'The navy is demanding twenty of my men who all have the papers required to exempt them from such an action; less if they take those Mr Pearce fetched aboard.'

The nature of the threat was then outlined; most importantly the frigate off their quarter was obviously heading away for a lengthy foreign mission.

'The captain has advanced that figure as a

92

compromise,' Fuller butted in, his look of concern seeking to convince her of his deep sincerity. 'I fear if he is forced to board us opposed, he will feel free to take many more, perhaps enough to make risky further progress.'

Emily had heard enough from John Pearce regarding Tobias Fuller to take his apprehension with a pinch of salt. 'But surely even I know that is not permitted.'

'Legitimacy is a distant concept out at sea,' Pearce responded. 'This fellow Warren cares not a whit for transgression.'

'I care, sir,' came the cry from below, 'for my ability to put my ship alongside that of our enemies and give a proper account of ourselves, as should you.'

Emily, when she moved to look out through the gangway, did so with a depth of purpose impossible to impede. Manners had even John Pearce step aside.

'Sir, I beg you introduce yourself.'

'Captain Phillip Warren, of HMS *Bellona*.'

'I trust you are aware of the law regarding the actions you are about to take?'

'You will forgive me, madam, for declining to dispute with you. I heard Mr Pearce advise you to return to your cabin, where I assure you, you will be safe.'

'Safe, sir? And if I do not choose to be safe, what then?'

'Madam, the task I am engaged upon is difficult enough; I would beg you do not make it any harder.'

'Perhaps, Captain Warren, I should introduce

myself. I am Mrs Barclay, wife of the late Captain Barclay, recently deceased in battle, who was held to be a most gallant officer.'

'He was that, ma'am, and you have my sincere condolences. I had the privilege of knowing him when we both served at the Battle of the Saintes in the year — '

The interruption was brutal. 'I know when that was fought, sir, you do not need to condescend to remind me. But perhaps you should be made aware that I am on this vessel through the good offices and at the express command of a man who has become both a good friend and a patron to me, Admiral Sir John Jervis.'

'Whose reputation does him justice. He is a fine officer with an attitude any fighting sailor can do naught but admire.'

'He has begged me to call upon the First Lord of the Admiralty upon my arrival in London, which I will most certainly do, to introduce Lord Spencer to the son of the naval officer who gave his life for his country.'

There was a bit of stutter in Warren's voice. 'Madam, I — '

She cut across him again. 'I would not wish to say that, on the voyage home, *Tarvit* was intercepted by an officer who seemed unclear on the limits to which he could go in seeking to man his vessel. I would also feel it incumbent upon me to write to Sir John and name you, as well as describe your actions this day, which even I know to be beyond validity.'

Pearce took in the view; the second boat

standing off, waiting for orders to board; the deck of *Bellona* with a clutch of blue coats watching intently to see the assault proceed and, no doubt, being the creatures they were, far from pleased at missing out. What he could not see, for Emily was in the way, was Warren's physical reaction to her words. To add to that, he was then surprised when she spoke once more, to broadcast what was a blatant lie.

'I am also, as was my husband, a close friend of Admiral Lord Hood. He was, when last heard, one of the Lords Commissioners of the Admiralty. Having retired from the Mediterranean he will wish, since he knew my husband well, to commiserate with me for my loss. He is bound to also ask of my journey home. Am I to tell him of your actions, sir?'

'Mrs Barclay, if your husband were still with us and here, he would say to you that prosecuting the war is of greater importance than such considerations.'

'I find it somewhat presumptuous, sir, that you feel you can tell me what my husband would have said. You may know him from service in the Caribbean, but I was by his side, even on the day he expired.'

'As I have said, you have my deepest sympathy.'

'But not the actions of one who would revere his memory. What will Lord Howe, under whose command he fought on the Glorious First of June, say when I tell him the tale, for he will wish to hear of it too?'

Pearce was grinning now. Emily was claiming

things that were palpably untrue, but Warren could not know that. In fact, he was the only one near the gangway who did know — Hawker, Byford and Fuller would be in ignorance. There was, of course, one other and he had to fight not to turn and exchange a look with Michael O'Hagan.

She was telling Warren of whom he could become an enemy or, at the very least, a captain who, marked by such powerful men, might find it difficult to move up the greasy naval pole from a frigate to a larger command.

Hood had hated Ralph Barclay, who was no client of his, but of his second in command, Sir William Hotham. There was a man Sam Hood ignored when he could and insulted when he could not. Before Barclay was lost, it became common knowledge in the Mediterranean Fleet that he had threatened Lord Howe for his imperfect handling of the Channel Fleet on the Glorious First and thus did not stand high in that man's estimation either.

It was with a strangled voice that Warren spoke again, proof that the threat had struck home. To make an enemy of one admiral was a bad idea; to do so with three, and the most powerful ones serving at present, was tantamount to professional suicide.

'I must, Mrs Barclay, thank you for reminding me of my proper duty. May I wish you future happiness after your loss. Coxswain, pull away.'

All Pearce saw was the man's back as his boat pulled back to the frigate, the other boarding vessel swinging round in his wake. Emily watched for some time before turning round, her face faux-serious: only John Pearce knew her well enough to discern her amusement.

'Now, gentlemen, I would say my son can sleep in peace.'

8

For a man like Cornelius Gherson, who craved comfort, good provender and respect, the journey from Leghorn had been awful. He had been stuck in various staging posts, obliged to wait for an onward journey at a price he was able to pay. This found him sitting atop a series of coaches in both mountainous terrain as well as an Italian midwinter, either covered in dust or drenched by downpours. What food he could afford at the stops to change horses, given his constrained budget, was of no great quality or quantity, too often leaving him with painful pangs of hunger.

From Leghorn to Rome had been uncomfortable due to the state of the rutted and potholed roads, which continued all the way to Milan. If it rained, that same road became a quagmire. Cloudbursts were often accompanied by lightning, so frequent in its flashes it seemed the ground around him was being bombarded with hot metal. He saw many a tree blasted as well as hayricks incinerated.

The real difficulties came when the conveyances began the climb into the Alps, heading for the Brenner Pass and Austria. The route had a proper carriage road, laid in the reign of the Austrian Empress Maria Theresa, so the movement was steadier but that did nothing to stop the temperature from dropping precipitously. There were times, despite his seagoing boat cloak and head-covering muffler, that left him convinced he was at risk of freezing to death.

The locals — men, women and quite often children — were obliged to keep the route clear, doing unpaid labour called the *robot*, this being an obligation owed to the Austrian state or their aristocratic overlords. Despite their efforts, winds created impassable snowdrifts even when the fall was light; there were times when the snow was so dense it was impossible to see a few yards ahead, which brought the conveyance to a halt.

That meant sheltering underneath the vehicle's body, this while those who could afford an inside seat huddled round a small stove, which they declined to share with the less fortunate. Nights were spent in barns shared with livestock, sleeping on dirty straw full of biting vermin, in the company of the kind of lower orders who barely ranked above the description of peasantry, added to which none of them spoke English.

Indeed, in terms of tongue, they were a polyglot set of individuals, with Germans of Austrian or Prussian extraction who could barely comprehend each other so different were their accents, added to Italians from various cities who spoke in a raft of local dialects.

Gherson had long detested Emily Barclay; he had taken great pleasure in managing to blackmail her into paying for his journey. But now he had the daily discomfort of hanging on to the rooftop rail to avoid tumbling off and breaking his neck. He was obliged to get out and walk at every serious incline, forced to carry his sea chest on his shoulder, so that feeling grew into an obsession predicated on a deep desire for revenge. Everything he suffered was laid at her door.

These multiplied in a man easily offended with things that challenged his self-worth. By the time he reached the Austrian capital, she had gone from the rare beauty, on whom he had for a long time harboured carnal desires, to the very essence of an evil sorceress requiring a stake through her heart.

His first task was to go to find a communal bathhouse — these had existed in the city since Roman times — where he could wash off from body and hair the filth of the journey, examine the bite marks from the fleas he had encountered, then shave off a week of growth with great care and change, possible since his sea chest contained several decent shirts, fresh breeches and a passable coat, while his good-quality boots, which he had kept wrapped in cloths in inclement weather, only required blacking to make them presentable.

Next he had to find somewhere to stay that would not clean out what remained of the coin that he had dunned out of Emily Barclay in Leghorn to pay for his onward travel. This took him back to the central square where the Italy coaches began and ended their journeys, as did those from all over the Holy Roman Empire. It was surrounded by inexpensive accommodation for travellers, none of it salubrious. He eventually found a place to lay his head and leave his locked chest: a tiny room he rented, paid for in advance.

Gherson had long wondered, having reached Vienna, how he was to progress beyond Hamburg. He had the means to get to the North Sea port, yet that would not provide to take him to England. He would have to seek a berth as a seaman on a ship bound for home, using the few skills he had acquired from his time as a pressed sailor.

Such a prospect did not accord with the Gherson sense of dignity and here he was in the capital city of the empire. Vienna sat at a crossroads which connected every part of Europe and the Levant, even including Muscovy, while the Hapsburg Crown Lands, added to the various imperial dependencies, encompassed a huge area and dozens of nationalities. Trade flowed in and out of the city from all directions, to the north and south, by the River Danube.

Reason told him this would bring travellers to the city in abundance, as well as those who wished to profit or take pleasure from its abundant activity. Having been a sharp in times past, he resolved to search for a mark, some dolt from whom he could extract the funds needed to get him to Hamburg in more comfort and, once there, purchase a cabin passage to England.

He reasoned one capital city had to be much like another and Vienna must attract the country-bred guileless in the same manner as London; best of all would be if he could find someone who came from England. The key was places where strangers might mix and, in this, there was no greater attraction than a coffee house. Being a city small in comparison, he found an area with an abundance of these dedicated to the same pursuits as at home: gossip, occasional conversation more elevated in tone and, at this time of year, merely the notion of keeping warm.

It took some wandering and much interrogation to locate one patronised by English travellers and traders, given his questions were usually met by incomprehension. He eventually came across a fellow with a few words in English who, with much arm-waving and confusion, directed him to a place near the Danube quays. This he entered discreetly, choosing a table that allowed him to both eavesdrop on conversations while keeping an eye on the door in order to observe comings and goings.

The place was both warm and smoke-filled, and since it could have been anywhere, and he could hear his own tongue spoken, Gherson almost felt at home. He paid for a supply of the brew and tried, with no success at all, to decipher an Austrian newspaper, while in reality using it to make his presence appear natural; staring at any part of the room or person would bring on attention he wished to avoid. But by careful manoeuvre he could use the papers to look at each corner in turn.

He was behind the newspaper, facing the door, when a voice interrupted his examination. *'Ist frei, mien Herr?'*

Gherson looked up to see a fellow with a snub nose in a round, rosy-cheeked face, a tricorne hat in one hand, the other pointing to an empty chair nearby, his pale-green eyes anxious.

'Forgive me,' Gherson said, 'I have no German.'

'You're English,' came the response, accompanied by a look of relief, quickly accompanied by a verbal one. 'Thank the Lord. I'm damned if I can get a proper handle on the language. Been practising such phrases for an age, ever since I landed at Lubeck.'

Gherson smiled in return, taking in the height — not great — as well as an impression of slight portliness 'You have achieved a greater degree of efficiency than I, sir. Given I did not even comprehend the question.'

'Damned difficult, German. Can manage a bit of French, but that's not of much use at present. But I say, what is the answer to my enquiry?'

'Forgive me,' Gherson spluttered, with a show of embarrassment caused by the continued gesture of the hand. 'Please feel free to take the chair.'

Gherson was not sure he wanted the fellow to pull it closer to him and his table, but that being done it seemed boorish to object.

'I take it, then, you're not native to Vienna, sir?' was the very silly question he asked, before he shed his double-shouldered cloak to reveal Gherson's first impression to be accurate. That exposed a somewhat slack body completed by a flabby belly, also showing clothing of decent quality but no finery.

'Passing through only,' Gherson replied, 'on my way back from Italy.'

'Damn me, there's a stroke of good fortune. I am on my way to that very place.'

'Grand Tour perhaps?' Gherson enquired hopefully; that meant deep pockets.

'Nothing grand about it, Mr . . . ?'

'Gledall, Charles Gledall.'

'Glad to make your acquaintance, Mr Gledall. My name is Arthur Boyce.'

'Likewise, Mr Boyce, but if it's not for a tour, I am bound to ask the purpose of your trip. Commerce, perhaps?'

'I doubt I could term it that. I carry a command from my employer that his eldest son, who is visiting Italy for the art, is to come home at once.' Boyce's voice dropped to a discreet level. 'To tell the truth, I think the young man in question is more interested in live flesh than that daubed on paintings.'

'A juvenile rakehell, then?'

'Not really. He is merely a wealthy young man with good looks, an excellent bloodline and active loins. It would be crass to condemn him for that which all of his age crave.'

'Sir, it does not diminish but stays with us. You will find Vienna accommodating in that regard, as is any other metropolis that lives off ship-borne commerce. I was accosted more than once by a trollop on my way here.'

'No doubt true, but I must restrain myself lest I fail in my task. I cannot disappoint my employer until I am sure his wishes have been met, which is a sore trial when travelling alone. Then there is, of course, my dear wife who would be mortified if I came home diseased.'

'Can I enquire as to whom it is who employs you?'

'That, sir, I must keep to myself. It is a name too easily recognised and one to which no scandal or enquiry can be allowed to attach itself.'

'I admire your loyalty, sir, to both your wife and your patron, which is rare in these times. I daresay such rags as the Observer would pay you a guinea or two for the details if, as you say, the family is prominent. But you must avail yourself of some coffee and tell me why you are not at present on your journey.'

'The Brenner Pass has been blocked by exceptionally heavy snow, as well as a fall of rocks.'

'Then I count myself lucky to have got through, for I have not long arrived.'

Boyce ordered a pot of coffee before embarking on what was close to an interrogation regarding Italy, the discomfort of travelling added to questions about what he should seek to see in the short time he expected to be there. Naturally this allowed Gherson to establish that his itinerary could take him all the way to Naples, obliged to pass through and stop in Milan, Florence and Rome to make sure his charge was not already on the way home.

'His father has written to him several times to say he should return but has been ignored. Hence my mission.'

'An expensive business,' Gherson opined.

'That it is. More coffee, Mr Gledall?'

'I really should decline. I am required to call in at our embassy to see if my funds have arrived.'

For a man who had no real story prepared, Gherson made one up with a facility possessed from an early age, first employed in lying to his father about the theft and sale of valuable metals. If that had been spontaneous, the ability to quickly fabricate had soon become a necessity when he found himself branded a thief and cast out onto the streets, to make his own way in the world.

It was not only a ready tongue and a ready ability to invent that had saved him. His primary gift was strikingly good looks, almost feminine in their gentility, which had many people take him under their wing — to later regret their generosity and the expense it had visited upon them.

Blonde, near-white hair, long now and inclined to swish, framed a face with smooth, unblemished skin and corn-blue eyes, to which was added a winning smile, easily turned sad and troubled. These gifts had seen him bed and live off many older women from a precocious age, though it often caused much trouble, given none were without a cuckolded spouse.

His story had Charles Gledall as the owner of an emporium close to the Bank of England and the wealth of the city, travelling in Italy, seeking out goods he and his partner could sell to their affluent clients. Pottery from the Capo di Monte manufactory in Naples, fine leather objects and blown glass from Venice, beautiful cloth from Florence as well as intricate metal goods from the artisans of Milan.

This was interspersed with invented recollections of places in the Italian Peninsula Gherson had never visited, sites to visit such as Pompeii and Herculaneum, the Coliseum and the Baths of Caracalla in Rome, the Ponte Vecchio in Florence and the Rialto in Venice.

These he culled from the recollections related to him by others. Added to this was advice and dire warnings about potential pitfalls, not least the number of villains to guard against. To paint a picture of a Latin intent to deceive or rob was not hard — it was the stuff of many a theatrical drama — nor was there any difficulty in imbuing them with near supernatural abilities in the underhand line.

'You experienced this, Mr Gledall?' enquired an enthralled Boyce.

'Came close to it many times, sir, and only innate caution and London savvy saved me: the knowledge it was never safe to trust in what one was being told. I say to you to always be on the lookout for dissemblers. The friendliest-seeming fellow will often turn out to be the greatest villain.'

'So you travel on for home?'

'I do, but with possible disappointment. My last stop was to be the Meissen pottery works, but I fear I may have to pass up on that.'

'Why so?'

'Simple, Mr Boyce. I have near exhausted my funds and my lines of credit by the quantity of samples I have sent back to my partner.'

'He has been slow to provide you with more funds?'

'I cannot say that. The war with France makes what should be straightforward fraught, but the delay is discomforting. I have been obliged to reside in what can only be described as inferior lodgings and will be stuck in Vienna likewise till the matter is resolved. Now, if you will forgive me, I must, as I said, go to the embassy and see if anything has come in from London.'

'In such a circumstance you must allow me to pay for your coffee.'

'That is most kind.'

'Mr Gledall, it is small recompense for the fund of information you have gifted me. I did fear to get dunned by cunning foreigners, especially in Italy, but I will feel safer now. You have told me what to avoid and I must, since I am carrying the funds necessary to get my charge and myself back to England.'

'If you remain stuck in Vienna, Mr Boyce, perhaps we can dine in each other's company. Perhaps tomorrow. I have a strong hope my needs will have been met by then.'

'A splendid notion. My informants say the Brenner will be impassable for several days.'

'Should I call upon you?'

'No', Boyce responded. 'Let us meet here, sir, rather than have you wander the streets of the city, for I am aware I have no knowledge of it and could easily get lost and I assume that too could apply to you.'

'Then it is settled. Three of the clock, perhaps?'

'A trifle early for my comfort, sir. Five would suit me better.'

'Five it is.'

Gherson stood, nodded and made for the

door, Boyce picking up the newspaper, which had been discarded, to likewise peruse it with incomprehension. Not for long; his companion was back by his side in a couple of minutes.

'Mr Boyce, I think some scoundrel has stolen my cloak.'

'Lord in heaven. Are you certain?'

'It was hung by the entrance and it is not there now.'

'This does not strike me as a den of iniquity, sir. Someone may have taken it in error, which means they would thus have left their own.'

'But how would I know which one that would be?'

'I suppose you must ask the proprietor.'

'I fear he will not know either.'

'But he will be appraised of the problem and, if your cloak has been taken in error, the fellow who took it will soon realise his mistake and return.'

Gherson did crestfallen very well. 'It may not be the case, Mr Boyce. The garment is singular and near to brand new, only just purchased in Verona, a special thickness and triple cape to alleviate the journey through the Alps and keep out the cold. I must entertain the notion that whoever took it did so intentionally.'

'Which will still require you to inform the owner. I am sure there are watchmen here to deal with such matters and he can advise you as to whom you must inform.'

Gherson sat down heavily in the chair he had so recently vacated. 'I must tell you, Mr Boyce, I have been less than completely frank with you. I had no intention of damning my partner, but I fear he has not been as assiduous as he should in sending me the funds I need to get home.'

'Which I assume leaves you at a stand.'

'It does indeed. I fear I may not be able to pay my share of any dinner we might have. I must keep my small reserve in hand.'

'The cost of dinner I can meet, sir. As to your circumstances, would you like me to advance you a small sum to ease your burden?'

'What gentleman could accept such an offer?' Gherson protested.

'Only a gentleman would refuse,' was the equable response.

Gherson pondered for a while. 'I would have to give you a note in hand so you can call in the gift on your return to England.'

'Naturally.' The green eyes, deeply concerned, changed swiftly to an amused look, which was enhanced by a slow smile showing good teeth. 'Not bad, Mr Gledall, which I assume is not your real name.'

Gherson's blood drained from his face and he felt a sinking sensation in his gut.

'Please do not worry. It may interest you to know that my name is not Boyce. I have to conclude we are both engaged in the same line of work. You are seeking to dun the innocent Mr Boyce out of the funds you need, perhaps to get home, perhaps to stay in Vienna. Maybe you even speak German.'

Gherson's look of shock softened and he examined 'Boyce', who continued in a less jaunty tone with narrowed eyes.

'I have been in Vienna a week now, and I have found it hard going in our game and hopeless within these walls. There are so few English folk here and they are sharp-minded and not of the type to be easily gulled, so finding a dupe is near to impossible.'

'So you are a sharp?'

'Please do not protest, for that is hypocrisy. I must say you were not of the kind I would normally have given consideration to. Your appearance did not lead me to suspect I could take you for much but desperation makes it necessary. Then to find you seeking to work me when you pulled the cloak gambit, one similar to the stolen coat I have in the past employed myself . . . '

'Who are you?' Gherson asked.

'Let us leave my name at Boyce for now. But do tell me, what was it you hoped to gain?'

Gherson took a long time to reply. 'I have to go home but I seek to do it in comfort, not sitting and freezing atop another coach with my bones rattling at every dip.'

'A worthy purpose.'

'And you?'

'I had hoped for some young fool on his way to Italy, one I could accompany in order to worm my way into his confidence, but the war has curtailed such adventures. Yet there are still some touring to the south and it was my intention to travel there and look for them. A fool is a fool wherever he is.'

'I sense that London might have become too hot for you. Why, otherwise, would you seek to employ your wiles abroad?'

'An easy deduction, sir, but it pains me to add, an accurate one.'

'So we find ourselves at a stand.'

Boyce cupped his round face in his hands, clearly in contemplation. 'I do have a solution, but it requires two people to execute what is needed and perhaps an element of violence. I have marked a Jew in the gold trade, who daily walks the streets that fringe their part of the city. He carries with him coin so he can deal on street corners — I think for stolen property — foolishly without any protection that I can observe.'

'One Jew?'

'He may be carrying a weapon under his garments, for they are voluminous.'

That did not suit Gherson at all: he had been all his life more visited upon by viciousness than a perpetrator of the same. 'Violence is not my metier.'

'Nor mine, but to paraphrase the Bard, need makes footpads of us all.'

Cornelius Gherson listened as his companion in misfortune outlined his plans, and very exciting they sounded. The Jew must carry substantial sums of money and it was possible that would be augmented by an amount of gold, for he was as likely to be selling as well as buying, that being the Levantine way.

Boyce described the promising places where an assault might take place, for of necessity, any transactions the fellow engaged in had to be clandestine: alleyways, the deep entrances to certain buildings. His voice rose and fell as he

112

sold the notion that both their problems would be solved in a few seconds of activity.

'And there is the added fact of us going our separate ways afterwards, you north and me south, which will confound any pursuit.' Boyce produced a gesture of humorous dismissal. 'Not that this city is any better provided with watchmen than London was before the Bow Street Runners. I do not fear a hand on my collar.'

Arrangements were made as to where to meet, with it made plain to Gherson that any weaponry required would be provided. Boyce reckoned he could get access to a pistol, though that would be more to threaten than employ; the sound of a gun going off was likely to attract too much attention. When they finally parted company it was dark, but they did so with a mutual commitment based on grim determination.

At cock's crow the next morning, Gherson packed a ditty bag with as many of his possessions as it would hold; his chest and a good deal of what it contained he would have to abandon. He then made his way to the square from which the coaches to the north were preparing for the first stage of their journey, paying what he needed for a rooftop place, knowing in doing so that might mean walking part of the way and, unless fortune favoured him, he would indeed need to get across the North Sea as a common sailor.

The fellow who called himself Boyce he would avoid like the plague. Gherson knew, from his own experience and activities, that when someone offered salvation or sudden riches, it was generally a way to enrich or save themselves. The best way to achieve that when committing a crime was to have to hand another person, one who could be sacrificed to the law and, if need be, to the gallows.

9

'Mr Byford. If I may speak with you. I require your assistance in a matter of some delicacy.'

John Pearce had entered the man's tiny lower-deck compartment with some reluctance, to find him sitting at his foldaway table, reading a tome so thick he assumed it to be some medical treatise. The confined space was full of shelving, some laden with books, others with jars containing the various ingredients he needed to make up curative potions. On a wall hung instruments from saws and pincers to the probes required to ease the plight of costive sailors, often employed on men who had an unwavering diet.

He was unsure how he stood with the surgeon and the look he received did nothing much to soothe him: enquiring but with no great show of interest. A slight fellow with light-brown wavy hair, worn long, he had, as suited his profession, a studied air. There was no doubt he took his duties seriously, while in the matter of Henry Digby, Byford laid the affliction at his door: if there was a case to answer, he was not minded to defend himself.

'If I can oblige you, Mr Pearce, I will.'

Those words were delivered with no trace of enthusiasm, which left Pearce wondering if he should even ask, since he would be ignorant of the problem. Alerting him could produce the very opposite result to that required. More than a refusal: active obstruction, yet Pearce felt he had no choice but to continue.

He did also entertain the notion, before deciding against it, of telling the surgeon he had brought the problem upon himself by an overhasty reaction to his being shifted to *Tarvit* from HMS *Flirt*. He had no expectation to be promoted to command when Digby lost possession of his wits, but he did half-hope for another berth in the Mediterranean to which he could shift with the Pelicans.

In getting Pearce out of his area of command, Sir John Jervis had killed the notion and with it an arrangement he might make with the new captain of *Flirt*. Every serving officer had his favourites and what he was hoping for was not uncommon: to swap a trio of hands from his new vessel and have his friends transferred so they were under his protection. Instead he had just taken them with him and now the chickens of that decision were coming home to roost.

'You will be aware that the crew of *Tarvit* are, once on shore, in possession of exemption certificates that render them safe from the press?'

'After our recent run-in with the navy, how could I be sure?'

Pearce smiled. 'Dry land is not the mid-channel. If the law is circumvented occasionally, it is dangerous to abuse it.'

'Your purpose, Mr Pearce?'

'The men with whom I came aboard lack that vital protection. They are, in fact, listed on the muster roll of HMS *Flirt*, still in the Mediterranean.'

That engendered a lifted eyebrow. 'Are you telling me they could be deserters?'

'It's a moot point, but it's possible. They came aboard under my orders and with my express permission, at a time when, in a sense, I was the temporary commanding officer of the vessel they left behind. Having got them to this point I have a continuing care for their welfare.'

'It would be a purblind fool who did not see there is a relationship between you that transcends naval hierarchy.'

'Is it so obvious?' Pearce enquired, in truth wondering more about himself and Emily.

'Noticeable. I rate your O'Hagan a good man, who has always been polite to me, but my instincts and experience tell me being a servant is not a role for which he is cut out. I once tended a bare-knuckle bruiser and I must say the scars he carries indicate such a one-time occupation. Then there are those knuckles on his hands. They do not grow to be so prominent unless they have been overly employed and certainly not in carrying a tray.'

Pearce just responded with a look implying it could be true, it could be false.

'And the other two, with whom you could be said to be overly familiar. Their names — remind me?'

'Taverner and Dommet.'

'I take it whatever you are about to ask for involves them.'

'If I have appeared to beat about the bush, forgive me. Their safety is of great concern to me. I would say as much, if not more, than your

117

dedication to your patients.'

'You prick my curiosity, sir.' The tome was closed slowly and Byford indicated a chest on which Pearce could just about perch. 'But that has been the case since the day you came on board at Leghorn. Added to that, I am not alone in my wondering — it has been alluded to by others.'

'Mr Hawker?'

'And Mr Fuller. When I say 'alluded to', I do mean in a casual way.'

'Then,' Pearce responded, lowering himself gingerly onto the edge of the chest, 'it is best that I satisfy it, at least to you.'

He was certain the surgeon had a partial inkling of what had happened regarding his rank and how it had come about; this would have come from Hawker, given the master could hardly not mention it after their recent run-in with the navy. Reprising that would not induce the feeling he wished to generate, one of an injustice requiring to be corrected. To do that he reckoned it best to start from the very beginning and that included his own background.

He spoke first of his radical father, Adam Pearce; of the peripatetic life he had lived as a youth, traversing the nation to hear delivered the parental message, repeated in pamphlets, damning wealth and privilege while calling for universal suffrage so that those affected by governance got the right to choose it.

Naturally the powers in place had little sympathy for the notion of the man propounding it; indeed, they had sought to silence him by

118

various stratagems, all of which failed. Finally one of Adam's pamphlets contained words that in their insinuations could be construed as a crime, which led to him and his son ending up in the Fleet Prison.

Released, Adam Pearce had gone straight back to his old ways, if anything emboldened by his recent experiences, ramping up his rhetoric and using what was happening in France, where the monarchy had been humbled, as an example of that which needed to be done., That was a step too far and flight to Paris, to avoid a potential capital sentence based on a spurious writ for seditious libel, became the only option.

'So we found ourselves in the French capital.'

'Hence your facility with the language?'

'I was fairly proficient prior to Paris. My father studied there as well as Edinburgh and was a fluent speaker who then became my tutor, yet being in Paris refined it. Nothing compares with immersion and necessity to polish a foreign tongue, added to which it was a golden time of social pleasures, before Robespierre and the Jacobin madness.'

John Pearce had come to full maturity in Paris, a city in happy ferment, where the rigid constraints of morality had ever been more lax than England even under Louis. Now they seemed, certainly in the circles he had grown to move in due to his father's fame, to be utterly free from the taint of hypocrisy in matters of the heart.

It had been an education for him in every sense: young, growing tall and reckoned to be turning handsome, though initially gauche, he was only too willing to be taken in hand by men of erudition and the youngster was a quick learner. More importantly, given he had the facility and stamina of his youth, he became an attraction to ladies of much experience in the art of dalliance.

'I see a quiet smile, Mr Pearce,' Byford said, unable, for the first time, to avoid looking curious.

'Recollection of stimulating conversations and pleasures innumerable. But to continue.'

His father came to see that what he had hoped for was being corrupted and he was not a man to remain silent. His comments and speeches no more pleased the new men in France than they had the powerful in London, which eventually meant a French prison beckoned. Added to that, Pearce's *père* was ailing: he needed to come home to be attended to by people he trusted, so his son was sent ahead to see if it was possible.

Pearce described how that had exposed him to danger, for the writ included him as an accomplice, and how he found the Corresponding Societies, which had been at the heart of radical thought, shattered by an alarmed, terrified and unforgiving government.

He found himself pursued by their agents over several days until, on a foul night, he had taken refuge in the Pelican Tavern, situated in the Liberties of the Savoy. This, he had to explain to Byford, was an enclave that ran alongside the River Thames upriver of Blackfriars, a place where those with a writ attached to their name could live without fear of the tipstaff.

'That proved to be a mistake. The tavern was raided that very night by a press gang.' He had to stop himself naming who had led it. 'It mattered not to the man in command that this was in total contravention of the law of the land or the rights of its citizens. I was taken up and so were the men you have referred to. Ben Walker, the fellow who interpreted for Raïs Hamidou, was another, as well as an older fellow called Abel Scrivens, now sadly deceased. Together we formed a group of mutual assistance and protection against arbitrary authority.'

It did not seem politic to mention it had been hard going, so he skipped over the reason they had parted from the frigate off Brittany, only to be pressed into service once more on the way home, which had bound them together even more. Nor did he mention the fight that had earned his promotion, or his shame at having failed his companions soon after.

'Suffice to say we have become a band of brothers, as it says in the Henry play. As such, we refer to each other as Pelicans.'

'You rose to wear a blue coat, though I am led to believe in a way not much appreciated by your fellow officers.'

'Another tale, too long to tell and of no relevance to that which I have come to ask.'

'You will have guessed Mr Hawker has availed me of it, though he has only the bare bones.' When Pearce didn't speak, Byford added, 'So I take it you have come to seek something on behalf of your — what did you call them — Pelicans?'

'I have. Our destination is Portsmouth.'

'Haslar and the hospital, to be more precise.'

That got a gesture from Pearce to imply it mattered little. 'I have to find a way to get them ashore in safety, in a situation where they could well be required to show certificates they do not possess. Added to which *Tarvit* is on charter. It may well be that the Navy Board has in mind some new task that will take it away from England in short order, perhaps another journey carrying stores to the Mediterranean.'

'Where your Pelicans, even with you there to plead their case, could face a charge of desertion if you cannot get them to safety?'

'I see you are ahead of me, Mr Byford.'

'Far enough to sense that you wish to use my good offices to save them, perhaps by slipping them into the naval hospital as patients.'

'Further ahead even than I thought.'

'Enough also to see that you are willing to make me party to a deception and one which could land me in deep water.'

'It is a lot to ask.'

'So much that only a fool would agree without giving it careful consideration.'

'Then you will give it that?'

'Mr Pearce, I have limited experience of naval life, but from what I have observed it is somewhat barbarous and in Sir John Jervis we have, by rumour and indeed repute, an admiral who often desires to set an example. He could well apply that to your friends. Such factors will affect my judgement. Now.'

Byford flipped open the book, which was as good a way as any of saying he wished to be left alone to think.

Making his way back to his own cabin, aware that if he had been on deck he would have been able to see the southern coast of England, Pearce shifted his thinking to his other problem. If the wind didn't turn foul, they would soon raise the Solent and surely be berthed off Haslar within a day. There Emily and Adam would be going ashore, but where would they head for?

He wanted her to travel, like him, to London, but suspected she would want to go straight to her parental home, there to play the grieving widow with her posthumously born son, to wallow in a mixture of sympathy and joy that at least she had her infant as comfort. Pearce could think of no way to stop her, even though he knew, if Emily ever got immured in that society, it would be the devil of a task to extract her.

It was a world which, socially, reckoned on a three-year widowhood before another suitor could decently pay court. To that would be added another twelve months before any mention could be made of nuptials, which would then be subject to a decent interval before they could take place.

John Pearce was contemplating five whole years perhaps before they could be a couple, in which he knew he would either go mad or, well aware of his nature, cease to hold to fidelity. To him it seemed like an eternity, added to which his son, given he would be sentient by then, would very likely be, to all and sundry, Adam Barclay for his entire life.

'You look grim, John-boy,' O'Hagan said as he stopped by the pantry door.

If only you knew why, Pearce thought, for he had been ruminating on how he had avoided the inquisitorial eyes of the women of Leghorn. Several had been made overcurious by the way he had aided Emily when it was obvious she was about to give birth, getting her away from the ball they were both attending, first to a carriage, then to the rooms she had taken near the port.

His action had been the spontaneous one of a man in love and one who knew, as others did not, the child about to arrive was his own. Being indifferent to what society thought of the affair he and Emily had conducted, he was happy to face and dismiss the opprobrium such a liaison would engender. Emily was very different: she cared deeply that she should not be shamed and also Adam should not suffer the taint of bastardy.

His excuse, of being a close friend to Captain Ralph Barclay, bound by a promise to look after his wife if anything untoward happened, sounded even doubly feeble when mentally reprised than it had at the time. In order to divert attention he had made sure, on returning to the ball, to be seen by those in whom his actions had aroused questions, dancing with a lustrously beautiful Italian Countess with whom he had enjoyed a previous liaison. It was an aid to deception that at the time had caused something of a minor scandal.

John Pearce could tell himself till doomsday he had only left with the countess to avert suspicion. But that would not hold when, in the early morning, he left a bed where he had enjoyed a great deal of carnal pleasure, this to make his way to *Tarvit* and get to sea, thinking he was going to pursue a woman and child who had departed previously in another merchant ship.

Emily, of course, was entirely unaware of his indiscretion, but that did not prevent him from feeling like a scrub.

'Michael, I think I need to confide in you.'

'Sure, I sense a sin in that.'

'You're too sharp, sometimes.'

'While you can be too blunt, John-boy, an' cause upset.'

'Something happened in Leghorn — '

'A whisper might be in order.'

And it was, as Pearce explained what had happened and sought to emphasise the need. If Michael had reckoned soft speaking was wise, that did not apply to laughter, which pealed out of his shaking frame, until he realised it needed to be suppressed, which made his jest wheezy.

'Never met gonads with a conscience, and sure, neither have you.'

'I'm thinking of being open about it, Michael,' Pearce hissed. 'Telling Emily.'

'Are you an eejit, or what?'

He outlined the hope he had conjured up. If he told Emily what had happened once, he might be able to convince her it could happen again and was almost bound to if they suffered an enforced separation. Such a thing might change her mind about returning to Frome.

'Never in life,' Michael asserted forcefully if quietly. 'You're likely to break her heart. She trusts you now, John-boy. Tell her and it has to be doubted she will ever trust you again,'

'So I must keep it secret.'

'Which I will do also, as would a priest.'

When Pearce entered the cabin he found Emily cooing over Adam, being quick to join her on the casement seats. In his mind he started several times to say something, only to reason Michael was right; the words he was contemplating employing would do more harm than good. In the end he was obliged to meekly ask if she still held to her intentions.

'How long have I waited to speak to you on this?'

'Weeks,' he said with a wan smile. 'It seemed best avoided, since it could not be resolved without contention.'

'Are you going to try to get me to change my mind once more?'

'If I did, it would only be to drive home my unhappiness at the prospect.'

Her lips pursed before she responded in a terse tone. 'Do you think it makes me happy, John? Do you believe I am eager to separate Adam from his father? For if you do, I must tell you I am not.'

'I had hoped being separated from me would also come into your considerations.'

A hand brushed his cheek. 'It will be a permanent pain.'

126

'Permanent?' was the stunned reply.

'For all the time it lasts, is what I meant.'

'I feel I'm being condemned to another spell in prison, with silken cords instead of chains and bars.'

'There will be ways that we can meet.'

'With half your family around and their neighbours gossiping about this strange visitor?'

'No, John, I have thought on it, for I have had the time to do so. As soon as I can I will write to our good friend Heinrich.'

'I can't see what purpose there can be in contacting Lutyens that will affect us being kept apart.'

'But I have. He loves us both, I know — '

Pearce produced a genuine smile. 'You more than me, I reckon, Emily. I do believe when you were nursing for him in Toulon, he had high hopes for his own suit.'

'Nonsense!' was her response.

This led her lover to recall that, if she was somewhat innocent now, she'd been a damned sight more so in Toulon, unaware in her provincial way of discerning what lay behind the way men looked at her. It was partly youth too; Emily had married young to a man twice her age and he was not himself much gifted with worldliness. If Ralph Barclay had been a successful sailor he had been a blinkered man.

That brought forth another untoward thought: Emily was a beautiful widow with a more than decent inheritance. Half the bucks in the West Country would have designs on her and he would not be there to see them off, a troubling train of thought broken by her continuing enthusiasm.

'My plan is that Heinrich should take a house in Bath for the season, shared with me and I will take one of my friends as chaperone, whom I know to be wildly romantic and one who will see us as the stuff of a novel. It will be perfectly acceptable that you too should be in the town to take the waters and, being Heinrich's friend, you should call upon him frequently. I know he will do everything he can to ensure we can have time alone.'

'When I observed you dish that fellow Warren, I suspected a devious mind but a spontaneous one. Now I see I am wrong: there is cold calculation in that pretty head of yours.'

'You make it sound disreputable,' Emily protested.

'Now there's a word that obliges me to remind you that tonight will likely be our last at sea. It is not the waters of Bath I'll be thinking of taking. Your delivery is long past, Emily, and it seems you are determined we should be parted. So I cannot but demand something by which to remember you.'

The deep flush on those slightly freckled cheeks was delightful and there was a moment when he thought she might protest, for it was true she still had the habits by which she had been raised and any mention of carnality troubled her. Emily, in her shy way, often found him overpressing as a lover, while deploring his language when he too frequently blasphemed.

'Then we must be sure to lock the doors,' was

the actual reply, delivered in a slightly husky tone. 'And we must also have care not to wake Adam.'

'Which you must guard against more than I, my love,' he opined, which was a pleasantly vulgar way of saying she was not one to be silent in pleasure.

The knock on the door made Emily jump, no doubt from the fear her thinking would be obvious to anyone who looked at her. It caused another blush when, with a grin full of mischief, Pearce, as he moved to put a distance between them, shouted, 'Come!'

'Mr Hawker's compliments. We's raised sight of the Needles.'

'Thank you for that. Please tell him I have certain tasks to complete and will join him when I have finished.'

At that point Emily dropped her head, seemingly to kiss the face of her son. In reality it was to hide her reddened cheeks.

10

He was on deck an hour later when Byford approached to take his arm and lead him aside, an action that got a curious look from Tobias Fuller, also present to gaze at the chalk-white formations which, as much as the Lizard itself, told returning sailors they were almost home. The surgeon pretended to point to the Needles as though asking questions, this while Hawker had the crew occupied in changing course to sail up the Solent, an affair with enough noise to make the conversation discreet.

'I have thought on your request, Mr Pearce, and am inclined to aid you. But first I must go ashore and look over what arrangements will be provided for getting patients ashore.'

'Is there not a jetty by the hospital?' The surgeon nodded. 'Then surely we will no doubt tie up there?'

'True, but I must request a boat to go ahead and make what preparations are needed for my genuine patients. I need to ensure they have beds and that I have the facilities to care for them.'

'The other medical staff?' Pearce enquired, airing another worry.

'I would not expect too much from them: they have their own people to care for and, from my limited experience of the hospital, they are not inclined to take on responsibilities that do not naturally fall to them.'

'But it is not impossible that they could conduct an examination?'

'Not impossible, no, just unlikely. These are my patients and I am with them until their future is decided. Also, while organising what is required, I can work out what to do for your Pelicans, who must also be accommodated and cared for as if they are genuine.'

'It seems insufficient to profess my thanks.'

'It is enough for me, sir. I will do my best to get your friends off the ship, but the difficulties do not end there. I am forced to enquire what you know of Haslar and its surroundings.'

'I confess little. I have seen it only from a distance and some time past.'

'Then let me enlighten you. When the hospital was built it was known that it would tend to men crewing the ships at anchor in Spithead, as well as invalids fetched from such theatres as the Mediterranean.'

'And I assume other commands?'

Byford nodded. 'It could have been located anywhere near to Portsmouth, but was constructed on a spit at the very end of Gosport Creek, which has one specific advantage. It is a very hard place from which a pressed seaman seeking freedom can avoid capture. The spit is surrounded by water on three sides, with only a narrow neck to pass through to get to open country. That leads to a flat area of featureless marshland dissected by numerous creeks.'

'You seem to know a great deal about it.'

'I have a passing interest in wildlife — birds, to be precise.'

'Which I guessed when I saw you employing a spyglass every time we were close to land.'

'Seabirds are a minor factor in what I observe, they being so alike, numerous and ubiquitous. Marshland is more interesting for variety, forests and hill country even more so. Gibraltar had some wondrous sights occupying the peak as well as the Spanish mainland. But that is not the nub of what I am seeking to impart to you.'

'You're telling me getting them into the hospital is only one part of it.'

'That narrow neck I spoke of is well patrolled for obvious reasons — both the roadway and the land to either side — with watchtowers, while concealment is near to impossible. Not only are there few places to hide, but it is rich in winged creatures, easily startled by any passing human.'

'At night?'

'A wise man does not cross an unfamiliar marsh in darkness, Mr Pearce. Those who live there would, I suspect, rarely do so and they must know what is sucking bog and what ground is firm and safe.'

Pearce was certainly disheartened by what he was being told; it made so much more challenging that which was already fraught with peril. Yet he forced a smile, to show a mood to the surgeon that he could not be discouraged.

'Mr Byford, nothing is without difficulty. If you can get my Pelicans onto dry land without discovery, then — '

'You must know even that is not without risk. Any one person could give the game away and our ship has many in number.'

132

'The crew?'

'Certainly, but — ' Byford looked towards Fuller; explanation of his point was not necessary.

'Leave me to deal with him.'

'Not with violence, I trust?'

'Heaven forfend,' Pearce replied with vehemence, which by the expression in response and the humorous look that accompanied it left the surgeon unsure. It was an ironic mode of speech in the circumstances.

'To disguise your friends without him noticing will be impossible and you have not formed, with Mr Fuller, what I would call an amicable relationship.'

'No, but I suspect he is less than honest and a less-than-honest man has much to guard against.'

'You harbour suspicions, as does Mr Hawker, but that is far from fact.'

'It may be close enough for my purpose. And by the way, let me thank you on my behalf and that of my Pelicans.'

'While I hope you and they will have reason to do so.'

Pearce moved away, calling to Fuller, who was surprised, this obvious on his blotched face as he turned, his expression leading Byford to think Pearce had his work cut out in that quarter.

And indeed he did; his attempts at a friendly discourse were not quite rebuffed, but there was no way he concluded it with any feeling that Fuller would abet what he had in mind, of which he was left in ignorance.

133

One positive was relayed to him by Michael O'Hagan: Pearce had noticed in the last couple of days, since encountering that Royal Navy frigate, the crew seemed to look upon and treat him with an even greater degree of respect than he had gained from the encounter with the Algerine. It was the Irishman who drove home just how powerful that had become.

'Sure, they've been venturing on how many that bastard would have shipped out.'

'It would depend on how short he was of hands. He certainly demonstrated an anxious air.'

'While this barky, close to home, in what looked to be decent weather, needed few to get her to a berth.'

'True.'

'So the guessing is they would have shipped out near half the crew, if you hadn't stood to prevent it.'

Pearce grinned. 'It pains me to say Emily's wiles and inventions had more effect.'

'John-boy, she didn't draw a sword.'

'Even you know women don't have to stoop to violence or weapons, Michael. They are born with a potent tongue.'

'Will you ever guess what it is I'm driving at? The lads are as one, and had a vote. They will do all they can to help.'

'How the devil do they know anything about it?' Pearce demanded, far from pleased.

'Ever known a secret to be kept on a ship?

This barky ain't no different from a ship of the line and nor are the fellows aboard lacking in seaman's nous. Weeks we've been hugger-mugger since Leghorn, an' they have known from the very start we're navy. That makes some wonder what we're doing aboard as well as what happens when we make Haslar. It only takes one to see the likelihoods and work out what's needed, to then rope in the rest. Not that it would have been that way afore, but it is now and to a man.'

'They will aid us?' Pearce asked with some uncertainty, after a reflective pause.

'Jesus, they'd have to,' Michael insisted, crossing himself as he took the Lord's name in vain. 'Who do you think is going to be carting our invalids ashore?'

'I had anticipated that Haslar would have orderlies.'

'Happen they will, but they will need aid for the numbers we have on board. And they might be layabouts at that, happier to watch than toil.'

'We need to talk, all together. Dare we risk it?'

'Dare we not?'

★ ★ ★

'You can't all three go ashore as ambulant beings,' Pearce insisted, having accepted what Michael was implying. 'Just walking and jesting won't serve. One needs a serious limp and another will have to play witless.'

'Part is made for you Rufus,' sniped Charlie Taverner, which got him a vulgar finger gesture

135

from the recipient and a sharp look from Pearce.

'One at least will have to be on a stretcher; Michael, given your size and being so prominent, I suggest it has to be you.'

'God help the poor buggers who have to bear his weight,' Rufus scoffed, seeking to establish humorous parity. 'Being in this pantry has added a bit of meat too.'

'Which is why you're ever sneaking in here for a bite,' Michael growled.

'Will you lot put your mind to what we are about?' Pearce hissed.

This was accompanied by a look at the canvas screen which, with the cabin door, stood between them and being overheard, this being the only place he reckoned they could talk. They were crammed into a space small in itself, but substantially reduced by Michael O'Hagan's bulk.

Yet what his Irish friend said was true: he always made a bit of extra grub for his Pelican mates while never asking John Pearce if that was to be allowed. So the sight of them sneaking aft was a common one, though they never did it in tandem or when Mr Hawker had the deck. It was only possible now due to the lack of work required for outside steering.

Everything needed aloft was set, with *Tarvit* making her way slowly past the port and anchorage of St Helens, home to part of the fleet and any number of fishing boats, some of which came alongside to sell their catch. They should make the main fleet base of Spithead sometime after the noonday gun, which would boom out from the Southsea shore. *Tarvit* would then head to the landing jetty, which served the naval hospital.

Byford had taken to the cutter and gone ahead to tell those who would receive his patients the numbers and names of those on his Leghorn manifest, plus a trio of badly wounded men picked up at Gibraltar — an excuse that was required, given there had been no fatalities on the way home.

What happened afterwards lay with John Pearce. Should they succeed in getting into the hospital he had to find a way to get them out and past that which Byford had warned him against. This would take place at a time when he was conflicted because, while he was dealing with that problem, Emily would be finalising the preparations that would take her away from him, an assurance they would soon be united providing little comfort.

Bath notwithstanding, she would have to come to London and the offices of his prize agent to settle Ralph Barclay's affairs, though she declined to say how long it would be before that happened. So much depended on what she encountered with her family and relatives, not least Ralph Barclay's sisters, now financially reliant on her. In addition there would be the difficulties of travelling with a small child; she could hardly come to where he was without bringing his son.

At least he should be there to meet her: Pearce had to get the Pelicans to London, itself a safer place than most, due to its sheer size. His destination would be, once more, the Liberties of the Savoy and the protection such a location should still provide. This meant, assuming he could get them off the Gosport headland, traversing a route full of prying eyes of a suspicious bent. Every coaching inn on the way would have some low-life creature who made his living from alerting the navy to those who could be on the run.

Nor was it easy to disguise such an occupation; any man who had spent a long time at sea acted, dressed and ambled in a very obvious manner. The motion on a ship, even a well-ballasted one on a calm sea, made walking in a certain way necessary to avoid a tumble. You had to roll with the canting, never-steady deck and it was near to impossible to quickly change to a different gait back on land.

Even if that could be disguised, there were other obvious signs of seaborne life. A ruddy complexion battered by winds and weather, hands ingrained with tar off every rope ever pulled, that commodity being required to stop them rotting as they were assailed by climate and salt water.

The only security Pearce could think of was their being in his company; his blue coat could deflect suspicion. That said, it was not foolproof; even a lieutenant had to be able to justify their presence if faced by a press gang and he knew from past experience such entities, for obvious reasons, patrolled the Portsmouth to London road, so that would have to be avoided.

'Might've found a way, John,' Charlie Taverner

said, now that Pearce had detailed the hazards. 'Had a word with one of the crew set to help, talkative cove as it happens. It seems not all the script they has on *Tarvit* is honest, which is why they's so grateful to you. Wouldn't say which is which, that being sensible, but some is sham. There's a hand in Portsmouth that can craft such papers.'

'Surely the press is on to that?' Rufus insisted.

'Half the bastards can't read,' Charlie protested with disdain, even although he struggled in that area himself. 'S'long as the emboss is genuine and the right paper is employed, I am told they hold water.'

'Sure, that would come at a price, Charlie.'

'Can't be too steep, Michael. I don't see many well-found 'tween decks on this barky. But there are those who don't want navy service at any price — grog and better pay put aside — and will pay the bill. They like the comfort of a trading ship.'

'What comfort!' With his ginger hair, pallid skin and heavily freckled cheeks, Rufus was prone to going red and he did so now in indignation. 'If we had a proper cargo we'd be sleepin' nose to tail. Even with what we has, I's breathing in farts every time I take to my hammock.'

Charlie's reply was the old saw. 'Nose too close to your own arse, Rufus, I reckon.'

'You two can't park your arses here all day,' Michael hissed. 'Happen the likes of Mr Hawker is used to seeing you nipping in for a bite, but staying longer will make others wonder, like that sod of an agent.'

139

'Which is the last thing we want,' Pearce asserted. 'Charlie: this forger, I can't walk around Portsmouth asking.'

'That would be daft, right enough.'

'So I need a name and a place and I want it before we tie up to the jetty, which I reckon we will do by two bells. You have scant time to prepare your roles and they have to be convincing enough to pass the scrutiny of any hospital orderlies.'

'They'll be former tars, John, for certain,' Charlie insisted, 'too old for service and we have to hope not likely to even look hard.'

Pearce considered telling them what Byford had warned him of, which made it almost certain anyone working in the hospital would not subject those coming ashore to excessive scrutiny. Why bother when you had no need to? That said, it would be unwise to be cavalier or careless.

'Even if they are, you have to look convincing, and that's not all. Byford reckons the hospital surgeons to be lax in their curiosity, but what occurs if one of them is about and examines any of you to find you whole?'

That was greeted by a trio of truly grim expressions; handed over, even with Pearce pleading for them, they would be sure of a serious flogging at least, and possibly much worse. Even with the former, they would be back aboard a King's ship before they recovered and as marked men, with no chance of ever getting off, even for a run ashore in a foreign port.

'And what if my man won't give up the falsifier's name?'

'Charlie, he must be one of the crew that has a forged certificate. Remind him from what I saved them. You've got a silver tongue, use it. Now get back to where you belong, while I try to work out how we're going to get you away once you're ashore.'

'One thing at a time, John-boy,' Michael cautioned softly as the other two slipped out. 'Let's reach the needed berth first.'

Pearce knew different: he had to think ahead; everything that could be done prior to landing was in hand, thanks to Byford, and it was doubly so now the crew were on their side. The key was the pair of loblolly boys who worked for the surgeon, assistants employed to carry out the daily duties of caring for his patients, some of whom could not move to wash, shave or evacuate.

They had been as vulnerable as anyone: when pressing, the navy did not employ discrimination. So they shared the mood of the crew, yet what they would do was more vital than just looking askance. If any Haslar orderlies came aboard to look over their patients, they had to show the Pelicans as part of the cargo and name an affliction.

Meeting over, Pearce made for the main cabin only to stop before entering, thinking there were still gremlins to deal with. Michael Hawker was a concern, but he had declared he would be going ashore to visit some Hampshire relatives once *Tarvit* had discharged her patients. Even if he was still on board for the transfer, Pearce felt he could deal with him, sure he could be persuaded

141

to turn a blind eye to something not of his concern.

But what about Tobias Fuller: how to go about keeping him from prying or exposing the subterfuge? No appeal to his better nature seemed feasible, it being doubted he had one. The answer was to keep him off the deck when the unloading of the patients took place. The only way he could think to achieve the former was to go to Fuller's screened-off cabin and physically threaten him if he moved, an idea quickly discarded, given it would only make him suspicious.

A possible answer came as he looked at the cabin door, which had him spin round to once more accost O'Hagan. 'Michael, what do we have in the way of food for a good dinner?'

'I picked up a basket of fresh cod from a fisherman as we passed St Helens, but if it's meat you're after, it would be salted.'

'Fish after soup will do, but I want food prepared. Another will have to serve it.'

Michael O'Hagan was too accustomed to the ways of John Pearce, who was given to sudden inspirations, to show any surprise at this, but he had one obvious question.

'And who would that be?'

'Find someone who is not afeard to wash. If the food is ready, all they have to do is carry things to the table.'

He then made for his cabin to get agreement from the one person he could trust to pull off what he had in mind. Emily needed to host the dinner.

11

'Mr Byford and I will be too busy to attend, but Michael Hawker will respond to an invite. Once alongside the jetty, his duties are over. Then there's Fuller, which is why it has to come from you. An invite from me he'd never accept. You, on the other hand, he could hardly refuse, given he makes a point of being on deck to ogle whenever you take the air.'

'You have noticed?'

'I did and have often wanted to challenge him, but he is scarce worth it.'

'You seem very sure, John,' she replied with a knowing smile.

'I've no time for teasing, Emily. You could say you feel guilty for not inviting him to the cabin before, due to the need to look after Adam. Then there's my presence. But now we are about to end our journey and will part company — '

Emily was not convinced even by his eager look or his sudden silence. 'And what if Adam does not oblige us by sleeping throughout this dinner?'

'The task is to get Fuller into the cabin and sat down. He's a bumptious cove and he will be flattered. I will show my face but no more and I can frown at what is actually an abuse of my rights as the ship's captain, which will set the required tone. Given the chance to gaze at you he will not dare rise to depart, even if the needs of Adam bring distraction.'

'You seem to forget I am heavily engaged in packing.'

'And have as much choice in terms of time as you need to complete it. Emily, if Fuller sees Michael, Charlie and Rufus being helped or carried off the ship, I have little doubt he will expose it. For them, if that happens? I need hardly tell you what that is.'

A quick explanation followed as regards what needed to be done by Michael: to get everything prepared, and once the guests were seated, to get below quickly and onto a stretcher, to which Emily opined, with a sweet smile, 'I will miss our gentle giant.'

Pearce had to force a smile of agreement. Michael was a giant, sure enough, but to call him gentle was stretching it. Capable of it, certainly, just as he was equally capable of outright violence — handy in battle, a damn nuisance in drink.

The note Fuller received told the toad that Mrs Ralph Barclay had been remiss in the previous lack of invitations to dine in the great cabin. Her excuse? It was not, in truth, an area over which she exercised dominion and previous suggestions had not met with approval from Mr Pearce. But, given the voyage was about to end, she felt it her duty to extend a thanks to those who had contributed to her comfort, which naturally included him.

Such phrasing laid at Pearce's door the lack of previous social interaction, which would touch a Fuller nerve and doubly ensure compliance. If

144

the sod didn't want him in his cabin, and it sounded as if he did not, surely Fuller would damn well make sure he was present.

And he was, eyeing a table already set, well before the appointed hour, knowing, no doubt, that neither Pearce nor Hawker could be present due to the pressure of their duties in docking the ship, the background noise of the vessel being eased alongside the jetty an accompaniment to what followed.

It was deliberate and annoying for a slightly chagrined Emily, wondering at his game. It was certainly not to display modesty. She was obliged to listen to boasts of his manifest skills. He reckoned no man could deal with the devious Johnny Foreigners better than he. As well as that he alluded to his extensive and elevated social connections. The latter she suspected were false; the former did not accord with what she had been told.

His chest puffed out, he swiftly moved on to his glittering future, for he wished to inform her his evident gifts had not gone unnoticed where it mattered, in the minds of those who employed him. They, it seemed, were keen to use him in a more elevated and responsible capacity.

'Which means I shall be pursuing my future career ashore, Mrs Barclay. This, I am glad to say, will very likely be my last sea voyage.'

'Will you not miss it, Mr Fuller?' Emily asked, driven by a need to say something and turn what was looking to be bombastic bluster into a conversation.

'I have done my duty in such a menial sphere,

145

madam,' he declared, waving a dismissive hand at his surroundings as though his own tiny cabin was more splendid. 'This is not where the real work is done in commerce. I know the syndicate for whom I labour have approved wholeheartedly of my activities in containing unnecessary expenditures. I was alerted before leaving England to expect a telling and continuing increase in their trust.'

The lean forward, the lower tone of voice, was an attempt to imbue what came next as the passing on of a confidence. 'I should not be surprised if a partnership will be mine in a couple of years.'

'Fully deserved, I'm sure,' was her laconic response.

'A vessel cannot sail on any enterprise, Mrs Barclay, without men of business putting the necessary things in place, capital and the securing of a profitable cargo. Such a task does not fall to sailors but to those who deal in the places where transactions are agreed. That, from now on, will fall to me and I am confident I will excel at it.'

'Really?' That was accompanied by a sup-pressed yawn. She might as well have let it happen and be seen: Fuller was not going to be put off by anything.

'I esteem Mr Hawker as a competent seaman,' was said in a way that implied the opposite. 'But his task is simplicity in comparison to those I will soon be called upon to undertake, merely to get his ship to where people of my ilk have said it should proceed with the cargo intact. I will be called upon to arrange lines of credit as well as to ensure what he transports is properly paid for once delivered — no easy task, you may be sure.'

'I feel we must be tied up by now.'

Emily was now looking at the skylight, really for a way to avoid his smug and pompous countenance.

'Of course, once ashore and in possession of the proper level of remuneration, I shall require a wife. There is a social side to such a position, which needs an elegant hostess to fulfil the necessary duties that will fall to a man on the rise.'

The gleam she saw in Fuller's eyes, as she dropped her head, nearly made her burst out laughing, its meaning being obvious and explaining his early arrival. He was seeking to tell her he would, in his imagined and well-funded future, be a desirable catch as a husband.

'I have to thank the Lord that my late husband left me so well-cared-for in the article of income that I can enjoy my independence. He was very successful in the accumulation of prize money, Mr Fuller.'

'How interesting.'

'Yes, he commanded a fine seventy-four at the First of June Battle.'

'A stirring victory which cheered the nation, and it has to be said a profitable one for those fortunate enough to have taken part.'

'Not that we were in need. He had, in prior service, taken several well-laden merchant vessels as a successful frigate captain, all carefully invested.'

Fuller puffed up like a pigeon, while a hand was used to ensure his hair was clear of his brow, then put to his neck to check his stock was straight. The most telling sign of excitement was the way his facial blotches became more obvious. His voice, when he spoke, was slightly hoarse.

'Mrs Barclay, you will forgive me for being so forward, but I feel we have so much in common. You have, I hope, noticed my admiration for you on those occasions when you took the air. It would delight me to return the compliment you are presently paying me and it would do me great honour if you would consent to dine onshore as my guest on the morrow, once we have both quit the ship.'

Emily was subject to a sinking feeling. She had sought to indicate she had no need of a prosperous husband and that had not only failed, but had encouraged the fool: he was seeing in his mind's eye a glorious matrimonial match in which his success and her affluence would be combined.

Shocked at the notion she might share anything with this man, Emily had nevertheless walked into a trap of her own making, one in which it would be bad manners to respond with a downright refusal. She was thus obliged to dissemble, alluding to her sleeping infant, secretly hoping either he would wake up or someone would appear to save her.

Thankfully Hawker entered, followed by John Pearce, he throwing the requisite black look at Fuller. It did nothing to diminish the man's self-regard; indeed, it seemed to lift him somewhat. Clearly he was of the opinion he had made some progress with this beautiful widow, a woman of wealth, who could obviously discern his qualities and could see the definite advantages of their being conjoined. He positively beamed at John Pearce.

'Mr Hawker,' Emily enquired, 'is our voyage now truly at an end?'

'It is, Mrs Barclay,' Hawker replied. 'We are tied up here until the afflicted are taken off and then we must anchor offshore and wait to find out what will be our next duty.'

'I'm sure Mr Fuller will be able to advise you. He has just been telling me of the need for application by men such as himself, to keep you poor sailors in employment. It seems you are mere pawns in a game in which men such as he exercise control. I have a notion he knows where you are next bound.'

The Fuller blotches stood out like red-coloured countries on a map. 'In my future position, ma'am, I will be able to do that. But not yet.'

'To which we must all look forward.'

Two of the men present got the sarcasm; Fuller did not.

'Lieutenant Pearce, it pleases me that you have joined us. You will, I hope, sit for a moment and take a glass of wine?'

'I still have duties to perform, Mrs Barclay. I must join Mr Byford and see the patients off the ship and into the hospital.' The deep frown told him she was not about to accept that; if he did not know why, he knew he had no choice. 'However, I can spare a moment.'

Emily indicated the bottle wrapped in wet cloth. 'Would you be so kind as to pour, then? It is, after all, your cabin; by rights, you should be the host. It is such a pity you say you cannot stay for even the first course.'

Pearce obliged with a bit of a scowl which, if it fitted the bill of the subterfuge being executed, was in fact caused by the knowledge Emily was deliberately guying him and she had not finished.

'I must thank you again for finally loaning it to me. And do pass a glass to Mr Fuller.'

Michael O'Hagan's replacement, recruited by Charlie Taverner, saved him. In a clean shirt and a checked bandana at his neck, he entered the cabin bearing a large porcelain soup tureen containing the first course, to a pretence of ignorance on behalf of the owner. Emily, playing her part, was quick to respond to his raised, questioning eyebrows.

'I hope you will forgive me, Mr Pearce, but I engaged this fellow to cook and serve, given I was advised he had done such work in the past. It pains me to say I found the man who attends to you, the Irish fellow, rather coarse in his manner.'

'He has served me well enough, madam, and it strikes me you have exceeded your position. It is not for you to say who does what in my cabin.'

'Come, sir,' Fuller protested, his glee at Pearce's discomfort ill-disguised. 'Surely the lady has a right to her own standard of provision?'

'Sir, in merely inviting you to what are my quarters, she has multiplied her questionable behaviour. So, you will forgive me. I'm sure I can find a duty more congenial than this.'

As Pearce made to leave he caught the eye of Michael Hawker, whose face bore an expression hard to read. By the time the turn had been executed, it struck Pearce he would be seeking to find a reason for what he was witnessing, and he had good grounds. If he knew Pearce had no regard for Fuller, what was going on between him and Mrs Barclay?

There had been no hint of dispute in the weeks at sea. If anything it had been quite the reverse: their friendliness and compatibility, albeit held in check, had been manifest, leading to speculation as to what lay in their future. Emily too had picked up the Hawker expression and, as they had with the threat of impressment from Captain Warner, her quick wits came to the fore.

'Lieutenant Pearce, I see I have offended you and I apologise, which I extend to your Irish servant. It would make me feel that this has been accepted if, once you have done what you see as your duty, you should rejoin us.'

It was through pursed lips that he replied. 'I will if my duty is complete, but I reckon it will take time enough that you will be long finished. Now, excuse me.'

'A fellow not much favoured by good manners, Mrs Barclay,' Fuller opined, with much pomp, as the cabin door closed and the soup was served, unaware that Pearce had gone to ensure

O'Hagan was on his way to where he needed to be, while making certain it was safe for him to do so.

Emily was later to tell John Pearce she had come close to biting off her own tongue. He then had to swear never to leave her alone in the company of such a bore again.

★　★　★

In the end, the transfer of patients proved ridiculously free from problems. There were Haslar orderlies but they were not of a type to sully their hands, happy to keep them away from the cold wind inside their tarpaulin capes and watch the crew of the merchant ship carrying out the labour. Their only duty, as they saw it, was the need to lead them to where Stephen Byford indicated each charge should be taken.

Henry Digby and his silent companion were first out, he attracting much attention, having declined to wear anything that might keep out the wind blowing off the sea. With a man either side taking a firm grip, he came down the gangplank dressed in the same manner as he had been throughout the voyage: a flapping shirt with no breeches or shoes.

When he espied Pearce standing on the quay, wrapped in his boat cloak, he burst into another diatribe of the kind he had produced before Raïs Hamidou, one which promised his one-time premier retribution for any number of slights and acts of insubordination. If the Haslar men, all old salts as Michael had guessed, had no energy for toil, they had plenty available to jeer at him.

'He'll be in good company for a bit, your honour,' said the senior man, who had been introduced to Pearce by the surgeon as an ex-master's mate called Bessel. 'We's a number of the raving kind passing through here on the way to Bedlam.'

'Do they mix with the other patients?' Pearce asked, seeking not to sound overanxious; a loose Digby wandering about would be a source of trouble to a trio he knew only too well.

'Never in life, your honour: we has a special cage for their like, barred so we can see they don't harm themselves. Good fun to poke them into a rant, though.' Bessel produced a belly-shaking chuckle. 'Lord alive, they do go off, some of 'em.'

Pearce, wishing to allude to the cruelty, was obliged to hold his tongue, not least because the moment of anxiety had arrived. Michael O'Hagan was coming off and it required four crewmen to carry his stretcher, not easy on a too-narrow gangplank, and it was clear they were struggling.

Pearce gave the Haslar men a meaningful look — he reckoned it would have been strange had he not — only to be faced with an ability long-practised by tars serving and retired, that being to avoid catching the eye of anyone in authority. If he knew he should be annoyed, he was not, more reassured there would be no trouble from that quarter.

It took an hour to get everyone off; Charlie

Taverner was brought down with an arm round one of the crew and staggering, giving a very good intimation of being unable to walk unaided. Pearce followed him to a place where they were unobserved to get from him a name and location, committed to memory before returning to his place on the quay to see Rufus, some twenty patients later, come ashore. The youngest Pelican did the witless act well, his eyes roving around, but seeming to register nothing.

Nor, when the patients were transferred, did the Haslar orderlies seem overkeen to act the nurse. His only worry now was the naval physicians, who might show some curiosity when they turned up to do their duty, with Pearce enquiring when that would be.

'Takes their dinner in Pompey, sir,' came the reply from Bessel, abetted by an embarrassed look and a touched forelock.

'So they will return in the evening?'

The look that got was of the nature that pigs might fly, the actual reply guarded in the extreme. 'They do like to take their pleasure, your honour, and the nights are short this time of year.'

If it was not stated, Pearce guessed what Bessel was driving at. Much drink would be consumed, enough to render the doctors more inclined to recreation than duty, which could encompass anything from calling upon a mistress or a visit to a bawdy house, of which Portsmouth had a surfeit. With that in mind he went to find Stephen Byford, now allocating cots to the last of his charges, to find they occupied two full wards with doors that, when shut, cut them off from the rest of the hospital.

'From what I have been told there will be no attendance by the Haslar doctors till the morning?'

'The rumble of their belly takes precedence,' Byford confirmed, when Pearce told him why.

'So I don't have to sneak my Pelicans out tonight?'

'I would guess even if some of the medical staff return, it will not be for an examination of any new patients. The orderlies have their own wards to attend to and will leave those we have brought ashore to me and my assistants.'

'I have to report to the C-in-C Portsmouth with my logs and despatches.'

'I'm told Mrs Barclay is entertaining Fuller?' Slightly thrown by the change of subject, Pearce could only confirm the truth. Byford's next words were laced with false wonder. 'You must be a very persuasive fellow, Mr Pearce, that you can get a lady of such charm and beauty to undertake that chore on your behalf.'

The locked eyes only held for a second, but it was enough to tell Pearce all of Emily's wiles and his attempts at deception had been for naught in Byford's case, very likely Hawker's as well. The surgeon must have guessed at his discomfort.

'Never fear, Mr Pearce. I am no gossip and if I were, it would only be to say how much I envy you.'

'I must go.'

'While I must see my charges fed. If it does not trouble you, given they can move freely, I

155

will employ your friends to aid us.'

Pearce nodded and left, on the way reprimanding himself for not removing his logs from the cabin. He had no desire to go back in case Fuller was still there. In that he was correct: the drone of the man's voice came to him as soon as he opened the door a fraction. Since the agent had his back to it the first sight Pearce beheld was of Hawker and Emily, both with set and unsmiling faces.

He hesitated to go further, wondering why it was that bores had no idea of the misery they afflicted on those too polite to tell them to be silent. It was as if they lacked discernment of the reaction to their words. Any sensible person would surely have taken from the stiff expressions a clear signal. People who were mean had a similar way about them, perhaps thinking themselves so clever that no one would notice the lack of a sight of their purse.

It was several seconds before Emily saw him peering through the door and her reaction was both loud and pointed as she cut across Fuller. 'Mr Pearce, you have returned. Can I take it I am forgiven?'

Fuller spun round to show a scowling face now wholly ruddy, no doubt from the consumption of wine.

'Mrs Barclay, I admit to being a touch brusque in my earlier behaviour. It is I who should be proffering an apology.'

'Damned right,' Fuller blustered, his voice carrying a slight slur. 'Never heard a lady spoken to like that in my life, sir.'

'Then you have lived a sheltered one, Mr Fuller.'

'Then I thank God for it, sir, just as I thank him he saw fit to make me a gentleman when he clearly did not accord such a status to you.'

'Since the apology was given to me,' Emily said, trying to sound emollient, 'I will say I am happy to accept it.'

Fuller's tone changed to one of mawkish regard as he faced his hostess with a lopsided grin. 'Graceful, indeed, and wholly undeserved by whom you bestow it on.'

'Mr Fuller,' Hawker interrupted, 'I do think it will not serve to comment on what has previously occurred. Mr Pearce is showing contrition, which is a manly thing to do.'

That had the chest puff out like a pouter pigeon, which was observed by Emily, especially since he was looking her in the eye, not the sailor. What followed was a crude attempt to establish, in order to impress her, that he was a man not to be trifled with.

'Mr Hawker, please be so good as to remember your place which, while not yet inferior to my own, will soon become so. It does not serve to have you check me.'

Hawker flushed and it was not wine. Yet for John Pearce it was the reaction that required concentration. He had tightly gripped the arms of his chair, tensed his muscles and looked to be about to get up and give Fuller that which he fully deserved. With his size and strength, if he had lost control of his temper, Fuller was in for a proper drubbing. This would do the sailor's career no good at all, which had Pearce interject quickly.

'I on the other hand am not constrained by such things, Fuller. Indeed, sir, you are occupying what I know to be my place at my table and I would be obliged if you would quit it forthwith before I feel the need to chastise you for your effrontery as well as your gross reflections on my character.'

The laugh had a trace of the manic. 'You, sir, are not my host. Mrs Barclay is, and given she and I are close to an understanding, you may whistle for your place.'

'Mr Fuller!' Emily shouted. 'I do not know where you get this talk of an understanding. Do I need to remind you that I am a recent widow?'

Adam John Pearce came in as if on cue, awoken by his mother's bark.

12

Unloading complete, the ship was then taken away from the jetty to moor offshore overnight as instructed by the naval harbour master. Come morning, Pearce required a boat to take him ashore and to the headquarters of the Commander-in-Chief, Portsmouth. Since Emily too was about to depart, he reckoned it would be seen as natural that he share it with her.

Given little Adam was held to be something of a mascot, while his mother was a kindly soul with a smile for any member of the crew she had encountered, the deck was crowded to witness the leaving. It was not a ceremony in any sense, but Michael Hawker was by the gangway to lift his hat and wish his much-esteemed passenger Godspeed, with a 'Hear him' from those assembled.

With Pearce any farewell was perfunctory, given no one had any idea if he would be returning to the ship for any other purpose than to collect his sea chest. One person who, if he was on deck, made a point of distancing himself from the departures was Tobias Fuller. As Pearce approached the gangway, logs and despatches tucked under his arm, he saw the agent examining the faces of the assembled crew, which alerted him to a fact he had not considered.

Michael O'Hagan was a hard man to miss. In

a situation where the likes of Stephen Byford could remark on the very apparent close connection between himself and the Pelicans, he had hinted that Fuller might have observed the same. Would he now wonder where the Irishman was, Charlie and Rufus too? Hesitation was for a fraction of a second, the conclusion being there was no time to do anything about it.

It was necessary, for the sake of appearances, that he make no overt conversation with Emily outside being polite. He sat in the thwarts facing the four men rowing, she in the middle cuddling a well-wrapped baby surrounded by her luggage. Pearce directed the cutter to aim for the sally port, really only for naval officers, so Emily could bespeak a conveyance to take her to an inn much patronised by the navy, The George in Queen Street, where she hoped accommodation could be provided.

There were willing hands on the shingle to unload the boat, as well as bear both lady and child over water to ensure her clothing remained dry, this for a shared tuppence as reward. An urchin was sent running to The George to ask if she and her baby son could be accommodated, this while her trunks were brought ashore, with the procuring of a dog cart to transport it.

With the news returned that she would be welcome at The George, Pearce was quick to dismiss the boat and send the crew back to *Tarvit*, allowing him to talk to her with a degree of intimacy, which would have been impossible in their presence.

'I will call on you once I have completed my

160

duties.' The look that crossed Emily's face then presaged what was likely to become commonplace, a flash of doubt as to the wisdom of what was being proposed, which had him add, 'Trust me to be discreet.'

'Something not much in your nature.'

'Admitted, but I have promised myself to try and respect your wishes.'

'Try?'

'You must appreciate how hard that will be?'

'You talk as if you're the only one to suffer, John,' she whispered, with a slight jerk of the head to indicate their exchange was being witnessed by those doing the porterage. 'It pains me too that such a display is necessary.'

'Then cast it aside and tell the world to go to the devil.'

'I cannot do that,' was the response, with a quick dip of the head towards Adam, driving home the reason. Lifted again, she said, 'I believe the man who owns the dog cart is ready to depart.'

'I will call,' was the forceful parting statement, with Pearce stalking off, his irritation very obvious in the manner of his gait. He did not see Emily bend her head once more to the swaddling clothes holding her child. It was not to kiss him this time or to blush but to hide the emergence of tears.

The offices of the C-in-C Portsmouth were in the high street and that, like all of the city, was full of bustle, the roadway covered in the dung — a sort of slurry at this time of year — of the hundreds of passing horses pulling every kind of

161

conveyance imaginable, mostly carts, but with the odd coach or shay. Pearce had to wait for a gap wide enough for the sweepers to do their duty before he could cross the road, a farthing disbursed as a fee for clean shoes.

His uniform coat got him entry to the flat-fronted building and the spacious hallway, but not much further. There an old fellow, balding, in a short blue jacket with gold buttons and a mean, crabbed countenance demanded he sign in before enquiring as to his business, the facts related doing nothing to soften his expression. A dismissive arm was waved to the right as eye contact was lost.

'There be a room o'er there in which you can wait until Captain Woolley is ready to see you.'

'And how long will that be?' Pearce asked, annoyed by the indifference.

'He don't consult with me about his tasks.'

'And here I was expecting to be shown straight into the admiral's presence.' If the sarcasm registered, it had no effect, beyond a huff and puff, which temporarily lifted the sloping shoulders. 'I am bound to enquire if there are any refreshments available?'

'You may send out, if you so wish.'

'You may send out, if you so wish, sir!'

That brought the head up with a jerk and there was a flash of anger in the heavily pouched eyes. Pearce could guess why: this old sod would have been given this plum job by an exercise in influence, possibly on the recommendation of a very high-ranking officer, so he had a high opinion of himself and his post.

He would grovel to an admiral and tip his hat to a senior post captain, but a mere lieutenant did not warrant even a courtesy. If John Pearce was not strong on the often ridiculous nature of hierarchy, he was not going to be condescended to by this bugger.

'I think it will be my primary duty, when I meet this Captain Woolley, to inform him that the fellow receiving visiting officers would benefit from a spell cleaning the heads. Which means I think it would be of a like advantage to us both if you address me properly.'

The 'sir' came out from somewhere close to his boots.

'Now, I cannot both wait to be seen and also send out for provender. So either undertake the task yourself, or find me someone I can instruct.'

Halfway through that sentence Pearce saw the look aimed at him, of a man sucking a lemon, shift to over his shoulder. This coincided with a draught of cool air as the door to the high street opened, that accompanied by the sound of stamping feet on the floorboards. He should have guessed from the changed expression before him, which went from testy to deferential, as well as a sagged body stiffening, that it presaged the arrival of someone of importance.

'Good day to you, Sir Peter,' cried the old salt.

Pearce heard the response as he turned round: 'I don't know what's good about it, man.'

The elderly admiral, identified by the mass of gold braid frogging his coat, was being relieved of his cloak by another lieutenant and scowling in the way that old folks do, a look that said things were very much better in his day.

'That cloak will need hot-sponging, Danvers,' Sir Peter barked, removing his hat and handing that over as well. 'This too.'

'They will indeed, sir, and I will see to it at once,' was the smooth reply.

The older man looked at the lieutenant before him, this only half-returned since Pearce was examining the man holding the admiral's hat and cloak well away from a wrinkling nose while his superior addressed the old salt.

'Some damned villain emptied a chamber pot on me, Riddell, the filthy swine.'

'What is the world coming to, your honour?' was delivered to the admiral over the Pearce shoulder. 'Folk too mean to pay for their night soil to be removed.'

'Hell and damnation, I doubt it was a mishap. I say it was deliberate. Get a party of marines round to the door of that dwelling, Danvers. I want whoever it was who tipped that pot to be given a drubbing for their insolence.'

Pearce wanted to laugh but knew he dare not, which left on his face a sort of rictus of mixed emotions. The admiral looked at him with his hooded eyes and demanded, 'Who the devil are you?'

'Lieutenant Pearce, sir, newly returned from the Med.'

'Ship?' was the next question, with a look at Danvers. 'Nothing has come in has it? I heard no gun salutes.'

'I was aboard a chartered transport vessel bringing back hospital cases to Haslar. I am

164

waiting to present my logs and despatches to the officer who deals with them.'

'Then you will oblige me by not cluttering up my hallway, young fellow.'

That was said as the admiral stalked off, to climb the central staircase with a sprightly gait that belied his years, leaving his flag lieutenant still holding his soiled cloak.

'I think you heard Sir Peter, sir.' The last word was so heavily emphasised it caused Pearce to spin to glare at Riddell.

'Just as I suspect you heard me, fellow. I will be in your anteroom, where I will expect to be delivered of a pot of coffee.'

A sixpence was extracted and slammed down on the counter as Pearce departed, throwing a sympathetic look to the still discomfited flag lieutenant.

It was a comfortable enough room: small, with a curtained window to the busy street outside and a fire in the grate, onto which Pearce threw another log before dumping his ledgers and papers, casting off his cloak and unhooking his sword.

Selecting an armchair with good light, he began leafing his way through the back copies of the *Gazette*, which lay on a low table. His coffee duly arrived, delivered by a pot boy from whichever house had provided it, he getting his copper reward plus an injunction to return at some time to collect his chattels.

The room was warm and the reading deeply boring when he got past the very old copy detailing the First of June Battle. The rest carried lists of promotions and few tales of the kind of actions to hold his interest. Soon Pearce, well inured to the sailor's habit of taking sleep when it was possible, was gently snoring, his head lolling against one side of his chair.

His dream was a melange in which he seemed to be unable to catch up with the vessel he was supposed to be aboard, the absurdity of his running on seawater taken as logical, as was the heavy weight of legs that barely functioned. Another trait he had, this from his peripatetic childhood, was to be wakened by the slightest noise, in this case the creaking door. He opened his eyes to see Danvers looking at him enquiringly from within the frame.

'I have been sent by Sir Peter to enquire if, while you were in the Mediterranean, you had any dealings with Captain Horatio Nelson?'

Pearce needed to blink several times, which allowed him to take in that which he had barely registered before. Danvers was of an age akin to his own, fair-haired with smooth features that indicated a comfortable upbringing; in fact, uniform apart, he did not look much like a sailor.

'Several, Mr Danvers.'

The blue eyes were fixed on his expectantly, as if waiting for elucidation. Pearce declined to oblige.

'In that case Sir Peter would like to see you.' Pearce looked towards the pile on the table, which elicited an immediate response. 'Riddell will care for those, and Captain Woolley has left for the day to raise Cain with the dockyard, so you would not have been able to report in any case.'

'Nice of Riddell to tell me.'

Danvers smiled, which rendered a good-looking cove even more comely. 'He is set in his ways.'

'True, he has perfected his bad manners.'

'If you will follow me, Mr Pearce, I will take you to the admiral.'

'Would you mind telling me admiral who?'

That got him a look which implied he had been on a desert island. 'Why, Sir Peter Parker, of course.'

'Ah,' Pearce responded.

This was to cover for the fact he had never heard of Sir Peter, which would be singular in a service where the names of senior officers and their exploits were common knowledge. He half-thought of asking if he was related to Sir Hyde Parker, who had acted as captain of the fleet to Hood, Hotham and now Jervis, but that would only expose more ignorance.

He followed Danvers, passing and giving Riddell a sour look, to follow the flag lieutenant to the first floor and a spacious room with three large windows overlooking the high street, these providing plenty of light. Parker was seated behind a large desk examining a pile of papers, appending a signature, before moving them to a second pile on his right side. He looked up when Danvers coughed.

'All right,' he protested irritably before putting his quill in the inkwell, sitting back and looking up, the expression one of deep curiosity.

Parker examined his visitor for several seconds, which was reciprocated, Pearce taking in the full cheeks and the prominent, slightly dropping nose. The buff waistcoat Parker wore was straining at the buttons, indicating a man who cared for his belly but, and this was telling, there was not a trace of malice in his expression.

'Didn't quite register the name downstairs, but are you that cove who got his step from King George?'

It would be an exaggeration to say that Pearce's heart sank, but the enquiry was unwelcome. How many times had he been in this situation where some superior officer asked the same question, before entering into a tirade at the folly and temerity of the sovereign? There was, however, no choice but to respond in the affirmative.

'My, you caused a stir. Never saw so much spittle flying in all my days and all of it to no purpose.'

'All I can say, sir, is this. It was not of my doing.'

'That I hold to be true, though it is questionable if it was wise of our monarch to do as he did.' Parker had been frowning as he said that, but then he suddenly smiled. 'Do sit down, Mr Pearce, and remove from your face that belligerent look.'

'It is habit, sir, when I am about to be chastised for the manner in which I came about my rank.'

'Not by me, young man.' He looked past Pearce. 'Danvers, be so good as to fetch us some

168

wine, then send someone to The George to bespeak a table. Mr Pearce, I think I requested you sit, do I have to make it an order?'

'No, sir.'

'I sent Danvers down to ask if you had come across Nelson. Your presence here indicates you answered in the affirmative.'

'I did have the honour to serve under the commodore and indeed, engage in various action under his command.'

'Then you can relate them to me over dinner. You probably don't know it, but I am the fellow who made him a post captain. I see him as a protégé.'

'Then, sir, you are to be commended on your wisdom. If I have jaundiced views on some officers, he is not one of them. I can add, apart from his application in fighting our enemies, he has never treated me with anything but kindness.'

'Which implies others have not.'

'No, sir, quite the reverse.'

Danvers entered, followed by a servant carrying a tray with a crystal decanter and three goblets, which was put on a side table. 'What presumption, Mr Pearce: my flag lieutenant, the cheeky young scoundrel, fetches three glasses?'

It took a look at a smiling Danvers to realise Parker was joking, this before he returned to the previous subject. 'It is easy for me to say to you that you must not mind the brickbats you get from other officers. It's damned hard to rise in the service and that fuels jealousy. I was on the receiving end myself when a callow youth, for having a high degree of interest.'

'I don't think I've ever had anyone admit to possessing that, sir.'

'Which is a case of not looking matters in the eye, fair and square. Lord knows there are any number of ways to clamber up the greasy pole, but none of them are easy outside some stroke of luck or the kind of action that got you your step. Powerful advocates are an advantage but they are not the whole case.'

Parker paused to look at Danvers to tell him to proceed with serving. 'So you have caused resentment, though to my mind, undeservedly so.' Pearce had to work to keep the surprise off his face as he took a glass of claret from Danvers. 'Daresay those that came up through the hawsehole were the most offended.'

'I think I had respect from Lord Hood, if not affection.'

That got a belly-shaking chuckle. 'If I recall him aright, Sam Hood does not do affection.'

'My subsequent relations with admirals did not live up to that, sir. It was all downhill from then on.'

'I am tempted to enquire what a mere lieutenant is doing conversing freely with admirals, but that would be seen as obtuse, given you are talking with me.'

Pearce launched into a potted explanation of the role he had come to play for Sam Hood, watched by a wine-sipping superior who had the good grace not to interrupt. Discretion demanded he pass over how different it had been with Sir William Hotham, though he did get in a

170

dig about his being shy in the fighting line, one to which Parker did not respond even with a flicker of the eye.

'And then you had Jervis.' The use of the surname denoted there was no love lost there, though it could be wishful thinking. 'Now there is an example of what I was saying. Jervis began life before the mast as an able seaman under Townsend and will claim to be a hawsehole admiral. The way he tells it, he has fought his way up to his present rank, but there is much stuff and nonsense there. He had some powerful folk giving him a leg up, Sir William Hamilton's mother and Lady Burlington being two — quite a formidable pair.'

Danvers coughed; it was obvious he found his superior unwise in being so frank.

'Never fear, Danvers, I'm too high up the list to let the likes of Jervis bother me, and besides, I doubt I have a chance of another active command.' He looked at Pearce and there was just a trace of bitterness in his tone. 'Being C-in-C Portsmouth is as close as you get to a yellow flag and still being able to hold your head high.'

'Sir John is singular in his method of command, sir.'

'Singular, Pearce,' Parker hooted, but it was only temporary humour, quickly replaced by a more serious mien. 'Now there's a word. I can imagine Johnny Jervis, who can be a crabbed sod at the best of times, being deeply offended by the mere proximity of someone like you.'

'It would please me to think so, sir.'

That got a flicker of the lips, not quite a smile. 'Which is why he would have shifted you into the command of a charter, to get rid of you. It's a common way.'

'I had that impression, sir.'

'Trouble is, Pearce, he's not alone in his opinions. I fear you might struggle for a new berth now you're home.'

'So I'm not staying with *Tarvit*?'

'I'll take a shilling to a guinea that in the despatches you fetched home, there will be a recommendation that you be beached.'

13

Hawker having departed not long after John Pearce, and those granted liberty taking the last of the three boats, Tobias Fuller was obliged to wait for one to return to take him ashore, his resentment at being so low in the pecking order for transport adding spice to many other antipathies. That said, there was no bar to going where he chose and the first place that beckoned was the great cabin.

Passing the pantry he registered it was empty, so he carried on and entered what was the man in command's private quarters. There was a slight feeling of discomfort as he recalled how he had so recently departed the previous day, but a night's sleep to a man of overweening self-regard had turned what had been humiliation into ill feelings based on the jealousy in others.

The table at which they had dined being broken up, with the excess chairs removed, Fuller registered the space in comparison to his own. Now Mrs Barclay was gone it included the two side cabins, one with the luxury of a private privy. The desk backing on to the casements was barren except for the quill sticking out from the sunken inkwell. Walking round it he occupied the captain's chair, to then enjoy a brief reverie that it was his by right.

Fuller closed his eyes and imagined himself chastising an imaginary John Pearce for any number of manifest failings, with the culprit cringing at the tongue-lashing. There was a second fantasy following, of his being able to bring the man down from his lofty blue coat to an able seaman's rags, with Captain Tobias Fuller RN ordering him brought up to a make-believe grating. Eyes closed, his imagination provided a swishing cat-o'-nine-tails, as well as heartening cries of pain.

Opened again he had to admit there was nothing he could do to harm John Pearce, the frustration of that bringing a look of deep anguish to his face. But Pearce had not been alone in discomfiting him over dinner and the expression cleared when he thought of Michael Hawker, to Fuller equally complicit. There was a man to whom he could do harm by merely reporting to his employers a story of questionable behaviour. Truth would not be allowed to interfere with effect.

A look in the drawers showed nothing of much interest, just a couple of ledgers and the usual accumulated detritus, so he rose and went to the side cabin that had been Pearce's temporary sleeping quarters. Most obvious was the cot affixed to the overhead beams, then the worn, working, everyday garments — a coat and breeches — hanging in an open closet.

His eye was soon drawn to the unlocked sea chest, and here was another indication of superiority of position: anywhere else on the ship a padlock would have been necessary; he had a stout one on his own. Fuller was too weak a man to deny himself a look, not that it revealed much of interest. Non-military clothing of good quality: shirts, breeches, dress pumps, stockings and the like; only two metal boxes of any interest.

The largest of the pair was securely locked and extremely heavy, giving off the sound of moving coin when shaken. The other was small and tight to open, needing an inserted fingernail, the contents, a small quantity of which spilled out, utterly puzzling. Why in the name of all that was holy would a man keep a tin of soil?

Back and seated at the desk he re-examined the drawers, pulling out one of the ledgers which proved to be the muster book. This listed the crew and their level of competence, from Michael Hawker down to the meanest waister. There in writing was their date of joining and any accrued competence that warranted an increase in their wages. This, with the other ledgers Pearce had taken ashore, would be used to establish their outstanding pay, given to them as tickets and usually discounted into spendable cash by some shoreside broker.

Flicking the pages he registered many familiar names. Yet when he got to the last, Fuller realised that there was one very obviously missing, which took his mind back to the empty pantry. O'Hagan, the Irishman Pearce had fetched aboard in Leghorn, and who looked no more a servant than that he had three legs, was not listed. The giant had not earlier been on deck either but Pearce had brought three bodies aboard, though he did not know the names of the other pair, just their faces. He sensed they too were not on the muster of *Tarvit*.

'There's some skulduggery afoot here, Mr John 'damn you' Pearce,' Fuller said out loud.

What it was, he did not know.

★   ★   ★

Across the water the Pelicans undertook the tasks previously carried out by Stephen Byford's loblolly boys; they, once the patients were settled, had been granted time ashore to take their pleasures. The trio saw to the washing and alimentary needs of Byford's charges, as well as feeding those who could not do so themselves, from a pail of porridge — in the absence of his normal help, personally fetched by the surgeon from the hospital kitchen.

Under different circumstances, Byford would have sought aid from the Haslar orderlies; having seen their stripe he was grateful not to have to ask. If help had been forthcoming from that crew, it would, he was sure, have been given grudgingly and with a hint of payment being due. That set aside, he did not want them on his wards where they might see that not all were invalid.

He had breakfasted with some of his colleagues, to find a mixed bunch of physicians who appeared to have no great attitude to care. Several were very old and cranky from long service: desiccated or plum-faced individuals who, by their words, saw themselves as put upon if required to provide their services. Those of middle years had that air of long practice, which indicated nothing to them would come as a surprise.

Two younger fellows, not long come from training at St Bartholomew's, if you excused their eyes puffed from lack of sleep and breath redolent of stale wine, were more animated, if wearily so from their nocturnal activities. They were happy to discuss their patients and the ailments with which they were afflicted, though the conversation was spiced with hints as to the best place across the water to get a decent meal or purchase the services of a clean bawd.

On Byford's return, the Pelicans — Rufus had been set to keeping watch — were lying on their cots, in place to continue with their subterfuge. They remained abed while Byford did his rounds, able now to tell at least some, the leg amputees being first, they would be discharged as soon as pegs of the right shape had been fashioned for them by the resident fitters, men who worked in round wood and the leather required to fit it to a stump which had, thanks to the voyage, time to heal and harden.

'Then there'll be a cook's warrant for you if you so desire and can find a berth,' was his cheerful message, not always so taken.

Those lacking an arm, and so useless aboard ship, would be discharged with a certificate which entitled them to a small pension from the Chatham Chest; not much, but enough to avoid outright starvation. To add to that there were tasks a one-armed man could carry out ashore, with naval service being a guide to a steady worker. Each already carried a written recommendation from their one-time captain to facilitate employment.

The three double-amputees of whatever limb, one fellow paralysed with a broken back, as well as those whose minds seemed troubled, would have to wait until relatives had been contacted to come and fetch them, which would take time. Generally this was certain to happen, given they too would be pensioned. Their families had likely depended on their pay, assigned by sailors on joining the navy. Now the new stipend, in no way comparable, would have to suffice whatever their circumstances.

Digby and the other deranged officer would be transported in a box cart to Bedlam if there was no sign of improvement in the coming days. Only when all were departed and the wards emptied would Stephen Byford be free to serve in another naval vessel in which to ply his skills.

For the Pelicans, the only question they wanted answered was some notion of how long they would be in the hospital, for the more extended their stay, the greater the chance of discovery.

'I have no idea. That is down to Mr Pearce.'

'Well let's hope he's getting a shift on,' Charlie said. 'We can't keep up this pretending lark for ever.'

'But, Charlie,' Michael hooted, 'is it not true you've been at that since the day you was born?'

'A sharp in the womb I were, it is true,' Charlie chuckled, taking the jest in good humour.

★   ★   ★

While that exchange was taking place, the man in question was snoozing in the anteroom of the Portsmouth Naval HQ. As his friends continued to fret he had met, talked and drunk wine with Sir Peter Parker. They were still anxious when he entered The George in the company of that officer to dine and he too was a tad frustrated.

Pearce wanted to be elsewhere, calling on Emily, then carrying out the errand upon which the Pelicans depended. This mattered little; Parker was not one to take no for an answer and Pearce had good reason not to upset him. He hoped to use his good office to defray whatever malice had been visited upon him by Sir John Jervis.

The coincidence of him being in the same place as Emily he could not put out of his mind; he had said he would call on her and here he was within shouting distance, for The George was not a large establishment, possessing only a limited number of rooms. These would have been full to bursting had it not been for the Admiralty rule that officers in command of warships must sleep aboard.

That did not apply to daytime eating. The room in which they were to dine was close to full, many of those present naval officers, though none below the rank of captain. That being so, Pearce, cloak removed and his hat taken, stood out for two reasons: his rank, but more importantly his host. A look round left him reasonably certain no one knew his name, which seemed to be confirmed as various officers stopped by to pay the C-in-C Portsmouth their compliments.

By the time the soup arrived Pearce was relating to Parker some of his recent service, first Genoa and the way the greedy and duplicitous merchants of that republic had driven Horatio Nelson to distraction. Parker was amused by the solution advanced by his one-time protégé: that he should put his frigate across the harbour mouth and, if not sink every ship in the harbour, at least enforce a real blockade.

'He was ever like that,' Parker acknowledged, as he went on to describe Nelson's exploits in the Caribbean as a young master and commander, eventually captaining a sixth rate. 'Activity was ever his solace. No officer I have ever come across has plagued me more to be doing something.'

Normally, Pearce disliked the naval habit of reliving battles and incidents that required courage or resource, but he found with Sir Peter it was less taxing. There was no hint of a boast as the admiral digressed on his own long career, which stretched from the War of Jenkin's Ear through every naval campaign up to and including the colonial insurrection.

'I felt for Sam Hood at Toulon, Pearce. Under Matthews, we got a bloody nose there in the year '44 and he didn't do much better two years past. Mind, we had the Dons and the French to contend with in unison.'

'They were part-allies only, this time,' Pearce said, recalling his conversation with Sir David

Rose, in which had been reprised the difficulties of holding on to Gibraltar. The previous siege, by the Spaniards and the French, had lasted three years and had only held out due to the ability of the navy to keep the garrison supplied.

Discussion of Toulon, which had been a place of conflict for both and Nelson too, brought Parker to his later successes in the Seven Years' War and against the American Revolution, wasted he insisted by the plodders of the British Army: generals who allowed themselves to be trapped at Yorktown. The conversation meandered on well past the roast fowl and the cheese, with Pearce getting anxious for the twin duties he was not acting upon, until Parker gave him an opening he had to take.

'Trounced de Grasse under Rodney at the Saintes, of course, but it hardly made up for the loss of the colonies.'

'Did you, sir, at that battle, come across a Captain Ralph Barclay?'

'Had a frigate, I seem to recall, but don't ask for the name. Never got close to him and it was not just rank. He wasn't the sort for intimacy, Barclay. No longer with us, of course.'

'It may interest you to know that his widow is at present here in The George.'

'Is she, by damn? I heard she was a rare beauty. Tongues wagged as to how Barclay managed to catch her, for he was no portrait.'

'She came back to England with me in *Tarvit*.'

Parker's eyes narrowed and the head canted to indicate interest. 'With you, Pearce?'

'Only as a passenger,' was the swift reply, to

181

deflect the way the older man's mind was surely heading, 'though I would say I could call her a friend. In fact, I did say I would call upon her to ensure she has settled in. I fear, if she was expecting me, I am going to be seen as somewhat tardy.'

Pearce had reckoned, after not very long in his company, Sir Peter Parker was a sly old fox who hid a sharp mind under a bluff manner; the look he was getting now confirmed it. He tried not to stammer in explanation.

'I grant you she is a comely creature, sir, very much so.'

'And of an age with you, I think, while you are, I assume, unwed?'

'But she is also a recent widow, with a child not yet two months old.'

'So there are proprieties to observe if there were attraction?'

'My mind has not been taken in that direction, sir.'

'Yet I sense I am keeping you from the obligation you mentioned and one you are keen to fulfil.'

'It was not an obligation, sir, more a promise to make sure she is not troubled in any way. She did confide the thought of returning home in her present estate induced a feeling of reserve.'

'Young man, I have listened to you, as you have listened to me, and I daresay you have formed an impression of my character.'

'One of generosity, sir, and a rare degree of understanding.'

'While you are decent enough but devoted

— by your own account of your travails — to insubordination. Your rank hardly merits notice, never mind attention from a flag officer, yet you seem to have managed to cross the hawse of three of them.'

'Thankfully,' Pearce smiled, 'it's not four.'

'Still, if I am right and Jervis has decided to recommend you be beached, that will be a difficult hurdle to jump and it won't be solved here, but at the Admiralty. Go to your appointment with Mrs Barclay, Pearce. If it is as I suspect it to be, such an association will do your service reputation even more harm than you have done it already.'

'It seems you reckon me to be sunk?'

'Perhaps, but if I can be of service to you I shall do my best for, if you have the esteem of Horatio Nelson, who is the bravest of men, there must be something worthwhile about you. That said, I will ask for an opinion in my next letter to him.'

'Thank you, sir.'

Sir Peter Parker nodded to him to go, then went back to the cheeseboard. Pearce made his way to the hatch in the hallway to ask for his name to be sent up to Mrs Barclay. Left waiting, he realised that it was getting dark outside and he had a vital chore to carry out for his Pelicans so he judged that Emily would have to wait.

Not that such a notion brought any certainty. Apart from a place and a name he had no idea where he was going, Portsmouth not being a town he knew well even in full daylight. That, once he had retrieved his hat, cloak and sword, led him back to the hatch and a second knock.

'My compliments to Mrs Barclay, but I've just realised I have another duty to perform. Could you send up a message to say I will call by in an hour or two? Also, could you point me in the direction of Caulking Lane?'

The directions took him back into the oldest part of the city. The lamps were being lit both within and without the dwellings and, if the street was still busy, this was diminishing as folk made their way to their homes, their hearths and their supper. Like all directions, what sounded simple was not, which had him ask a couple of passing strangers the way to make sure he was not getting himself lost.

Caulking Lane was a one-dog-cart-wide alleyway and, by the time he came to the corner where it joined Broad Street, the daylight was diminished enough to make it a gloomy passage. The dwellings here were a jumble, with no way of telling who lived where, which obliged Pearce to retreat to the corner and ask a trio of men stood there if they knew the place of one Quill Perkins.

'Who's asking?' came from the tallest of the three, whose face was so in shadow it was hard to pick out his expression.

'No one you'd know, friend.'

'So why would I say?'

'Happen I want to do a bit of trade with him.'

'From what I've heard, he don't just trade with any cove passing by, at this hour especial.'

Pearce could not keep the impatience out of

his voice, much as he tried. Partly it was the
need to get his business done so he could return
to The George and Emily, added to which he
had consumed a decent amount of wine with Sir
Peter Parker which did nothing for restraint.

'If you can point the way, I'd be obliged,
friend. If not — '

The response was not quick in coming, and
was preceded by a bit of whispering before the
tall one spoke. 'Low door, halfway down this
side. There's a knocker, brass it be, in the shape
of an anchor, you can't miss it.'

'I assume by his name he's a scribe?'

'That's so.'

'I thank you.'

Pearce had to peer now as he moved down the
alley, there was so little illumination. In the end
it was by touch and fluke he found what he was
looking for. The rap of the brass anchor on the
backplate was magnified by the narrowness of an
alley that had no right to the name 'lane', while it
was frustrating there seemed to be no response.
He rapped again and called out the Perkins
name, that too echoing.

'Who's 'at?' came through the wood eventually.

The voice sounded elderly and hoarse, the
accent local. Pearce decided not to say he was
navy and certainly he thought it unwise to name
his rank. The notion had him wonder if he
should not have come here in uniform at all
— still, that was hidden by his cloak. To disguise
himself even more, he spoke with a drawl like
that of Stephen Byford.

'I've been told you can aid a sailor in holding to his freedom.'

'Who a' told ye?'

Pearce cursed; he had forgotten to get a name from Charlie. 'I came in with the morning tide on a barky called *Tarvit*. A couple of me shipmates said I should come to you for what you did for them.'

'Names?'

'Would you know them, friend?'

'I would if I scribed for 'em.'

Pearce was at a stand. He could not just conjure up a couple of names; that would be worse than admitting he had none. 'I'll speak the truth to you. I have no need of your services myself, but I have three shipmates who need it bad. They would scarce dare walk the streets at a time like this, so they have charged me to deal with you and provided the coin needed to transact on their behalf.'

'Your name?'

No point in lying. 'Pearce, John Pearce.'

The rattle of bolts and chains being moved was a relief, aggravated by the number, for here was a fellow who had no notion to be surprised. The first crack of light from a held lantern had Pearce prepare to move forward, but he stopped dead when he felt the ring of cold steel at his temple. The next thing he felt was a hand on his back pushing him through what was now a wide-open door.

14

It was easier to see the hunched man holding the lantern now, in a room better illuminated by a couple of tallow wads flickering in sconces on the walls. His rheumy eyes were fixed on Pearce with an expression of wariness and his voice, when he spoke, came out as rasping.

'Search 'im.'

The cloak was pulled back to reveal his sword, quickly removed. Hands were run all over, pockets and waistband, probably searching for a pistol, given a small Queen Anne piece was easy to conceal. The sight of his uniform did nothing to soften the look in the eye of the fellow he assumed to be Quill Perkins; quite the opposite, it brought to his throat a half-rattle sound that would not have been remiss in a dog.

The others, he had to assume those he had questioned at the corner, stayed behind and out of his eyeline; he guessed that in the area of warren-like alleys and passages in this, the oldest part of the town, they must have been able to alert the scribe to his approach through some circuitous route.

Pearce sought to get some sense of his surroundings, without any excessive eye movement. The increased light, added to a modicum from a glowing grate helped. The smell was of burning coal under a chimney that did not draw too well, in a room that was small, the ceiling low and beamed in oak, with whitewashed walls long neglected and soiled by smoke. A single flick showed an unmade bed and a big chair, another the shape of a high desk and a stool, to the right of the fireplace. The feathers of several upright quills picked up the glim.

'The name you gave?'

'Was the right one, just as the errand is as I described.'

'You'se not a tar, you'se an officer.'

'It would be foolhardy to deny it.'

'The blue coat will do nowt' to protect you, matey.'

Pearce made a determined effort to keep his voice steady and his manner calm in his reply. 'Do I require protection?'

The response, like the threat, came from behind. 'Face down in water you can die as quick as any man.'

'And if it was known I was coming here?'

'Then you never arrived, friend.' The last word was larded with mockery. 'I can stand witness to that and, any road, we made sure you had no cove dogging your heels.'

The lantern holder spoke again in a wheezing way, indicating he was not young and ever short of breath. 'You come here askin' for a service no officer needs an' that might say to me you've been sent to worm me out for a rope.'

'If I had come as an officer to have you arrested, it would have been with a file of marines.'

Again the man behind responded, this time scoffing. 'Which would have been seen comin' a mile off, to find the place empty and us long gone.'

Pearce was wondering what services Quill Perkins provided, given there was no attempt to deny the forging of exemptions. He would have the normal trade of a scribe, writing letters and pleas for those who could not pen their own; good business in a port full of illiterates. But the level of precaution, men watching out for trouble, was surely not warranted by chucking out a few false documents. Yes, those who needed them would pay, but that was hardly a rich and steady source; indeed it was more likely to be intermittent and meagre.

'I have come alone and seek only what I have been told you can provide by men who carry them now: sailors who trusted me as a friend with the name and location.'

That lie came out easily as he sought to increase the sincerity in his tone. 'I have three men, friends in good times and bad, who could be classed, if collared, as deserters. They cannot move from where they are presently and I have come to get for them the means that will ease their plight.'

'My, he's got a fine turn of words, Quill.' This was accompanied by the barrel, of what Pearce presumed to be a pistol, being pushed into his back.

He turned his head just enough to speak over his shoulder. 'A fine turn of fact.'

'Sayin' it don't make it true,' Quill rasped.

'What else you do is no concern of mine.'

'What is it you're a'saying?'

'That you are probably engaged in activities that leave you to have more to fear from the government law officers than you have from me.'

In the few seconds he'd had time to think, Pearce had made certain deductions. This Quill was a forger of more than that which he sought, so being a scribe was his cover for more nefarious activities. That could be false claims for monies owed, bills of exchange or concocted wills, but the one that sprung to mind was forged lottery tickets.

Such criminality would explain the precautions as well as the fact he did not act alone. A falsifier of such scrips would require protection, not only from the law but from other felons seeking to purloin his products. He would also need others to sell his item, men who would do the dealing and share in the illegal earnings, which would explain the association with the trio who had been idling on the corner to keep an eye out for trouble.

Selling forged lottery tickets was a hanging offence, dangerous work even for the fleet of foot who could outrun the law. It would make no sense for the man producing them to do the vending as well, especially since this one looked too old to put up much of a fight, and besides, sounded as though running would kill him.

Quill alone he could have dealt with in a fight to get free, but how potent and numerous were his companions? He had no idea if there were two toughs or three behind him. Logic would indicate one must have been left to keep watch, so he maybe had only two to overcome, but there was a pistol and he could not assume it to be unloaded, while his sword was probably out of reach.

'He's fathomed too much, Quill,' was hissed into his ear. 'He's got to be seen to.'

'He ain't fathomed anything,' the older man protested.

'The gibbet rope ain't no respecter. It won't just be you that will be dangled.'

'Quill, I suspect you are not a man inclined to violence.' That was a guess, but a good one judging by a slight change of expression and a brief loss of eye contact. 'Your companions are right to be wary, but I have a tale to tell that will bend your thinking. All I ask is the chance to relate it.'

'Got to give 'im that, Whacker.'

The protest was swift. 'Ain't gonna help you givin' him my name.'

Quill began to cough, a throaty exercise full of phlegm, concluded with a gob of spit aimed at and hissing in the grate. 'You said my name free enough.'

'That he had a'forehand.'

'Let him talk,' Quill insisted. 'Makes no odds. If he's false, then we can do whatever we has to.'

'You can't believe a King's officer is goin' to tell you truthful?'

'Not always an officer,' Pearce countered. 'Once, and not so very long past, a pressed man serving before the mast.'

That took the old man aback. 'Away with ye.'

John Pearce did not hesitate; he started talking, for there was no doubt the fellow called

191

Whacker would happily club him unconscious before stripping him of his clothing and throwing him into the sea to make of him an anonymous corpse. Who would remark on a floating, naked body with nothing to identify them in a place like this? And that would only be if he was found and not washed out on the tide.

If Portsmouth was anything like the Thames, drowned cadavers were not objects to be too closely examined unless a name could be put to them, even if they had obviously expired from violence. Too often those fished out and unknown ended up on a surgeon's slab to help those training to master their trade, with the finders pocketing a guinea for their trouble.

In telling his tale, he had to leave out many details of the night he and his troubled friends had been pressed and that applied to subsequent events. Finally, he came to the point at which they might accept he was telling the truth, the incident that had got him his step and had at the time been much talked about.

'Do you recall the fight that saved HMS *Centurion* from certain capture by the French?'

He saw a flicker of recognition in the eyes of Quill Perkins, which was not surprising in the premier port of the King's Navy. Battles and nautical exploits did not exist as the sole province of men who served in warships. Those who built and repaired them had an interest too, as would everyone who lived off the prosperity the navy brought to the fifty-gunner's home port.

That particular contest might be too far in the

past to be easily recalled, so to make sure it was, he related every detail of how it had come about as well his role in the action, not eschewing downright exaggeration to enhance it. If he had ever been disinclined to boast, he needed to do so now: John Pearce had a strong inclination to survive.

'Heard of it right enough,' Quill acknowledged, when Pearce stopped. 'So you're tellin' us you was the midshipman cove all were talking about?'

'I am.'

'Could be made up, Quill, learnt by listening. I remember it being a well-talked tale at the time.'

'On the spur, Whacker?' the old man replied, with a less aggressive tone of voice. 'And spot on, as I recall. I reckon not.'

'My three companions were with me then and they are with me now.'

'Don't see 'em,' Whacker scoffed.

'They are in hiding.'

'Where?' Quill demanded.

'Haslar.'

Which occasioned more explanation as to how they came to be there, as well as his original plan to get them to London and back to the safety of the Liberties until he had been advised of what he could get from a visit to this house.

'If your script is as good as I've been told, they have no need to worry about that.'

'Haslar, you says?' asked Whacker.

'Yes.'

'Ain't as clever as he thinks, Quill.'

'No, he's far off it.'

'What does that mean?' Pearce enquired, with some trepidation.

'It means the Gosport shore is locked tight, mate.'

Pearce took a chance to turn and look at the fellow called Whacker, who had uttered those words. The first thing to register was his matching height, second that he did indeed have a pistol. But it was no longer aimed at his back; it was hanging by his side. The other, even if it was ill lit, was a well-scarred face dominated by a cratered nose and several gaps in his teeth, obvious as he spoke.

'Same as Pompey, maybe even worse, so many seeing Haslar as a way out.'

'How many do you think seek to get free from here?' Quill rasped, followed by a hacking cough. 'You can't get out of Pompey without you has to cross a bridge and they is manned by fellows who can spot a tar a mile distant, even dressed female as some have tried. Haslar's even harder, a prime place to seek to do a runner from. The marines there are on watchtowers and wise to every trick ever thought of. It's fer certain your lads would be picked up, to be locked away till their certificates could be proper checked.'

'I was told they hold up.'

'For passing along,' Quill insisted, 'not for too close a look by a beady eye who knows the marks. A medical scrip would serve better for where they's at.'

'It might if they were invalids.'

It was Whacker's turn to wheeze at his own

194

sally. 'Cut off a bit of flesh, happen. Hobble them out.'

Pearce was facing Quill again. 'I have to take a chance on your forgeries. I have no choice.'

Whacker spoke again, this time right by Pearce's ear and in a near whisper. 'That depends on your purse, friend, an how deep you'll dip.'

There was no mockery in 'friend' now. 'What does that mean?'

'There's more'n one way out for those with the means. Twenty guineas will see your shipmates clear, if'n you can go to the price.'

'How?'

Whacker tapped that cratered nose.

'The way is there,' Quill added. 'Word on it.'

Was that an assertion he could accept from what had to be a ripe set of rogues? Aware he was under keen observation, he made a point of appearing studious, sensing the changed atmosphere in the room. It was not really friendly and still wary, but he was no longer being threatened, which meant they believed he was telling the truth. But were they?

If they did know a way for a man to desert from this part of the world, his first thought was that it would not be gifted to many. What sailor had that kind of coin to lay out even after a fleet victory? The second was the possibility of a trap, twenty guineas being probably enough to match a month of selling forged lottery tickets. A careful man could live for a year on such a sum.

'I could run to that if I was sure it was the way.'

195

'Afore we say how, the sight of the gold would ease our concerns.'

'Meaning you still mistrust me, while asking me to trust you and that pistol you're still holding.'

'It would be good business, Whacker,' Quill interrupted. 'Best kind, and simple.'

'Simple it ain't, Quill, but you know it can be done. But sayin' how is taking a risk when, with this cove and his tales, we's takin' one already. Best if we see the payment, I say.'

'Who but a fool carries around that amount of coin?' Pearce enquired.

'You brought gelt of those certificates.'

'A guinea a piece I was told.'

'How would he know that, Whacker, if'n he hadn't been set right by those in I dealt with afore? I say he's on the up.'

Whacker gave way, but with reluctance. 'On your head, Quill.'

The striking of a bargain was far from easy, given the continued mutual suspicion, but when Pearce departed it was with an arrangement in place that might make possible that which was necessary. He paid for his three forged certificates, these to be brought to the agreed rendezvous, where he was to meet with Whacker on the long pebble strand that ran between the town and the near ruin of Southsea Castle.

The man who came back to The George was still unsure if he had done right, so was in no mood to be told that Mrs Barclay had left a message to say she had retired for the night and would thus be unable to receive him. A return to

Tarvit in the dark, using a hired wherry in an anchorage packed with shipping, looked fraught with misadventure and he'd had enough of that for one night.

'Do you have a room?'

That was answered in the affirmative, with the caveat that it was not of the best or most comfortable. The truth was driven home when he found himself in what might have served as a linen cupboard in times past. The cot would have accommodated a dwarf, which for someone of Pearce's above-average height led to an uncomfortable night.

He awoke stiff and far from rested, sending for a barber, given he first had to attend on Captain Woolley at the Naval HQ and he lacked the means to wash and shave. A foul mood was partially relieved by breakfast and the notion he had the time to call upon Emily before the King's Navy.

While consuming a good meal he ran over the bargain made the previous night, and the more it was examined the greater seemed the risk, though he could not be definite. It might be a trap to rob him, given the sum he would have to get from his chest would certainly justify it, but what was the alternative? Eventually draining the last of his coffee, he decided the plan had emerged in too spontaneous a fashion to be dismissed.

Coaches arriving at a place like The George was not something to be remarked upon, even at this early hour. It never occurred to him that it would apply so soon to Emily and indeed it was fortuitous that, appetite sated, he departed the dining room to call upon her, to find her in the tiny area set aside to receive and deal with guests.

She was by the hatch in the act of settling her bill, while the porter was busy taking her luggage out through the front door. Adam, wide awake, lay in a basket on the floor, staring up with those large blue eyes at whatever took his attention, his father being the object as he stood over him.

'Mrs Barclay, you are in the act of leaving already?'

Folding the bill she had just paid, Emily was already turning when he spoke, so her head jerked up. The expression of surprise mingling with discomfort did nothing to aid a mood barely restored.

'Lieutenant Pearce, how odd it is to see you about at this hour.'

'Naval habit, and I was on my way to see you, given I was too late to call upon you last night.'

'I retired early,' she replied, nodding towards the basket. 'I'm sure you'll understand that my clock is set by the sleep needs of my child. You will know from being on board ship with him these last weeks, he does not go through the night and is an early riser.'

'But such an early departure?'

He might as well have accused her of seeking to avoid him but no actual reply came as she glanced towards the porter coming back through the door. She would also be aware of the owner of The George, sat inside the hutch from which he ran the lodgings, which got him a glance from

Pearce to indicate that if he was eavesdropping, it was not welcome.

'The motion of the coach will put him back to his slumbers I'm sure, Lieutenant, which will render him less likely to be fractious on what will be a long day's journey. I hope to rest at Salisbury tonight.'

'I do think after the time we have spent in each other's company, a little less formality could be permitted.' Pearce dropped his voice as the porter carried out the last of Emily's possessions, while the curious face had disappeared from the hatch. 'We're alone, but not for very long, Emily.'

The cold response hurt deeply. 'I think you will find that ashore, the need to avoid too much familiarity would be best. What passes in the confines of a ship at sea will not pass on terra firma.'

'Say you've forgotten something and go back to your room to give me some time with you.'

'That, sir, is a shocking suggestion,' she hissed, before resorting to a normal voice. 'I believe the coach is ready to depart. If you wish, you may bear the basket for me and say farewell to the child whom you have come to know so well.'

Emily had turned away as though that was not a request to be refused, to speak over her shoulder as he obliged, following her out of the door.

'I do recall, however, you mentioned the possibility you might take the waters. I may myself go to Bath, if for no other reason than an abundance of physicians reside there who will

199

ensure my son does not succumb to any noxious ailments.'

'How will I know?'

'I have the address of your prize agent, Alexander Davidson. I will write to you of my intentions.'

The coachman was on hand to aid Emily into the conveyance, an expensive private hire that must have been arranged the day before. The man held out a hand for the basket, to be told by a jerk of the head his aid was not needed, which allowed Pearce to clamber in and raise it up so he could kiss his son, before laying it on the padded seating beside Emily.

'No doubt you will ask God to forgive you for this cold charade, Emily. If you feel he does, do not assume the same will so easily come from me.'

The look he got from the box seat for the slamming of the coach door was responded to with a furious glare that obliged the coachman to look away. A flick of the reins and a call had the two horses begin to move.

If he had looked round, once in motion, all the coachman would have seen was Pearce's rigid back as he strode back into The George.

15

John Pearce was still not in the best of moods when he was faced with the old sod called Riddell, but if he saw him as a target for his ire that was disarmed by a high degree of obsequiousness. Any man Sir Peter Parker esteemed enough to feed better be shown respect. His logs and despatches were produced in a trice, with an offer that they should be carried by him in person to the office occupied by Captain Woolley.

On entering the room, once Riddell had placed his things on the desk, Pearce found himself faced with an elderly officer, heavily built and with a sedentary air exacerbated by bloated cheeks. Woolley had a full head of white hair set off with heavy whiskers and was soon found to be hard of hearing.

Invited to sit, he observed the man carefully as he gave the logs a quick perusal, before ringing a bell to summon a clerk who would no doubt give them closer examination in an attempt to spot obvious anomalies. They would then be passed up the chain to the Admiralty where a fine-tooth comb would be employed by men whose sole task in life was to make miserable the lives of serving officers.

'Being a chartered vessel, Mr Pearce,' Woolley boomed, in the way the deaf do, 'they will, of course, go to the Navy Board not the Admiralty.'

'Then I hope they will note the parsimony of the owner's agent, sir. It is my contention he risked the safety of the ship and its passengers and crew.'

Pearce was sure Woolley had not heard that properly, even if he was nodding: there was a slight air of confusion in the eyes, quickly masked by the need to untie the ribbon holding the despatch from Sir John Jervis, in truth from his executive officer, Sir Hyde Parker. This he read head down, only to look up and make an attempt to compose his features.

'I daresay, sir, the name now rings a bell.' If it rung one with Woolley, it did so only when repeated in a louder voice, the truth acknowledged as Pearce added, still with force, 'I daresay I am no longer to command *Tarvit?*'

The large head nodded, as the letter was waved. 'You are to quit the ship at once, Lieutenant.'

Was there any sympathy? Pearce could not detect it but then he could not see malice either. There was nothing to keep him here; conversation would have been limited anyway by Woolley's hearing affliction, but the captain had the decency to shift uncomfortably. It was plain he did not have much to say in the way of polite conversation to this tainted officer.

'Then our business is concluded, Captain Woolley. I will go back aboard to collect my dunnage and make up the necessary paperwork to claim what I am owed in pay.'

The response to that was a noisy clearing of the throat and with nothing more to impart to a man now concentrating on his desk, Pearce stood and left. Sure Riddell was unaware of the cloud under which he laboured, Pearce requested the means to write a note to Sir Peter to say his fears had been confirmed.

It also advised him that he would, in due course, be calling at the Admiralty in London to seek a place, not with much in the way of hope. But if the admiral could see fit to support such an application he would be grateful.

Back outside and making his way to the sally port to bespeak a boat, Pearce, even if he had expected it, could not keep his anger from boiling up. This had him cursing everyone from Jervis through to Hood and Hotham, and all the way back to Ralph Barclay, only to realise why he was so upset. Naval service had come to represent the only way he could see to make his way in the world.

And it was more than that. For all his blaspheming opinions on the navy and the way it was run, he could not avoid the truth either: if it had not all been plain sailing, indeed at the very outset it had promised hell, there had been times when he had felt thoroughly at home, not least when action beckoned. Never to be admitted to anyone was the pleasure he took from the way his blood flowed at the prospect of fighting an enemy, surging even more when the chance came to outwit them as well.

There was no hatred of the French in this; if his father had taught him anything it was that there were good and bad in all races and he had seen both in the flesh when resident in Paris.

Another parental dictum had named all war as folly, for the main victims were those with nothing to gain.

What were they doing, his father would ask, the rank and file of soldiers and sailors, putting their lives in danger to keep a man no better than they, whose blood was the same colour and consistency, sitting on a padded throne surrounded by grasping offspring, to which those close to his person grovelled for the flummery of place and profit?

His son had come to realise there was a tinge of hypocrisy in that opinion. Adam Senior, as he had to be called now, had his own areas in which he loved to do battle: universal suffrage, great land holdings stripped from the rich to be broken up and given to the needy, many of whom existed in a state near to starvation. The duplicity of governance in which the true protection of the law was only for those who could afford it.

That message should have been music to the ears of those on whose behalf the man known as the Edinburgh Ranter pronounced. If it had gone down well at times, it had often proved to be the opposite. How many times had he and son John been forced to make a quick exit from some place in which Adam had aired his views at a public meeting, only to be booed? And on occasion, these hurried departures brought hard on their heels and seeking, if not blood, then certainly some form of violence, the very people he was trying to help. The paradox was that those who wished to hear his message, and were willing to feed and accommodate the pair in order to do so and at some length, were those with much to lose: people of means who knew the system was rotten and were genuinely looking for ways to change it for the better.

Nothing demonstrated the disappointment of old Adam's world view than the outcome of the revolution in France, not least its effect on him. From a bright dawn it had descended into barbarism. Adam hated the trappings of monarchy but he had abhorred what he saw as the judicial murder of the King and Queen of France, soon to be followed by some of the best minds in nation.

The bloody way it had progressed was something worth fighting against and if that had moderated with the death of Robespierre the governance was still a travesty. France was now being run and Europe threatened by a cabal of regicide cronies whose main interest was in lining their own pockets.

'Where to, your honour?'

The request broke that angry train of thought. 'The merchant vessel *Tarvit*,' Pearce commanded, adding the berth number.

'Aye, sir,' was the automatic response, which cheered him a little. This was a navy cutter, with the task of transporting officers to and from their ships. At least here, even if it was not to be for long, he was still given the respect due to a King's officer.

★ ★ ★

Tobias Fuller had missed John Pearce by not much more than a minute. Had he not done so the agent might have had a hard task in giving a reason as to why he was visiting the headquarters of the C-in-C Portsmouth, a place in which he had no discernible business. That said, it was far from easy to convince the old doorman that what he had to impart was serious enough to warrant disturbing anyone, let alone a man as busy as the person who could deal with it: Captain Woolley.

'Should you deny me a hearing, it may be that an officer of your service will be allowed to seriously transgress.'

'That officer being?' Riddell enquired.

'Fellow,' was the supercilious reply, 'you're not of a rank or position that allows me to vouchsafe you that information.'

The arch tone ensured Fuller was kept waiting on a hard seat in the hallway till past noon, indeed until Riddell reckoned he could keep him hanging about no more. Comings and goings tended to increase with the needs of the naval belly and the old salt had no notion to be asked the identity of this civilian, who frowned mightily at the sight of anyone passing by. Eventually Fuller was let in to see Captain Woolley, where he was obliged to shout his information.

'I have no idea of the exact nature of what it is Lieutenant Pearce is about, but I suspect it to be nefarious. He came to us at Leghorn with a trio of fellows all aboard took to be navy. They are no longer on the ship and I fear Pearce may have contrived to have them desert.'

That brought a grave expression to Woolley's

face, for desertion was a serious business, second only to mutiny in the canon of crime. The navy came down heavily on those who ran for the simple reason of example. Those contemplating the act must be shown the severe consequences they would suffer when caught, and it was made plain there was no amnesty or alleviation through time.

Britannia even risked war to get men back. A goodly number of deserters had run in the Americas, or got to that continent by various means, which led to every vessel flying the flag of the so-called United States being subject to search in an attempt to get them back, against which Washington threatened retaliation. Years of freedom and a claim of citizenship were no bar to being forcibly brought aboard a Royal Navy ship.

'I believe an officer seen to engage in such a practice would be dismissed from the service.'

'That is so,' Woolley replied; Fuller's accusation against John Pearce made the matter doubly grave. He rang once more for his clerk, who entered to receive his instructions. 'Go with this fellow, who will take your deposition, Mr Fuller. It may amount to nothing and it is to be hoped that is the case.'

If Woolley saw that the man before him disagreed with that statement, it did not register. 'But if it turns out there is a case to answer, you will have the gratitude of both the navy and the nation.'

'To act honestly, sir, is its own reward,' was the self-satisfied response.

A hand was cupped over an ear. 'Sorry, sir, what did you say?'

'Good day,' was Fuller's reply; he had no patience for repetition.

As soon as the door closed behind him, Woolley rang his bell again, to ask that an officer of marines be fetched from their billet. What Fuller had said about Pearce being involved was serious enough to require an immediate answer as to the truth.

★ ★ ★

'I can do nothing, I have told you.' Stephen Byford was annoyed and, though he would not admit it, a bit worried for his own part in the affair. So being faced with the trio of Pelicans asking him what was going to happen did not help. 'You depended on Mr Pearce yesterday and you must do the same until all is resolved.'

'We could be outed in a blink,' Rufus said.

'Not if you continue to be careful.'

'So you would say not to try and get away ourselves.'

'Taverner, I do not have the answer to that question.'

'Name's Charlie,' came with a grin.

'Sure, we have to just hold on,' Michael insisted. 'It were never goin' to be easy and you can wager John-boy is doing his best.'

'Another day at most, Michael,' Rufus countered. 'Then it has to be thought on serious.'

'So it's back to your cots.'

'Who'd have thought it, Mr Byford,' Charlie said, with a look of wonder. 'Told to lie abed all day, which there's not a tar born who don't dream of, and we're griping.'

'Well you best shift, there's orderlies coming in a short time to take the leg amputees down to the workshops.'

'Any hope you could go aboard the barky and find out what's goin' on?'

'No.'

★　★　★

When John Pearce entered the great cabin it was to feel acutely the fact of its emptiness; no Emily or Michael, and certainly no Adam or all the accoutrements that went with infancy. That thought was the most telling and depressing of all and it took a while for him to get his mind back to the matter at hand and how it was to be dealt with.

The option to just arrive and hope for the best had to be discarded. He had to get to Haslar and alert the Pelicans to what was proposed so they could be ready and in the right place. Stephen Byford would have to be appraised also, so as to have a story ready to explain, which he could be obliged to do: that three seemingly sick men, too weak to walk, were somehow missing.

To take the money now or later? He reckoned it best to have it on his person in case something untoward came up, so he went to the side cabin to fetch it from his locked money box. Just about to lift it out, having shifted some clothes to expose it, he spotted the slight trace of dust on the rim of the chest.

Many things could appear from nowhere on a ship but dry earth was not one of them, which had him lift the box quickly to feel its weight and check the lock was secure, the sense of relief palpable. Yet that did not explain the earth and it was only when he saw the old, now battered tin he had carried for years that an explanation became possible.

Not that it was cheering. The only way dust could have been spilt was if it had been opened and he had not done that for an age, the conclusion obvious. Someone had been rifling through his possessions, but whom? He felt the crew would not enter the great cabin by custom, and besides — most of them were, he assumed, still ashore.

Still, it had been foolish to leave it unguarded, done so by habit, given Michael O'Hagan ruled the roost in his absences and no one in their right mind would seek to take him on. Still wondering, he took the metal box to the desk, sitting prior to opening it, a quick count of the contents establishing he had not been robbed.

As he stared at the jumbled gold, the results of the success of the action in the Gulf of Ambracia, Pearce was forced to admit that he was looking at, outstanding pay apart, very nearly all he possessed in the world. That was not a pleasant thought, driving home, as it did, his need to find some way of earning an income. Another fact rendered the matter no better. The Pelicans depended on him and what he was looking at might have to support them all, and for how long he had no idea. It was easy to despise money when you had it, the very opposite when the possibility of poverty beckoned.

Emily wanted him to share in the wealth she had inherited from Ralph Barclay. Employed in the navy he could hold out against that. Could he if he were never again to get a berth, with nothing coming in but a lieutenant's half-pay?

'One thing at a time, John,' he said to himself, as he counted out the twenty gold coins, guineas because they had been paid over by English traders in the Adriatic port of Brindisi. They weighed heavy in his hand until he extracted a spare leather purse with which to carry them, reassuring himself with other words spoken out loud. 'A small price to pay for what I owe my friends.'

Taking out paper and dipping his pen he wrote a note which, sanded and folded, he propped up on the desk. Having locked his chest, and with his own pistols and the means to load them in a ditty bag, he went on deck to ask for a boat, as well as a couple of hands to bring up his dunnage.

'You're a'leaving us final, Mr Pearce?' asked the carpenter, a man who had stayed aboard: one of those too wise and long in the tooth to throw their wages away on Portsmouth pleasures.

'Afraid so,' was followed by the very necessary falsehood. 'The navy has other uses for me.'

'You have our gratitude, sir; it is hoped you know that.'

211

'I only did my duty.'

'I reckon you might not know how many who wear your coat don't, an' want for respect cos of it.' The carpenter, by the name of Prowse, the senior deck member of a merchant crew, smiled to expose toothless gums. 'If'n they sought a boat they would be told to whistle for one passing. What lads are still aboard will be happy to take you where you want to go.'

'Haslar first.' That got a nod, for he knew why that would be. 'Then the sally port.'

'Hope the sod that replaces you has your ways.'

'There's ever sadness in leaving a ship and crew,' Pearce responded, even if he knew it was not true; it was the proper form.

'Aye,' was the reply, as Prowse went to rustle up a man to fetch his chest, as well as a crew to row the boat. As he stood waiting a whip appeared and, when it was brought on deck, he lashed his sea chest on with practised ease, ready to be lifted over the side to the jolly boat, now bobbing below the gangway.

'My compliments to Mr Hawker. I have left a note on my desk thanking him for his companionship and his excellent seamanship.'

As Pearce was being rowed across the anchorage towards Haslar, a boat carrying a captain of marines and four Lobsters was leaving from the sally port, bound for *Tarvit*.

16

The fellows rowing John Pearce did not need to be told he was departing their ship; what would his sea chest be doing sat in the middle of the jolly boat if it had not been the case? Yet it was a measure of the sense of hierarchy that existed, even in merchant service, that none saw it as right to talk to him of it. This had him seeking to break the silence, if for no other reason than to take his mind off his own troubled reflections.

'I hope it does not inconvenience you that I wish to be taken to Portsmouth once my visit to Haslar is complete?'

'Not at all, your honour,' said the closest rower. 'Happy to oblige. We'll be getting our own run ashore when our mates come back aboard.'

'That's if they do come back,' opined another.

The sally from Pearce got everyone nodding. 'It will be with sore heads, I reckon.'

'An' sore pricks a few weeks on for some. Happen we'll need Mr Byford back on board with his mercury and his probe.'

The thought of that treatment made all wince, which had their passenger reflecting on the way men such as these risked their well-being. There were an endless number of fleshpots in the port — and not just this one — few of which could be classed as safe. A greater number of tars got ashore at Portsmouth, not just the normal fellows trusted to be given liberty, this for the very reason outlined by Quill Perkins.

It was a damned hard place to get away from, which meant his attempts to distract himself turned full circle, so it was as well the Haslar jetty was close. As they pulled alongside Pearce reached into his ordinary purse to produce a couple of shillings.

'Two men to guard the sea chest, taking turns. There should be enough there to get some victuals for all from the hospital kitchens.'

'You're a gent, your honour,' was the reply, which had Pearce thinking it might soon be the only title to which he could lay claim.

Byford he found in the workshops where the pegs were being fashioned for the leg amputees. The labour involved for this was not so much with the wood, which was only a matter of length and strength: the real craftsmanship went into fashioning the cups, which would connect to the stumps. These were made of a mixture of soft leather to fit against the skin, this set inside a metal cup, joined to the peg, and finally there were the body straps to keep it in place. These were objects of high quality and precise measure, provided by the navy: aids to movements that would have been unaffordable for most otherwise.

In a corner, away from those working, Pearce outlined to Stephen Byford what needed to happen and why, aware of the look of deep concern that furrowed his brow. There was little doubt as to the cause: he was being dragged deeper into the matter than he had originally envisaged.

'I took the precaution of not listing them as patients, Mr Pearce.'

'A good thing.'

'Only if no one was counting the unloading.'

'I saw no tallyman on the jetty.'

'There was no need to account for their food, either. The listless, by not eating, provided for them.'

'You seem to have taken every precaution, but I sense you are deeply worried.'

'What you propose to do is fraught with risk.'

'I have no choice, even if I acknowledge you are right.'

'They cannot get out of the ward unless I let them by unlocking the door.'

'Accepted.'

'And if they are apprehended before — '

Pearce interrupted, 'We have to trust that will not happen. I can guess you are reviewing your involvement in my scheming and for that I cannot blame you. But the game is on and I cannot, dare not stop it.'

'They need to be at the end of the jetty at eleven?' Byford asked to a nod from Pearce. 'Then let us compare our watches and ensure they show the same time.'

★ ★ ★

'Permission to come aboard?' This request came from a major of marines, stood in the prow of a boat.

The carpenter, who had watched the cutter approach and knew very well what it contained,

215

was the one to reply. 'Who's asking?'

'Are you blind, man?'

'I can see what, but not who.'

'Major Keller of His Majesty's Marines. Please call for the ship's master.'

'Ain't here,' Prowse replied, 'nor is the naval officer we had.'

'It is him I've come to see.'

'Too late, then.' Prowse reckoned it time for a bit of exaggeration. 'He shipped out with his dunnage not a half-hour past.'

'I still need to come aboard.'

There was not much choice; in this anchorage, entirely naval, he had the right to do so.

'As you wish, though I'd be obliged for a purpose.'

'Deserters. So I will need to see the exemption certificates of the whole crew.'

'Hope to Christ you're in dire need of spectacles.' This was muttered under the carpenter's breath, before he added, in a normal voice. 'Half are ashore.'

'Then I'll settle for what I can see now and leave the rest till time permits.'

It was not just him that came on to the deck but also the four Lobsters and their Brown Bess sea service muskets, to stand and close off the gangway, as if some soul would be daft enough to try and get off.

'If Lieutenant Pearce is no longer here, I am obliged to examine what papers and logs he has left behind.'

Prowse just nodded at him to carry on but, in truth, his mind was racing to make sense of this and to get ahead of what it portended. A search for men run from the navy was not unprecedented, but it was rare in harbour. The explanation was not hard to arrive at: it must have to do with the men Pearce had fetched aboard in Italy.

'Best I gather the hands,' Prowse said. 'Save time.'

There was a gathering already in place below decks, brought on by the sight of the marines, those with Quill Perkins' certificates the most nervous. Yet oddly that applied to all; a genuine exemption did not relieve the bearer from the worry it might be declared false. In the world in which they lived, anything could happen and it was held it was likely to be commonly unpleasant.

'Not a peep,' Prowse hissed. 'Pass it on. Any names mentioned, we never heard 'em. Play the chump.'

'Ditchin' might be best, Prowse. Save us.'

That got the speaker a glare. 'Not so. The steep tub is big enough for us all an' I for one have a mind to stay out of it. Best we all do the same. When fault spreads, who knows where it ends up?'

In the cabin, Major Keller, sent by Captain Woolley, was examining the muster roll, in his hand a slip of paper bearing the name of Michael O'Hagan along with the words 'two more?'. His problem was simple: with half the crew ashore there was no way to mark off all the names with the men they belonged to. Best concentrate on the one he knew, so he took the muster and went

217

to find the crew, calling to join him two of his men, one of them a corporal.

'I be obliged to have a name.'

'Prowse, Ship's Carpenter.'

'And the master?'

'Mr Hawker. Taken a run ashore to see family.'

'Anyone else in authority?'

'Not aboard. There's the owner's agent, but he went ashore this morning.'

'So I will be required to deal with you for now.'

'Looks like it.' Prowse saw the marine's face turn to a frown; he was obviously not getting the respect he thought his due, which was not a good idea. 'Just tell me what it is you want, sir, an' I will bend all to provide.'

'I will call out a name and each member of the crew will answer to it as his own. Then my corporal will examine their certificates. You will answer to the names of those missing.'

The corporal was ordered to lay aside his musket, and right away Keller began to read. Considering himself shrewd, he did the calling out as it was listed, that being the date of joining, to have either the man acknowledge and show his paper or for Prowse to shake his head. O'Hagan, Michael, he slipped in without a change of tone, halfway through, looking up first at the sailors assembled, all still and silent, then at the carpenter.

'Mr Prowse?'

'Major?'

'No response from anyone or you.'

'Name don't mean 'owt.'

'It's listed here.'

Which I take leave to doubt, was the thought of Prowse. 'Odd that. There's no man of that name ever sailed on this barky.'

'And if I say different?'

'Can't see how?'

Keller called out the name again with a hard look at the line of sailors. Getting no response he beckoned to Prowse and they moved away enough to talk without being overheard. There the marine was adamant that a fellow of that name had been aboard since Leghorn, and two more if what the navy had been told was true.

'Can't say I can see how anyone would say that to be the case, your honour. I am certain no one named that served on *Tarvit*.'

'We have one fellow saying he was and you saying he was not?'

'Either he's a'lying or . . . ' Prowse paused and his face took on a look of enlightenment. 'Might have been posing as one of the invalids we dropped off at Haslar.'

'Why would an invalid be on the muster?'

Prowse held out a hand. 'If I can see it.'

'Take my word,' was the sharp rejoinder. 'Now let's carry on.'

Keller started calling out names again, everyone owned up to or admitted, until the end was reached. He was frustrated, and gave a poor impression of hiding it. One more possibility existed and he turned to his inferior.

'Corporal, the certificates?'

'All good, sir.'

'Right names, as I called them?'

219

'Yes, sir.'

'O'Hagan,' he shouted, spinning around in an attempt at a second surprise. He was greeted by a sea of blank expressions, which had him stomping towards the companionway calling for his men to follow.

Keller departed to report to his superiors, having left no doubt of his intention to return again on the morrow, leaving behind a buzz of conversation. The men of *Tarvit* had done what was needed, but the concern still existed it could all come back to haunt them.

* * *

John Pearce had finally got to the end of his explanation of both the difficulties he had discovered in the matter of exemptions, as well as the solution. Byford would let them out of the ward and they were to make their way to the end of the jetty at the appointed hour. There boats would be waiting, the larger of which they would help row to the mouth of the Hamble, past the watchtowers of those seeking deserters. Quill Perkins insisted it was better, safer, to go west than east. The second, smaller boat would take him back to Portsmouth.

'You paid these folk, John?'

'I will do, Charlie, when I see the boats.'

That got a sniff of doubt. 'Never was much of one for trusting strangers.'

'Nor I,' O'Hagan hissed. 'Sure, you might be setting yourself up for a club on the head, with your gold the prize and you weighted to be chucked out at sea.'

'I know that, Michael,' he replied, 'but I will be armed.'

'Jesus,' he crossed himself, 'there'll be more'n two to deal with if a pair of boats need rowing.'

'Then I use my sword,' was the impatient response. 'I know the risks, just as I know that doing nothing is worse. Are you going to act as I say or not?'

It was not necessary to affirm it; the Pelicans knew there was no choice.

'I must go ashore and get myself a room, hopefully at The George and of more comfort than I had last night. You must make your way to Winchester, a route will be provided, and find a place to lay your heads. Keep an eye on an inn called the Old Vine and watch out for me. I will travel tomorrow if I can and then we will join together and head for London. I have brought all the small coinage I have: golden guineas, even halves, would draw too much attention.'

The coins, silver and copper, were handed over to be rattled in O'Hagan's hand, with neither of the others objecting that he was the man to hold it. 'Till tonight — and Michael, feel free to pray.'

'Not just him, John,' Rufus asserted. 'All of us.'

Crossing back to Portsmouth took Pearce past the stern lights of half a dozen first rates, hundred-gun leviathans that formed the back-bone of the Line of Battle Fleet. He was noting their names, HMS *Caledonia* getting a particular look. Would he ever step aboard one of these warships again — not that he hankered after one of such size?

If smaller vessels were cramped, they promoted a sense of camaraderie and, it had to be said, were not tied to the apron strings of an admiral. He could recall the freedom and independence he had enjoyed, even when not in command, which now looked like it was gone for good. It was a gloomy and apprehensive lieutenant that came ashore to bespeak a dog cart to carry his chest.

★   ★   ★

'Are you sure, Captain Woolley,' Keller shouted, 'that your informant is telling the truth?'

'No, Keller, I'm not. And there's no need to shout in that manner. I can hear you perfectly well.'

'Of course, sir,' was the required reply, delivered with little diminution of tone. 'But he may just be mischievous. He is, after all, a civilian.'

Those in uniform, of whatever service, had an unhealthy disrespect for those not so blessed. Civilians had no sense of honour, which was the mark of both an officer and a gentleman.

'Which makes me reluctant to pursue this by seeking the Pearce fellow ashore. It will mean sending my men to everywhere in the city he can lay his head.'

'Will he do that? He's just been beached, Keller. Not much point in hanging round here. Might have set off for somewhere else already.

Have to say, though, the cove who told the tale was convincing.'

'I can do the rest of the crew tomorrow, sir, and then perhaps check on Haslar, just in case they slipped ashore there.'

'Make it so. I'll send to the most popular inns with Pearce's name. If nothing transpires, we can forget it. I have no time for wild goose chases.'

Unlike me, Keller thought.

★   ★   ★

Pearce had no idea the room he was given had been occupied by Emily and Adam, a small space — there were no large suites at The George — but a damn sight more comfortable than that which he had previously suffered. Weary, and having ensured he would be called in time to eat, he lay down to sleep and dream, none of which were anything but disquieting.

The servant carrying his tray of food woke him in good time and he ate heartily. Knowing — or was it hoping? — he would be out all night, he shaved and, given it was cold, dressed in several layers of warm garments, but not so excessively as to hamper movement. The edge of his sword was examined for sharpness, more by habit than need: Michael had always seen it was keen.

The loading of his pistols was done with care for he knew it not to be without risk. He would need to carry them in that state and only cock them when and if they were drawn. But the hammer was lightly secured. If it slipped, stuck in his belt, it would be he who suffered.

It was necessary to wait until past twilight before he left the room, to creep downstairs and exit through the rear, slipping past the stables and making sure his departure was not observed by the grooms. Then, hat brim pulled low, he headed south, glad when he cleared the new developments being built in Portsea — many houses for naval officers — to make the pebble strand that led to Southsea Castle.

'Now't there but a corporal and four men,' Quill Perkins had said, 'who will sell you a tot of rum if you like, for they ever wait for their pay, poor buggers. They won't stir for 'owt, Jacobins landing hard by included. Our boats will be just far enough off not to be spotted in the dark, but it's scarce needed.'

Pearce wondered, as he strode along, his feet scrunching on the loose pebbles that made walking a struggle, under a sky that was a mix of cloud and moonlight, whether the forger had the right of it. If the cloud cover broke completely, there was enough starlight to see by, never mind a half-moon.

The head of the beach being lined with grass-covered hummocks and trees, it was from them that Whacker emerged, to softly whistle and call Pearce to him. When he got close the rogue retreated into the darkness of the woods and this, Pearce reckoned, was the moment he would find out if he was to be dealt with straight or crookedly. His heart was beating as he pulled back one side of his cloak to take hold of the right-hand pistol butt, yet he was wary of drawing it out. Right at the tree edge he

224

stopped and waited.

'A'feared is you?'

'Cautious.'

'Bound to be.' That was the voice of Quill Perkins. 'No man in his right mind wouldn't see hazard. If you'se got a hand on a pistol, know we has one on you.'

'Trusting.'

'I need to see the coin.'

'And I need to see you, Quill, as well as my certificates.'

'Don't see as how you can read 'em in the dark.'

'Then show me the boats.'

The soft whistle that followed produced an immediate result. One prow, of a cutter-sized boat, appeared just as a gap in the clouds opened up to illuminate it, the sound of half a dozen feet and its keel on the pebbles setting up a din Pearce was sure could be heard a mile off. The second boat was fetched, the first now safe at the water's edge with Quill emerging from it, his face ghostly but smiling.

'You got to trust us friend; you ain't got no choice. Hold out your hand.'

Doing as he was asked, Pearce felt papers being pushed down on to his palm. 'I took a liberty in changing the names: close to the originals, but not the same. If your lads are King's Navy their monikers are listed somewhere. Best if exemptions carry different.'

Feeling for the delivering hand, the purse was passed over, he assumed to be weighed. 'You can't see that either, Quill.'

'I can feel it, friend, and my hand tells me you have come with the needed. Now I reckon both boats are in the water, which is where you need to be, and Godspeed.'

'Would it offend you if I said I hope not to ever see you again?'

'Never in life.'

17

The stern lanterns were unshaded as soon as the boats pulled away from the shore with Whacker on the lead tiller; seeking to be invisible would only bring on suspicion, not allay it. They were crossing an anchorage full of craft plying to and fro, all with lanterns on a sternpost, coming and going from anchored vessels and containing those who had no other means of getting ashore or back to their ship whatever the time of day.

It was also best to row with purpose, as if there was a destination, for there was known to be the occasional cutter full of marines patrolling, to what most folk would see as no purpose, doubly so on cold nights. It was commonly held to be the malicious jesting of naval officers looking down on their red-coated confréres: a deliberate ploy to drive home who wore the garment of superior colour.

Steering was dictated by the lights ashore — Portsmouth to one side, Gosport to the other — with the black maw of the entrance to the harbour in the middle. Once past most of the warships, all in some measure illuminated, they headed for the long row of lights on three levels that were the windows of Haslar, throwing out the results of numerous candles.

'Time, friend.'

Pearce had to move close to the stern lantern

to check, which told him it was just past an hour of the First Watch. That passed on, he heard the shout that told the following boat to put down its tiller and circle; they were too early.

'You're sure?' Pearce asked in a whisper.

'Allow I know my own patch,' came out as a vexed growl.

The detour was wide enough not to draw attention and, once straightened again, Whacker asked for another time check. That provided, he instructed the rowers to haul in the oars and muffle them. Stationary, the boat rocked heavily on the swell as cloths were tied to the blades to kill the sound of splashing water.

Happy all was complete and the right time had come, Quill's bruiser gave the order to 'haul away slow'.

He shaded the lantern over his head which, in a patch of water less busy, given the second boat followed suit, left only the Haslar lights and the overhead illumination to work by, slow-moving cloud occasionally blotting out moon and stars to plunge them into darkness.

As he listened to the muted sound of dipping and lifting oars, Pearce found it frustrating to be in the hands of others. He was accustomed to being the man making the decisions in what was very like the kind of boat raiding he had done in the recent past. Recalling those occasions occupied his mind and made the suspense bearable, until the man in charge told him it was time to call out and make sure those they were to pick up were ready and that it was safe to pull alongside the jetty.

'John-boy here,' he called.

The answer was a low whistle, which had Pearce pat Whacker's shoulder as a sign to proceed. There was no rushing: it was still to be done with caution. It was as well the sky was momentarily clear, which silhouetted the darker shade of the jetty.

'Pelicans?'

'To a man, John-boy.'

'Is it safe?' Whacker demanded, with no attempt at gentility.

'Not a soul in sight. Pull along a bit to the ladder.'

'Then, friend, say a quick word to your mates and change boats.'

As Michael, Charlie and Rufus came down the wooden ladder, the second boat pulled up on the seaward side. Pearce waited until the Pelicans were settled, moving to speak in a hurried whisper and make sure they knew what had to be done next.

'This should have been sorted a'fore,' was the impatient response. 'I've no mind to be had up for your blether.'

'All paid for?' whispered Michael.

'It is.'

'Then when we get to where we're going, happen I'll give that eejit a clout to teach him some manners.'

'Just get there.'

'Sure, have I not got enough saints in my corner for all of us?'

Pearce moving caused both boats to sway, but as soon as he was aboard the smaller boat the oars were used to push off, to then be dipped with the same caution as had been used on the approach. Whacker acted likewise, quickly disappearing into the gloom. Further out the oars were shipped again and the muffling removed, with an unknown voice requesting the lantern be unshaded once they were back in the water. From then on progress was normal.

He was put ashore just out of the arc of twinkling lights that delineated the urban area of Portsmouth, to walk back to where he had started. The hour rendered it impossible to enter The George in the manner in which he had departed. This obliged him to knock and wake the cudgel-bearing fellow set to man the door for the night, to ensure the place and those accommodated were not robbed.

The residue of his earlier meal was still on the table, most notably the half-empty bottle of wine and he helped himself to a decent glass. Certain he would not be able to sleep, so many and various were his thoughts, he nevertheless undressed and lay down to think over the events of the night. He was asleep in minutes.

★   ★   ★

'Mr Pearce, sir.' The voice came through the door to be heard by a man sitting writing a letter. 'There be a marine officer downstairs asking for to see you. Would showing him up be in order?'

Looking around the room and thinking it too small to receive visitors, and with his bed not yet made, he replied in the negative. 'I will come down presently.'

His letter to Emily was unfinished but he sanded it anyway so it would not inadvertently get smudged, wondering as he did so what business an officer of marines could have with him and failing to produce an answer. It seemed appropriate, however, to check his appearance prior to leaving and that extended to a habitual brushing of his best uniform coat just before he put it on.

The man who had come to see him was pacing to and fro in the tiny hallway, the first sight Pearce had being of his highly polished shoes, silver-buckled, his stockings and the bottom of his snow-white breeches, another two steps picking up the tail of the red coat. Those shoes turned at the sound of his tread, so his visitor was facing him when he finally descended.

What Pearce observed then was a red face, bright blue eyes and a lumpy skin texture, the whole of which hinted at ginger hair, but if it was that, it was hidden under a tight powdered wig. The pose — hands behind back and body rigid, added to a determined stare — indicated impatience, as if Pearce had kept him waiting. The brusque voice gave the same impression.

'Good day, sir; you are, I presume, Lieutenant Pearce?'

'Since you sent for me, sir, I doubt I'd be anyone else.' That sharp reply induced a look of amazement, it being unexpected. 'Can I ask who it is I am addressing?'

'Major Keller, sir, sent by Captain Woolley to

undertake enquiries regarding a report we have had — a very alarming one.'

'On the subject of what?'

'It has been imputed to us, by an informant who called upon Captain Woolley, that you have aided and abetted a trio of common seamen to desert the King's service.'

'Imputed by whom?'

'That I am not at liberty to say.'

Had he kept a straight face? Pearce hoped so but he reckoned the small hall of The George, even not busy, was still a place in which any exchanges could be overheard by those who ran the establishment, which would never do.

'It may be better to carry on this conversation in the parlour, Major Keller. Since I most vehemently deny this accusation, it would not do to have the matter too publically aired.'

That confused the marine, who was struggling to follow the logic of two entirely unconnected points, as Pearce added, 'And, of course it would be remiss of me not to offer you some refreshment.'

There was no waiting for agreement; Pearce was already heading for the parlour and, upon entering, seeking and making for what he thought to be the most discreet corner. There he stood until Keller appeared, a hand indicating a seat, taken with seeming reluctance.

'What will you take, sir?'

'Nothing.'

'Then you will not mind my ordering a pot of coffee.'

Did this Lobster discern that Pearce was

playing for time, allowing himself to think through what he was being accused of — nothing but the truth? Yet how did it come to be known? Someone was telling a tale and he ran through a gamut of possibilities, which even extended to Quill Perkins who, now he had his guineas, might be looking for a second bite for informing on him.

'Now, sir,' Pearce said, as he sat, not looking at Keller but summoning a servant. 'I think I am entitled to some kind of explanation.'

'That, sir, is moot. I reckon it is the service that requires clarification. But the plain case is this. We are told that you fetched three sailors from the Mediterranean aboard the vessel of which you so recently had command — '

The held-up hand stopped Keller, as Pearce placed his order, his voice silky as he enquired, 'You're sure you won't join me?'

'I have already declined, sir, have I not?'

'Indeed. We were, I believe, talking of the hospital vessel *Tarvit*.'

'We will be talking of a fellow who goes by the name of O'Hagan. There are two others whose names are as yet unknown, but we have been assured that you are connected to them, perhaps with a familiarity not befitting an officer dealing with common seamen.'

How to deal with the identification of Michael, while being glad Charlie and Rufus were unmentioned? Deny all knowledge? Was that wise, given so many people had seen their close association and it was not just the crew of *Tarvit?* Many people must have observed what

233

Keller was alluding to and they were not all in the Mediterranean. Added to which any muster of the ships on which he had sailed would show the name of O'Hagan on the roll.

'I seem to recall the name,' came after a pensive moment and studied pose.

'From where, sir?'

'A sailor, of course; small fellow, nimble topman and rated able, but my memory does not extend to the ship on which we both served.' The conversation was interrupted by the arrival of a pot of coffee as well as the presence of the fellow who brought it, with Pearce feigning enlightenment. 'Now I have it: HMS *Larcher*, an armed cutter, which I took out to the Mediterranean carrying despatches to Lord Hood.'

'And where would this fellow be now?'

'No idea.' That was at least the truth; he knew where he should be going, but not where he was. 'Might not even be alive, but if he is I reckon he would be with the Mediterranean Fleet, though in which vessel I could not say. I lost HMS *Larcher* in a fight with Barbary pirates and the crew was broken up.'

'We have been told he was here in Portsmouth, aboard *Tarvit* and acting as your servant. A brute of a fellow, by all accounts, not small, who was singularly unsuited to the job of waiting table.'

Keller mistook the look of anger in the face before him, unaware Tobias Fuller had sprung to mind. In mentally ticking off names it had to be him, the only other possibilities people he was sure would not ditch him. If it had been any of the crew — the only other likelihoods, Michael Hawker and Emily having been swiftly dismissed — they would not have alluded to his suitability as a servant.

'This, Major Keller, I find preposterous. Those who attended to me on the voyage home were provided by the ship's master, Mr Hawker. I'm not sure I could name them.'

It was now Keller's turn to look pensive. 'The vessel brought home casualties?'

'It did. The serious cases.'

'A good way to smuggle people as afflicted stowaways, would you say?'

'If there were such people, I have no knowledge of it. Dealing with them was the province of the surgeon and his helpers.' Coffee poured and cup to his lip, Pearce watched the marine carefully. 'But if it was the case, they would no longer be aboard, sir: they would have been shifted into the naval hospital the day before yesterday.'

'It is my intention to make that my next port of call.'

'This implies you have already searched *Tarvit*.'

Keller tried to hide his surprise at the deduction, which to Pearce was so obvious it made him doubt the mental agility of this marine. Also plain was that the crew had not told him anything. There was a look then of a man who felt he had been outwitted and had not enjoyed it, followed by puffing cheeks, a glare and Keller getting to his feet.

'Mr Pearce, if this accusation had been made

against any other officer, I doubt it would have been given a moment's credence. Yet such is the matter of your rank and your reputation — '

'Have a care, sir,' Pearce snapped, cutting Keller off. He stood himself and at speed, which obliged the major to take half a step back 'I have made your acquaintance for the first time this morning and that does not permit you to mention such a subject.'

'There are those, sir, who would say it is germane.'

'And they, sir, are like you ignorant. I would beg to doubt you have the faintest notion of how my promotion came about and what actions I have engaged in subsequently. I have never been shy in the article of personal engagement with our nation's enemies, and there I have a reputation of which I am proud. So I must tell you that neither your rank, nor the colour of your coat, will protect you from the consequences of too loose a tongue.'

'Damn me, sir, are you threatening me?'

'It would be more accurate to say, Major Keller, that you are threatening yourself. You call upon me with accusations of a base nature and from a source you decline to name, to act as if they are true when they are patently false. If you have been aboard *Tarvit*, then the truth must have been made plain to you.'

'I have yet to visit Haslar.'

'Where I have every confidence you will find nothing either. Now, I bid you good day and suggest once you have finished your business you call again with an apology — not only from you, but from Captain Woolley as well.'

'I'm damned if I'll apologise for doing my duty.'

He was talking to Pearce's back; he was heading back to his room to think what to do next and it was not long before he saw the only way to deflect attention from him was to discredit Fuller. That could only be done in one place, so he headed back to Sir Peter Parker's headquarters to enter and demand to see Captain Woolley.

'He's at the weekly conference, your honour,' Riddell protested. 'With Sir Peter and the officers of the port.'

'Then drag him out, man, or I will go in and fetch him.'

It was bluff but, delivered with real force, it broke the old salt's resolve. 'All I can do, sir, is send in a message and even that might get me keelhauled.'

The switch of tone, the softening of both mood and voice, was immediate. 'I would be most obliged, Riddell, if you could see your way to doing that. And please accept my apologies for being too brusque with you. I have just been most seriously traduced not an hour past and it has affected my manner. Since you are not the culprit it is remiss of me to berate you for something that is not of your doing.'

The leathery wrinkled face cleared of obvious worry. 'Gracious, your honour, gracious.'

'Captain Woolley?'

'Happen if you pen a scrip, your honour,

which would mean I was obliged to enter the room.'

There was a desk and the means to do so against a wall and Pearce sat to compose his request, his point an insistence that the honour of the service was at stake. He added that he would not depart until Woolley had obliged him. It was some time before the old captain emerged, to move to greet Pearce with a stiffness that testified to his sedentary occupation. Hard to believe he had probably at one time been a sprightly fellow in command of a ship.

'There's damned effrontery in this,' Woolley cried, waving the slip of paper. 'Who, sir, do you think you are?'

The reply was loud enough to echo throughout the building. 'Given that to which I have been exposed, I make no apology.'

Woolley spotted Riddell, who was making a poor fist of not eavesdropping. The flustered captain ordered Pearce into his office, where he immediately put his desk between him and his angry caller. He was about to speak, no doubt to castigate further, when Pearce cut him off in a voice so loud it would have bypassed a deafness greater than that which afflicted Woolley.

'Have you read my logs, sir?'

'No, I have not.'

And nor will you, Pearce thought. That will be left to your clerk, the demand following that the fellow be fetched and the papers with him.

'For within those, sir, you will find daily complaints aimed at a fellow called Fuller, agent to the owners of *Tarvit*.' A quick allusion to the lack of ballast and how it had affected the trim of the vessel raised Woolley's thick grey eyebrows. 'He risked the ship to save pennies and I have no idea if it was to line his own purse or that of his employers. All I will say is this. I made him aware of my intention to find out on more than one occasion and alerted him to my log entries on the subject.'

'Mr Pearce,' the older man said, with an ineffective wave of the hand.

'Would my suspicion be correct that the accusation levelled against me by Major Keller came from that source?'

'I must decline to answer.'

'Sir, you have just done so and confirmed it. Can I say it shocks me you believe the word of a civilian, and very likely a less than honest one, against that of a King's Officer? Even one, as Major Keller was foolish enough to allude to, who carries a certain amount of baggage. Fuller is seeking to ditch me, in order to divert attention from his own misdeeds.'

'Major Keller?'

That was put to Pearce in a softer manner, indicating he had succeeded in sowing doubt.

'Is, I believe, on his way to Haslar to seek some fellow who does not exist.'

'Then I must await his return.'

'He will find there nothing to aid this folly.'

'In which case, Mr Pearce, the matter will be closed.'

★   ★   ★

Pearce departed with a hope, but no certainty, that the matter would not be pursued. It would have eased his mind if he had heard Captain Woolley, on his way back to the senior officers' conference, give a firm order to Riddell:

'If a fellow by the name of Fuller calls and asks for me I am not available.'

18

'I was obliged to hang about for two days, Heinrich, which bore heavily on my Pelicans, as well as swing by Haslar to thank Stephen Byford. But he held the line and Keller went away empty-handed, so I have a strong hope the matter is not going to be pursued.'

'The journey?' Lutyens asked.

'Passed without incident. We did encounter an officer and some fellows of the Press at a village called Camberley, but my coat kept them at bay. Had we taken the direct route through Guildford, I don't think we'd have got off so lightly.'

'And where are our friends now?'

'Safe in the Liberties and wondering what to do next.'

Lutyens stood and went to the sideboard to pour himself a second glass of wine, Pearce declining a refill. 'John, they cannot bide there for ever.'

'No.'

'And what of you?'

'It would be a lie if I said I had any certainties at all, and that applies to my personal concerns as well as my service ones.'

Lutyens leant backwards against the furniture, glass in hand, his head on his chin in contemplation, his free hand pulling at his rather pointed nose. With an expression sometimes giving the appearance of confusion — not aided by his now wearing spectacles and his small stature — many people had taken him in the past for a person of no consequence, none more than those who had only seen him as a run-of-the-mill ship's surgeon.

Nothing could be further from the truth: the likes of Stephen Byford, competent as he was, would have admitted in a blink to be in the presence of a superior fellow in the medical line, both in matters of the head and the body. He had taken service aboard HMS *Brilliant* not to just carry out the normal duties that fell to his position, but to undertake a study of the mental state of sailors, both those pressed and those who volunteered.

How did a man not born to the sea adapt in a setting so different to life ashore? What was the effect of a hierarchical discipline acknowledged to be harsh on such people, officers and men alike? What made those who manned the ships such eager fighters, and were there those who put out a pretence of being eager to engage in battle?

Pearce knew from his letters that his findings had been presented at The Royal Society, to much acclaim and at much enhancement to his reputation. Not that he was short on that to begin with: if he looked unprepossessing Heinrich Lutyens was very much the opposite, a leading light of St Bartholomew's and a fellow called to attend upon Queen Charlotte if she felt indisposed.

His father held the position of Pastor at the

Lutheran Church in London, to which the Queen, being German, went as a frequent worshipper, King George and the royal offspring very often accompanying her in her devotions. His new abode in Harley Street attested to his status as a fellow to consult, for the connection to royalty brought many wealthy folk to his door.

'I take it they are living on your generosity,' Lutyens said finally. 'Board and lodgings?'

'What choice do they have, Heinrich? There are still warrants out for Charlie Taverner and Rufus, though it is to be hoped they are ancient history, while it could be foolish for Michael to go back to that which he did before and dig ditches with only a forged protection to keep him safe.'

'You said they were sound.'

'I have been told they are sound, an opinion I have yet to observe tested in practice.'

'Which obliges me to enquire as to how you are found?'

'That I will let you know when I have called upon Davidson. He has been in receipt of my pay and any monies I have garnered, except that which I fetched back from the Mediterranean.' Pearce grinned. 'Somewhat less than that with which I set out.'

'You have ever been cavalier on the subject of money, John.'

'Appearances, Heinrich. I am as conscious of the need for income as anyone.'

'I'm sure that when it comes to supporting Michael, Charlie and Rufus, Emily would assist. She is, after all, a wealthy woman now.'

The tone of friendly conversation evaporated. 'It's Barclay's money.'

'Ah, Barclay,' Lutyens said, moving to sit down once more, then cross his legs and lean backwards, eyes aimed at the elaborate plaster-work of the drawing-room cornice. 'What a vexatious fellow he was in life, and now he is to be that in death.'

'I fear the vexation has moved from him to Emily. Try as I might, I cannot get her to see sense.'

'Surely you mean your view of what constitutes sense?'

The smile took away any unkindness; Lutyens was a true friend and had proved the fact many times in the past. A series of images ran through John Pearce's mind as he sipped on his wine: of their first meeting, if it could be called that, on a cold February morning. The surgeon of HMS *Brilliant* was required to inspect the unfortunates brought aboard by Ralph Barclay, that basilisk presence watching for signs of unwarranted sympathy.

On that same morning he had espied Emily for the first time and had been struck by her beauty and youth; how much had that affected his life? As much, perhaps, as his being forcibly inducted into the King's Navy. Michael O'Hagan was a stranger to him then, as were the others who became a group just to support each other.

A less pleasing image, as bad as Barclay, was the one now in his mind of the slug, Cornelius Gherson, who had also come aboard having

244

been saved from drowning in the River Thames. What had become of him?

★ ★ ★

Asked, at that moment, Cornelius Gherson would have insisted on one thing. He hoped never again to be exposed to the smell of pinewood in its raw state. It had filled his nostrils for a full two weeks: valuable cargo of seasoned planks from Scandinavia that would go into panelling the better rooms of the fine town houses springing up all over the capital.

The *Melissa* had been packed with it to the point where, for the crew, there was scarce room to stretch out and sling a hammock. The outbound cargo having been grain, the ship was also beloved by rats. They had infested the vessel and, with their previous abundance unloaded and thus starved of easy food, they made bold enough to take an occasional bite out of human flesh.

They had to if they wished for sustenance, given the victuals on the *Melissa* had been beyond poor and meagre which, with sharp-set sailors, left nothing for rodents; hunger nearly had Gherson chewing the pine. The captain, a Scottish martinet called Cullen, was also the owner and a man who saw every penny expended as blood drawn from his very veins.

The voyage was over now and he was thankful to be back on home soil. With the last, lashed bundle swung by the derrick to land safe onto the dock, Gherson went to gather up his meagre

245

belongings, as well as to wash as well as he could and dress his hair so he looked passably presentable, before going to collect the docket that would see him paid.

He could not but help look at his hands as he stuffed his ditty bag, ingrained with tar in a way that they had not been for a long time, since his first weeks on board HMS *Brilliant*. That was before Ralph Barclay had come to see his ability with figures, as well as finding him a kindred spirit when it came to peculation.

When he reflected on the journey from Italy, Gherson reckoned there was not a conveyance in existence on which he had not travelled and none in any comfort: coaches, carts for hay, winter vegetables — even one carrying bovine slurry — and not forgetting river barges. All had taken him part of the way in varying degrees of misery. But he was in London now, a city he knew like the back of his hand. As for future prosperity, he had worked out a way to ensure that would come his way.

'Food and small beer?' he asked, incredulous, as he saw that the captain/owner had deducted for keeping him so poorly fed and watered. 'There was scarce enough to feed a mouse.'

'You've now't to complain aboot,' Cullen protested in his Caledonian burr. 'You got a free crossing from Hamburg, did ye no, an' why should I feed a body when I's doing them a good turn?'

'You sir, are nought but a thief.'

Cullen, fat-faced, with grey skin topped by wild pepper-and-salt hair, came halfway out of his chair, a fist raised. 'Withdraw that, snotdrop, or you'll feel my temper.'

For a coward like Gherson, it was incumbent to apologise and take the pittance he was given.

'Make your mark,' Cullen growled, pushing forward the ledger.

'I shall sign it with my damned name.'

'Writing, is it?' asked the captain, a devious look in his eye. 'Might have a place for a body who can do that. What are you like with numbers, laddie?'

Now far enough away to ensure he could avoid a blow, Gherson replied firmly, 'I know enough of them to see when I'm being robbed blind by some Sawney Jock.'

The roar followed him down the gangplank where he made for the booth at which his docket would be rendered into coin. The money-teller offered to hold part of it for him. 'To keep it safe.' Gherson declined; he knew the reason. Sometimes those leaving their payment did not return.

All he had to do now was get out of the dock area and past the crimps waiting to suck him into promised pleasures and vices, which would see them have in their pockets by nightfall the small amount he now had in his. Also to be watched out for were the hail-and-well-met fellows, who would offer to buy him porter and victuals, saying they were keen to hear stories of the romance of the sea. They made their way, having got their mark hopelessly drunk, by offering up dupes to the navy for reward, in an area the London merchants and shipowners had made sure press gangs could not operate.

Watchmen were guarding the dock gates, sharp-eyed and full of suspicion, there to prevent pilfering; his ditty bag got a searching look but no interference. On the outside of the gate he leant against one of the brick pillars to examine the scene before him, to spot the loungers or those who seemed to be moving in circular fashion to little purpose.

This was a milieu in which he had grown to manhood and nothing had altered, so what would have been mysterious to others was as plain as day to Cornelius Gherson. The clothing, the wary looks mixed with the false insouciance allowed him to sort out those waiting to prey on the gullible from people going about their legitimate occasions. As he made his way, and being very obviously fresh off a vessel, he did suffer the odd approach, but a bold look was enough to deter any attempt at familiarity.

Long consideration had been given at sea as to what he needed to do and how it was to be accomplished. First he must acquire some decent clothing into which to change. That took him to a part of the city, the narrow Star Alley close to the Tower of London, where there was a market. Here goods were traded: often stolen property, as well as by those fallen on hard times seeking to raise some coin by vending their possessions.

In a crowd it was not easy to spot what he sought, but in a shifting body of souls he espied an unmoving, empty-handed fellow of hangdog expression and posture, which marked him as out of place. More importantly, he was reasonably clad, holding his cloak open for coat and breeches to show, while looking sadly but expectantly at passers-by in the hope someone would engage with him.

There was no hasty approach; first Gherson must spot who else was interested but hanging back from trading in the certain knowledge that, whatever price this young man sought for, most likely, his clothing, it was falling the longer it took for him to sell. Two wary-looking coves were spotted, stood still for no purpose except pretend indifference. If one made to trade he must move first.

Idle speculation was natural; how had this fellow fallen on hard times? Gambling was common, as was a woman. But if he was country, not town, come to taste the pleasures of London, it was just as likely he had been dunned out of his funds by some sharp, one of which had, not so long in the past, been the man watching him.

The shuffle of feet from one of the competition had Gherson move forward quickly, his voice hearty. 'Hail, fellow, what brings you to this place?'

The misfit had the wit to look suspicious. Close to, Gherson saw the reddened eyes, which could come from weeping or an excess of drink, as well as the fluff that passed for growth on the chin.

'I sense misfortune.'

The voice had the croak of thirst. 'You sense correctly, sir; I have been most cruelly used.'

'Not unknown in the Great Wen. Do I mark you rightly as a stranger, a visitor?' Getting no reply, only a vacuous look, Gherson gently took an arm. 'I will assume it and, in order it should not be repeated, sir, I urge you to move from where you stand. There are eyes upon you that have you down for a mark.'

'Mark?'

'A word employed by the villainous to identify one easy to separate from his funds.'

'Then they are wasting their time, for I have met the kind, sir. A most pernicious fellow who promised me much and — ' The poor fellow sobbed, unable to continue, which got him what might have been a pat on the back, but was in fact a slight shove to move him on. The next words came through tearful snuffles. 'I am left without the means to return home and face my disgrace.'

'Parental, would it be?'

'My father, yes.' That got Gherson a crabbed look. 'But, how do you know that to be the case?'

'It is a tale too common. Would I be right in thinking you have come here to sell something?'

'What I wear, which being of some quality, will provide the funds to get me home.'

'To?'

'Dorset.'

'My geography is limited, sir, but I sense from your demeanour it is a distance.'

Gherson, as that was affirmed, had managed to get him out of the alleyway and to a spot less crowded. 'You were left with nothing, I take it?'

'Cleaned out when in a drunken stupor.'

Another sob. 'I have been a fool.'

'But not singular in that. Now, I see you as much of a size to me, so I suggest that if you wish to trade, an honest fellow like myself will see to your needs better than those who haunt the Star Alley.'

'A kindly trollop said it is where I should come, said that it is where I would get an honest transaction.'

Gherson had to look away then; the notion of a whore being kindly was not one to which he felt he could subscribe. Getting rid of an empty purse and a wailing booby was more likely.

'Would you object if I placed my foot alongside your own, to measure your boots, which I note are finely made, if in need of a burnish?'

'Those I cannot sell, lest I will likely have to walk most of the way.'

'Which risks seeing you robbed, sir. Fine boots are prized by evil minds, which would leave you barefoot. What misfortune it would be to have been stolen from not once, but twice. I will set you a bargain. I will buy all your outer garments, boots included, and give you my clothing as replacement.'

The young dupe looked down at Gherson's footwear, which had once been quality but were now very much down at heel, lacking the buckles which he had sold in Germany. 'I grant they appear worn, but they will suffice to get you to where you need to be, without some rogue seeking to deprive you.'

It took much persuasion but Cornelius

251

Gherson had ability in that department, his only regret, when they found a discreet place to exchange clothes, that he had to part with nearly all of his money. In times past he would have been carrying the means to crack this booby on the head and move on with his funds as well.

His eye had not been as accurate as he hoped — the boots pinched — but it was appearance that was all. He needed to look like a fellow who could pay for what he required. His next port of call was on an old Jewish acquaintance called Israel Meyer, who operated from a basement room in Clerkenwell Green. The sign outside on the railing identified him as an engraver.

'Gherson!' The dark ringlets that framed his Levantine face shook in surprise, his voice having the sibilant hiss of his race. 'I had you as meat for the maggots. There's word around you was sought and not for talking.'

Gherson thought on that, but concluded there were any number of people who would wish to do him harm and had been for years. It went with and was a hazard of his past life.

'Been abroad, Israel.'

'To profit, by the look of you.'

'It is for that I have come. How are your hands?'

Meyer cracked his fingers; he had done business with Gherson before and it had paid well. 'Still supple.'

'Then let me tell you what I need.'

★ ★ ★

Gherson spent the whole of the rest of the day with his Jew, even prevailing upon him for a bed and a bought breakfast. In good spirits and on a full stomach, he presented himself at the offices of Ommaney and Druce, Prize Agents, with a particular desire to see the latter. To say Druce was reluctant would be an understatement and for more than one reason. But it was not wise to decline and, having kept Gherson waiting while he composed what he had to say, though a servant was ordered to keep him supplied with wine, the one-time clerk to Captain Ralph Barclay was shown into his chamber.

'Mr Gherson, a surprise.'

'Can it be that, Mr Druce, when we have done so much good business together? Who should I come to see on my return to London but you? I do believe I am owed some commissions.'

'Obligations that we will meet.'

'Nothing more?'

'I admit to our association, but that connection is now, sadly, no more. It was through your late employer and, given he is no longer with us, I am preparing to deal with his widow.'

'Even if she is not the beneficiary of his estate?'

'The late captain, surprisingly for a naval officer, left no will and she is his natural heir.'

'But that is not true, Mr Druce,' Gherson replied, reaching into his pocket to produce a parchment document tied with a red ribbon, the handiwork of Israel Meyer. 'I have here that very document entrusted to me before we went into battle on that unhappy day.'

'Let me see,' replied a doubtful Druce, the document being handed over to be opened and the wording studied. 'Mrs Barclay wrote from the Mediterranean to say that there was no will.'

'Perhaps she thought it lost, Mr Druce.'

'The writing?'

'Is mine, naturally.' That got a quizzical look, as Gherson added, 'Who else would he ask to compose his will if not me, his clerk, who dealt with all his correspondence? But I think you will note the signature, which is that of Captain Barclay.'

Druce examined the document once more. 'I see you are also the witness.'

'Correct.'

'But not mentioned otherwise. The late captain left you nothing?'

'Would that not be irregular, Mr Druce, to witness a will from which you would receive advantage? You will also have seen that Captain Barclay, and I must say on my advice, appointed your firm as executors.'

The implications of that were obvious; to act as executor to such an estate would be very profitable. The prize agent held up the parchment. 'I will need to discuss this with Mr Ommaney. It seriously affects dispositions we have already made.'

'Naturally,' Gherson said, with a slight smile. 'But on another matter, as I acted to keep you in a position to control the late Captain Barclay's affairs, I believe I am due recompense for my activities.'

The mutual stare was not hostile — that was too risky in a delicate situation — but neither was it benign. No words from Druce were necessary to tell Gherson that some exposures on the estate, most pressingly canal trust shares, required to be discretely unloaded — investments of a highly speculative nature. Barclay, had he been in full control of his own affairs and had he been possessed of an interest in matters financial, would have been unlikely to approve.

Even if he had never fully trusted him, Ralph Barclay had left Gherson to handle the day-to-day running of his money as well as the ship's books. As long as he was kept informed of what was being done in his name, and that the actions would not cause him difficulties, Barclay was content. Gherson had made an arrangement with Ommaney and Druce, the latter particularly, which had left them free to speculate to their own profit, a portion of the rewards of which were now due to him.

'That will require to be calculated.'

'An advance of what is owed will suffice — say five pounds?'

The nod was slow in coming.

'One more thing. I feel it would be wise to write to Captain Barclay's sisters, as I will myself, and advise them that they are the true beneficiaries of his estate and not their sister-in-law. After all, we cannot have the man's widow running up huge bills on his credit. You might also support me in my contention that I, as the fellow who saw to their late brother's affairs and was trusted by him to do so, represent the best person to carry out the same function for them.'

Paid and told to return the next day, Cornelius Gherson went outside to immediately pay off Israel Meyer. That done he soon covered the short distance from the Strand to Covent Garden, where he was determined to avail himself of good food, fine wine and the services of several whores, this to rub from his mind the miseries of his now completed journey.

He also wished to wallow in the joy of paying Emily Barclay back for having visited such vicissitudes upon him. It had taken time to get the will right, even longer for Israel Meyer to become fluid, and satisfy him, in the execution of Barclay's signature, which he knew so well from memory. Even if his word and the will were not believed, the trouble he would cause would be very satisfying indeed.

19

Edward Druce was in a quandary; in truth, that extended to more than one, all being related to the man who had just departed his office. Cornelius Gherson had been a useful tool in the article of making profits for himself and his partner, but he had also been a personal concern for the one with whom he had dealt due to the way he had cuckolded Druce's brother-in-law, Alderman Denby Carruthers.

Sitting fingering the document he had just been given, a problem he had not been required to consider for over a year reared its unwelcome head. His wife's brother was a hugely successful city trader, quite possibly a future Lord Mayor of London. Several years ago, late in his fifth decade, he married an attractive woman, twenty plus years younger than him, which, if it had prompted some ribald comments at the time, had come to be a curse and one which extended beyond the immediate victim.

Gherson had been employed by Carruthers, which was easy to see in hindsight as a mistake, though only if you had no idea how charming and appealing the rogue could be. Perhaps with a less touchy and proud fellow, someone might have advised Denby that to take into his house as a clerk, the place from which he ran his affairs, a young and handsome fellow who claimed to be honest but might be unscrupulous, was a risk. So it had become.

For Druce, his first involvement — one he now severely regretted — had seemed innocuous at the time. Carruthers had asked him to find for him some men willing to do what had to be a less than legitimate service in the collection of a debt. Unaware of the true nature of what was required and with his strong naval connections, Druce had recruited a quartet from one of the London press gangs, sailors of the most thuggish sort, and sent them to his brother-in-law.

To admit the whole thing had spiralled out of control was to underrate the case. Druce knew now what he had not bothered to find out before. The hard bargains he had provided were required to rid Carruthers and his wounded vanity of the fellow who had not only seduced his wife but had also, through her, stolen a serious amount of his money.

If he had succeeded, Edward Druce would barely have been aware of Gherson's existence and would certainly have had no recollection of his name. What jests were the Gods embarking upon when the fellow turned up as clerk to Ralph Barclay, a client of Ommaney and Druce and, quite suddenly, given his successes in the taking of prizes, one of value?

It had soon turned from a perceived jest to a deadly conundrum: his brother-in-law discovered Gherson was alive and wanted him found, with no doubt or equivocation this time of what would be the outcome should that occur. This was the point at which Druce realised in what he had become involved, yet that tied him to whatever his irascible brother-in-law had in mind and it was inadvisable to protest.

So he had set out to satisfy two competing aims: first to deceive Carruthers by employing a thief-taker on his behalf, one well versed in finding those seeking to hide from the law. But the instructions to him were to enter into a pretend search: look but do not find, a task made simple by the fact that Gherson was serving with Captain Barclay, either safe aboard a warship in harbour, or at sea.

Quite apart from a desire not to be a party to murder, Barclay's clerk had become valuable in his own right, he being flexible in the article of honesty which provided the means by which he and Ommaney could use the Barclay money as they saw fit and without undue scrutiny. Barclay's death, Gherson's turning up in their Strand office, was bad enough; the will he had produced only added to the difficulties and made it incumbent that the problem be shared.

'I admit, Francis, it is something I kept private. It seemed politic at the time but in hindsight . . . '

Francis Ommaney was a corpulent man as befitted his prosperity and, with such a full face and fleshy jowls giving the impression of a jovial sort, it was not possible for him to fully convey any distress he might be feeling. But his partner knew him well enough to concentrate on the eyes and the way they were avoiding contact, a sure sign he was troubled.

'We are obliged to consider what effect it may

have on our firm, Edward.'

'Which is why I have aired it, Francis.'

'I feel it would have been best if I'd known of this earlier.'

'You too have your own concerns and arrangements, into which I do not enquire. Anything you undertake, which does not affect our partnership, I see as none of my business.'

'This could hardly be said to fall into that category.'

Druce spread his hands and adopted an apologetic air. 'It did not begin that way and what it has become could not be anticipated. What we must consider, now that it has become a serious problem, is this. How are we to deal with it?'

'We?'

'I cannot do so alone and still be sure to meet my obligations to our ongoing affairs.'

There was a degree of trepidation in that statement; Ommaney had already parted from one partner in a messy break up, one which proved expensive to both parties. Unstated now, and something that would ever be held private, was the debt Druce owed to his brother-in-law for the funds by which he had been able to match Ommaney and set up the present joint venture.

Did this grant Ommaney grounds to split from Druce, with the costs falling to him to possibly be followed by a call from Carruthers to have his loans repaid, he being hard-hearted and coldly ruthless in business? He was relieved when his partner made no mention of it, going straight to the nub of the problem.'

'I see two questions, Edward. The first is the production of a will we were told did not exist.'

'Given who produced it, as well as its convenience, I would not be surprised if it were a forgery.' That got a raised eyebrow. 'He did, after all, act as much for us as for Captain Barclay.'

'What obligation do we have?'

'We owe Gherson a certain sum of money in commissions.'

'But not officially. I assume the monies put aside for him are not recorded in the accounts.' That Druce acknowledged. 'So the will is the crux of the matter?'

Ommaney rose from his chair and began to pace, head down and deep in contemplation, a steady progression from the window to the wall and back again, which turned into the need to vocally speculate in what was, by nature, a sonorous voice, reflecting the girth of the belly as well as his self-regard.

'Please forgive me if, in running over the problem, I allude to matters and possible outcomes of which you are aware, especially your notion he may have faked that will. Now you inform me he cheated your brother-in-law, both in the counting house and his bedchamber. Yet in his dealing with us he has proved useful.'

Ommaney stopped abruptly and fixed his partner with a stare. 'Can we ignore the will?'

'Difficult. He proposes to alert the late captain's sisters to its existence, which he also expects us to do and, even if we doubt the validity, we have no proof and therefore no choice but to comply. It is beyond the bounds of reason to think, with so much at stake, they will see this as anything other than heaven-sent. In short, the will, to them, will be taken as valid. Gherson is going to suggest that, as their late brother's clerk, he is in the best position to get them their due.'

'While we are bound to do the same to Mrs Barclay, Edward, who is guaranteed to claim it to be a false document.'

'Which renders it, even if we chose to declare it a forgery, a matter that can only be decided by a court of law. The question is, then, which side do we take?'

'Which must be the one most suited to upholding our reputation?'

'We have a concern in Gherson. He has been privy to the actions we took and on which he advised Captain Barclay, able to assure him they were both sound and to his advantage. To cross him would possibly be to make him an adversary, able to cause us difficulty by revealing matters best not aired.'

'Which could make it politic for us to continue the association.'

Druce responded unhappily to Ommaney's point; it was not a prospect to please him. 'I would reckon that as inimical to our reputation.'

'Mrs Barclay,' Ommaney mused, 'without access to the inheritance, will struggle to fund a case in court. If we did support this will, we would have the estate to draw on for lawyer's fees, back her and it would only pay if she were successful.'

'So you are advising we should stick with Gherson?'

'What I am saying, Edward, is we either back Gherson and deny Mrs Barclay what is very likely her due, or act for her claim, while alluding to some quite clear outcomes in terms of losses or gains.'

Druce got another hard look from his clearly troubled partner as, puffing as if out of breath, he resumed his seat. 'You hired a thief-taker to search for Gherson, you say?' The truth of that explained, including the monthly bill Carruthers was charged for the service, got a response much more cynical than anything hitherto spoken of. 'It might be in our interests for your man to actually find him.'

'Francis, you are forgetting the nature of what I am almost certain my brother-in-law intends.'

'Far from it, Edward; I am speculating, as I must — seeking the best outcome. If Mrs Barclay did challenge the will it would be bound to become a public sensation: such disputes always are. Can we, in a civil action, agents acting on behalf of a whole slew of naval officers, be seen to be standing against a naval wife, the widow of a brave man killed in battle and with an infant child?'

The treble chin hit the chest as an alternative thought occurred to Ommaney. 'That said, the sisters would be a possible counterweight in the sympathy line.'

'Perhaps better than we know. Barclay originally had me employ Hodgeson to hunt for his wife, from whom he was clearly estranged.'

263

'If that could be established, it would dent the compassion.'

'Gherson would know all about the matter,' Druce admitted, his face showing signs of a thought process hitherto unexamined. 'I must add that despite his best efforts, Hodgeson failed to find her. Also her letter, alerting us to his death and her inheritance, was sent from Leghorn.'

'What was she doing in Italy?'

'I have no idea.'

'When did she travel there?' Ommaney asked only to get a negative shake of the head.

Silence reigned for a full half-minute as the concomitant of that was digested; a husband and wife separated, her turning up in a foreign country, which made extreme a thing that otherwise could be described as commonplace. It was Ommaney speaking once more who nailed the way both minds were working.

'Are we not bound to enquire if she went to Italy alone, or ran away with a lover, perhaps?'

Druce spread his hands again, his expression acknowledging the possibility.

'Could it be Barclay is not her child's father?'

'If one is conceivable, Francis, so is the other.'

'There we have an avenue that it would be wise to pursue, but with absolute discretion. If we decide to act for Mrs Barclay it would not do for her to find out we've been making enquiries into her recent past and even more so into her morals. But what if we did back her and such a truth emerged later? We would be a laughing stock.'

'So, Francis, your conclusion?'

'Whatever happens, Edward, we must be seen to be acting responsibly and above board.'

'Of course.'

'But I fear whatever we do must fall to you.' The message was clear in both the words and the look that accompanied them; you got us into this mess, you get us out, the thing not stated the consequences of failure. Ommaney hauled himself to his feet. 'We have a choice of ways to proceed and as far as I can see no need for an immediate decision.'

With Ommaney departed, Edward Druce was left contemplating that which had been thought upon, with no clear idea of how to proceed, but aware of one thing not aired in the notion of ditching Gherson. What would Carruthers say if he realised he had been dunned out of the money to pay Hodgson and kept in the dark as to the truth, even worse if he discovered he had acted to shield the scoundrel from retribution?

In this there was no one to turn to: his wife Elisabeth was extremely fond of her older brother, not inclined to see him as he was: headstrong and arrogant. Many times Druce had hinted at such traits only to have them brushed aside as nonsense, with references to Denby's charm, wit and generosity, not least in the article of financial provision.

Denby's wife had never been seen as suitable, not that anyone could be to a sister with a sibling mote in her eye; Catherine Carruthers was seen by Elisabeth Druce as a mistake, though one any red-blooded man could make. She had never truly been accepted in the Druce house and was now rarely brought into their company, being more or less confined to their city abode.

If this all blew up, it could have a devastating effect on his domestic harmony; he could not see Denby behaving as though nothing untoward had happened between them, nor would he be able to say what any break was about, given that could only make matters worse.

The betrayals and folly of Catherine Caruthers had been kept between the two men and were not to be publically discussed, certainly not with his own wife. And how could he say to Mrs Druce that he had aided her beloved brother to contrive at a killing and, the attempt having failed, he had been obliged to enter into a conspiracy to correct the error?

What about Gherson himself? If he was to be kept from retribution for his cuckoldry, he would have to be told he was in danger and from whom. If Ommaney and Druce plumped for the Barclay sisters, he was the only one who could convince a judge or jury the will was genuine. To keep him alive he would need to be spirited away and hidden somewhere safe. As a witness in what would be a high-profile civil action, he would be no good dead.

Never had the lesser of two evils as an expression been so apposite, with no notion of which was worse. Such troubled thoughts had to be put aside as he picked up and dipped his quill. The letter he would send to Emily Barclay had to be carefully composed. He was required to alert her to what Gherson had brought in,

266

while reserving any hint that she would not continue to be their client.

It was while penning the address that he had a subconscious nudge that went back to previous speculation; if Emily Barclay had been adulterous and the child was not her husband's, could Gherson be the only one who knew? Surely there must be others? Did he not have Hodgeson available, a fellow well able to seek out information?

Druce knew him to be in London and not, as he often was, on some extended travel in search of his imaginary prey. The Barclay letter was put aside, the quill now employed to compose a very short note. Druce then rang a bell to summon a servant. The message was to be sent round to the lodgings of Mr Hodgeson, asking him to call upon the office on a matter of some urgency.

⋆ ⋆ ⋆

'Mrs Barclay?' Hodgeson remarked with some surprise. 'We are speaking of the same lady I was set to find afore?'

'We are.'

'Would it be on behalf of her husband again?'

'Captain Barclay is no longer with us.' The look that got from the man supposedly hunting Gherson spoke volumes, for there had been more than a hint of violence in the affair. 'I'm surprised you failed to note it. There was a description of the battle and his unfortunate death in *The Times*.'

Hodgeson's lack of a reply and stoic look was

enough to tell Druce he was not a reader of that newspaper, nor very likely any other.

'Then I am bound to ask what it is you're after, sir?'

'It is a delicate matter, Mr Hodgeson.'

The explanation was comprehensive but Druce could pick up, from the little the man was showing in response, that it was not a proposition that found too much favour. Hodgeson had spent his life as a thief-taker and quite a successful one, an occupation not without risk, in which he sought and tried to apprehend felons for the reward their capture entailed. Spying on people it was not.

'If her man is now dead, on whose behalf is such information being sought, Mr Druce?'

'We require it for our own internal purposes.'

'And what about this Gherson fellow?'

'That can be put in abeyance for the moment,' Druce replied.

As he said that, he experienced a slight feeling of unease. Gherson had said he would seek to represent the trio of Barclay sisters. To facilitate his case, he might well turn up in the vicinity of Emily Barclay himself. Matters were tangled enough without his presence adding more complications.

'You may draw on the administrator with whom you normally deal, to provide any expenses you may require.'

'On the usual account, sir?'

'No, this one will be paid for by us.'

Hodgeson gone, Druce was left with his own thoughts. For all the impact the putative contest

268

would have on Ommaney and Druce, it was he who faced the most difficulties, a choice between being an accessory to a heinous crime or to take part in what was very likely a blatant attempt at fraud.

Hodgeson would be in Frome in a couple of days. Perhaps he should encourage Gherson to go to Somerset as well, given he would at least be out of London and safe there. Then, depending on which way they bent, a neat solution could be contrived, one which could either satisfy Denby Carruthers or the party they chose to represent, while ensuring the business of the agency or his domestic harmony was not in any way impacted.

It was a matter of which he would have to think, which did not obviate the need to finish his letter to Emily Barclay. As a precaution, he decided not to mention Gherson's intentions as regards her sisters-in-law; that might smack of some kind of involvement.

20

A visit to the Admiralty, even if it was held to be a waste of time, while simultaneously being highly unusual, was very necessary to John Pearce. With his friends safe for now in the Liberties, he had to find out if he could get employment and, by doing so, take them with him, not least because his purse would not last long if it had to keep fed and watered four souls.

The usual form for a lieutenant when seeking a place was to write to captains with whom they had previously served, asking first if they had an opening and, if not, had they an acquaintance who would take someone on their recommendation. If that proved fruitful, then the approach to the Lords Commissioners, happy to facilitate the wishes of those in command of their vessels, tended to be a formality.

For the average person of his rank, years in the navy gave them ample contacts to pursue — not an advantage he possessed. Having spent most of his time in the Mediterranean, there were no senior officers serving in home waters he knew well enough to enquire after a berth. Any attempt to return there would certainly be blocked by Jervis.

Indicative of his rank was the long wait before he was granted an interview, not with Sir Philip Stephens but with the Second Secretary, William Marsden. It was soon obvious on meeting the man that he was not inclined to be helpful. Marsden was Irish, but with a refined manner of speaking, which did not match the rougher argot of Michael O'Hagan. He was a dry functionary, with the skin colour of an indoor man, who looked down his rather long nose at Pearce with barely disguised disfavour.

'It is common, Mr Pearce, to write in seeking a place, not to turn up in person. Even post captains, men of seniority, show respect to the fact that the Admiralty and the office of the Lords Commissioners is busy.'

'Then I am gratified to be seen doing something unusual, Mr Marsden,' Pearce replied, making no attempt to hide his pique. 'I have found a man gets nowhere in life sticking to habits long formed, which I hope will give you some measure of how eager I am to be employed.'

'Eagerness is not the only quality needed in a naval officer.'

'If you mean, sir, can I bring to you a list of recommendations — the answer is no. If required to do so, I could count on the good offices of Commodore Nelson and Sir Peter Parker, whom I dined with a few days past.'

That got a look of curiosity but no actual comment.

'Yet I would have thought my record of activity, as well as the number of actions in which I have participated, added to more than once being in command of an unrated vessel, would be sufficient to show I am worthy of something.'

Marsden looked at the papers on his desk,

which Pearce reckoned to be his service record. Within the building there toiled away clerks who dealt with the mass of documents and logs without which the King's Navy could not function. These included reports on the standing and abilities of officers junior to the commander of a man-o'-war, captains being likewise rated by their admirals.

As a means of control it worked against free thinking: challenge a superior, even when he was obviously wrong, and an unflattering appraisal would follow to end up here. To be outspoken once was held to be unwise; to be continually so was likely to kill off a budding career faster than a cannonball in the belly.

Pearce could only assume his to be unhelpful. Were Digby's reports contained in the folder? Early opinions might be flattering, with the likelihood of the latest being praiseworthy non-existent. It was almost certain Sir William Hotham would have submitted an appraisal of his abilities as a master and commander, guaranteeing blatant antipathy.

That said, the officer being assessed had the right to see such opinions on his character and challenge them. Anything too egregious and Pearce could demand a court martial, something which Hotham would avoid like the plague for fear of what might emerge. But what would Hood have said about him? Surely crusty old Sam would have been fair?

'Having read your record, I cannot think any captain would welcome you into their ward-room. The list of those who find you insubordinate outstrips any praise.'

'So there is praise?'

'Not enough, and latterly none at all.'

'Sir John Jervis?'

'I will be frank with you, Mr Pearce: his despatches, only just come in from Portsmouth, make it clear he had no regard for you at all and questions your right to be in the service as anything other than a common seaman.'

'Perhaps we should pass a copy to His Majesty.'

'I see you choose to be jocose.'

'Mr Marsden, this I do know. The expansion of the fleet in these last three years has left the navy short of everything but post captains. How many midshipmen are at present serving as acting lieutenants? Since I am in rank and intend to remain, despite the opinion of Sir John Jervis, you must be able to offer me something?'

'What the navy is short of, Mr Pearce, is seamen. The men brought in by the Quota Acts do not provide the quality required. Every locality required to provide hands sends us their dregs.' The look on Marsden's face changed to one that hinted at illumination; Pearce reckoned it contrived. 'There is a need to expand the Impress Service, of course, to counter that. If such a task finds you willing there may be a place there.'

* * *

'Sure, you're sunk to the bottom of the tub if they offer you the Impress Service, John-boy.'

'Of which I do not require to be reminded, Michael.'

Trying to think of alternatives, Pearce let his gaze wander around the low-beamed and smoky Pelican Tavern. It was nothing like as busy as it had been the night he was pressed, but it still enjoyed enough custom to set up a buzz of conversation. Looking at them he could not but wonder how many were here just to partake of a pot of ale, set against those who had little choice. They would be, like Charlie and Rufus, afeard to set foot outside the area for fear of arrest.

The ancient Liberties of the Savoy encompassed what had once been the royal palace of John of Gaunt, Duke of Lancaster and brother to Edward the Third. In that respect, even though the building was long gone, burnt down by rioters in the reign of the second Richard, it still came under the legal jurisdiction of the Duchy.

That it was an anomaly was obvious, but it was one which remained as well as the protection and sanctuary it afforded from the bailiffs of the common law. It was a godsend to many, who would otherwise have ended up in the Fleet prison. His attention was brought back to the table by Charlie Taverner.

'Had a talk with some of the Thames boatmen, John.'

Seeing Pearce looking at him expectantly, Charlie was quick to scotch his hopes.

'Now't goin' there. They're as good as a guild, so it's father, cousin and son when it comes to being a bargee. Rowing for hire likewise.'

'But . . . ?'

Charlie then behaved in a manner all had come to know well, imparting some nugget of information as though it was a secret, when it usually turned out not to be that at all. He would lean forward, quickly shift his head left and right and drop his voice.

'They are accustomed to be queried on it, natural.'

'So?'

Michael asked this impatiently; the Taverner follow-up was always a pause, then another pretend shift of his eyes, as if ensuring he could not be overheard, taken as annoying for on most occasions — and this was one — there was no one even remotely close.

'I told him we had protections.'

'Which you were bound to do, Charlie,' Pearce snapped, as tired of the game as O'Hagan. 'Scarce worth engaging with them without you have that.'

Charlie sat back, a look of offence on his face. 'With that tone coming at me, I'm a wondering if I should say what I learnt.'

'Suit yourself,' Rufus said, with a look of disinterest.

'You have the right of it there, Rufus,' was Michael's response. 'It's Charlie up to his tricks.'

Pearce had to smile at the response. The last thing Charlie could abide was that he not be taken as serious, so there was a clear conflict showing in his features. A brighter cove would have spotted the indifference was feigned but he was a man with a blind spot, though not stupid; he was gifted within the sphere in which he had lived, working the Strand and Covent Garden as a sharp.

Likewise he had the easy manner and quick sense of humour to be liked aboard ship, but he just could not abide a void when it came to talking. John Pearce had often wondered if his dislike of silence had contributed to him being under threat of arrest; had Charlie talked himself into trouble? As of now, he could not keep silent.

'Ever heard of a place called Shoreham?'

'Why would we?' asked Michael.

'Should have done. Surprised we never heard it mentioned on any barky we served in. Hard to fathom it being so furtive, when what goes on there is known on the river. Mind, the bargees have protections too, so happen that's how they got to hear of it, with folk trying to recruit them for service.'

'Will you spill, Charlie? I feel my fists getting tight. What in the name of Jesus are you on about?'

The angry tone was at total odds with Michel crossing himself, but there was no mistaking the look in the eye. Nor could any of his friends miss the slow smile that came to Taverner's cheeks. It might just as well have said 'I've got you', out loud.

'Letters of marque.'

'What about them?' Pearce asked, his tone equally impatient, for he had some vague recollection of hearing the name of Shoreham mentioned.

'That be where the Channel privateers have taken to laying up when not cruising.' Another pause, a full grin. 'Found it best to have a home of their own, one not used by the navy. And to a man the crews have certificates.'

'An' the Impress all over 'em,' Rufus scoffed.

'No so, young 'un.' That got a sour look from Dommet; he was the youngest but hated to be talked down to because of it. Charlie did it often to rib him. 'The press don't go near the place.'

The silence that followed, added to Charlie's knowing grin, had Pearce snap at him. 'This is like drawing teeth!'

Michael O'Hagan made no attempt at a soft tone as his fist came up off the table. 'Sure there's more'n one way to do that.'

'Will you hold up,' Charlie protested. 'I ain't goin' to pass on what I found out if I's going to have a fist under my nose.'

'Let him play his game, Michael,' Pearce sighed. 'We're in no hurry to go anywhere.'

Charlie tapped his near-empty tankard on the tabletop. 'Another wet would aid matters.'

'Then it's just like our first encounter, Charlie,' Pearce responded. 'You dunned me for ale then.'

'It were easy done, John, very easy done.'

Pearce signalled with his own tankard that all four should be replenished. The serving girl whose eye he caught, hips like a horse and far from comely, came quickly with her large pitcher and poured, ignoring the come-hither looks from Rufus; if she was not an attractive wench, he was a needy lad.

'From what I's been told, those that holds letters of marque are able to put words in the right ears, powerful ears at that. So Shoreham is never visited by the Impress. It has a set of sandbars that provides for a safe berth at anchor, though being tidal is a bugger to get in and out of.'

As Charlie was speaking John Pearce was culling his memory for what he knew about privateers and it was not much. Now that Shoreham had been mentioned, he vaguely recalled others raising the name, not that he had paid much attention. He had met one fellow in Leghorn, but he had not been one to go to sea: more the kind to make his money from either supplying those who did or selling their cargoes.

He did know they were, as a breed, not much loved by the King's Navy — hardly surprising since they competed for the same spoils and sailed the same waters in search of prizes. The dislike was made stronger by the fact that letters of marque, granted written patent powers by the Crown, sailed to where they wanted and when, which naturally took them to the most productive hunting grounds. The navy rarely had such freedom.

The English Channel had to be one: on a French and Dutch coast dissected by innumerable rivers that led to the inland markets, the best and cheapest way to transport cargoes, despite the risks, was over water. Leghorn had been another, a harbour full of their sleek boats ready to set sail and prey on the same kind of trading vessels using the Mediterranean.

Profitable it must certainly be, but it could not be without risk. If a privateer vessel came across any kind of warship and could not get clear, there could only be one result, given they were armed to fight merchantmen. Nor would the crews be treated well on capture; galley service in some enemy port was their likely fate.

'Captains take on the hands they want at an agreed share of the spoils, which can be good.'

Pearce had to bring his mind back to what Charlie was saying, to hear described a possible way out of the dilemma he faced.

'Now we has certificates, even if they're sham an' that be a risk. The shipboard navy sometimes hoves by seeking deserters an' that can't be gainsaid by the captains or owners so they give them up willing.'

'Are they not of the same ilk?'

'No, Rufus,' Pearce replied; this he did know. 'Some own their boats but others sail them on behalf of syndicates with deep pockets and no desire for risk themselves but a deep love of profit.'

'I says we should be lookin' to go there, John.'

'Charlie's right.'

That was quickly interrupted by the man himself. 'Don't hear them two words often from that throat.'

'We can't sit here for ever,' Michael added, 'an' deep as your purse is of now, John-boy, it will soon run dry the way Charlie there sinks his ale.'

'There's a way to go, Michael.'

'An' what if another Barclay happens along?' Seeing his friend about to protest O'Hagan was quick to counter. 'You can say to me it won't be so, which is when I say to you the opposite. You came back from talking to that Admiralty cove, who told you the navy is serious short on hands. What did we meet afore soundings but a captain so short on crew he was willing to transgress the law?'

'We ain't safe here, John,' Charlie concurred, gravely, 'and if Michael has the right of it, I would not want to be relying on some pretend exemptions with the likes of a second Ralph Barclay. Ignoring them would only be part of it. If our true identities were rooted out — '

If he thought what was being said to be unlikely, Pearce knew why it was being laid on so heavily; his friends were not happy to exist on his generosity, which showed, particularly in the case of Charlie Taverner, how far they had come from the life they once led. Nor were they now wedded to idleness.

'I say we make for Shoreham an' see what's what.' Charlie's statement was backed up by serious looks from the other two, clearly in agreement. 'We need your blue coat to get us close, John, but I would say it is not the garb to be wearing when we get there. Lookin' like a gent will serve better.'

'In all this, are you including me?'

'Sure there's now't for you in the King's Navy, John-boy. That you said plain.'

'An' a private barky needs more'n a captain to sail 'em, I reckon.'

Looking at Charlie, and hearing the murmur of approval, Pearce was thinking of his other problem and how that would be affected if these

280

three were right. What was being proposed had no hint of delay; if they were going to try for Shoreham they wanted to do it quickly and it did solve a problem.

There was little doubt in his mind the Pelicans would be welcome. If the navy was scratching for seamen, privateers could not have an abundance and certainly not of prime hands, which is what his friends had become. They would be occupied, paid if good fortune attended any cruise they embarked on, and it would keep them together.

For himself that was tempting. Yet he had to make some arrangement with Emily so that he knew what he could and could not do in the future to keep both his sanity — he avoided including his fidelity — and their relationship intact.

The solution, though he did not share it, came easily. He would accompany them to the south coast and, as King's officer, albeit not in uniform, help them to seek a berth by recommendation, revealing his rank as well as the details of his service.

In his own case, he would go no further than putting out some feelers for the future and return to London. Left in Shoreham his friends should be as safe as they were in the Liberties and if they struggled to find a berth right off, well he was supporting them here and he could do the same there at no extra expense.

'Then let us do that. Get your dunnage together while I go back to Harley Street and fetch some suitable clothing. I will also bespeak a private coach.'

'What need of that?' Rufus asked.

'Charlie says Shoreham is barred to the Impress Service.'

'I did.'

'But I will take a wager with you there are men of that stamp on the outskirts of the area into which they are forbidden to go, waiting there for just as the likes of you three to come sailing by.'

'A private coach will avoid them?'

'I will keep on my uniform coat until we reach the town and damn any press man who seeks to impede us by taking on the mantle a certain Mr Marsden offered me. I shall claim to be from the Impress Service and bound for Shoreham in search of deserters to man my ship.'

Rufus was confused. 'But you don't have one, John, an' no chance of such to alter.'

'Sharp as ever,' was Charlie Taverner's mordant comment. 'If a blue coat says he's got a ship and is seeking hands, who is goin' to dispute with him?'

21

The journey to Shoreham was uneventful, taking the Pelicans into a one-time important port, now fallen into a relatively tidal backwater. Pearce and his friends had not been long in the taproom of the Red Lion Inn, where they stopped to rest and have their horses fed, before their ears were assailed by those they met, to tell them of a history which had seen medieval armies and supplies depart the estuary of the River Adur to do battle in France.

It was not that now; subject to much silting and shifting sandbars, it was fallen into disuse as a major home to shipping and trade. As he walked the riverbank down to the sea, having left Michael, Charlie and Rufus nursing pots of strong and rough cider, Pearce could see that most of what was tied up there, by size and design, was engaged in the coastal trade, ships that would carry what was grown in the fertile hinterlands to the markets of larger cities, where it could be sold.

The other boats also bespoke the activity in which they were engaged; fast-sailing small brigs and sloops with the kind and level of armaments required to overawe vessels carrying none. With deeper hulls these were sat mid river, either tied up to mooring posts or, nearer the sea, to a mooring chain, which hinted at strong tides and potential inundation by the waters of the English Channel.

Finally, before retracing his steps, he had a look at the eastern spit, one of two, which kept out the sea, wondering if it held at a high spring tide and against the kind of wind powerful enough to produce a surge. Whatever happened, such occasions would be rare; in the meantime Shoreham provided a safe haven for letters of marque, with the added advantage of being close to the shipping routes of those they sought to interdict.

His destination was The Star, another hostelry and the one he had heard was patronised by the crews of the privateers. Entering, he was subject to much examination and a palpable drop in the buzz of conversation. In a buff coat and wearing a tricorne hat, quickly removed, he excited only a slight level of interest before those occupying the tables and benches went back to what they had been engaged in hitherto.

Looking about the place, not easy given the density of smoke hanging under the low beams, he felt, apart from the outside temperature, he could have been back in Leghorn. There he had found the need to visit the privateer part of the port and the same kind resided here. If the garb was akin to a tar, blue water sailing in a merchant ship, the faces told a different story; these were a harder crew by far than their trading counterparts, more like King's Navy.

The search he was undertaking sought a table — there was ever one — where the leaders of such creatures congregated. The clue was in a touch of sartorial flamboyance; not only better

284

quality clothing, but that which was designed to state their entitlement to their vanity. He espied it by a second doorway, which probably led to an alley, open to let in light and allow out the fug of tobacco.

So determined was his progress there was no mistaking to where Pearce was headed, so it was not just the quartet at the table who noted his course. As he weaved through the tables it led to a second but slight diminution of the hum of talk. He saw one fellow in a crimson coat edged in gilded braid — a rather old-fashioned and piratical type of garb — catch his eye, then very slightly jerk his head to alert his companions, one of whom, to redcoat's annoyance, made a point of looking.

'Would it be possible, gentlemen,' he said, once close to the table, 'that I could prevail upon your company?'

'To what purpose?'

'I hope, one to your advantage.'

Eight eyes were on him, in faces that close to, in a trio of cases, seriously lacked refinement. For all their clothing these fellows looked to be what they were: hard bargains, scarred individuals with good clothing providing only a shimmer of quality. Redcoat was of a finer breed, with a face to make proud a Roman emperor: square chin, high cheekbones and a prominent nose with a high bridge. The eyes under a prominent pair of eyebrows, picking up the light from the open door, were bright blue and steady.

'Are we to be obliged with a name, sir?'

'Mine is Pearce. Yours, sir?'

'Faulkner,' came after a slight hesitation.

'To our advantage, you say?' asked another: coat of brown velvet and a coarse scarred visage.

'I represent a trio of prime hands, men who can hand, reef and steer, who are seeking employment.'

'Represent?' Faulkner enquired. 'Are we to deal with agents these days to crew our ships?'

'Fees charged,' guffawed a third fellow: a beanpole, thin as a rake in both body and face.

'If I may be allowed to join with you?'

Faulkner, after a swift look at his companions to ensure no objection, nodded. Pearce pulled a chair from another unoccupied table to take a seat. 'I will happily call for pots of ale if it suits.'

'Wet your own throat, matey.'

These words, croaked enough to resemble shifting gravel, were spoken by the man who'd had his back to Pearce as he approached and, since he had been addressing Faulkner, no attention had up till now been paid to him. He was defined by the scar that ran from his forehead to his cheek, the missing eye obvious in what was an ugly face even without the blemish. There was another scar on his throat, which looked like a burn mark.

'Hospitable as ever, Toad,' Faulkner said, in an amused way. 'Never a man to be open-hearted to a stranger.'

'I say to this fellow, state your business.'

'Which I will happily do, sir.'

With the rasping voice, the snappish one was well named in his soubriquet; he did indeed sound like a marsh toad seeking a mate. The single good eye was unwavering as he looked at Pearce, who sought to deflect his clear irritation with a winning smile; it achieved no change of expression.

'I have brought to Shoreham three fellows, ex-navy, who are not only, as I have said, competent seamen but are also handy in the fighting line. They seek a berth in which money can be made and since that is your trade, they would seek a suitable place.'

'Are we to assume,' Faulkner asked, 'these fellows to be deaf and dumb, so much so they cannot speak for themselves?'

'They trust me to act for them and secure the very best terms.'

'You're short, Toad,' said the beanpole.

'That be because I has a care who I takes on board, Cecil. Won't have any old Tom, Dick or Harry. I needs men who can think as well as fight.'

'Then the trio I am proposing would fit that bill. They're bright fellows and great guns in a fight. I think if you saw them, you would sense their mettle.'

'And just who are you, Mr Pearce?'

Knowing it would come to this, he was well prepared and he waved his hat to attract attention to the table. 'I will tell you, but the story you will hear is bound to outlast your present dregs, so I will order a refill.'

⋆ ⋆ ⋆

'I had to be open,' Pearce insisted, 'and, as I expected, telling them I was King's Navy, even after being pressed, did not sit well.'

Tempted to describe the shocked looks and very physical signs of alarm, Pearce decided it made no difference, so he went on to state the terms of employment, which were general throughout the privateer fleet.

'Thirty-three percentums split three ways between owners, masters and crew paid on each quarter day, the first one held as promissory. If the captain owns, he will hold that share as well and it is my thinking such a reward will make for eagerness.'

'What did you say on the protections, John?' Charlie enquired.

'Said you possessed them without telling where they came from.'

Rufus looked worried. 'And you weren't pushed on that?'

'I doubt they care much if you are lifted out from their ship by the navy. They will hope to be holding a sum of money owed to you and that will be forfeit. Besides, there's no offence for them to answer to having taken your word.'

Each got a long look intended to elicit agreement.

'I am going to recommend a fellow called Maartens, name spelt in the Dutch manner on his insistence, because he is the owner/master. Ugly, one-eyed brute but I sense an eager hunter.'

Had he been asked to explain, all Pearce would have been able to say was he had a feeling in his gut. Faulkner was too smooth and his conceit sat ill with his chosen occupation. Beanpole Cecil had too much about him of the antipathy alluded to by Julius Caesar in the Bard's play, a kind of keen untrustworthiness, while the fourth fellow at the table had remained silent.

'If he does not suit, you have the freedom to shift your hammock.'

'And what are you going to do, John-boy?' Michael asked.

'I am going back to London, Michael, where I will try to sort out certain matters of a personal nature.'

'Mrs Barclay?'

'Who else? Then, when that resolves itself into a solution I will take stock. I do have one other avenue to pursue.'

The way it was said did not invite enquiry.

'Is it to be goodbye, John?' Rufus asked, his look surprisingly crestfallen.

'No, it's until we meet again. Now, pick up your ditty bags and I will take you down to The Star.'

If John Pearce had sounded sure in answer to Rufus, once in his carriage and heading up the slopes that led away from Shoreham to the South Downs, he could not but wonder if, in his actions, he had cut himself off from the only people with whom he had a mutual bond. There was Emily, of course, but he had no idea of the direction in which that relationship was heading.

* * *

'I must go to London at once.'

'My dear, you have barely arrived and surely

289

matters will resolve themselves without your presence. It can be dealt with by letter.'

Emily looked from her mother to her father, standing silent at and leaning on the mantle, his face drawn and looking so much older than she recalled on her wedding day. He was anxious and his daughter knew why. Her inheritance had lifted from his brow a sword that had hung over the family for years, namely the entail Ralph Barclay had held on the home they occupied at a peppercorn rent.

Now this shock of a will had come from London. Would he have to fawn upon the sisters in order to ensure continued tenancy? He had walked on eggshells round Ralph Barclay, flattering a fellow, with his rough naval manners, scarcely worth the compliment. Never to be admitted was his own guilt in encouraging his daughter to wed him, a man twice her age and not really the match he had envisaged in reverie.

If Emily had been able to see into his mind she would have come upon the castigation of his own soul, plus the certainty that God was paying him back for his previous sin. How quickly matters had gone from joy to gloom; his beautiful daughter home, the curse of the entail lifted, she being now wealthy and in possession of a lusty boy child.

John Raynesford had carried the burden since moving into the house and often, even if he knew his wife to be aware of it, alone. It was never referred to, but for him the calling in of that entail, which might well have happened had he discouraged Ralph Barclay in his pursuit of his daughter, meant that which every person of his standing in the world feared most: a drop into penury, for his income would not run to a property rental at normal rates.

'It may be best I accompany you, my dear.'

'No, Papa!'

The response came too hastily and the shock of her response cleared his countenance slightly, taking years off a face now lined. He was a bookish man and Emily reckoned not robust, while her mother was a flutterer most of the time, though more steely when she carried out her duties in ministering to the poor. Her love for them both was unconditional, as it should be.

'I will not need help to set this matter straight. The supposed will is a construct and should be easy to deal with.'

Did he see the lie? Emily could not tell, but neither could she admit that, if her father did accompany her, seeing John Pearce would be impossible. If she required help, he would be there to provide it and she reposed more trust in his will to fight for her rights than her father.

'Emily, you are of the fair sex.'

She knew he was trying to be stern and it had always come out as false; he had never had much of a handle on parental discipline, being too kind of heart to impose the necessary sanctions.

'Papa, I have twice been at sea in a ship of war taken by the enemy and I have survived. I have tended to men wounded in battle and held the hand of one who expired, as well as survived the shock of widowhood and the pleasure of childbirth. Whatever I was when I left here as a newlywed, I am not now. I am also a mother who will, with tooth and claw, protect her child and that which is due to him.'

How do you say to someone you love that he would be useless anyway? He would be inclined to seek a compromise, for that was the way he had lived his life, which would render him a liability. The will was not a true document; Gherson was a slug and she intended to see him taken to Tyburn and strung up for the crime of forgery.

'Now we must bespeak a coach and get Adam's things together.'

'You cannot surely take the child, Emily?'

'Mother, I cannot not take him.'

This was said as she swept out of the room; any explanation would have been a tissue of lies and Emily had never been a comfortable dissembler.

★ ★ ★

'You don't lack for effrontery, laddie.' Henry Dundas accompanied these words with a withering look. 'And the word 'demand' sits doubly ill.'

'You do not see a debt?'

'Not within a length of miles.'

In his pomp as Minister of War, Dundas, also the closest confidant of William Pitt, seemed absolutely sure of his ground. The allusion by John Pearce that he owed anything to the family was not well taken. Yet he had blenched slightly when he was reminded of how old Adam Pearce had died and why. When it came to the writ that had sent father and son running to Paris, it was from Dundas's machinations that the act had been promulgated.

'A word from you and the Admiralty will give me some suitable position; not a ship perhaps, but some shore appointment that will provide income and stability.'

'You never struck me as one wedded to the latter.'

'People change.'

'Not in my experience. Once a troublemaker, always so. And I think you overrate my influence, not that I'm inclined to exercise any on your behalf regardless. Earl Spencer and I are as close to mortal enemies as it is possible to be and sit in the same government. He's Portland's man and Billy Pitt had to shift his own elder brother to give him the navy. He tells me I am always seeking to impose upon his prerogatives, as if he knew anything about the abilities of the admirals for whom he has responsibility.'

'I would be obliged if you would tell me, if I am not to be a sailor, what I am going to do?'

It was the wrong thing to say, speaking as it did of pleading, Pearce being sorry for the utterance as soon as it left his mouth. It smacked of desperation. Seeing Dundas fill with air in order to point this out, he was quick to cut across him, speaking so loudly it was not far off a shout.

'I have acted for you in the past and at some risk to my person. I therefore think I'm owed some form of recompense.'

293

In terms of voice level, Pearce was answered with equal force. 'While I recall that you took a large sum of money to the Vendee and not all of it was accounted for. I could have you locked up.'

'Only if you admit to having misappropriated government funds.'

'Damn your cheek!'

'Raised voices?' said William Pitt, from the doorway he had just occupied. Then he looked at who was visiting Dundas and his grimace was immediate. 'I can see why, Henry.'

'Demanding help, Billy, as though he has any right to that.'

'I have been kicked out of the Mediterranean by Jervis and he has sent home a despatch advising I have no right to employment in the navy. Given he is not politically a bedfellow of yours — '

'He's a Whig, certainly,' Dundas interrupted.

' — I thought you might welcome the chance to confound him.'

Pitt produced a humourless smile. 'You see yourself as standing in equality with a vice admiral? My, the navy has changed.'

'I think it is time I bid you good day, Pearce.'

Dundas got a glare, not that it affected him in any way. His response was a look of indifference. His visitor was not surprised to be leaving empty-handed; it had been a close to futile call brought on by extreme need, not any substantial hope. He stood to leave, making for the doorway still occupied by Pitt, irritated by the way the man did not move yet rendered curious by the pensive look on his face, lowered to his chest initially but lifted finally to look.

'Mr Pearce, wait in the anteroom across the hallway.'

'For what reason?'

'As of this moment I am not sure, but I would be obliged if you will indulge me. Ring the bell and ask for some refreshment if you wish.'

Pearce tried to stare Pitt down as an act of defiance at being so ordered about. But the King's First Minister was looking past him at Dundas, his eyebrows raised in a quizzical way.

'What do you have in mind, Will?'

'First and foremost a private conversation, Henry. Then we shall see.'

Pitt stood aside with a gesture to John Pearce, one which told him to leave the room.

22

Called back in to the room some twenty minutes later, Pearce was asked to take a seat facing both men, they holding full glasses of wine; an empty bottle sat between them with a second opened but he was not offered a chance to imbibe.

Seen together the contrast was very obvious; Dundas, in his fifties, somewhat stocky in his build, with a countenance that hinted at long experience, as well as a deep and devious mind. That contrasted with Pitt: slim, aesthetic and fastidious, who looked to be more of a younger son than a seasoned politician who commanded the House of Commons. John Pearce had to remind himself that when it came to being cunning, they were not master and pupil, but a pair of like minds.

'We may wish to engage you upon a particular service,' Pitt said.

'One suited to your abilities,' Dundas added, both men looking at him expectantly.

Pearce declined to respond to what was an obvious invitation to ask what this particular service to which he was suited entailed. Being seasoned debaters and aware that he who speaks first often loses an argument led to a period of silence. This was finally broken when their visitor laughed out loud, to which a clearly irritated Dundas reacted badly.

'I can assure you what we have in mind is no

cause for amusement.'

'I never thought it would be, but the notion of you contriving something suitable for me leads me to suspect my survival is not of paramount concern.'

Pitt's response carried a trace of resentment, which was unusual for a man so commonly urbane. 'You malign us, Mr Pearce, especially when we may be talking of the survival of the nation.'

Hyperbole or genuine concern? Pearce could not tell, but he watched Dundas closely as he took up the baton. 'The war is bankrupting us. So much gold has been shifted abroad, the country is short on specie and transactions are being conducted with notes in hand, which drives people to hoard their guineas and shillings, making the whole worse.'

'As of this moment,' Pitt added, 'we are fully expecting some kind of rapprochement between France and Spain, which could bring about a run on the banks.'

'Because of Manuel Godoy?'

'You know of him?' Dundas demanded, as though it mattered. 'It is not a name much bandied about in the coffee house.'

'I stopped in Gibraltar on the way home. Sir David Rose told me of the way he was inclined after the Pyrenees treaty. He was strengthening his defences in case.'

'Sir David is governing an island at great risk,' Pitt acknowledged, 'and one, if we are correct, we would struggle to support outside the navy, and that is stretched thin. With the Low

Countries overrun and the Dutch joining them in their so-called Batavian Republic, it means a second powerful fleet in the North Sea so they can be contained. The armies of the Revolution are poised on the borders of Italy, and I fear Austria, as an ally, is not as solid as she should be with the subventions we are paying her.'

'Having seen the Austrians at first-hand I would have said you should have saved your coin. I believe you have utterly wasted money on Piedmont, for they will run at the first whiff of grapeshot.'

Pitt took up the case. 'The reports from that theatre support your contention, but not paying for the military strength of others would be the worst of two devilish problems. What troops we have have been deployed elsewhere, so we must fund others, even if it is for mere show.'

Pearce could not resist a dig at Dundas, Minister for War. 'From what is being said in the coffee houses, most of the soldiers we did possess are occupying six feet of Caribbean earth, having expired from yellow jack.'

Pearce directed a wolfish smile at the man who had sent them there. If he'd expected Dundas to blush with shame he was disappointed. 'How easy it is, laddie, for those not charged with making decisions to question the actions of those who do.'

'I'm sure the sugar lobby is grateful for your concerns.'

That struck home as a barb, one often set against Dundas and Pitt. Those who either had plantations in the sugar islands, or derived revenues from them, were highly vocal, well organised and quick to remind Whitehall of how much the taxes on sugar supported the activities of the state.

'Our main hope is that France is exhausted too,' Pitt said, changing the direction of the conversation, to cut across a companion about to blast Pearce for insolence. 'They have been living off their paper assignats for a long time now, increasingly worthless to the point where they may require to be repudiated. This presents us with an opportunity.'

'To do what?'

'Make peace,' Pitt responded. 'If Spain joins with France, and we have strong grounds to believe that is becoming increasingly possible, then our situation deteriorates significantly.'

'The French situation too,' Pearce posited with a wry look. 'Spain could be more of a liability than an asset to the Revolution.'

'For a mere naval lieutenant, laddie, you have a tendency to wallow in high policy.'

'While watching you flounder in same,' Pearce snapped. 'If the war is not proceeding well, who should bear responsibility if not the Minister for War?'

'I can't abide this, Billy; I feel the need to place my boot fair and square on this poltroon's arse and send him back to the gutter from which he sprang.'

'You're welcome to attempt it if you are prepared also for the consequences.'

The two men exchanged angry stares, Celtic blood high and no fellow feeling from one

Scotsman to another. The relations between a Pearce and a Dundas had always been high-coloured, which had been the case before John was even born. His father had engaged in many a row with this man, the radical orator versus the master political manipulator from Edinburgh, who brought to the Tory government of Pitt the entire parliamentary voting power of Scotland, thus keeping him in power.

'I doubt you two wrestling will get us very far,' was Pitt's dry comment, before he addressed Pearce directly. 'We require someone to go to France and talk to certain people, who we have heard might incline to an end to hostilities as well as an overthrow of the Directory.'

'And you have me in mind?'

'It occurred to us that you might fit the bill.'

'Might,' Dundas added.

'Why not send an embassy?'

'I'm sure you can guess.'

Given his antipathy to Dundas and a desire to bait him, Pearce had not thought on the matter being discussed and the proposition being put forward. He sought to do so now, not that it took him long to come to a conclusion. Pitt, in order to prosecute the war, had been obliged to form a coalition with a section of the Whig party, a faction led by the Duke of Portland.

If that fell apart it would bring down the government and him with it, so what he and Dundas were proposing had not been discussed in certain quarters, namely with Portland and those people holding the ministries he had demanded as the price of his support, the most important one being the Lordship of the Admiralty.

'It has to be someone you can repudiate if the attempt is exposed.' Pitt canted his head and pursed his lips, while Dundas sat like a statue, both an affirmation of the point.

'And what do you have in mind as reward for this service?'

'Shall we talk first of the advantages you possess in your mere name?' Pitt asked.

'You're Adam Pearce's son,' Dundas barked.

'I have already reminded you this very day of how he met his end.'

'For which I have already offered you my condolences,' said Pitt.

That was true and acknowledged but Dundas declined to join in the commiseration. 'That was under a very different regime. The case is altered.'

'Is it, Dundas? The Directory is composed of regicides to a man. They may have slowed the Jacobin slaughter and sloughed off their previous skin, but I doubt the guillotine is completely idle. If they feel their position to be under threat, it will be working flat out once more.'

'Your father's good name has been restored,' Pitt insisted. 'As has that of many a victim of the terror. Émigrés have gone home in numbers, so the composition of society is much changed. The Chamber of Deputies has been relegated to useless bluster and matters are being decided upon in salons and corridors. What would you do if you found yourself able to talk with people of some stature and get a hearing that might

301

bring an end to hostilities?'

'By offering what?'

Dundas had got control of his passions so he spoke in an even tone. 'Not just offer. Seek, too, some indication of a way to bring about what both countries desperately need.'

'Before something formal, a proper govern-ment initiative, can be put forward?'

Again that induced the kind of silence that passes for confirmation. These two gave an outward appearance of calm. Pearce could only hope to match it as he ran his mind over the difficulties. How was it they knew there was even a chance to invoke a treaty of peace?

'You have spies in Paris?'

Dundas declined to reply; they would certainly exist and would be under his control and budget.

'Use one of them.'

'One of whom? As of this moment you are without employment and with no prospect of getting any without influence being exercised on your behalf, which is what you came here to try and alter.'

'Am I then talking to people who can alleviate that?'

Pitt replied with a smile. 'We could hardly ask for any kind of service without we rewarded whoever undertakes it.'

'I'm curious as to how much of that you are willing to grant?'

'Something that is very likely not in our immediate gift,' Dundas replied. 'But ask away.'

'I am a naval lieutenant by profession now. What could I seek but employment?'

'And that's what you would want?'

John Pearce nearly said yes without hesitation. Since Leghorn and thinking on his relationship with Emily, he had seen sea service as a way to occupy the time that must elapse before she would be willing to publicly acknowledge him as a potential husband and one in which he could support himself. Ashore he would be open to endless temptation and that was an article in which he now knew himself to be less than stalwart.

Yet he had the feeling, in this room, he could perhaps ask for more. William Pitt, on coming across him and surprised to do so, only saw the possibility of employing him a half-hour past. Both he and Dundas had only that amount of time in which to discuss what had to be an important subject and one close to their heart with him as part of it.

Which implied they were both keen to see such a mission undertaken, but dare not canvass widely for a candidate to meet their needs. There was also the fact that Dundas had sent Pearce on a secret mission to France previously and provided ample funds, those he had alluded to earlier as not being properly accounted for.

If it had not been an unqualified success, no blame for a less than perfect outcome could be laid at his door, which meant he might be the very man they were looking for, unexpectedly before them and free to do their bidding in a situation that demanded that nothing leak out.

Dundas would be very guarded with whom he shared any information, not just on this. Pearce suspected he would keep most of his ministerial colleagues, even Tories, in ignorance of what intelligence he was receiving, feeding them only that which suited his devious political machinations. He had to remind himself to include Pitt in this, it being too easy to fall into the trap of thinking the First Lord of the Treasury to be some kind of Dundas puppet. He was a man in possession of an acute partisan and Tory brain, more likely a prime mover than a marionette.

'I would have to consider both what you propose as well as what might persuade me to undertake any task you have in mind.' Pitt was about to speak, but a hard look from John Pearce stopped him. 'I have to also think it may well mean being open with me as to whom I must contact in Paris.'

'And if I say no to that?' Dundas asked, surprisingly without much passion.

'Then it might qualify for my answer too. No man in his right mind would go into the lion's den without he knew how to proceed and I can assure you I am in full possession of my faculties. I am bound to ask if you have contrived a way to get anyone to where you want them to be and a method which ensures they arrive in one piece?'

Pitt managed a slight smile. 'That sounds to me as if you're doing more than considering what we propose.'

'You may take from my words any impression that suits, but do not mistake necessary speculation for agreement. It is very easy to hatch schemes in rooms such as these, without any consideration of the means of execution.'

'That's an inappropriate word, Pearce,' Dundas chuckled; it gave the impression he favoured the idea.

'What would be inappropriate would be to go charging off half-cocked, which is what you seem to want someone to do. Worse, as far as you are concerned, is that it almost invites exposure. I doubt the Portland faction, even if they lauded your aims, would be pleased to find out you are acting without their knowledge.'

Pitt looked away then, casting his eyes to the ceiling; Dundas flushed with a look that seemed to promise another blast of temper.

'Nor am I fool enough to leap in with both feet without I give it due and proper consideration. I would need to know how you are to get me to Paris, who I have to contact and how deep the mood is for an end to the war amongst those with the power to affect matters.'

'Are you saying, Lieutenant Pearce, that if we could meet the objections you just raised, you are minded to consider it?'

There was a very slight sense of pleading in Pitt's voice, but Dundas was less inclined to beg. 'I would hate you to leave here with the impression we are supplicants.'

Pearce had to hold back then; Dundas might deny it, but he suspected that was precisely what they were. He would have to be careful in what he demanded, but was there a limit? Before coming here he had been in a quandary as to how to proceed, feeling acutely the loss of his friends and the ongoing difficulties with the woman he loved.

Then there was that craving for activity and Pearce had to acknowledge that his heart was lifted at the prospect before him. Yes, it would be dangerous but what a prize! To be the instrument that not only ended a war but possibly one who set the clock back to a more ordered world both in England and France.

'Are you saying you have alternatives, Mr Dundas?'

'We always have those, Pearce, and you would do well to bear that in mind.'

It was politic to agree, even if he was not sure he believed it.

'Would you be reassured,' Pitt asked, 'if we were to tell you we have the makings of a plan that will give a chance of a good outcome?'

'Make sure it is one that survives contact with the reality. Also that it does not leak out to your political foes or even your supposed friends.'

'Absolute discretion is essential, Pearce,' Dundas barked.

'How odd,' came the smooth reply. 'You wish from me a particular service, yet you decline the courtesy of addressing me properly — not an error committed by Mr Pitt.'

'Be satisfied that you get it from such a source.'

Pitt butted in. 'How you are addressed is not germane. I return to my previous point. This notion we have appears sound, but if it is to proceed it must be secret even before there is an outcome and remain so afterwards. My colleague is merely seeking to point this out to you.'

'Think all you want,' Dundas added. 'But talk to no one.'

I could ditch these two, Pearce thought. A word in the right ear and there would be the devil to pay and no pitch hot, which was tempting. This was set aside as bringing to him no perceived advantage. He could only give up what he knew and hope for reward; here he could make it part of his terms.

'I think enough has been said for now.'

'I agree,' Pitt acceded, 'but I would ask you to provide us with an answer swiftly. We feel we have a very small window of opportunity and such things close rapidly. If I have not driven home to you the importance of the stakes then I have failed, but be assured it is of great import.'

Pearce was on his feet, looking from one to the other. 'Very well. I will let you know.' He departed, his mind in a whirl, leaving the two politicians to refill their goblets and drink deep.

'Will he do as we require, Henry?'

'Of course he will, Billy. I know my man and he'll not be able to resist. Think on what the outcome might be and if it all goes wrong someone of the stature of John Pearce is a small price to pay. God forbid they connect his name to that of his sire. It will be a poniard for certain.'

Pitt managed a full smile. 'It's so enjoyable playing games with people who reckon themselves cleverer than us, is it not?'

'It is, Billy.'

'What do you think he will ask for?'

'The moon, and we can promise it. Delivery

will remain at our discretion.'

Dundas began to chuckle; very soon both men were laughing.

23

Edward Druce had not enjoyed a good night's rest for three days; too many avenues in which to proceed jumbled his thinking and at the base of that was the prospect of ruin. Naturally the face of Cornelius Gherson swam through his dreams and, unwelcome as it was, it could not be evaded. There was his partner too, a fat, smiling presence, in reverie his cynical way of thinking regarding the Barclay estate running up against a more honest and upright Druce.

The ogre was Denby Carruthers, a snarling beast ready to tear out the heart of his upright brother-in-law, who had only sought the best for all concerned. Such a nocturnal character assessment did not survive wakefulness: Druce knew himself to be just as conflicted as Ommaney, so the notion of his being upright and truthful died with the dawn. But the problem and how to resolve it stayed with him as he coached from Kennington to the Strand.

His arrangement, that Gherson should return the day following his first visit, had not been met, so there was a faint hope he had been waylaid by some footpads and thus, as a problem, disappeared. Such an expectation evaporated when he entered the premises. There he found a dishevelled-looking ne'er-do-well reeking of his manifest debaucheries, whose sole purpose in finally calling was to seek more money.

'How can you have disbursed so much, so soon?'

'You have to take account of my months of deprivation, Mr Druce,' Gherson pleaded. 'Short on funds and no pleasure to be had. A man cannot live in that manner, and anyway, I have been generous.'

'You appear to be making up for lost time.'

That got a leer. 'There's more to cover, sir, mark it.'

'Have you written to the Barclay sisters?'

'Not yet, Mr Druce; what need is there for haste?' Before Druce could reply there came what was close to a demand for wine to whet a dry throat. That supplied and the first slug taken, Gherson spoke again. 'It matters only that Mrs Barclay is aware of that which I brought to you.'

Looking at him, Druce made up his mind. No reliance could be placed on this scoundrel either in life or in court. Any residual doubt he had as to the legitimacy of the will evaporated. A man, however deprived he claimed to be, who could not control his passions would likely go down and take everyone with him.

'While I am prepared to indulge you — after all, the firm is still in your debt — it is also the case I may need to find you, Mr Gherson.'

'I do not stay far, sir. There is all I need in nearby Covent Garden.'

Drink and whores, Druce thought as he penned a note to pay Gherson another five pounds, which would not sit well with Francis Ommaney; there was a shortage of coin in the country and the firm was minded to hang on to that which it had, issuing promissory notes until the situation eased. But the places where Gherson was indulging his lechery did not accept paper.

Should he have sent Hodgeson away? Would it be wise to call upon him to return? Druce decided against, for he had one problem easily solved and one that would be difficult to deal with. The mere mention to his brother-in-law that Gherson was to hand would see that problem solved. But if Gherson let on about his association with Ommaney and Druce, another would rise to haunt him.

Francis Ommaney's head came round his office door; he never beat Druce to his desk. 'Did I hear that Gherson has finally turned up, Edward?'

'He has. I think we need to talk, Francis.'

★   ★   ★

It took Emily Barclay three days to depart for London, in the coach with her and Adam the box she had brought back from Italy containing her husband's papers. One whole day had been taken up in consulting with a local attorney, as well as going over the investments with her father, who had the kind of deep interest in such matters that is gifted to those who long to indulge in speculation, but are forbidden by circumstance.

There were no glaringly egregious errors, but a feeling of things not being utterly above board. A letter went off to Heinrich Lutyens, with a request to be accommodated, taking advantage of an offer already made. Another had gone to Alexander Davidson, whom she knew to be prize agent to John Pearce, asking if he would be prepared to take control of her affairs.

The third letter went to Ommaney and Druce, to alert them to her coming and giving the address at which she would be staying. The final missive was to her lover, and it pleaded that when they met, due discretion should be maintained in public.

'Not a trace of affection, Heinrich,' he complained. 'Regards she sends me.'

'It may have been written within sight of her family.'

'Nonsense.'

'You will both be under my roof. I daresay you will get as much affection as you can handle.' That got a wide grin from Pearce, quickly suppressed as being too obviously salacious. 'Do you intend to tell Emily of the foolish venture you're contemplating?'

'Lord, no. In truth I should not have been open with you.'

'While I am aware that what advice I have proffered is likely to be ignored.'

It would not have been polite to say to his friend he had only been consulted as a sounding board, off which Pearce could bounce his ideas: a way to bring clarity to confused thinking. One thing that had emerged was a way to marry up his aspirations with the needs of Pitt and Dundas, and that had grown to become what would be a demand on this very day, for he was due to meet with them.

'It will not look out of place if I accompany her to Davidson's. She must wish for him to be in charge of her affairs.'

'The firm who handled Barclay's prize monies has a sound reputation.'

*　*　*

One half of the sound reputation was trying to persuade the other to a course of action that would protect Druce as well as the firm, the difficulty coming from not being entirely open. A financial debt to Carruthers could not be mentioned, but it could be stated with some confidence that to make an enemy of such a powerful figure was unwise. Eventually Francis Ommaney was persuaded on the course suggested.

'Very well, Edward. I will play the part assigned to me. But blame me not if it fails to be believed.'

Once alone, Druce penned a note to Denby Carruthers, one in which he stated he had made a most alarming discovery on a matter in which they both had an interest. Would his brother-in-law call by Kennington this evening to discuss it?

*　*　*

If Heinrich Lutyens greeted Emily with genuine affection, it was obvious to her that did not extend to babies. Adam was of course acknowledged and she was informed that he had engaged a nurse to attend to him while Emily went about her affairs. But there was no billing and cooing over the infant and no desire at all to hold him. Medical man he might be, but he would not consent to be present when the boy was fed.

'It is hoped he will sleep now,' Emily said, when she rejoined him in the drawing room. 'I do hope I am not keeping you from your affairs?'

'I have come to be the master of those Emily, and am thus very fortunate of my time as well.'

They had a lot to catch up on; letters purveyed only so much, so an hour was spent in Emily recalling her adventures while Lutyens interjected occasionally to mark some act of his, which he admitted sounded mundane beside what she had endured. There was, of course, a ghost present, or to be more accurate, absent.

'When will John return?'

'I have no idea, Emily. He had some important business to transact and he could not wait on the expectation of your arrival.'

Said like that it was taken as avoidance.

'I have wounded him, Heinrich, but I have no choice.'

'Ah,' replied a fellow who had no desire to talk of their relationship. 'I am sure when he returns you will find yourself forgiven.'

'Will I? It is all very well for him, a man, to say appearances do not matter, but it is my sex that bears the brunt of approbation. I have family, too, and he has none.'

'For which he should be pitied.'

'It may be part of his attraction, but John can be awkward.'

★   ★   ★

He was being that right at the moment Emily spoke those words, and Dundas was aghast. 'A command?'

'Why not? Master and commander is a rank I've already held and lesser men hold it.' That got a look to imply such creatures in his case did not exist. 'I am being asked to negotiate with what I assume will be people of stature. How can I do that as a mere lieutenant? I should be made post and a full captain.'

'How am I to ask for such a thing without Spencer demanding not only to know why, but also what business it is of mine? I don't run the Admiralty and he does, quite apart from all the naval lords who will, I reckon, resign rather than accede to such a request. I told Billy you would ask for the moon, but not even I thought of this.'

'Those are my terms. If you decline to meet them you must find another to do what you require. In addition, I require a trio of protection certificates for three men I shall name.'

Pearce knew the post captaincy to be unlikely; he only mentioned it to render master and commander seemingly reasonable. He had a strong belief that Dundas would negotiate, which proved to be well founded. The haggling went on for some time and the first demand was left hanging until after the mission had been completed, this on the very good grounds that

Earl Spencer would not be made suspicious by the request. Dundas was not a man to give way easily but after an hour of toing and froing, mixed with other offers of preferment that Pearce turned down — he had no desire for a government sinecure that would have his father turning in his grave — the terms were agreed.

'With whom am I to talk?'

'You will find that out in good time and that has not yet arrived.'

'How do I get to France?'

'We had in mind that you should be captured.'

'Am I allowed to say that seems fraught with uncertainty?'

'Take my word for it, it's not.'

'Am I to be enlightened as to how that is?'

'That we can do.'

Dundas stood and went to a side door, one Pearce had assumed to be a cupboard. It was not: it led to a windowless room from which emerged a slight-looking fellow in poor-quality clothing and of a somewhat unremarkable face: round cheeks, evenly spaced eyes, an inconspicuous nose and a small mouth. His expression, being non-committal, suited the whole.

'Mr Oliphant, this is Lieutenant John Pearce, about whom I have told you.'

'Pleased to make your acquaintance, sir.'

'Should I be pleased to make yours?'

'You insisted we needed a plan,' Dundas said. 'Here is the first part of it. Perhaps, Samuel, you would care to explain.'

'Happily so, as long as you assure me it is safe to do so.'

316

'I trust him and I will guarantee you can too.' It would be fair to say that shocked John Pearce, a fact which was obvious. 'Whatever else you are, you're a man of your word. And so was your sire. But know this: you must follow what instructions you are given until you are face-to-face with those to whom we need to negotiate.'

★ ★ ★

Pearce arrived back in Harley Street and entered to the sound of wailing from an upper floor, which was music to his ears. He took the risers two at time as he followed the sound, to burst in on Emily in a bedroom, cradling his crying son, with another woman in the room, obviously the nurse Lutyens had said he would engage. He rushed to Emily's side and took Adam from her with such intent as to make complaint impossible.

It had to be admitted afterwards that his presence was of no help; if anything, when he took Adam and tried to console him, the sound and distress increased to a crescendo, but no child cries for ever and eventually it died away and his father could wave him to and fro and bask in the delight of his situation, only the presence of the nurse making things awkward.

'What does she know?' he asked when the woman departed, her duties for the day completed and Adam in a basket for the time between now and his next feed.

'I doubt she has any enquiries as to the parentage,' Emily said, her face clouded. 'You

317

could not have made that more plain.'

'While I doubt she has the faintest idea of who you are, if Heinrich did as I asked.'

'He did, introducing me as Mrs Raynesford.'

'Am I allowed to be Mr Raynesford once more, Emily?'

She blushed so easily. To be reminded of the first night spent together in the New Forest should have been an occasion for unmitigated joy; it had certainly been that at the time but he knew it was the implications of the use of that name that was embarrassing her. She was always seemingly reluctant to make love until the actual moment arrived.

'Heinrich?'

'At St Bart's.'

'Then we are alone for the first time since the Solent, Emily, and Adam is sound asleep.'

'Then let us ensure he remains so,' Emily said, taking his hand to lead him to another bedchamber.

★   ★   ★

'Denby, I was as shocked as you appear to be now. To have searched high and low for Gherson only to have him turn up in the Strand at our very office.'

Druce had a keen eye on Carruthers' expression; did his brother-in-law believe a tale that even Druce found far-fetched? His explanation stretched credulity but he could see no alternative but to try it. Gherson had to be sacrificed if matters were to be resolved and he could at least reassure himself he would have no actual hand in what would follow.

'We have a separation of clients as a matter of course and Ommaney dealt with this Barclay fellow. I have to say, if he had not been killed, I would still be in ignorance of the fact that he employed Gherson as a clerk. No wonder we couldn't find him.'

'Did Ommaney know?'

'He says not. His client was Captain Barclay and it was to his name all matters were addressed. It was under his hand that all replies were received so who his clerk was meant nothing. You will not quibble when I tell you that your affairs were never discussed with Ommaney: they were private between you and me. Even the man I hired to find the scoundrel did not have any idea why.'

'Yet we have a list of sightings, none of which proved to be true. I cannot say your thief-taker was a good investment.'

'It may be he was prone to exaggeration, I cannot tell. But he came across to me as an honest fellow.'

'An honest fellow who has lived off my money.'

'If you feel dunned, Denby, I feel it my duty to offer you recompense.'

Denby Carruthers was a dark-complexioned man, one who often looked angry by nature and he was certainly that now. Yet the offer of repayment was waved aside.

'Covent Garden, you say?'

'That's where he said he was going. I doubt he

will be discreet if his boasting is anything to go by.'

'Well,' Carruthers sighed, 'I thank you, Edward.'

'Can I ask what you intend?'

That brought a smile to a face not much given to the expression. 'He requires to be chastised, does he not, for the crime he committed against my person?'

'And the extent of that?'

'Now, why would you concern yourself with such things? I will find him and I will deal with him.'

Druce could not plead for leniency; to do so would only expose him. And he knew the matter might not rest: if Gherson was interrogated he would be bound to name him, not Ommaney, as the man who dealt with Barclay. In all the thoughts he had engaged in, all the twists and turns of the conundrum, Druce had never found a way out that involved no risk, so it came down to which was the least perilous, with a possibility one would not arise.

Ommaney, if asked, would say his partner dealt with the affairs of Ralph Barclay. As long as his brother-in-law left his retribution to others, no mention of him might surface. Having done what he had planned to do, he could with a clear conscience go to his desk in the morning and write a letter to Harley Street, to tell Mrs Barclay that the will had been outed as a clear forgery and the matter laid to rest.

★ ★ ★

The letter arrived as the trio were eating breakfast, with Adam cradled in his father's arms, his blue eyes entranced by the passage of food from the plate to the mouth. It asked Emily to call upon him at any time this morning, preferably after ten of the clock. Appraised of the problem with the will, John Pearce had declared right off it had to be a forgery, only to be intensely annoyed with Emily when she told him of how she had paid Gherson to depart Leghorn.

'The fellow I knew would have taken the money and still exposed you.'

'I acted as I needed to at the time, John.'

'Which only encouraged him to more felony, as you can now see.'

'Well, the matter is at rest. After I have called on Mr Druce, I will see your man Davidson and arrange a transfer of my affairs. I would also have him examine the accounts with a more practised eye, to see if they have been well handled till now.'

'And then?'

Her eyes dropped. 'I will return home.'

'So nothing is altered in that regard?'

'It cannot be.'

She waited for an argument, which did not come; Pearce had told her nothing of where he was going and why. In fact, her returning to Frome was a blessing, though a pretence of misery had to be displayed.

'Forgive me, John.'

'I cannot hide that it stretches my ability in that regard.'

It was mid morning before Emily Barclay arrived at the offices of Ommaney and Druce, to be told by a clerk that Mr Druce was not in the office.

'But I have an arrangement to meet with him.'

'I fear he has good reason to be absent, madam. He has just this hour been advised that his sister-in-law, Mrs Catherine Carruthers, has been foully slain, stabbed to death last night by a villain who goes by the name of Cornelius Gherson.'

He took Emily's shock as being related to the notion of murder and put aside what he had been about to say: that the perpetrator had been here in this very office the day before. He was, of course, unaware that this lady before him knew of the connection between Gherson and Ommaney and Druce. Given what had so recently occurred, it would have been unnatural not to wonder at a whole skein of associations.

'Please ask Mr Druce to write to me when he is able to see me. And add my condolences.'

24

The news that Emily was not departing as planned did not come as welcome and nor, when he was told what she had learnt, could Pearce believe Gherson, a man likely to faint at the sight of a pricked finger, could stoop to bloody murder. Not that he could bring himself to care that the sod would hang if it was true, given he had more pressing concerns.

He was due to coach down to Deal the following morning with Oliphant to be taken aboard a frigate, and he needed an excuse to deflect her enquiries. Heinrich Lutyens was no help; he was of the opinion his friend should be open and tell her everything.

'You intend to risk your life yet you are not about to tell the woman you love, moreover the father of your infant son?'

'She will worry,' Pearce protested.

'With good cause.'

'Heinrich, I risked my life every time I saw and engaged an enemy and, it's fair to say, it was not always by my choice. I have been gifted a chance to alter everything that stands in my way. If I have become a sailor by accident that is what I am now.' The pressing tone was dropped, as Pearce added, 'It's the only skill I possess.'

John Pearce did not have much experience of lying to Emily; arguing with her yes, but dissembling was a new and a far from pleasant feeling. Nor did he know if she believed him in what was a wholly made-up tale. There was no way to mention a future naval career without too many questions, given she was aware of his standing with the Admiralty.

'I must have some form of occupation and have decided on becoming the captain of a letter of marque.'

'Not noble, I seem to recall from conversations in Italy; very much the reverse.'

'I was never much one for nobility.'

'I heard them named as brigands and pirates.'

'Then I shall seek to change the perception by my exemplary behaviour. Michael, Charlie and Rufus are already aboard one and I will certainly have them sail with me.'

He even asked her to be an investor in a scheme that could be highly profitable if properly pursued. That to him, he insisted, would be a proper use of Ralph Barclay's money, not, as she intended, a gift on which he could live.

'There are people I must see in Dover, then I must go to Shoreham in order to ensure our good friends are well and satisfied with their situation. I had to leave them there with little knowledge of how they found it.'

'How long will you be gone?'

'A few days at most,' he lied; in truth he had no idea.

Having spent the night together, Emily departed to see to Adam, at which point Pearce dressed as the lieutenant he was and hauled out and began to pack his sea chest, unaware of what he would need and obliged to take all he possessed. He was caught in the act: Emily was standing in the doorway to the bedroom watching him and her expression was not encouraging.

'How long have you been there?'

'Long enough to wonder why you're taking that with you.'

The laugh was forced and false. 'I never travel these days without it.'

'Even if it would be here on your return? And why are you in your naval uniform?'

'Perhaps I best be honest.'

The truth was not well received, Emily biting her lip as he concluded telling her where he was going, even as he insisted there was little danger.

'You set out to deceive me, John?'

'I set out to save you from being concerned. I am engaged upon a particular service and one that might lead to an end to the present conflict. Come sit on the bed and I will explain.'

She listened without interruption, but Pearce could hear the way her breathing altered once she had realised the magnitude of the risk he was taking. Nor was she seemingly comforted by the reason.

'Is what I have so tainted you would rather risk your life than accept it?'

'I have told you any number of times, I cannot live as a kept man and especially not on the source of those monies.'

There was a temptation then to add the other reason, until he recalled Michael's admonishment to say nothing.

'Would you have me an indoor man, Emily? Ever since you first met me you have known my attitude to risk. It is no different to that day, on the deck of *Brilliant*, when I spoke to you, a common seaman addressing the wife of the captain. I knew it was forbidden.'

'Knew, John?'

'It was not hard to guess, though I admit to my act being spontaneous.'

'What you describe now does not reek of spontaneity.'

'This is not so very different: it's something that will place me where I need to be for my own self-esteem. I think if I became a country squire, as you originally had in mind, you would come to despise me.'

'The country is not an idle place.'

'But it's not my place.'

'Sometimes I wonder if you have anything of that kind. You spent your youth wandering; perhaps it is in your blood.'

'There will be a hack calling for me very shortly. I must go and I would like it to be with your blessing.'

'Would you join me in a prayer for your safe return?'

If he felt hypocritical, it was a small price to pay to say yes.

★ ★ ★

The first question was asked before the hack left Harley Street. 'So, Mr Oliphant, tell me of yourself.'

'To do so would fly in the face of all common sense, Mr Pearce.'

'Is your name really Oliphant, I wonder?'

That got a sardonic smile. 'It is the one I hope you will address me by. From the moment we reach the ship to which we are to be delivered to the French coast, I am your servant. You may choose Oliphant without the mister, if you wish, but I will answer just as readily to Samuel.'

'If you're a servant, it is of a higher power than I.'

'Mr Pearce, you must not enquire and that is for your own security, for you cannot reveal that which you do not know. I will give you a background, which I would like you to commit to memory. It is that of a man taken to sea as a boy, who became your servant on a ship, which we will agree upon. It will be my task to use the journey to Deal to ensure you have what facts are necessary, while you must instruct me in some nautical information of which I admit to being woefully short.'

'I think I will have to teach you a sailor's gait. Even a servant rolls as he walks.'

Oliphant smiled, though he clearly meant what followed. 'At least, as a servant, I know I don't have to dirty my hands with tar.'

'You're not as ignorant as you suppose.'

At the regular stops to change the fast-trotting horse Oliphant was attendance personified, seeing to his master with an attitude that, if it bordered on the servile, never quite descended to that level; here was a man, to the casual eye, who was familiar with the ways of his principal. Likewise he kept an eye on the chest lashed to the back of their conveyance, to ensure no pilfering. At Canterbury, for a longer stop, he had the civilian coat fetched out into which Pearce must at the right point change.

Darkness was falling when they passed through the Parish of Sholden, which Oliphant informed him was the last before Deal. This told Pearce he knew the places and the route well. Tempted to ask how many times he had been this way before, he held his tongue, something he realised would now have to become a habit.

The naval yard for the Downs lay on the shoreline, entry secured by Pearce's blue coat without him giving his name or rank. He was admonished to remain in the hack and change into his buff coat, a bag produced for the one he was wearing, while Oliphant went off to make certain arrangements. He soon returned with a couple of sailors, old and no longer sea-serving by the look of them, who unlashed the chest and carried it to a boat tied up to the jetty, with his supposed servant carrying his own ditty bag.

'HMS *Circe?*'

Oliphant addressed this to what Pearce took to be a midshipman, but the minimal amount of available light rendered that a guess. The call being answered in the affirmative, his sea chest, as well as his supposed servant's dunnage, was lowered into the cutter.

Oliphant whispered. 'Time to board, sir.'

The reply was equally soft. 'After you. Senior officer last.'

'Noted.'

If the men rowing, as well as the mid in command, were curious at this clandestine behaviour, it was too dark for enlightenment. Pearce was fixating on the name of the ship, HMS *Circe*, thinking it was a poor omen to have as a name the witch who had lured Odysseus and his men into a trap with her potions to turn them into pigs. Was that what he was facing, a brew concocted by Henry Dundas?

The boarding of the frigate was without ceremony — no whistles, no officers on deck — with Pearce being shown to the great cabin to meet the captain, who pronounced the whole thing a rum business in a voice larded with disapproval.

'I have been advised not to ask your name so I won't. Accommodation has been arranged for you in the wardroom, my premier having vacated his quarters. It will be up to your servant to see to your needs. We weigh at first light.'

* * *

It was strange to lie abed and hear the ship coming to life, to visualise rather than observe the frigate weighing anchor and heading out to sea. Mentally he registered the calm waters of the Downs, rendered so by the great sandbar of the Goodwin Sands, just as he knew by the increased motion of the ship the point at which they came out into the open Channel.

Oliphant fetched him breakfast and since he had the premier's quarter galley he had access to a private privy. Left alone to ponder, he had to wonder at how Dundas had contrived a frigate when he was forever denying he had any influence at the Admiralty. The more he thought on Oliphant the less likely the man seemed. He was aware inactivity was making him brood and he fought to see the better side of the situation, all his thoughts accompanied by an acute ear for what was happening on deck.

Daylight, which was punctuated by the sounds of practised swordplay, morphed into a second night aboard. He knew from the position of the dropping sun on the casements they were on a southerly course and he could not but wonder where they were headed. Oliphant, who had been in and out several times, came in carrying his naval coat.

'We are about to go ashore.'

'Am I allowed to know where?'

'Of course. We are off the Seine Estuary and the captain is about to launch an attack by boats on one of the Le Havre quays. His task is to destroy commercial shipping and if possible cut out a vessel or two.'

'And this was planned by whom?'

'Mr Pearce, I think I have alerted you already to the fact there are certain questions best not asked. That is one of them. We go in with the boats, but luck will not permit us to return. Your coat.'

'So I am navy again.'

'We are both navy and I am a fool of a servant who will not let his master out of his sight. I think, if you harken to the noise of feet on the deck, it is time to go.'

'My sea chest?'

'The captain will ensure it is returned to

Harley Street. We take nothing but that which we would require for a cutting-out expedition. You will find what I believe you tars call a hanger as well as a pair of pistols on the wardroom table.'

'Everything thought of?'

'I have never known that to be possible.'

Pearce followed Oliphant out and picked up the weapons in a wardroom entirely deserted, hardly surprising if there was action proposed; even those not taking part would be on deck, if only to encourage their mates.

'You, sir.' The voice was recognisably that of the captain he had met the night before; there was insufficient starlight for a true identification. 'Please obey any instructions given to you by the officer in command of your boat.'

'Aye aye, sir.'

'You are navy, I had it so in my mind.'

'Least said, sir,' Pearce responded, wondering what the reaction would be if he did know his name. The answer was a throat-clearing growl, followed by, 'Godspeed to you all.'

It was Oliphant who struggled getting into the boat; Pearce accomplished it with the ease of long practice but it was a credit to the fellow's discretion that he did not curse in any way as he slipped off the wet and weed-covered battens, taking silently the assistance he was given by the sailors, as well as their humour directed at this lubber.

The oars were muffled, taking John Pearce back to that crossing of the Solent, and like then the pace was measured. There was a lantern in the rear of the lead boat, only occasionally unshaded, with obviously a man in command who knew where they were headed. The cry to haul away was evidence they were close to whatever the object was and that produced yelling and screaming from everyone in the raiding party, this as the pace markedly increased.

There they were, the silhouettes of masts and rigging against the starry sky, but it was not long before illumination increased. Pearce was aware of the fizzing fuses before the bombs were thrown and watched as the lit end arced through the night sky to burst into explosive flame on contact with wooden hulls or decks. Now they were alongside those craft with men clambering from their boats, using ropes on the end of grappling iron to get aboard.

'With me, sir,' Pearce said to Oliphant, for this was his element. 'And stay close.'

There were hands to help them onto a deck and, now that torches had been lit, enough light to have them shepherded across to the quayside where they could gangplank down onto dry land. All along the quay ships were being set alight in a frenzy of seeming mayhem until a voice cried out in a loud shout to tell the raiding party to get back to the boats, the reason clear.

From the direction of what lay ahead, the town most likely, the darkness was punctuated with another line of torches, and a lengthy one, which indicated a strong body come to repel this attack. Oliphant had a grip on Pearce's arm, which irritated him.

'You are back in command. Tell me what I

need to do and I will do it.'

'Very well. We must wait until the boats have departed and yell to be rescued. It must look as if we have been left behind. Your name is your own and you are third on HMS *Circe*.'

'And then?'

'Unless someone is too free with a weapon, we become prisoners. Now begin to shout to be saved and at some point fire off your pistols, though with a care as to where you point them.'

The frigate's boats were pulling out of the circle of light created by the fires they had started as Pearce and his so-called servant began the requisite pleas to be rescued. Pearce discharged with the muzzles elevated high enough to do no one any harm, this as the line of torches came closer.

'I think it now politic to raise our hands in the air.'

Pearce dropped his pistols and did as he was bid, as the furious faces of his enemies and soon-to-be captors became visible. Those with muskets ran past him to fire their weapons into the darkness, which produced cries he reckoned to be more dramatic than real; the British tar loved to guy his friends, never mind his foes.

Both he and Oliphant were roughly handled and subjected to screaming imprecations that were so fleck-filled as to be incomprehensible, this till someone who had to be an officer gave an order to be calm, followed by a demand that they identify themselves and the ship from which they came.

'I believe you speak French, Mr Pearce. Best

in that case you answer. And I believe it is common to give up your sword.'

Wondering why this had never been mentioned before, he did as he was asked, speaking to a fellow with epaulettes who had come close enough for much of his face to be visible under his hat. The information was taken without much in the way of response until he was asked in French for his parole. The officer did not wish to bind the arms of a brave man.

'I give you my word I will make no attempt to escape.' It was with savage delight, given the feeling he was being manipulated, that he added, 'I cannot, of course, speak for my servant who may seek to abscond.'

'How very noble, sir,' was the response as Oliphant's wrists were bound.

The route to the town was not empty for long. As soon as the citizenry had decided it was safe, they had come out of their houses to jeer and spit at these *sals Rosbifs*. The building to which they were taken, in which were now hundreds of torches, was of stone and decorated with elaborate masonry work, not that they were allowed long to wonder at its purpose.

A set of steep stairs took them down into a narrow, damp corridor and then to a barred, rusty doorway which was shut noisily behind them. Pearce, once his companion had been released from his bonds, was informed that they would be interrogated come the morning.

'Well, Oliphant. How would you say we are progressing?'

'As well as can be expected, sir, under such

trying circumstances.'

Their talk brought to the bars a scruffy torch-bearing soldier to glare at them. They were glad of him, for the light showed a pair of plank-like boards that would serve as beds.

25

What passed for an interrogation came the
following morning, really just a series of
questions to establish how these two had come
to be where they were, posed by a French naval
captain who had along a clerk to take notes.
Pearce listened closely to his manner of speech
and detected a degree of refinement; this was no
petty officer jumped up to a captaincy by the
Revolution. Surely he had been a royal officer,
perhaps one of the many who had recently
returned to France after the end of the Terror.

Since only Pearce spoke French, the enquiry
was conducted through him, with a clear
statement that Oliphant, as servant, had little to
contribute in the way of information. Given the
Frenchman had no English, that also allowed
him to speak to Pearce without being understood.

The story was straightforward: they had taken
part in a boat raid to burn commercial shipping
and become stranded when the raiding party
withdrew, a mistake by someone for which they
must pay the consequences. The Frenchman
doing the asking did not seem to object to
Oliphant interjecting to ask questions, which
were posed in a querulous voice, denoting a deep
degree of concern. They were anything but.

'Have you mentioned the name of the ship?'
he moaned, wringing his hands.

No being too close to '*non*', Pearce had to ask why he should, the point obvious: surely that should be kept secret? Oliphant was quick to add another seeming plea. 'Will we ever get back to HMS *Circe*, your honour?'

The interrogator might lack English but he knew the designation of a British naval vessel when he heard it. He turned to his clerk, who favoured him with a nod; the name had been noted. Then it was rank, service, a demand to know the name and size of the vessel on which they had come to the Seine Estuary, number of guns, who was the captain and what were the future intentions. All were answered with a negative.

The man was thorough: one set of queries was soon followed by the same questions differently phrased; they answered again, those notated no doubt for a future comparison. Pearce was then told they would be held here in Le Havre until news came from Paris with instructions as to where they were to be sent. Throughout Pearce had turned to Oliphant to make sure he knew what was going on, asking for permission, given on the grounds that his servant was clearly in a parlous state. This allowed Pearce to ask that they be kept together.

'This man,' he said, patting his supposed servant on the shoulder, 'has served with me for years. You may find it unusual that any officer's servant chooses to accompany him on a raid that is bound to involve fighting and violence. But he made a vow never to leave my side and it is one he has held to.'

'You do him honour, monsieur. I will include in my submission a request that he remain with you.'

'It is as I suspected, sir,' Pearce responded, with something of a verbal flourish. 'The French Navy upholds the tradition of the service, even in such troubled times.'

That got a half-bow and a smile. 'I ask that you hold to your parole, monsieur. Where you are now held is not a prison and it would trouble me to have to put all of my men on duty to prevent your escape.'

That provided, Oliphant asked what the exchange had been about. 'What's he saying, your honour? Is he worried the crew from *Circe* might come back for us?'

'Will you be quiet man,' was the sharp response, which brought a smile to the lips of the French captain. Pearce reckoned, even if he did not understand the words, he recognised the sentiment and agreed that was the correct way to talk to a servant. With another half-bow he said his farewells.

'Why in the name of the devil did you name the frigate again?'

'I doubt it did much harm, Mr Pearce,' was the calm reply.

What followed was a week of ennui; no activity apart from a daily, hour-long walk in the courtyard of the building, overlooked by windows that at first had faces wondering at this pair of rogues, though that did not last as they grew accustomed to the sight. The provision of food was basic: bread and cheese mainly with occasional fish heads, but no hot water or implements to wash and shave.

With two prisoners locked up together it would have been common for the pair to exchange stories: background, families, where they came from and how they had got to their present impasse. Not with Oliphant; he was a ready listener if Pearce wanted to talk, but with nothing coming back at him, he decided to keep his own counsel.

In a situation of confinement any change in routine is welcome. The sound of boots on the stone-flagged flooring, in the darkness before dawn, had both men on their feet to see appear under torches a quartet of marines, and quite smart fellows at that, properly attired and their uniforms spick and span. They were soon joined by an officer of the same service, who addressed Pearce in English.

'Lieutenant, please make ready to depart.'

'Make ready, sir? I am ready since what you see is what I possess.'

'Bring your man along. He is to travel with you.'

'To where?'

'Paris. You are to be interrogated there on the grounds that you may very well be a spy.'

Pearce looked at Oliphant, who said in an alarmed tone, 'What have you been about, your honour?'

'I should have thrown you in the sea,' Pearce snarled, angry that those words seemed to back up the contention of espionage.

The door was unlocked and the two were

escorted out to a closed carriage, into which they were hustled, the marines' officer heading for another carriage, one that looked well sprung. There was an open cart, which Pearce suspected was for the escorts.

'Well, Mr Pearce,' Oliphant said, his voice cheerful as the conveyance rocked into motion, moving at a fair lick. 'We are on our way.'

'Given you're so cheerful, you do not see it as wise to tell me what it is you know?'

'It is never wise to do so when you are unaware of precisely what lies ahead.'

'But you have some notion?'

'Please don't ask, Mr Pearce. It gives me no pleasure to deflect your questions; indeed, it is uncomfortable.'

'Not as uncomfortable as the thought of being taken for a spy and having my head removed.'

The response was calm. 'Yes, that would be a cause for concern.'

With that Oliphant closed his eyes and lay back in his seat, the message plain. Pearce had little option but to do likewise in a conveyance out of which he could see nothing. The officer accompanying them was happy to say they were stopping the night at Brionne and he was decent enough to ensure Pearce was allowed the same kind of food as he was being served himself.

That did not apply to a servant and he took savage delight in watching Oliphant consume his thin gruel, washed down with cider, while he dined on pigeon and fresh vegetables, set off with a decent local wine. Yet if anything Oliphant appeared amused, as if he had anticipated this behaviour and that led, on the second night in Évreux, to a sharing of the better victuals.

'What a gent you are, your honour,' was said in a country voice and with a touched forelock.

'Damn you, don't you guy me.'

'My pleasures are few, Mr Pearce. Please don't deny me that which I can find.'

'I think I smell a metropolis,' was said the following evening and Pearce had to reckon him right. Disembarkation took place in another courtyard lit by torches in iron sconces on the walls. This was a more substantial affair than what they had endured in Le Havre and, given the number of locked and heavy doors through which they passed, more of a proper prison.

The surprise came when they were shown into a spacious well-furnished apartment; a roaring fire filled a huge grate in a substantial main chamber with two cubicles off to the sides. It was furnished with a long oak table, chairs as well as armchairs, a writing bureau and, most surprising of all, a separate privy. The closet had a stone basin and above that a mirror, into which Pearce looked to examine over a week's straggling growth. Oliphant had looked unshaven, but even with touch, he had not realised how unprepossessing he looked.

The marine officer, who had never identified himself, spoke to remind him of his parole, which was fully expected to continue here.

'But the Temple is not an easy place from which to abscond, monsieur, so it is more a formality than a necessity. I have ordered hot water to be fetched and you will be shaved first, with food following shortly. I hope you will find your confinement more comfortable than that which you have suffered up till now.'

Then he departed, leaving the two of them alone. Pearce turned to his companion with a look that was far from at ease and that was to do with where they were now incarcerated. If that marine had been paying close attention when he mentioned the Temple he would have observed the shock his officer prisoner felt, for this was a building he knew well, if only from the outside.

Once the medieval home of the Knights Templar, it was a massive structure steeped in history and blood. It stood almost alongside the Bastille in the annals of French confinement, a place where enemies of the regime had been locked up very recently before being taken by tumbril to the guillotine. It was from here that King Louis and his queen were taken to their execution.

'I do not like this, Mr Oliphant. I have a deep fear I have been led into a morass of which I know too little.'

A hand was held up for silence as the heavy bolt-studded oak door swung open. In came two fellows carrying bowls of steaming water, one of the two, once it was placed on a side table, indicating that Pearce should sit. His coat got a look that insisted it be removed, which was obeyed, and the fellow then began to strop a razor on the leather strop hanging from his waist.

'I may not even make it to Madame Guillotine,' he remarked as he sat down.

'Oh, I shouldn't worry,' came the reply as

Oliphant was passed a razor. 'If the French want to dispose of you, I reckon they will put on a public show. If my gullet is to be sliced, it appears I must do it myself.'

Pearce's face was washed with a cloth, then out came a brush to work up a lather and, as it was applied to his chin and cheeks, his nostril filled with the odour of an expensive musk, one which took him back in time to the Paris he had known when his father was in his pomp. Then it was a city of pleasure, where the Revolution had not yet interfered with its famed sense of luxury or imposed its bloody morality.

The strokes were swift and expert and, as if in other times, a small pair of scissors were produced to trim the eyebrows as well as the ear and nasal hairs. Finally from under his apron the barber produced a small brush and some scented powder, the chin dusted to remove any trace of damp.

Pearce stood and made to retrieve his coat, only to get a look of distaste. It was taken from him and put to a significant nose, which brought to the barber's face a look of horror. He shook his head and immediately left, garment held away from his body.

'I should not be surprised if you get a fresh shirt, Mr Pearce. Truly there is a gap between the treatment afforded to an officer and that of a servant. I shall be obliged to maintain my present stink unless you plead on my behalf.'

'This is all very strange, Oliphant.'

'Shall we just say that *Circe* has worked her spell?'

That was like a flint being struck. 'It's a code word.'

'Caught up at last. I really thought you would have smoked that earlier than this.'

'I lack your devious nature. What happens now?'

'I have no idea.'

'You expect me to believe that?'

'It troubles me not one jot if you don't, and while I have some hopes I have no certainties. Perhaps, if you were to ask for a change of small clothing for us both, it would indicate which way the wind is blowing.'

Food came next and Pearce did ask a rather stiff fellow, who was wearing a black high-collared coat and a proper stock at his neck like a major-domo, while clearly overseeing the setting out of food and utensils, for what Oliphant had requested. He got a swift nod, his supposed servant a rather sour look, but it seemed to be agreed as fitting that an officer could not share his accommodation with a servitor who stank to high heaven.

'I was given to understand that the people of France were close to starvation.'

This was a pertinent remark given the spread on the table. It was with no sympathy at all that Oliphant, tucking in heartily, replied.

'The peasant may need to live on short commons, Mr Pearce. I never to this day have met a man with power who suffered to starve or even hold back on excess. Revolution has not brought alleviation for the masses and nor has it done anything to prevent those who are intent on filling their belly and lining their purse.'

'You sound quite the radical.'

'Perhaps as much as you are yourself — that is, if you are your father's son.'

'That is a reference you have not made previously.'

'No, for it means nothing in the present circumstance. In another time and another place it might be an entertaining discussion to engage in.'

Pearce waved a hand over the table and the food. 'I was wondering if this angers you.'

'I have no time for that, as of this moment.'

'Who are we here to meet?' That got a lifted eyebrow. 'Come, we have not travelled the distance we have to test the cuisine.'

'Would you believe me if I said once more that I do not know?'

'No, I would not.'

'Then why would I bother to answer your question? We are in the belly of the beast, Mr Pearce, and what will spring from that is a hope not a certainty.'

'You know what I would love to do now, Samuel? Take a dip in the sea.'

'What a remarkable notion. Quite mad.'

* * *

The summons came with a sponged and clean uniform coat fetched by the major-domo, who indicated he should follow once he had put it on. A look at Oliphant got him a nod and a reminder of the name of the frigate that had transported them to France, accompanied by a look that told Pearce nothing else.

The route he followed was by an endless series of corridors until, through a partly open door Pearce spied an altar covered with lit candles, this accompanied by the odour of burnt incense. Fully open there was a high beamed ceiling and walls decorated with images of Christ and the Disciples. Behind the altar was a Christ-bearing crucifix.

The floor was mosaic and patterned in symbols, both heraldic and cabbalistic, which had to hark back to the Knights Templar who would have worshipped here before the order was destroyed by the Valois kings. Even with no religious beliefs to speak of, Pearce was aware of a sense of presence, as though there was indeed some higher power to which man must answer.

'Enough,' he said to himself. 'You'll be as daft at Michael O'Hagan if you let this get to you.'

The black-coated escort indicated the confessional, an elaborately carved split structure that stood against one wall, on either side two-man-high candle stands with guttering flames at the top. Odd that he felt a residual objection, as if he disliked Catholicism more than religion, which must be a hangover from the small amount of Calvinism he had absorbed in his childhood.

He pulled aside the curtain and entered the right-hand part of the confessional, to take a seat on a narrow board. To his own right was a heavy gauze and from there a hatch slid open showing the very slightest outline of a human head. In a low voice the question was posed in French.

'You have a word for me, I believe?'

'Circe,' was imparted, more in hope than certainty.

'That is good.'

The voice was even, but distinctive as well as refined, and Pearce had the feeling he might have heard it before. His time in Paris had seen him meet men of affairs in the salons of the women, like the banker's daughter Germaine de Staël, who were sure they ruled Parisian social and political life. The men who actually held the power were inclined to flatter them while eyeing the younger ladies who had no interest in such a subject.

'I have matters of which I must inform you, grave and disturbing.'

'To whom am I speaking?'

'Let it be enough that I represent the interests of the true France.'

'I'm listening.'

'What do you know of Louis XVII?'

'I know he is a young boy. That his parents were guillotined and he has not been crowned but kept prisoner. No one is sure if he is dead or alive.'

'He is lost to us, monsieur, last year, but they fear to let it be known. He resided in this very building, monsieur, kept in less than healthy surroundings and looked after by ogres who cruelly tortured and neglected him, and because of that became gravely ill. When he expired from his maltreatment he was buried in secret.'

'That makes me angry as well as sad.'

Pearce meant it because he had agreed with

his father about one thing: bringing down monarchs was to be welcomed and encouraged, murdering them merely for their birth and bloodline was not. It was barbarous, but that was what the Revolution had become and son John reflected that his father, watching the descent into judicial murder, must have wondered that all he had fought for in his life, the betterment of the common man, was for nought.

'It is soon to be the anniversary of that sad day. I am hoping you have been sent to us from London to say that, should that be seen as an occasion for the redress of the events of the past, any popular uprising will be welcomed by those with whom we are presently at war.'

What to say? He was an emissary not a spokesman and there were many more opposed to the Revolution than Great Britain. 'I can only speak for London, monsieur.'

'The source of gold that pays all our foes and, we hope, will support our aims.'

'They would welcome peace, of that I am absolutely sure.' Pearce felt a bit of a fraud as he added, sure he had to say something fitting, 'I have had such an assurance from the highest counsels in the land.'

'And a Bourbon restoration?'

That made him sit back. Surely that could not be the aim? It was their blindness and folly that had brought about the original upheaval. The reply was more diplomatic, that not based on any certainty and there was a high degree of speculation too; he really had no idea. How would Pitt, the defender of parliamentary manipulation, handle it?

'It is for the legislators of France, answering to the people, to decide how they are governed. That, of course, must apply to those who have been overrun by your armies. What has been seized by force of arms, cannot be held.'

Pearce was feeling pleased with himself; if he had been out of his depth on his first day at sea, he was even more so now. What in the name of creation was he doing thinking and acting as if he had the power to decide anything? The need to concentrate on what was being said chased such thoughts away.

'The anniversary will act as a tocsin for those who are loyal to the late King's brother.'

It was hard to keep out of his voice surprise at what he was being told. 'A counter-revolution?'

'Nothing less.'

'And you wish me to convey this message back to London?'

'You must wait until all is in place. When we are sure of our plans and the time at which they will be executed, you will be free to return home and request that England acts with us so we can bring back to Paris he who will be crowned as Louis XVIII. We will speak again, but now you will be escorted back to your chamber.'

Pearce looked back as he was escorted out of the chapel, but no figure emerged from the priest's side of the confessional.

26

On the way back to the chamber that passed for his place of confinement, Pearce sought to make some sense of what it was he was involved in, not easy because he now realised he had been sent forth naked. Dundas had been vague about the purpose of this mission but what had just happened drove home that he was out on a limb.

That was not an entirely strange place to be for a naval officer; at sea, faced with circumstances and needing to act, individual judgement was required simply because there was no way to apply for guidance to a higher authority. That applied doubly so to commanding admirals, who had to make decisions that could impact on national policy, knowing the consequences could be dismissal.

In recalling the fact, he determined to find out what he could and his only source of available information was Oliphant. It seemed to Pearce the man knew what was coming as soon as he saw his face, on which he made no attempt to disguise his feelings. A finger was held to the supposed servant's lips and a warning, roving eye hinted at their being spied upon.

'Why bother?' Pearce barked, which got him a furious wave to be quiet.

Oliphant made a great play of going round the interior walls and tapping them, then putting an ear to the stone, which his companion watched with total disbelief. Every time Pearce made to speak that hand came up again until finally, tour completed, Oliphant indicated he should come close.

'We cannot be too careful, Mr Pearce.'

The hand that took Oliphant by the shirt and pushed him against the wall showed no care whatsoever, though Pearce took the admonishment to possible eavesdropping by hissing his words; there was no need to shout when his nose was within inches of his quarry.

'Now, you will tell me your real name. You will tell me what this assignment is about or I will call in those guarding us and have you removed from my presence, which will probably have you plying an oar on a galley in Toulon if you're lucky, for it is at least warm there.'

There was no alarm in Oliphant's eyes, but there was calculation; when, after several seconds, he did whisper to respond, it was in perfect French and asking to be released as what he was experiencing was very uncomfortable.

'Only if you accede to my demands?'

The nod was likewise calmly delivered. Pearce took away his hand and stepped back a single pace, hoping to convey by the look in his eye that he would not be deterred. It was a moment before Oliphant spoke again, in English and still whispering.

'My name is of no account.'

'To me it is.'

'Then I admit it is not my own, but that is all I will say.'

'For fear I will reveal it?'

'For fear you might be made to reveal it.'

It did seem to Pearce slightly odd that he had never considered the notion of being tortured, but it hit home now: he was on a clandestine mission in a foreign and dangerous country that would not scruple to tear his limbs off if they required him to reveal secrets.

'My task was to get you to this place and I succeeded. What happened then was to be a matter of judgement.'

'Yours or mine?'

'I assumed yours, with my advice.'

'Given on what grounds?'

'That I would know more of the nature of what was proposed.'

'You were sure something was to be proposed?' A nod. 'Which implies you are better informed on what the situation is in Paris than either myself or Dundas.'

That obliged Oliphant to blink; it was almost as if he was beginning to realise that John Pearce was no simple sailor, which had been an impression easy to arrive at up till now. He was a man who had a brain, added to powers of deduction, and one who decided to drive home the point.

'That also indicates to me that your name, your real name, is one that if used, might be recognised by our captors.'

'It might be an idea if you informed me, Mr Pearce, of what you have just been about.'

Pearce described the confessional and the conversation, trying to discern any telling reaction but getting none. Oliphant's eyes gave nothing away, which was fitting in a man who must be a spy. With that in mind, it made sense that he had held back information. Between leaving HMS *Circe* and getting to the Temple any number of things could have happened to thwart the aim. Even naming the frigate as the code word had been held back until Pearce had finally rumbled it for what it was.

'I take it you would have told me before I left?'

'I was just about to, but I reckoned you had it finally.'

That brought a crabbed look to Pearce's face; this finally meant he had been expected to realise its use before. He'd not been as sharp as he needed to be.

'So what happens now?'

'I am happy to proffer an opinion, Mr Pearce, but that lies with you.'

'Even if I have no idea on how to proceed?'

It was Oliphant's turn — Pearce could not think of him any other way — to appear confused.

'Surely you have your instructions?' The slow shake of the head in response changed the look in the man's eyes from one of calm to one troubled. 'You were given none?'

'I was told there were people in France prepared to work for peace. I was to make contact and ask under what terms that could be brought about. Then I assumed I'd report back, my journey facilitated by those with whom I had spoken. All of which I would have told you before if you had asked me. But then I now realise that in this line of work, as you so rightly pointed out to me, information shouldn't be divulged that does not have to be.'

'And where does that lead you, Mr Pearce?'

'Judging by the look in your eye and the tone of your voice, to the same place as you.'

'Such a way of proceeding has been used in a way not originally intended.'

'Which does not bode well for our prospects. Nor can I say that success would bring me any joy. My father railed against monarchy all his life and was extensive in his condemnation. While he decried Britannia, he knew at least there were checks on the power of the Crown; not so France. I cannot see myself as an agent of the means to put the Bourbons back in Versailles with their powers restored.'

'While I had no idea that was the purpose of the undertaking. It was imparted to me that you had connections, through your name, to people who might act to check the powers of the Directory, which might at least have led to the war being pressed less forcefully.'

'So we have both been manipulated. But I am bound to ask to what end?'

Oliphant was silent for a long time, the two men only two feet apart and giving the impression of one waiting for the other to speak, this while a whole host of possibilities were being examined.

'Mr Pearce, I am experiencing the stench of manipulation.'

'Which does not require a strong sense of smell. The question is who is pulling the strings? Given you must know more of what happens here in Paris than I, it seems to me you would be better placed to make any deductions.'

'While it occurs to me there are conspiracies too tangled to unravel.'

'Nevertheless that requires us to decide on a course of action.'

'Quite the reverse, Mr Pearce,' Oliphant insisted, looking around the chamber, the point obvious: they were prisoners with no chance of escape. 'It requires us to play whatever game we are in to the end. Only then will we know what we need to do.'

'Which would serve if I had patience as a virtue.'

'Acquire it, sir, for not to do so will tempt you to risks best not taken.'

A second summons came the next day and Pearce made another trip to the confessional. There was the same voice, this time asking questions as to what plans had been made to assist a Royalist uprising. Many moves must be made by Albion that would sow alarm in France, enough to make the prospect of peace more attractive than war.

Given time to think and Oliphant as a shrewd aide, Pearce dissembled, claiming that he must hear what was required, then carefully compare it to what he could offer in the way of assistance, before coming back with the outline of a plan. Surely those who proposed to rebel — the word was badly received and had to be substituted for those who propose to restore — must give some indication of where any action by the British government would be effective.

355

'They seem to think we have soldiers by the several thousand to spare,' Pearce reported, after his fourth visit in a week. 'I have been given at least half a dozen places from Flanders to Aquitaine where they expect us to land troops on some pretext of invasion, this while the armies France has humbled these last two years take the offensive in the East and south to march on Paris.'

'And the navy?'

'Launch an attack to capture Brest and Toulon, which I am assured are awash with sympathisers and should fall to us easily.'

'That might be true.'

'You're speaking with the same level of ignorance they are showing, Oliphant!'

The brusque response was not well taken, forcing Pearce to both apologise and explain. Toulon he knew from personal experience, Brest only by hearsay but it had to be as much, if not more, of a formidable prospect.

'Any naval base needs deep water and the ability to be easily defended, for to site them otherwise is sheer folly.'

He went on to describe the mountains surrounding Toulon that, thanks to mobile artillery batteries, had obliged Lord Hood's fleet seeking to take the port to remain in the Outer Rade. The long arm of the bay that helped form the Inner Rade made it a difficult harbour to enter and depart swiftly.

'Which you have to be able to do if the assault does not succeed.'

'But was that not taken by an internal coup?'

'It was,' Pearce replied and, given he'd had a hand in that event, he went on to describe how touch and go it had been. 'It comes down to who commits the fewest errors of judgement — in other words luck — and Brest, I am told, is even a nightmare for the French to get in and out of safely.'

'I bow to your superior knowledge.'

Over the last few days, and he had not shared the feeling with Oliphant, he had been constantly reminded of what had happened when Sir William Hotham sent him under the command of Henry Digby to the Gulf of Ambracia. The similarities had seen him sit in silent contemplation and it now became apparent this had not gone unnoticed.

'I observe you meditating, Mr Pearce, and wonder what it is you're cogitating upon?'

He was reluctant to let Oliphant know and was saved by the opening door from replying or lying. He asked for a moment and approached Oliphant for a discreet word.

'I think I must indulge their fantasies. You?'

He was pleased the man thought on it for several seconds before nodding in reply. Pearce went down to the confessional making up in his mind outrageous scenarios of what could be done, until he checked himself and decided to play it long.

'I think you must decide on a point of incursion and not seek to spread the effect.'

'That will be a difficult matter of which to persuade my friends, monsieur.'

'Nevertheless persuade them you must.

Britannia has not the means to meet all your hopes. If it is not enough, a greater effort must come from your own side.'

'I cannot tell you how much that disappoints me.'

'I have to be a realist, monsieur, for I see no purpose in impossible dreaming.'

The silence from behind the gauze was long, with Pearce struggling to place the voice and realising he might be himself indulging in fantasy. How long was it since he had been in Paris and how many hundreds of conversations had he either taken part in or overheard?

'I must consult and come back to you. These are matters beyond my knowledge.'

'How close, monsieur, are we to acting rather than talking?'

'Further today than we were yesterday.'

'I am also bound to ask what means you have to get myself and my servant back to where we can put into motion whatever plan is agreed?'

The response sounded quite hurt. 'We got you to this place, monsieur; please be assured we have the means to get you out of France again.'

'I asked out of curiosity, not doubt.'

'Good. Now I must be gone and you before me. Until tomorrow or perhaps, given what has to be decided upon, the following day.'

Which left him and Oliphant doing what had occupied much of their time: pacing the chamber, Pearce reading some books he had been given while his supposed servant declined; he might speak and read the language but he did not wish to be seen doing so. The first surprise on the appointed day was that Pearce was not summoned, but told to expect a visitor.

He heard the sound of quiet singing before the tall, elegant individual entered the chamber and that definitely stirred a memory, albeit as yet a far from firm one. When the figure appeared in the doorway, with an amused cast to his eye, Pearce could not hold back his astonishment.

'Monsieur de Cambacérès!'

'It pleases me to see you remember me, Jean.'

Oliphant had shrunk back into the only bit of shadow in the candlelit room, and throwing a glance in that direction seemed to amuse Cambacérès even more.

'Creatures of the night, Monsieur Bertrand, often recoil at illumination.' He then turned his attention back to John Pearce. 'You have been mixing in some dangerous company, young man, and not just in this chamber.'

A servant appeared behind Cambacérès with a tray holding a flagon of wine and goblets. The instruction for the man to lay it on the table and be gone was done without a word being spoken. He then moved to a chair and sat down, indicating that the other two should do likewise.

'When you say dangerous company — '

'Traitors would be the appropriate description.'

'Even if they see themselves as patriots?'

'An argument we could have for many an hour. But I am curious as to how you see them, Jean?' He looked at Oliphant. 'You would not care, Bertrand.'

Try as he might, given the use of the name,

Pearce could not avoid looking at the man.

'There is a type of person so wedded to conspiracy that ideology or passion for any form of politics does not enter into their thinking. But you, Jean? I find it strange that you would become part of a plot to restore a king.'

'I came looking for a way to bring about peace.'

'I visited St Sulpice before coming here and stood over your father's grave, to ask him to forgive you.' Pearce did not know if the visit was true but he reckoned the request an invention. 'When you say peace, this, of course, does not apply to the bloodbath some people wish to release into the body politic of France.'

'For which I would decline to be held responsible.'

'No, that would rest with your political masters. Let us pour the wine and at least you and I can drink to an old association.'

'You know of my gratitude.' That got a jerk of the head from Oliphant/Bertrand, which required an explanation as the wine was poured. 'Monsieur de Cambacérès helped me bury my father. I still carry a tin containing some of the earth in which he was interred.'

'Let us drink to his memory.' Two goblets were raised as Cambacérès alluded to the third not being so. 'Of course, you did not know Adam Pearce and I doubt you could have abided his honesty.'

'I am wondering what happens now?' Oliphant asked.

'Indeed.'

'While I,' Pearce insisted, 'am more curious as to what has happened up till now.'

'Ah. The little plot we hatched. It was like a seagull tapping the ground to bring up the worms. A hint through certain people of a plot to overthrow our government. But who could be planning such a thing?'

Régis de Cambacérès, a revolutionary and regicide, was setting out to be entertaining, with mock surprise at the seriousness of the question.

'And how were we to find out when so many people are so undecided at which way to act, weathervanes who will spin with the prevailing wind? If we try to expose them ourselves they disappear.'

That came with an appropriate gesture, fingertips to lips then flying away. 'But if they thought they were in communication with friends, enemies of the Revolution, they would have to meet and plot, and when you meet and plot in Paris it cannot be done without those set to guard the nation noticing such a gathering. Then there arrives from England the people they need to meet in order to ensure that what they require will be both welcomed and supported. But of course they will not come if they have no idea of a plot being hatched so they must be alterted to the possibility. And here you are.'

'Clever.'

'Why thank you, Jean. You were always an attractive fellow, but it was as much your intelligence as your handsome body that made you so.'

'While I have always appreciated your restraint.'

'I am not much given to fighting for that which I wish to be given freely.'

'Am I not following my father to a bloody demise?'

Cambacérès looked shocked. 'No, Jean, we are more civilised now.'

That got a guffaw from Oliphant/Bertrand.

'Ah yes, there are those who would remove your head, but wiser councils prevailed. There was a plan for your escape and it has to be said it was a sound one.'

'How did you find that out?' asked the pretend servant.

'By methods that should you continue in your chosen profession, will one day be applied to you and, I must say, sensitive as I am, that is one I would watch with some interest.'

'So?'

'You will escape from this Temple and the city.' A glance sideways. 'Both of you.'

'And after that?'

'Drink up, Jean; this will be the last wine you will enjoy for some time. How nice it would be to spend some time with you, to perhaps persuade you that what I could offer you would not be unwelcome. But!'

He was on his feet quickly for such a big man. 'Make ready to leave tonight and, if I believed in God, I would ask him to speed your journey.'

'Do you believe him?' Oliphant asked, once Cambacérès had departed.

'I have to. We have no choice.'

27

If it was done by Cambacérès he was as good as his word, yet Pearce was never to know whether it had been the original plot to get them out of Paris, or one he had contrived in a sudden emergency, given the whole thing was carried out in silence. They were ready early, before darkness fell, not that either man had much to carry: some hoarded food, a bottle of wine and a serious degree of worry that the whole thing was a trap.

'What do I call you?' Pearce asked.

'Stick to Oliphant.'

'Why not Bertrand?'

'Because that's not my real name either, Mr Pearce, and I have no intention of enlightening you as to what is.'

They waited for some time but eventually the door was unlocked, to be opened so slowly they prepared to defend themselves. Pearce's watch told him it was just past midnight as it swung open to reveal a fellow in a black cloak and a large hat who, in his exaggerated gestures, could have been a performer in some play from the Italian canon. Everything seemed exaggerated: the admonishment for silence, the wave to follow, the constant halts with extravagant bodily expression of alarm.

Finally, having traversed a series of doors, corridors and passageways, few of them properly lit, they came to a postern gate which, once opened, led out to what Pearce knew to be the Marais, a district of cobbled narrow streets and fine palaces that the nobility who built them called *hôtels particuliers*.

In between these huge mansions there were houses and hovels and there lived the meaner folk, who either saw to their needs or existed off their scraps. But it was soon apparent that the most important feature of the Marais was its proximity to the River Seine, hard by the *Île de la Cité* and the towering spires of Notre Dame, visible against the night sky.

Pearce and Oliphant were led down narrow, dank passageways to the riverbank, where a barge-like boat was waiting to take them out of the city, which should have been forbidden due to the curfew. The sentinels set on the Pont Neuf were either asleep, ordered to turn a blind eye, or had been bribed to ignore their passage. Yet it was no easy matter for whoever was steering the craft to get it through the narrow arches, where the river, not far from in spate at this time of year, set up dangerous currents and eddies that were hazardous in daylight and deadly in the dark.

Paris was asleep, the few pinpricks of light not enough to identify buildings or landmarks, and progress was swift, taking them out past the inner city gates and the riverbank towers. The next obstacle was the arched wooden bridge at St Cloud, a suburb that in past times had formed part of the outer fortifications of the French capital.

That too was passed under without incident and, as the Seine swung north, the strong current on a windless night did the work of propulsion. Assuming they were to be boated all the way down to the coast, both Pearce and Oliphant were about to settle down for the night when the boat swung into the riverbank and a small jetty, with ropes being cast to the torch-carrying men on the bank to haul it in so they could disembark.

'*Chevaux.*'

This was the only word used as something in the nature of a document was pressed into Pearce's hand, he noting that the boat had already cast off, disappearing into the night. They followed a flaring torch, to where sat two saddled mounts with large panniers. Closer to the light Pearce could see he had not only been gifted a map, but a pile of the paper assignats, so derided by William Pitt as near to worthless, with which to pay their way.

'Where are we to go?' he demanded.

'Where are we now?' asked a querulous Oliphant in English, the question translated and asked by Pearce, who noted with some irritation his companion was still not going to speak French if he could avoid it and wondering why.

'Close to Épinay,' was what came back. 'The map is marked with the route north through Beauvais to a final destination, monsieur, at the port of Gravelines.'

That was an unwelcome one to a man who had been there before and had good cause to regret it.

'Travel on to Arras. You will find clothing in the saddlebags as well as directions as to where you should go and whom you should seek out when you arrive. Our man there will find you a boat to England. Wait till dawn to change, when you should be in the Forest of Compiègne and able to do so in safety.'

'Best wait here, surely, until daylight?'

'Non,' was the panicky response. 'It is dangerous to delay. You must head north-east by the polar star. Here is not safe.'

'What say you, Oliphant?'

'Well, your honour,' he replied, in a servile manner, again sticking to English, 'I only does what you tells me to.'

'Your playing of a part is cancelled.'

'When I am ready and I feel safe.'

'What are you like on a horse?'

'Tolerable.'

'Then we will walk first. I have no mind to deal with you falling off.'

It actually made sense; riding in the dark was rarely a good idea. There was a road of sorts, not very well maintained now that the *corvée*, the obligation to repair the roads, was no longer imposed on the locals. They were soon hemmed in by trees with the odd break, these, Pearce knew from the past, forming avenues laid out to allow hunting parties into the deeper areas of the Forest of Compiègne.

It had been, until the year '89 and the fall of the Bastille, a royal preserve, kept full of game for the daily pleasure of a court and a king blind to the forces that were about to sweep them away. The horses were surer of foot than those leading them, so did not stumble on the ruts made by the traders' carts that must pass through daily on the way to the city.

Pearce suspected dawn would bring them on to the road, as well as wake those travellers who had camped by the side in forest clearings, folks whose campfire embers glowed, while their dogs were wont to bark at those passing in darkness and warn their owners of an untoward presence. As soon as he saw the first greying of the sky, he led Oliphant into the trees, deep enough for them to be in near total darkness and there they waited.

'I do wish you would stop telling me what it is we must do,' Oliphant complained.

'Habit,' Pearce replied, with a grin he knew would not be seen.

'A bad one, since I reckon to be more adept at this game than you.'

'I am open to suggestions if you have any, but I have yet to hear you proffer one. All I have is you still playing the dim-witted servitor.'

'Well, one would be this. What is it we are about? I have travelled through France before. It is not possible to do so without being stopped and questioned by every citizen who thinks he has the right to know another man's business and that, in my recollection, means just about everyone.'

'While I know we cannot stay here,' was the reply, as Pearce watched the sky, no longer starry, for evidence that the light would eventually penetrate the forest canopy. 'In a

367

moment we will see what clothing has been provided. That will give us some notion of a tale to construct should we be questioned.'

It took time before they could even properly see each other and the first thing to do was eat their hoarded food, not much more than a couple of chicken legs and some stale bread to be washed down with wine. The mood was not good, for without talking about it, both men could imagine there had to be many difficulties ahead. France had never been like Britain, where people moved freely from one place to another; it had always had internal borders.

Prior to the Revolution there had been customs barriers between the various regions, places where taxes could be levied for passage. The people who once manned them had quickly morphed into National Guards and were just as awkward as they had been in a previous existence. Pearce had prior experience too of the need to show papers and was not in the mood to think their onward travel would be simple.

That was immediately lightened when they opened the panniers, to find they had been provided with soldiers' uniforms and ones that not only fitted but conferred status. Pearce became a captain of cavalry and Oliphant an ensign. A small pommel saddlebag revealed more: a set of sealed despatches plus an order signed and under the seal of Lazare Carnot, a leading member of the Directory and the man in charge of the military, with instruction that these officers were not to be impeded.

'Capitaine Gerard Moreau.' Pearce said,

reading the *laissez passer*. 'Almost a promotion.'

'Cambacérès must desperately want to bed you, Pearce. You know his tastes, I take it?'

'He has never made any secret of his proclivities, but he has also never made any untoward advances, while he has to me been very kind in the past. So let us just thank our good fortune, change, and be on our way.'

It was not as easy or as swift to travel as it would have been for a genuine pair of French officers. They would have been able to use the resources of the National Guard to demand a change of horses at every conurbation to speed their passage. That was reckoned too dangerous, so there was as much walking as riding.

To this was added frequent stops to rest the mounts and let them graze, while some of the assignats, a fair amount at each exchange, were used to buy oats as well as food for themselves. Luckily the weather held and they did not have to contend with downpours, which would have made progress much more uncomfortable. That said, four days in the saddle left both men sore, in their backsides and thighs.

All the way to Gravelines, Pearce had regularly consulted the instructions they had been given as to how to make contact. Whatever it had been called before, their destination was now the Rue de La République, within the walls of a fortress Pearce knew well, one of those star-shaped bastions surrounded by canals designed by the Marquis de Vauban and replicated all over Europe; there had been one of a similar design in Leghorn.

It was a place to be approached with some caution, for, as Pearce had pointed out to Oliphant, on his previous visit the town and port had been at the front of the French incursion into Flanders and thus had an atmosphere that was feverish. Now there was no front; the Revolutionary armies had swept all the way north to overrun the Dutch Republic.

But it was still a military outpost, so no one at the southern gate seemed inclined to question a pair of French officers, even unshaven and on weary-looking mounts, assuming them to be on their way to the headquarters in the citadel. A look at the number of soldiers, both acting as sentinels and in the streets, told Pearce the port was still a well-protected possession of the Revolution. Was it, as he remembered it, also still an entrepôt dedicated to servicing the needs of English smugglers?

The address, to which they required directions, proved to be a large house with high double gates leading to a courtyard. There was a domestic door on which Pearce hammered. It was opened to reveal a very attractive young lady indeed, of blonde hair and even features under a crisp white Flanders bonnet. She looked at his dust-covered uniform then held out a hand, into which Pearce placed Carnot's *laissez passer*.

That examined, she called out in a musical voice then indicated the double gates, which soon swung open. Once within and those closed, they were hidden from view, to be greeted by an elderly fellow of stooped posture and low-on-the-nose spectacles, who invited them to follow him into the house, this while a servant saw to the horses.

They were led into a well-furnished parlour, where he too took and examined the pass bearing Carnot's signature and seal. 'Messieurs, you will be in need of food and the means to rid yourselves of the filth of travel. My daughter Eugenie will see to your needs, if you do not mind being attended to by a girl.'

Both Pearce and Oliphant having sized up the daughter, the assent was so swift and eager, they looked to see if the father had noted it. But he was too preoccupied, probably with what he had to do next.

'It has not been possible to make arrangements in advance of your arrival; the time was not known. So I must go down to the canals and see if the right craft to take you home is either available or anticipated.'

'A *contrebandier?*' The question surprised their host and he gave Pearce a look that, over his spectacles, bordered on the deeply suspicious. 'I have been here before, monsieur, but in a different guise and almost in a different life. I know how the port and town makes its revenues, but it is of no consequence to what we are engaged in.'

Almost an invite for the fellow to talk of whom he represented, it was not accepted. Yet the eyes, watery with age, were capable of a glare, which left Pearce in no doubt he had erred in mentioning having been here previously, creating suspicion where none should have existed.

'You really must learn not to be so open,'

371

Oliphant chastised him as, washed and shaved, they sat eating what one of the household servants had fetched for them: a fresh ham and a loaf of bread, to be washed down with strong local beer. 'Never tell anyone that which they do not need to know.'

'It pleases me to say that in your occupation, I am an amateur.'

'Not something I need to be informed about. Now, do we discuss once more, and finally decide, what it is we are going to say if we do get back to England?'

That had been talked of on horseback and various avenues explored. Pearce wanted to tell Pitt and Dundas they had been taken for dupes, humbugged like the silliest coves ever drawn by Hogarth, this by a set of Frenchmen sharper by far than they — drawn into a trap designed to bring to the surface and to expose those who were plotting a restoration.

Oliphant did not take to that notion at all, and pointed out to Pearce for the umpteenth time they were both in need of the good offices of the same pair of politicos for future employment. He had also speculated that Pitt and Dundas knew exactly what they were doing when they conjured up the mission.

'But that alters little. It will not do to accuse them of duplicity, nor does any man wish to be told he's been humbugged and led by the nose into a trap, which to my mind is worse.'

'So you're sure we were supposed to survive this assignment?'

'Not really,' had been Oliphant's reply. 'Yet I

also cannot believe we were set up to be sacrificed.'

'Perhaps not you, but me?'

'I do not mean to offend when I say you overrate your importance. Dundas commands the Scottish vote and moves armies, Pitt is the King's First Minister and must bend our sovereign to see sense. How much time of theirs do you think you command?'

Pearce had been obliged to acknowledge it would not be a great deal.

'Best to assume they had no idea it was a construct, even if it was. We go home and say there was the outline of an uprising, which we sought to encourage. But it was betrayed, probably internally, yet enough escaped the net to help get us out of France.'

'Cambacérès?'

'Should not be mentioned. So the possibility exists that enough dissatisfied folk remain to carry on the work with the suggestion that perhaps it is now time to turn our minds to encouraging them to continue their efforts.'

'Even if it's not the truth?'

'Positive news, Pearce, and for me continued employment. That is better than being told you're a fool. And that is what you are, if you think they will ever admit to your other contention.'

'Very well.'

That came with a sigh; Pearce wanted nothing more than to laugh in their faces.

When their nameless host returned, it was only to say that matters were in hand, but nothing was as yet certain and nor would it be till the following day at the earliest. So the pair partook of an awkward dinner in which it was obvious, in a desultory conversation, just how much could not be referred to.

The daughter played shy, which was in contrast to her attitude on first acquaintance. Pearce tried to watch them both closely for clues, aware that his companion was seemingly content with things as they were, concentrating on his food. This was something he had often done throughout their association, which left Pearce wondering if he was a man accustomed to being on short commons.

He longed to know whom it was their host represented and he had to conclude, given his prosperity, it was unlikely that he was a Jacobin, which led to a whole host of conjecture and a train of thought that lasted well beyond dinner and provided him matters to gnaw on as he tried to sleep.

There had been originally a plan in place to get them back to England, but it seemed bizarre that Cambacérès had just allowed it to go ahead. Was it possible he was part of the royalist plot, because nothing could be said to be impossible? Yet it was unlikely given he had voted in the National Assembly for the execution of King Louis and was tarred as a regicide. But if he was, he could also have joined in with the conspiracy for the purposes of betrayal.

Had there been behind them, as they rode north, men sent by Cambacérès and the Directory, seeking to find the very people in whose bed he now lay? Had they been sent out as lures? Would his host and that comely daughter be arrested as soon as they were got away, a thought that, if it was troubling, left him with no notion of what to do about it?

The only conclusion he could reach was that on both sides of the English Channel he was dealing with men so devious, it was possible they did not know their own true aims, if you excluded political and personal survival. How different that was to the simple life of a sailor — a notion that did not hold for long, as he reprised his memory of Ralph Barclay as well as the many times he had felt manipulated by senior officers.

It was impossible not to speculate on what might happen on his return. Would Dundas keep his promise? Was it possible to serve once more with his fellow Pelicans? Could he resolve his differences with Emily? If not, how would his future take shape? Such reflections were so depressing he forced himself to be optimistic.

If he looked back on his life, how many times had he been in what naval jargon had as the 'steep tub'? Yet he was here, healthy and, if he could get back to England, with some kind of future, which was well worthy of looking forward to rather than subjecting it to unknown concerns.

If not the navy, he would have to find a way to carve out a life for himself and did he not have strong and true friends, a woman who loved him and a son? The last thought John Pearce had as he slipped into sleep was his determination to make young Adam, and his mother, proud.